THE FIRST GENTLEMAN
OF THE UNITED STATES

THE FIRST GENTLEMAN OF THE UNITED STATES

C.S. TABOWN

INDEPENDENT PRODUCTIONS AND AVIATION SERVICES

Dedicated to my two families:
My Australian Family - My wife Sharon and our two boys, Ty and
Austin, whose love encouraged me and whose support
allowed me to complete this work.

And to my American Family, the Van Voorhies. To Jim who took a
shine to me and took a chance on me;
to Christine, the mom I always wanted but who became a trusted
friend and confidant;
and to their two beautiful daughters and my sisters, Cheryl and Pam,
whom I watched grow up into remarkable women.

If not for all of you, this humble offering would still be bouncing
around my head.

Contents

The Joint Select Committee Convenes

The image of the president's body lying on the floor next to her bed was shocking. She had been in office less than five months; hardly time to make the Executive Residence her own. Alongside her was the body of secret service agent Henry 'Bruce' Lee, the hero of the attempted assassination of President Daniel Troup two years before. Somewhere, along the chain of custody, someone had leaked this photo to the media, and now it was being seen on every news bulletin and in every newspaper and blog. It was all anyone could talk about. The country's most popular president since Kennedy, along with the hero of the US Secret Service, were both dead.

Michael O'Rourke—Mick to his mates—was in his US Army uniform at his lawyer's insistence. He stared at the picture of his dead wife on the front page of the *Washington Post* that lay in his lawyer's open briefcase. Embarrassed, his counsel quickly closed it. He did not want his client any more nervous than he may already be, although he did not appear to be nervous at all. In fact, it was quite the opposite. His client, the one accused of assassinating America's first female president and her secret service agent, appeared calm. This worried the veteran lawyer and his firm. His client's cool demeanor may not work in their favor, especially today as the whole country was baying for the death penalty which, it seemed, may well be the sentence.

No. In fact, Mick's sang froid, would serve neither of them well.

The Joint Select Committee was to hear testimony today. Mick and his lawyer sat in a part of the marble hallway partitioned off from the public by rope barriers. US Capitol Police stood guard, maintaining order. The media, thirty yards down the hall, were stumbling over themselves trying to get just the right picture. So much for social distancing.

A few other men and some women stood in small groups nearby. They were to testify before the committee also, most likely about his alleged role as a member of a foreign intelligence service. Mick watched them. Some were obviously lawyers; a couple were FBI, proudly wearing their ID badges for all the world to see. Others were less obvious but probably from some other branch of the 'three-letter' intelligence community. CIA possibly... or perhaps NSA. He thought he recognized one person who had attended a Department of Homeland Security meeting at the White House. It was hard to tell when everyone was wearing masks in this new age of Covid. So, who knows?

What Mick did know was that no matter how smart he might look in an army uniform, the bruises could not be hidden. The beatings he had suffered at Fort Leavenworth while he was in federal prison, at the hands of both guards and inmates, had left him with deep lacerations and heavy bruises, which now had that yellow and green tinge. They did not heal quickly.

Soon, two dark-suited men and an officer from the Capitol Police emerged from the hearing room and stood next to Mick and his counsel.

"They're ready for you," said one man with venom. His hatred was almost tangible. Though Mick could not see his mouth behind his mask, he could almost imagine the sneer on his face.

Mick's lawyer began gathering his papers and said to him, "Are you ready? Just remember everything that we've discussed, just be honest and say as little as possible. We don't want them doing some creative editing on the news. Single word answers: 'yes', 'no'."

The army officer stood up, his uniform slightly askew, favoring his good ankle. He looked down at his counsel, still seated and still gathering his notes. He spoke in his Australian accent, the only thing that really gave him away as not being from the States.

"You know, back in colonial Australia, we had these guys known as bushrangers. They'd be the same as outlaws in the American west," he said. "They'd rob stagecoaches and hold up banks and post offices, and generally make a nuisance of themselves, that sort of stuff.

"This one bushranger, Ned Kelly, made an iron suit that was bullet proof, which was pretty smart. But he didn't make iron pants, which was pretty dumb. When the troopers went to arrest him, he came out shooting... so they shot him in the legs. He went down, was arrested, and was sentenced to hang."

The lawyer listened, wondering where this was going.

"Well, before they put the noose around his neck, his final words were, 'Such is life'."

"What's the point?" asked his lawyer.

"We only have a brief stay on this planet. You can't tell what life is going to throw at you or where you'll end up," came his fatalistic response.

With that, Mick straightened his uniform, tugging down on his tunic, and then placed his hat under his left arm. He motioned to the two dark-suited men and the man in uniform and swept his arm towards the huge mahogany doors that led into the chamber.

"Shall we?"

They were led into the chamber, and what seemed like a hundred cameras started following him. He tried not to limp, but his fractured ankle was not healing well and probably never would. The crowd, on either side of the aisle, watched them walk towards the witness table, in front of which thirty or so men and women with cameras knelt, snapping away. The accused, his image being beamed around the world, was an injured man trying to hide his pain and trying to maintain some semblance of dignity.

On the podium behind a long table sat twelve members of the US Congress, senators and representatives, chosen for this committee. They each sat behind nameplates, appropriately separated, looking very serious and watching the group as intently as the audience in this chamber... and the millions around the world! All the committee-members sported an American flag on their masks. Cameras clicked, sounding like a nest of rattlesnakes in the pit before the podium.

Mick and his counsel were led to their table and took their place behind two chairs. The Australian leaned towards his lawyer, who seemed to be the only person on his side and whispered, "It would be good to have some iron pants right now."

"Major Michael O'Rourke, would you raise your right hand," demanded a man in a uniform holding a bible.

Mick whispered to no-one in particular as he raised his hand ready to take the oath, "Such is life."

2

Inauguration Day—Beijing

Five months earlier...

The Beijing winter had its grip on the city. It had been a cloudless day, but the ever-present smog leached any color from the sky, leaving it a washed out gray. As the multitude went about their lives looking forward to a subdued Spring Festival, when the country would welcome in Chūn Jié, the lunar new year, the bitterly cold north wind snapped at the faces of the 'faceless' millions. And the cloudless gray day would soon succumb to the dark and starless night. The less fortunate that were unable to find warmth or shelter, or who were suffering the effects of the virus, would not see the new year's celebrations.

But at just before 1:00 a.m., in this particular room of Zhongnan-hai—the old Imperial Palace that was now the headquarters of the Chinese Communist Party—the General Secretary of the People's Republic, Jaw-Long, sat in comfortable shirt and slacks. Surrounding him were high-ranking military officials from the People's Liberation Army, and a few button-suited bureaucrats from the Central Committee. The air was warm and the atmosphere electric in this room in which only the most trusted and senior members of the Party were allowed. Some sat, some stood, but all were watching the TV upon which they saw the president-elect of the United States take the podium to receive the oath of office.

On the other side of the world, Washington DC, like Beijing, was in the grip of winter, and like in Beijing, the sky of the US capital was cloudless. But the Washington sky did not suffer from smog like in Beijing, and it sparkled a brilliant blue on this inauguration day. The puffs of mist from the mouths of the unmasked bore evidence that it was icy. However, the people who had gathered in front of the Capitol Building did not seem to mind because they were about to witness history being made.

The camera panned over the crowd. Women, wearing scarves, beanies and mittens, were crying with joy, for about to be sworn into office as the most powerful leader in the free world was a woman. Many wore the same mask that the president-elect had made famous. Others wore no mask, showing their defiance of the virus. After a tumultuous campaign full of emotion and angst, and against the backdrop of a deadly pandemic, America's first female president was to be inaugurated with her new husband by her side. He was a foreigner but who captured the hearts of Americans during the campaign. And though he was Australian, it was for love that he gave up his army career and his life in Australia.

This romance had captivated the world in general, but particularly in the States where the new 'first couple', a term that had been coined even long before the election, had featured on the covers of tabloids and tell-alls; and on *E News* as often as it did on *Fox News*, such was its entertainment value.

The defeated Democratic Party candidate and his supporters complained that the sobriquet 'the first couple', was an unfair advantage during the campaign. It, like the engagement and the wedding, was as fabricated as a mind-numbing reality TV show. And like reality TV, the masses lapped it up. The Democrats grumbled that these 'Republican stunts' were manufactured to 'polish a tarnished brand'.

Be they Republican stunts or not, they worked!

Even though the representative from Georgia had already proven her credentials and had served her constituency well—just as she had served the country well as an air force officer—it was only those who were politically interested that understood what a good candidate she actually was. The great masses of the disinterested were captivated by the story, not the politics. But this was how the politically disinterested became the politically involved. The voter turn-out was testament to that.

The tabloids and the news shows pushed the romance to spice up their political coverage. It was almost a *fait accompli* that she would win the popular vote against the old white man and his black female running mate. It didn't seem to matter that her views and policy intentions were sound, rational and more unifying than those of the incumbent president, or those proposed by her opponent. The public was more interested in the fairytale, not the facts. For America, this was the closest they had to a royal romance. And not since the days of Camelot had there been a positive feeling about the next administration.

Now, in the cold January air in Washington DC, women wept, and the crowd waved the Stars and Stripes. Even a few Australian flags could be seen standing out in the crowd just for good measure, showing their support for the soon-to-be First Gentleman of the United States.

* * *

The Chinese officials in Zhongnanhai watched the TV with anticipation as the camera focused on this man, this non-American, soon to be the husband of the President of the United States. The General Secretary watched him intently and, taking a bottle of champagne, poured himself a glass.

"Tonight, one of our own will go to sleep in the White House." He held up his glass toasting the scene on TV where the oath of office was being given.

The president-elect made her solemn oath to protect and defend the US Constitution, and when she uttered the words, "...so help me God," the moment had finally arrived. A woman had just assumed the 46th Presidency of the United States.

The outgoing president had been very subdued for the past week. Rarely had he tweeted his displeasure, which was very much out of character. This may have been at the insistence of the Republican Party, or, as was preferred, the 'GOP', the 'Grand Old Party'. Suffice it to say that his vitriol—that had been a hallmark of the campaign—ceased after Thanksgiving, leaving a peaceful December.

Now, as President Troup stood on the steps of the Capitol Building to see a woman, almost half his age, assume the office he so desperately wanted to keep, he did not even try to force a smile. His annoyed and somber face spoke volumes.

The Army band played the ruffles and flourishes, and soon the familiar sounds of '*Hail to the Chief*' boomed while the crowd cheered.

She mounted the podium and waited for the band to stop and the crowd to calm itself. Around the country, and around the world, millions waited for this woman's inaugural speech. Would it have the gravitas of a Churchill or Kennedy oration?

"My fellow Americans," she began, the crowd hanging on every word.

"As president I would like to honor and thank our servicemen and women, past and present, who have made countless sacrifices for our nation, with so many making the ultimate sacrifice so that we may live in a free and open society. In times of peril, we look to our God, and we look to our allies and friends, and we, as a freedom loving people, draw strength from both.

"Now, as I take the office as President of the United States, I am aware of the challenges the world has placed before us, and the trials we face as a nation. But I am heartened by the steadfastness of our people, and of the strong and deep bonds we share with the allies of America. And it is in that spirit that I would like to honor one nation in particular, Australia, a country that has stood by the United States in every time of our greatest need, by making this act my first official act as Commander-in-Chief." (In Australia, at 5:00 a.m. Eastern Summer Time, cheering could be heard in those houses that were watching.)

With that, an army general standing nearby stepped forward with a small wooden box. The crowd that had gathered in Washington for this ceremony was murmuring so loudly that it could be heard on the podium. The president looked at her husband. She indicated to him that she wanted him to come forward and to take a position next to her. Turning to the crowd and the cameras, she made sure that the microphones would capture her words.

"May I ask the First Gentleman of the United States to step forward."

Mick had to think for a second. The title 'First Gentleman of the United States' had been used many times in passing, and in briefings, and in the media, and in countless gags and spoofs by stand-up comedians and comedy shows leading up to this moment. It had become something of a joke; a reference to a fictional person. But now it was real. The president had just summoned him forward by that title. He took position next to her. She looked up at him and smiled. Was this a photo opportunity for the world to go with the president's first address? An image, and a speech, that would go down in history? If so, it was a great idea. He had to refrain from putting his arm around her waist, even though the urge was so great.

"Mister O'Rourke, please raise your right hand." He stood there, momentarily bewildered at what was happening. He had helped his wife with her inauguration speech, much to the chagrin of the Party's speechwriters, and he was expecting her to make what would be history-making words, words over which they had both labored. But that was not happening. Instead, the president was going 'off-script' and was asking *him* to step forward and to prepare to take an oath. The crowd and dignitaries continued their confused murmuring. This was definitely not what they were expecting during this momentous occasion.

Then it dawned on him what was happening! His face turned from a quizzical expression to one of great seriousness and solemnity when he realized what was about to take place... when he realized what she meant when she said, "her first act as Commander-in-Chief." His back stiffened instantly, and he came to attention. His right hand shot up, elbow bent at a perfect ninety-degree angle, just as Jack Nicholson's had done in the movie *A Few Good Men*. The general opened the little wooden box to reveal two small, bronze metal badges in the shape of oak leaves.

"Repeat after me: 'I, Michael John O'Rourke, do solemnly swear that I will support and defend the Constitution of the United States against all enemies, foreign and domestic; that I will bear true faith and allegiance to the same; that I take this obligation freely, without any mental reservation or purpose of evasion; and that I will well and faithfully discharge the duties of the office in which I am about to enter. So help me God.'"

The president recited the oath perfectly. It was obvious that she had rehearsed it many times. Mick had no hope of remembering it verbatim. One of the aides whispered the oath *sotto voce,* just loud enough for him to hear. He repeated it while the crowd watched in awe. In Australia, those that had stayed up to watch the event also watched in amazement, especially his former army comrades. Never before had America, or the world for that matter, seen such a spectacle, and the Democratic Party cynics cried foul once more. One could almost hear them yelling at their TVs '...another Republican stunt!'

"...that I will well and faithfully discharge the duties of the office on which I am about to enter. So help me God," said Mick, snapping his arm down and standing at attention. He paused, his breathing shallow, trying not to move. The general held the box for the president who took the two oak leaf clusters and, reaching down gently, took her husband's hand and placed them in his palm, giving his hand an affectionate squeeze. He was in civilian attire, so pinning them on him would be inappropriate.

"May I welcome you, Major Michael O'Rourke, into the United States Army and ask that you faithfully serve the flag, the president and the people of these united states."

The newly appointed Major O'Rourke, US Army, remained at attention sporting a serious countenance. He then saluted his wife, his Commander-in-Chief, who was smiling proudly... and the crowd went nuts.

"Thank you, Madam President," he said for the whole world to hear. "I shall."

She leaned forward and kissed him on the cheek... and the crowd cheered wilder.

In the warm room in Beijing, at 1:05 a.m. China Standard Time, the generals, admirals and bureaucrats could not but hide their joy. The man in the comfortable shirt and slacks was smiling.

"And so now we own America," he said.

3

On the Barbie

Dothan, Alabama. Three years earlier. Before the virus.

Mick bounded up the six or so stairs, the wine bottles clinking in his hand. The night air was heavy after the rain. At the top he pressed the doorbell, checking his appearance in the window's reflection. He looked up and down the street, still wet from the storm earlier in the evening. A small coupe cruised by, its tires making that 'wet road hiss' as it passed.

In a parked car nearby, a man smoked a cigarette, reading a magazine. He looked Asian, which was unusual here in rural Alabama. Mick caught his eye and raised his chin in acknowledgment, the way men do with each other as if to say 'w'sup?' The Asian fellow merely looked at him and nodded and started the car and drove away.

The door opened and Ben, smiling, welcomed him. "Hey buddy," he said, beaming. "Thanks for coming." Ben put his hand on Mick's shoulder and ushered him in, calling out to his wife, "Mickey's here, honey!"

Ben was dressed casually, not really befitting the dinner party being thrown. Jeans, a T-shirt that had obviously been worn at some time while he had been painting, boat shoes and no socks. He was immediately berated by his wife.

"Sweetheart," said Jessica, the attractive strawberry-blond with just the hint of some laugh lines near her eyes and carrying just a little bit of weight that seemed to complement her, "will you *please* get dressed!"

Jessica, or Jess as she preferred, rolled her eyes and turned to her dinner guest smiling and, after rubbing her hands on her apron that protected her beautiful, cobalt blue dress, reached out to draw him in for a kiss.

"Michael. Thanks for coming. At least *you* know how to dress for dinner," she said and pecked him on the cheek. Jess never called him Mickey like Ben and his other American friends. She preferred to call him Michael.

"Don't get too close," she said. "I'm covered in flour." She smelled of Crisco and fried chicken. She was exquisite.

Mick offered her the bottles.

"Oh, thank you. You're a doll. BEN! Please get dressed! Honestly!"

Ben was Mick's 'stick buddy' from years before. They were both army helicopter pilots and, as is often the way in military flight training, two trainees are paired up with one instructor. They would compare their performances; study together; quiz each other; and encourage each other. They would share in each other's successes and provide solace when things were not going as well. Strong bonds of friendship would often form between stick buddies, and in this case this is what had happened.

Michael O'Rourke—nicknamed 'Mickey Rawk' by his American friends in a misspelled and mispronounced homage to the Hollywood actor—was a Major in the Australian Army. He had come to the United States five years before to train on the giant twin-rotor Chinook helicopter at the US Army's School of Army Aviation at Fort Rucker in southern Alabama. After qualifying he headed back to Australia to fly them for the Australian Army.

Benjamin 'Ben' Theodore Johnson the third, was a second-generation US Army warrant officer, a Chief Warrant Officer Grade 4, a CW4 or 'dubya 4', whose father had been a chopper pilot during the seventies. Ben was only three years old when his father was killed in a helicopter crash in the aftermath of the invasion of Grenada. He was piloting a UH-60 Black Hawk helicopter for the 160th Special Operations Aviation Regiment when it crashed off the coast of the island. His body was never recovered. Years later, Ben would be flying the same type of heli-copter, UH-60s, at the same base going through the same training, just as his father had done twenty-three years before. After flying the Black Hawk for seven years he began his conversion training to the twin-ro-tor Chinook at 'Rucker' where, as a Chief Warrant Officer Grade 3, he was paired with an Australian Army captain, also a trainee. Their friendship grew from there.

Though Mick was the more senior, the formalities associated with rank were often dispensed with between stick buddies, and particularly between the Chief Warrant Officers and the commissioned officers. The latter knew precisely how important the former were to a capabil-ity and an appropriate amount of respect was afforded their significant expertise, even at the cost of military formality.

But Mick and Ben had not had to contend with that. They were stick buddies from two different armies under training. That was five years ago, and they had been friends ever since, separated merely by a continent and the Pacific Ocean.

After the death of his father, Ben's mother left Savanna in Georgia and moved back with her parents in Maryland. His grandparents had had a significant impact on his life. He was handsome in the typical American boy-next-door look. Fair-haired with a crooked smile and good build, although he was also sporting a small 'pot' belly that could only really be seen if his shirt was a little tight. He was relaxed and thoughtful and had married his third girlfriend—a family friend also from Maryland—who had been studying business at Georgetown Uni-versity in Washington. Their romance blossomed when he was on tem-porary duty at Weide Army Airfield in Maryland after his grandmother had set them up. From there he was posted to other units while Jess re-mained in DC and Maryland. It was a long-distance marriage for four years and they hated it. She completed her studies, including a post grad, but decided to follow her husband regardless of where his mili-tary career took him. She had had dreams of attacking the corporate world... but decided that she'd prefer to be the supportive wife to her army officer husband. This didn't really impress her parents, but they had a soft spot for Ben, so it could have been worse.

Now, five years after becoming friends, and after flying for their respective armies, both had returned to Alabama, and both were now instructors teaching the next generation of army pilots to fly. Ben was posted to Fort Rucker and was living in the nearby town of Dothan. Mick's exchange posting with the US Army was for two years, and when he and Ben found out they would both be at 'MotherRucker' together for those two years, they were both delighted.

Mick was at Ben's place two or three times a week and tonight Jess was holding a dinner party. Of course, their favorite Australian had been invited. Mick, however, suspected that she had other designs.

He looked around. He was the last to arrive and soon Jess was leading him by the hand to the guests milling on the back deck. He could not help but feel as though he was being led to his doom... or more precisely, an embarrassing and clumsy set up with some equally unfortunate single female friend of Jess's. Jess and Ben had no kids. It had been a hard pill to swallow seeing as how she had given up a business career in the hope of living an interesting life as a service wife and mother. Now she had to be content with being a service wife: no kids; no career... but she was happy with her friends, which included her husband's Aussie mate, Michael, who was now her 'pet project'.

In the garden there were some kitsch 'tiki' torches. While they seemed be a throwback to the seventies, they actually created a nice atmosphere in the warm and humid Alabama night. The cicadas were singing their trill song now that the rain had stopped (it reminded him of home) and fireflies glowed and disappeared near the bushes lining the backyard. Ben had emerged and put on some music: *Sweet Home Alabama* to start... the stalwart song of this once Confederate state. It was the 'Alabama anthem' and it seemed to waft through Dothan's suburban streets every Friday and Saturday night without fail.

Mick looked at the other guests. Five women; four men. Yep! This was a set up.

"Which one, Jess?" he asked her. She turned and smiled at him. She put on an affected, unauthentic southern accent, totally unconvincing from a yankee.

"Wah sir. Ahm sure ah don't know what you mean."

"I can count. I'm here to even out the numbers," he said. "So, which one is she, Jess?"

Jess merely smiled and took him into the crowd of couples and introduced him. All the guests were very polite and were interested in the fact he was Australian. Some said that they would 'put another shrimp on the barbie' for him and laughed at what they thought was a funny joke for an Aussie. Mick didn't have the heart to tell them that that TV commercial never aired in Australia and so it was only popular in the US. Oh, and it was more than two decades old! But he let them have their fun.

They were watching the news bulletin about the attempted assassination of President Troup the day before. He had been at a rally in New England when a gunman with a pistol rushed the podium, firing. One of the secret service agents overpowered him but was shot in the process. The bullet was not stopped by the agent's bullet-proof vest. Fortunately, it was a small-caliber pistol and the agent's injuries were not life threatening. The TV news showed him being taken away in an EMT ambulance and he was now being hailed a hero.

Some of the guests were discussing the agent, Henry Lee. It was obviously an anglicized name as he looked Chinese, possibly Korean. Apparently, according to the news, his colleagues nicknamed him 'Bruce' after the movie star and martial arts expert. (What was it with the Americans and their movie star nicknames?) His face was on every news bulletin and a somber President Troup would bumble through his interviews trying to articulate his admiration for the secret service agent.

Jess interrupted the TV and the talk of the assassination to introduce Mick. One of the women seemed to be intrigued by the images of Troup and Agent Lee and was transfixed by the news story. Jess interrupted her fascination with the story so she could present her Australian friend. She was an attractive woman with almond-shaped eyes and medium-brown hair. She had a slim build—fit and athletic—around thirty, it was hard to say. Her ethnic background and physique made her look younger than she was. Her eyes were a light brown, almost green color and her skin had a touch of Naples yellow to it that gave the appearance of a healthy tan. She was stunning. It was as though Mick was making his debut to society and was being presented, like a débutante, at a cotillion.

4

The Debut

"Leigh Buchanan, I would like you to meet Michael O'Rourke. He may have an Irish name like yours, but he's from Australia."

Leigh held out her hand. "Oh, I know you are from Australia," she said. "Jess has been talking you up since she concocted this sham dinner party."

Jess protested, and even appeared to blush slightly... as though her perfect plan had somehow been discovered.

"I figured as much," said Mick. "I mean it wasn't half obvious," he said looking accusingly at Jess, before turning back to his hostess' friend. "I'm pleased to meet you, Leigh."

"Actually," she replied, "my friends call me Maye. That's my actual name. Leigh is my middle name. Please call me Maye," and she held out her hand.

Mick shook it. Her skin was soft, but her grip was not limp. She smelled wonderful. Jess beamed. Her matchmaking seemed all but complete. Both Maye and Mick gave her a look of exasperation... as if to say, "We know what you're trying to do." But if Jess recognized that look they both gave her, she didn't seem to care. She continued to smile inanely until she saw her husband appear in an outfit that, in her opinion, was totally inappropriate... and in a flash she was gone to wreak havoc in his life, or perhaps to dress him herself.

"Jess tells me you're instructing at Rucker. Chinooks?" said Maye as she took a sip of her wine.

"Yes. I'm posted to the Chinook training battalion of the 223rd Aviation Regiment as a foreign exchange instructor. I have about another year-and-a-half here, then back home to Australia," he said. They were both distracted by Jess and Ben discussing his outfit. Perhaps discussing is not the right word because that infers a two-way exchange.

"What do you do?" he asked.

"I work in DC," she answered quickly. It seemed she had the answer ready to go, as though she got asked that a lot.

"Are you a beltway bandit?" he asked, referring to the nickname of businesses and lobbyists that had offices on Interstate 495, the Capital Beltway. It was a uniquely Washington term.

Her smile lit up the room and her head cocked letting one of her earrings dangle, revealing themselves amongst her long hair.

"How do you know what a beltway bandit is? That's very obscure for a foreigner to know."

"Oh, I know a little about a lot of things," he said smiling. "Actually, I just know trivia."

"Well, I'm impressed!"

Their talk was interrupted as Jess came out and began ushering the guests inside. She came over and, interlocking her arms into theirs, led them both to the table.

"I've got you two sitting on either side of me," she said, still beaming.

5

Smooth

In actual fact, the dinner was quite enjoyable. Ben had grilled some ribs and Jess had done some chicken and the wine was flowing.

Jess had proven to be surprisingly restrained in her matchmaking. Mick had expected her to be shameless, but for some reason she had not. In one way that was a shame, for Maye seemed to be reluctant to open up. She was polite; a good conversationalist, but the conversation was more about her asking questions of Mick than the other way 'round. And when Mick tried to get her to talk about herself, she was not as forthcoming. She adeptly deflected some topics and concentrated on others. She was considerate, charming and intelligent—not to mention extremely attractive—but it seemed that she was not too inclined to speak much about herself, or what she did.

But what he did discover about her intrigued him. She was formerly a pilot in the US Air Force and flew C-130 Hercules transport aircraft. Originally from San Francisco she was stationed in Georgia at Dobbins Air Force base for a few years and got to like living in Georgia. She bought a house just north of Atlanta, and now that she was no longer in uniform that is where she called home when she was not in DC. Oddly enough, Maye was Ben's friend first, having met in the Officers' Club while they were both stationed at a joint military base in Texas, but Jess and Maye had formed a very strong friendship since. It seemed that Maye wanted to distance herself from having too many military friends after she had left the air force, so Jess was a good mix between civilian life and military life. And both being childless while everyone around them had begun starting families, well that just made their friendship stronger. Jess would often go to DC when Ben was on an exercise that took him away. It gave her a chance to visit her parents and friends in Maryland, and spend some 'girl time' with Maye in Washington.

Mick got the impression that she had previously been in a serious relationship, possibly married, but that relationship had ended. From some clues and looks exchanged between Jess and Maye, he suspected that domestic violence may have played a part. But as far as what job she did now, when pushed, she would merely say, "I sort of do a bit of troubleshooting for key stakeholders that my organization represents. I engage in a lot of customer relationship building."

Mick knew something strange was going on. Every now and then, when he asked Maye a personal question about her life now, he could see Jess give a furtive glance towards her or Ben... as if it was a touchy subject. Mick knew better than to push it, although it did make the conversation somewhat stilted.

"So. Maye," he said looking into her brown-green eyes, "you seem to be reluctant to tell me exactly what you do, so I won't ask. All I can think of is that you're some sort of spook... or possibly in the witness protection program," he said jokingly.

"You got me," she said. "I'm on the lam after killing a guy in Tucson! I had to kill him... he was asking too many questions."

Even though this dinner was a blatant setup, Mick was enjoying himself, and particularly this intriguing woman.

6

Not So Smooth

Around midnight Mick decided to head home. After the dinner, and plenty of wine and cosmopolitans, the girls had thrown off their shoes and were dancing to a Sophie B. Hawkins' song screaming to each other 'Damn! I wish I was your lover!' The sober husbands now had to contend with their drunken spouses but would, perhaps, get lucky later that evening... or if they weren't so lucky, they may have to hold back their wives' hair as they threw up into the toilet.

When Mick went to leave, the wives came up and each gave him a big, and perhaps even slightly inappropriate, hug. They all then returned to the living room to turn up the music and start dancing while their husbands merely waved and shouted their goodbyes across the room returning to the heated discussion as to whether the Atlanta Braves had a chance this season.

Standing off to the side, patiently waiting her turn to say goodbye, was Maye, who had stayed sober. "While we both know that this was a set up," she said, "it was really nice meeting you. I hope we get a chance to meet again when I'm next in Alabama."

"How often do you come down from DC," asked Mick. He was kind of hoping she would say 'often'.

"I spend most of my travel time in Georgia when I come down from DC to see our stakeholders," she said. "It's a three-and-a-half-hour drive to here from Atlanta, so I don't regularly come to Dothan... but when I can, I do."

"That's a shame that you're not often here," he said. "Maybe next time I can get more details of that guy you killed in Tucson," he said with a grin.

Maye smiled. Mick could see how exquisite and exotic she looked.

"Maybe I'll tell you how I got rid of the body," she said, "but you have to buy me lunch first!"

"If I also buy you dinner, will you tell me how you beat the rap?" asked Mick.

"Lunch *and* dinner? You're on, Aussie!" She held out her hand. While the other women were giving hugs, Maye offered a goodnight handshake along with a beautiful smile. Mick was pleased about that. The hugs were fake, but Maye had taken time to wait to say her goodbye away from the others. A handshake meant she wanted to leave a dignified impression... and while he would have liked to have felt her body against his, and smell her perfume, he was glad that all that was being offered was a hand. He took it and, almost without thinking, kissed it. As soon as he had done that, he regretted it. How cheesy! How sophomoric! He immediately apologized.

"I'm sorry. That was such a stupid thing to do. That was so corny." He took her hand and gently shook it. "It was nice meeting you. Have a good trip back to DC," he said and turned for the door, escorted by Ben just as Jess spirited the beautiful Maye away.

"What the fuck was that?" asked Ben. "You kissed her hand! That was pretty lame, dude!"

Mick merely shook his head, disappointed with himself.

"Yeah, that *was* pretty lame."

Ben laughed and put his big, meaty hands around the shoulder of his Aussie mate and pulled him in.

"But she's hot, huh?" They stopped to look at her, now talking to Jess who was sporting a full glass of wine and being very animated. Ben shook his head admiring Maye and said, "I would totally hit that," he said. "Too bad I can't now!"

Mick watched her smiling at whatever Jess was saying, admiring her long straight hair and gorgeous figure. Who was this mystery woman? Maye gave Mick a quick glance and, seeing him looking at her, flashed him a smile.

"Yeah... she's something, alright," said Mick, enthralled.

7

On the Tarmac

Mick stood on the edge of the airfield tarmac watching the return of the gaggle of aircraft; the afternoon's wave of flight training as army pilots—some experienced, some brand new—learned the complexities of the Chinook. Even though he was himself very experienced, he still watched with awe at these huge and ungainly machines dancing in the air, his stomach reverberating to the slap of the rotors.

The Alabama heat was oppressive. Humid and hot, just like back home in northern Queensland. The sun cooked the concrete which, in turn, baked the air. A Chinook taxied to a nearby parking spot shimmering in the heat haze coming off the concrete, and after a couple of minutes its massive rotor blades wound down. Soon, the two pilots emerged from the cargo ramp at the aircraft's rear and walked towards Mick as the crew chief and aircrewman tied down the blades and readied the aircraft for the maintenance team.

One of the pilots was Ben. He had just finished the day's instruction and was taking Mick out for a drink at the Officers' Club. Soon, after the post flight de-briefing and paperwork, they were driving down the base's roads towards the O's Club, a cold beer and some hot wings.

8

The Officers' Club

The cool air-conditioning of the club instantly took the edge off the stifling Alabama heat. Around them, other officers mingled, some with their families and kids. Ben went to the bar and Mick sat in a booth as one of the young girls chose a song on what would once have been called a 'juke box'. Soon the latest boy band's lollipop music was blaring, totally out of place amongst the many military uniforms and olive-green flying suits in the club.

Ben returned with two beers.

"Hey man," he said, reaching to the vacant table nearby to grab its bowl of pretzels and nuts. "Jess wants to know if Maye has called you. She gave her your number."

Mick, on hearing this, became a little excited.

"I hope you don't mind that she did that. I mean, I was supposed to ask you and I totally forgot. She did it anyway, I guess."

He took a gulp of ale and grabbed a handful of pretzels, trying to seem nonchalant about it.

"Yeah, that's fine. She can call me if she wants to," he said. He didn't want to appear that he was excited at the thought of speaking with the woman who had so intrigued him.

"Mate, I have to ask you: what's her deal? What does she do?" Mick took a gulp of his beer, trying not to look too interested, but he was eager to know more about this woman.

"She works for the government," said Ben, almost cagily. "I'm not sure exactly what her day-to-day job is, but she spends a lot of time in Georgia. In fact, she's heading to Atlanta later this week and wanted to catch up with Jess on the weekend. If she drives down, you should come over!"

Mick's mood was elevated even higher.

"I'll see what I'm doing. I was going to head down to the Gulf but if I change my mind I'll drop around and say G'day." That was a lie. He had no intention of going to the Gulf of Mexico. He was going to binge watch some TV.

"You'll say Good Day," laughed Ben trying unsuccessfully to say the Australianism. "Anyway, Jess has been pushing for her to give you a call, so she may or may not call you."

The hot wings arrived, and they both took one and began devouring them, hot sauce smearing their lips.

"So. Mate," said Mick, "tell me the truth. Did you and her ever...?"

Ben finished his chicken wing and leaned in towards his Australian friend, as if to reveal a secret.

"Yeah, a long time ago. She was in this bad relationship, and I helped her out. Her ex was an absolute asshole. A typical fighter pilot jag off! She slept on my couch for a while when she left him. He beat her up pretty bad. We had to get a restraining order on him, and his CO found out and that became really messy. The asshole sneaked into my garage and keyed my pickup 'cos he thought I was putting it to her. He denied it but I knew it was him. I kicked his ass."

"Well, did you?" asked Mick.

"Damn straight I kicked his ass. Almost broke my hand doing it. To tell you the truth, I was trying to punch the fucker and I missed and hit the door... but then I landed a few good ones on his pretty-boy face and kicked him in the balls." Ben laughed at this and grabbed another wing.

"I mean, did you sleep with her?"

Ben munched his wing and lifted a finger to indicate that he had, once.

"It was just once not long after we first met. We were both drunk and she came on to me and I weakened. She was technically still married. I was actually married. Jess was in DC finishing up her post-grad at Georgetown and Maye and I were at San Antonio. I think her husband got a posting there, so she managed to also get a posting to Lackland in a non-flying position to do a language course, or something like that. I was flying sixties doing some instructing with the Texas National Guard unit there. It was a drunken mistake. Whatever you do, don't ever tell Jess," implored Ben, suddenly stopping in mid-bite.

"Do you think Maye may have told Jess that you two did?"

"I doubt it. I mean I would never have heard the end of it from Jess. She would have had my balls on a plate. Plus they're best friends now, so I doubt it."

Mick took a wing. These buffalo wings were terrific. He had become a fan of them from his previous trips to the US.

"Mate, can I ask you something else?"

"Sure," said Ben, licking the red sauce from his lips.

"I tried to ghost her on the web and I got nothing. I found nothing on social media or anything from her time in the air force. There is no Maye Buchanan or Leigh Buchanan. I found a couple of Buchanans who were air force pilots but they were males. Surely she'd have to be on the 'net somewhere?"

"So you Googled her, huh," said Ben with a 'big shit-eating grin' on his face. "I bet you want to Google her brains out!" he said laughing hysterically at his undergraduate *double entendre*.

Mick immediately regretted asking him. This teasing would no doubt go on for a while. Ben took another wing and began to eat it, but as he did the smile vanished from his face. He realized that Mick's previous ambivalence was him being coy. Now his Australian buddy had just let slip that he had been looking her up on the internet.

He was looking right at Mick, assessing him and the situation. He quickly summed up possible outcomes and his face suddenly took a serious expression.

"Listen, man," he began, using the chicken wing for emphasis. "Maye's situation has some serious baggage. I would recommend that you don't get involved with her if that's what's going on in your head. I told Jess that you weren't interested because I thought you weren't. I mean, you haven't mentioned her since that dinner party. I just assumed you didn't give a hoot 'n a holler about her. That's why I told Jess that it was OK for her to give her your number. I just figured that because you weren't interested in her, then it wouldn't go anywhere. Now I find out you Googled her, and you want to know if I fucked her!"

Ben threw down his half-eaten chicken wing into the basket with the rest of them and looked at the ceiling in exasperation.

Licking the sauce from his fingers he said, "You're a grown man. You can do whatever you want. But remember, you have a career in the Army back in Australia. If you start anything with her, I'll tell you right now, she *won't* leave the US and move Down Under with you... so you'd be starting something that will only end in you both being hurt."

Ben put his elbow on the table and his forehead in his hand. He gazed down at his beer. Mick was taken aback at this sudden change in the demeanor of his friend. "What the hell is going on?" he thought to himself.

"Fucking women!" said Ben. "All they want to do is match people up and make everyone one half of a relationship. Goddamn it! Bitches be crazy!"

Ben looked up at Mick.

"Man, you're a good dude. If it was anyone else, I'd say, 'Go for it!' But trust me, this one will not end well for either of you." He grabbed his beer and downed the rest in one gulp.

"C'mon, man. Finish your beer. I'll take you home."

9

Home Invasion

The car ride back into Dothan was subdued. Mick was puzzled as to why his friend, normally so laid back, had taken such a serious turn on this subject. There was obviously more going on. He wondered if there were, indeed, deeper feelings by Ben for Maye, or vice versa. Was this jealousy? If so, it was seriously misplaced. After all, Ben was married to the wonderful Jess. He seemed happy. She had sacrificed a potential career so he could pursue his. She was attractive and vivacious. Hell! Mick had a slight crush on her and thought Ben was incredibly lucky. This whole thing with Maye was extremely odd. But Ben was his really good friend. If Ben said that it was a bad idea, then there had to be a reason... and jealousy was the only thing he could think of.

The car pulled up in front of the townhouse Mick was renting. Grey with white trim, it was typical of the style found in new sub-divisions in Dothan. There were six of them in this row: the six-pack formation with a shared driveway and lock up garage underneath. They sat in silence for a short while.

Ben turned off the engine and turned to look at Mick.

"Man, like I said, you are a grown man. If Maye Leigh... I mean, if Maye calls you, then you decide what *you* want to do... but my advice is to not get involved. Go out with her to catch a movie or whatever but leave it at that. I can fix you up with one of Jess's other friends if you need some company while you're in the States. Hell, she's got some friends who'd love to bag an Aussie. But Maye has got some real baggage. You need to think of your career 'cos getting involved with her is trouble."

Mick got out of the car. He was puzzled. Why was Ben harping on about his 'career'? So what if he hooked up with Maye? Surely her past can't be too bad. Ben drove off honking his horn goodbye. Mick waved and walked up the driveway towards his condo. Perhaps Maye had some emotional issues. That's it! She's had emotional baggage... maybe from her marriage. That's why Ben was worried. Maybe she was even mentally unstable!

He headed up the stairs, opened the door and turned on the air conditioner. The afternoon sun had turned the condo into a sauna but if there was one thing that the Yanks were good at it was controlling the temperature, and it wouldn't be long before the place was icy cold. He put his keys and phone on the breakfast counter and grabbed a Coke from the fridge. He heard his phone buzzing and looked at the caller ID. Area code 770. Where the hell is 770? He'd seen that somewhere before. He picked up the phone, and as he pressed the 'answer' button he remembered. 770 is Atlanta.

"Hello?"

"Hey, is that Michael? It's Maye... Ben and Jessica's friend."

Mick paused for a second, letting it register who he was talking to.

"Ah, crap!" he thought to himself.

10

A Two-Way Street

They spoke for ages. Mick glanced outside and saw that it was dark. "You know we've been on the phone for almost two hours?" he said to her. Ben's dire warnings were still echoing in his mind, but he had to admit that speaking with Maye had made those concerns disappear. She had opened up somewhat about her past and her air force career. What she liked and what she didn't like about serving in uniform. She spoke highly of Ben and of Jess and of the time Ben helped her out when she was having some marriage problems and when she split up with her ex.

Mick decided not to divulge that he knew about the domestic violence and that Ben and she had slept together. He would let her lead the topics of discussion. Mick deftly steered it where he thought it was safe: her childhood in San Francisco, why she wanted to join the air force, her time at the air force academy, her flight training, flying C-130 transports to and from Afghanistan and Central America, her time as a government representative for business opportunities in Asia, her MBA studies, and other safe topics. They talked about her house on Lake Allatoona in Cherokee County, north of Atlanta where she hoped to retire, but she spent too much time in DC (although she still didn't talk about exactly what she did there). Often, whenever Maye was back in Georgia, Ben would find an excuse to fly up to the Georgia National Guard unit that was also located at Dobbins Air Force Base, with Jess coming along for the ride. Ben would concoct some reason to make the flight and he could grab a couple of single guys to crew the aircraft with him and let them have some time in Atlanta to get away from small-town Dothan. There was never any shortage of volunteers. There were plenty of aircrew who jumped at the opportunity to spend a weekend in Atlanta. This gave the guys a treat and it gave Jess some time to catch up with her friend. Something that both she and Maye really appreciated.

The more he learned of her the more he was impressed. Even somewhat in awe of what she had achieved in her life. There came a pause in the conversation. Speaking with her over the last two hours had been incredibly easy and enjoyable... but now he was at a loss for what to say. She decided to fill the void.

"So, do you want to know why I killed that guy in Tucson?" she asked jokingly.

"I know why," said Mick. "'Cos he asked too many questions... so I'm not going to ask."

She laughed. He liked hearing her laugh.

"That's too bad. I was going to tell you all about it when you took me out to dinner," she said.

"So you're coming to Dothan?" Mick asked, immediately wondering if this was a good thing or a bad thing. At the moment everything pointed to the former.

"Yep," she said. "I'll be there this weekend. Is that offer of dinner still on?"

"I thought it was supposed to be lunch," said Mick with a little anticipation.

"Yes, it was... but I've decided that your conversation skills have allowed you to graduate to dining after dark," she said. "I don't like having too much to drink at lunchtime."

"So we're drinking, are we?"

"You are over 21, aren't you?" she asked playfully.

"Why? Do you prefer younger studs?" As soon as he said those words, he regretted it. It sounded immature and something you don't say if you're trying to impress. It was the whole 'kiss her hand' thing again. He needn't have worried. Maye took the reins.

"No. I prefer real men with experience who can show a girl a good time... like the one I'm speaking with," she said.

Immediately, Mick got excited. This flirtation was now officially two-way! Ben's warning was now a distant memory.

II

The Wine

The dinner had gone well. Now they were heading back to Mick's car in the warm night air. Sleepy Dothan did well in providing just the right eatery for the two. Not too formal, but not too casual, it was the perfect location for a first date.

Mick was curious to see if Maye would open up even more given their long phone conversation, and she had. It turned out that she worked for a Federal Government department that sought out the needs of voters in Georgia and did its best to push the decisions through Congress, or at least that's what he gleaned from her explanation, although he still wasn't sure.

Her boss was some big shot in DC, and she was responsible for an area in Georgia that saw her virtually commuting back and forth often. She stayed in Atlanta mostly, at a company condo, but whenever she could she would visit her house to the north of the city and that's where most of her clients lived.

She told Mick about her time at language school in the air force where she learned Mandarin. It helped that her grandmother was Chinese—that explained the almond-shaped eyes—and she enjoyed the challenge of learning the language. Soon after she finished her language course, she left the active-duty air force and transferred to the Air Force Reserve after she was offered a job in DC with one of her former language instructors, and from there she did some corporate work for him liaising with government bodies that wished to do business in Taiwan. She was then head-hunted and took up the government job.

She opened up about her ex-husband. He was a controlling, violent man who blamed her for his career being stalled when she was stationed in Texas and he had felt obliged to go with her. Even though he made the decision to follow her, he blamed her for his stalled career. Soon the verbal abuse turned to verbal abuse and drinking, and then drinking and beatings. Her time at language in San Antonio became a morbid game of trying to hide or conceal the bruises before putting on her uniform and going to class. That's where she befriended Ben. He was by himself in Texas as an active-duty army member working with the Texas National Guard while Jess was still in DC at Georgetown University. Of course, Maye's husband immediately suspected that she and Ben were having an affair, which was not true. (Mick knew that on at least one occasion it was). She also made the decision that after five years of marriage it was time to leave him, and it was Ben who gave her a safe place to stay.

When the chain-of-command became aware of the domestic violence and the restraining order she had taken out on her husband, things really became ugly and out of hand. Her husband claimed that it was all a lie and that she was faking it. But she had photographs of the injuries and could prove it. She told Mick that she had never sought medical attention from the base military center, but went to clinics that were out of the way. San Antonio was a military town and too many people knew too many in uniform. She did seek psychological assistance and she had the psychologist report provided to her chain-of-command. That was when she moved into Ben's spare room.

"At first Jess hated the idea of some strange air force woman staying at her husband's apartment while she was in DC and so she was on the next plane to Texas to find out for herself what the situation was. When she arrived and met me and heard the story of the violence and abuse, she became very protective. I think she saw I wasn't a threat to her husband, and it was both of them that went with me to get my furniture. That was when Ben and my ex got into a fight. The asshole even damaged Ben's pickup truck one night when it was in his garage and they got into another fight. Of course, he has always denied everything and was posted away. We had our lawyers sort out the divorce, and I decided to buy a home near Atlanta, and I haven't seen or spoken to him since.

"After that, Ben and Jess became my best friends and Jess has been on a quest to try and fix me up ever since. That was the reason for the dinner party."

I2

Single Entendre

They drove back to Mick's place and parked in the driveway outside his condo, next to Maye's car. Neither of them wanted to get out of the car. What was to happen next?

"I've been dominating the conversation all evening," said Maye. "What about you? Tell me about your childhood."

"It's pretty vanilla. I was born in Sydney in a middle-class household with middle-class parents. Dad was a middle-level executive, and my mother was a middle-school teacher. My grades were fair... one could say they hovered around the middle of the class, and..."

"OK, smart guy," she said. "Let me ask you this. Would you ever leave Australia and live somewhere else?"

Mick thought a moment. This was a rather pointed question to be asked on a first date. Was there some ulterior motive to it? Was she sizing up possibilities so early in their relationship? Hell! You couldn't even call it a relationship. It was a first date!

"I've been all over the world and I consider Australia to be my home and the best place in the world to live. But if I had to move, then I'd move to the US. I like Americans and I like America. I find the place comfortably familiar and the people I like being..."

He was cut short. Maye's lips were pressed against his. She had grabbed his chin and turned it towards hers and kissed him passionately, cupping the side of his head with her hand. He reciprocated and

38

let his tongue just gently explore her lips. It was sudden. It was exciting. It was arousing. She smelt of vanilla and spices. Obsession? Most likely.

She stopped kissing. His expression must have been one of shock because she looked at him and then almost started laughing.

"I'm sorry. I just had that urge to do that right then and there."

"Hey! Don't be sorry," he said. "You can't fight your urges!"

Maye sat up in her seat. "Probably, but tonight I have to. I have the urge to stay with you tonight but that would not be proper on a second date."

Mick was confused. "You mean first date."

"I consider our phone conversation to be our first date," she replied. "I had more fun talking to you for those two hours than I have had on many actual first dates. So then this would be our second date."

It wasn't logical, but who was Mick to argue with this goddess? He just wanted to kiss her again.

But instead, she kissed him on the cheek and got out of the car leaving him panting and aroused. Before she closed the door she bent down, the neckline of her dress falling down enough to expose her bra holding in her breasts. Mick could not help but glance down to peek but caught himself, bringing his gaze up to meet hers. She was smiling. It was obvious that she saw what he had inadvertently done, that he tried to glimpse her breasts, and now he was embarrassed, and she could see it. She merely bent over even more, so that her dress revealed more of her chest. She kept a firm gaze on his eyes, and it was obvious she knew what she was doing. There was no question that she was in control.

"You know, in America, if two people have a third date, it usually implies that something is likely to happen," she said. "Did you know that?"

"Yes," he replied. He knew of the unwritten rule that a third date meant sex. "That is a uniquely American thing. That's not the same back in Australia."

"Well, you're not in Australia now, Kangaroo Boy! You're in the land of the free and the home of the brave. And when you're in America, it's rude not to follow the customs of its citizens," she said with a wry smile.

She cocked her head slightly and grinned. "Like I said, I consider this our second date. I'll call you... so keep your phone handy!"

And with that, she walked to her car, turned and smiled and drove away. He sat there stunned. The cicadas were singing—just as they did the night they first met. From now on, cicadas would be his favorite sound.

13

The Dodge

For the next week Mick tried to avoid Ben at the battalion. His dinner with Maye had been a secret and he didn't want to have to answer any questions from his good friend. Fortunately, Mick was on day training and Ben was doing night training, so their programs only overlapped for an hour in the late afternoon. During this hour, Mick tried to find jobs that would take him away from the training rooms, and he would return the next morning with notes and messages waiting for him from Ben, wanting to catch up for a drink.

Mick didn't know what he was going to say to him. For all he knew, Ben may already know that he went out on a date with Maye. Mick didn't know if Maye had told Jess—she probably had; you know how women are—and, of course, then Ben would know. Until he knew one way or the other it was probably safer to avoid him.

It was Thursday. There was no training next week, so his company had given all its members a few days off. Mick had six full days to do whatever he wanted. What he really wanted to do was to go to DC and see Maye. Although she still hadn't called him since their date. This had played on his mind a bit. How interested in him was she really? "I mean, couldn't she find the time for a quick chat in the last six days?" he wondered.

Walking out to the parking lot Mick pushed through the door into the hot southern sun. He ran straight into his big American mate who dropped his helmet bag onto the grass.

"Mickey! Man! I've been trying to catch you. Have you been avoiding me?"

What did he know? Mick wondered if he should just come clean or if he should try and get out of this situation. If he admitted he went on a date, would Ben be disappointed? What was the relationship between Maye and Ben? Why was he so adamant that Mick should not get involved with her?

"Sorry mate," Mick replied. "I've been busier than a pickpocket at a kangaroo convention."

"Hey. Jess wants to know if you want to come around for dinner tomorrow night. I'm not flying so I've got the evening off. We can get a head start on the weekend!"

Mick didn't know how to say no to this. If he went there he would be trapped and given the third degree by both of them... especially Jess. Ben could see the hesitation in his friend's face.

"Give it some thought. We'd love to have you over. I'd better get moving or I'll be late for evening brief."

Phew! It seemed Mick had been given a reprieve. Ben picked up his helmet bag and started towards the door to enter the building. Mick considered just telling them that he was busy and heading away for the weekend.

"It'd be great to have you over, buddy!" yelled Ben as he walked backwards into the building. "I know Jess would love to see you. She's dying to know how your date went with Maye last week!" he said with a smile and a wink. The jig was up. *Obviously* Maye and Jess had talked... why would he think that they hadn't? And Ben? Of course he knew! There's no way Jess would have kept that little bit of gossip to herself.

The fact that Ben smiled meant that he was either happy for his Australian mate, or that he was ready to really twist the knife when they were together next. Hmm. Going to dinner at their place could be quite excruciating, but he was eager to discuss Maye with the two of them and find out more about this incredible woman.

He headed to his car. Why hadn't Maye called him?

I4

The Swerve

As he headed out the gates of Fort Rucker towards Highway 84 to Dothan, his phone rang. He looked down at the screen and saw the 707-area code and almost swerved off the highway. Pulling up under the shade of some pine trees, he answered. The voice on the other end of the line was as sweet as a mint julep on a hot summer's day. (It looked like the South was having an effect on him!)

"Hey, you!" he said, trying to sound cool while trying to hide his excitement.

"Hey yourself," she said. "I don't know if you've spoken to Jess, but I had hoped to come down to Dothan this weekend."

Had hoped? This could only mean that hope had been lost of her coming to Dothan.

"No. I haven't spoken to Jess. I just ran into Ben, and he said that you and Jess had spoken."

"Yes," she replied. "We had a long chat. She wanted to know all the gossip."

Mick was enjoying this. As much as it would have been nice for Maye to come to Dothan this weekend, to know that he had been the subject of conversation was a good consolation prize. At least it was now out in the open.

"Anyway, I have to go away for business, so I just wanted to let you know in case she told you I was coming down."

Mick's heart sank. He was going to suggest that he head up to Atlanta if that was where she was going to be.

"Where are you going?" he asked.

"Canada." There was a pause. Mick was disappointed. Cars sped by on the highway. At this time of the day there was a minor rush hour as soldiers left the base. Maye continued hesitantly.

"I, um. I don't suppose you'd like to join me?" Mick was stunned. He was elated. Words failed him and he was left mute. Not only was this intriguing beauty calling him, but she was also inviting him on a long weekend away. Don't forget! It would be the third date, too! That meant a 'dirty weekend.'

"Well?" asked Maye, not hearing a response. "Are you interested?"

"Are you fair dinkum?" he asked.

"I don't know," she replied, "I have no idea what that means."

"It means, are you for real? Do you really want me to come with you to Canada?"

As soon as he said it, he regretted it. (Why was he always regretting things that he had done or said with this woman? He seemed to regress to being a clumsy teenager with her). But his question did sound a little desperate, though he didn't care. He was about to agree to go away with a goddess on what promised to be dirty weekend. Ben would probably not approve... m'eh!

"Yes. It would be great to see you again," she said. "Have you ever been to Vancouver?"

Mick noticed the cicadas were singing their shrill song. He loved Alabama!

15

My Own Room, eh?

He had arrived at the hotel by airport shuttle after catching the non-stop from Atlanta, only to find that he had been booked into his own room. Maye had arrived some time earlier and had reserved a room for him. He had his credit card swiped and headed up to the fifth floor to freshen up before going to meet her. He was a bit put out that he had his own room and wondered if the 'third date' was just something they said in films.

When he got to his room there was a message waiting for him under the door. It merely said 'Room 505. Knock twice only.'

He had a quick wash, sprayed some cologne and brushed his teeth. He couldn't wait to see her. He walked down the hall and knocked on the door. Two sharp raps. It opened and there, looking exquisite, was Maye. She pulled him in and kissed him passionately.

After a few long seconds they stopped and looked at each other. She then took him through the door that adjoined the next room where her bag was and where the TV was on with the sound turned down.

That was weird! Why book three rooms? What was going on? Maye could see the puzzled look on his face and sat him down.

"I need to be honest with you before we go any further," she said. She made him sit on the bed next to her and she held his hands and looked into his eyes. Her passionate welcome and inviting demeanor notwith-standing, it seemed that the mood had changed almost in an instant.

After what seemed an inordinately long time for Mick, she said in a hushed voice, "I'm actually a man."

Mick's face must have been a study in horror. He even recoiled slightly. He had just had his tongue in her, no wait, *his* mouth! Maye tried to keep a straight face but she could not, and she burst out laughing.

"The look on your face was totally worth it," she said, and kissed him. He, shocked and still not comprehending what was happening, sat frozen while she pressed her lips against his rigid face.

Grabbing his hand, she placed it on her breast and said, "These are real. You can put your heart back in your chest. I am all woman... and a very funny one, even if I do say so myself!"

Mick laughed. His heart was beating hard, but it wasn't because of Maye's joke. He was just happy to be with her. And hey! He just copped a feel! That was a bonus, even if he had almost soiled his pants.

"But in all honesty, there's something I do need to tell you." Mick was now a bit nervous at whatever this revelation was to be. Was she still married?

"I have not been totally honest about what I do for a living." Uh-oh. Is she a stripper? Or worse, a tax agent?

"When I said I worked for the government, that wasn't a lie... but it also wasn't exactly the truth." Mick's mind began to race. Was she a spook? A spy? That would explain a lot. She was a linguist. She had booked three rooms in a hotel out of the country. She was ex-military but now worked for the government in DC. Yep, she was definitely a spy. His mind did some rapid calculations, and the answer was the same: This was not good.

"I do work for the government. Well actually I work for the people." She paused and looked down and then back into Mick's eyes. Slowly she said it, measuring each word carefully, "I'm a member of the US House of Representatives. I represent the 11th Congressional District of Georgia.

She let it sink in for a moment or two and then stood up. With an air of the ridiculous, she placed her hands on her hips, raised her chin and looked off into the distance, saying mockingly, "I am the honorable Miss Young, Representative from the Great State of Georgia."

16

An Alias

Mick rapidly tried to process this information. That would explain the to-ing and fro-ing to DC and Atlanta. It also explained her reticence to admit what it was that she actually did. It also somewhat explained the three rooms. After all, she didn't want the media to catch on... although the two of them were in a hotel in Vancouver which is a long way away from the Deep South. She stayed silent for a few moments to allow Mick to grasp the situation. He was calculating her past and her present and any potential future that may involve him... but he kept coming back to her past and present. He didn't know much about her; she had managed to avoid any deep questioning.

What it didn't explain was why Mick couldn't find Maye Leigh Buchanan on an internet search. Surely such a young and beautiful congresswoman would have featured on any search engine. He asked her why she didn't have a profile online.

"I do, but it's under my maiden name. I'm Maye Leigh Young. Buchanan is my married name and I've kept a personal account and a Texas driver's license in that name so I can book hotels and hire cars without arousing suspicion. The other name I use as a representative in Congress. Besides, most of my friends know me from my air force time when I was Leigh Buchanan anyway so it's not so hard to keep that identity, but my birth name is Young.

Mick thought that it was a bit much. Sure, it's good to have one's privacy, but fake licenses and aliases seemed to be over the top. But who was he to judge? After all, he wasn't an American and he certainly wasn't a congresswoman who had escaped a violent marriage.

She reached into her bag and pulled out a glossy pamphlet. On it was featured a picture of her, smiling, standing alongside a man in a suit with perfect teeth and a fake tan. It said: 'Your Republican Representatives of the Georgia Northwest: Congresswoman Maye Young and Congressman Morris Turner. 11th and 14th Districts, GA.'

"I'm sure you understand that with you I have to take certain precautions. The Party wouldn't look too favorably on one of its members being out on the town with a strange man. It's bad enough that I'm a divorcée. But it seems that I fill some sort of demographic that appeals to conservatives. It helps that I'm a young woman with a military background. Apparently, I tick a few boxes," she said. "I need to be careful because everything you do, especially if you're a woman, is scrutinized by the men who want to sideline you, the ultra-conservatives who want to judge you, and the women who want to destroy you."

Now that the truth was out there, what was Mick likely to do? Would this be the end of any potential relationship? Both of them sat for a moment contemplating it. In reality it was Mick who was doing most of the contemplating because Maye had already thought about this for over a week, wondering whether or not to pursue it. Speaking with Jess didn't help. Jess adored Mick and she adored Maye. There was no hope for an objective viewpoint from her. Ben, on the other hand, was much more rational, and he had told Maye that it wasn't a good idea to get involved with Mick, just as he had advised Mick likewise. Mick now understood why Ben was so adamant. It wasn't jealousy, it was logic and reason.

Mick thought about the hotel they were in and the three rooms. It made sense now. "So that's why we're in Vancouver. You don't need a passport if you drive across the border."

She nodded. "It's also as far away that we can get to from Georgia and Washington. The chances of anyone recognizing me here are slim. We can be free to have a good time."

Mick thought for a few more minutes. The TV screen showed the local weather with a scene of Vancouver Island as its backdrop. Tomorrow it was going to be twenty-two degrees Celsius. A beautiful day in Vancouver.

17

Your Time is Almost Up

Maye patiently waited for Mick to consider the situation. "I need to think for a bit," he said.

"Sure. I know it's a lot to take in... but if it helps, I really like you and find you fascinating and smart," she paused momentarily, "and very sexy."

This last comment caught Mick's attention and he looked at the beautiful Maye. While this was not the most romantic setting, after all the only light in the room came from the half-drawn curtains and the blue glow of the TV, Maye still took his breath away. He had been thinking about her almost constantly since their last encounter and it had started to affect his duties. He had been distracted during pre-mission briefs and whilst they were flying. On more than one occasion the crew chief had to repeat what he had said over the helicopter's intercom because Mick's attention was elsewhere.

Now Maye had dropped this bombshell which filled in almost all the previous blanks. Maye could see he was looking at her in a different light; with more clarity now that he knew that she held a public office. Any possible relationship would need to be considered with that in mind. She decided to be bold.

"Michael," (she hadn't called him that since Jess's dinner party—Mick had insisted on being called 'Mick'—and it lent an air of seriousness all of a sudden), "you may not wish to get involved in my life. It is a complicated one and with you being an active-duty member of a foreign military, it would become even more complicated. So I wouldn't blame you if you just wanted to part company as friends and we can go back to our own lives as they were before Jess set us up."

"Ah, yes. Jess."

She continued as she sat down next to him and took his hand in hers. "I am very much attracted to you, but I don't want to complicate your life, so here is what I propose."

Mick was not sure where this was going.

"I think that while we're here in Vancouver, at least for the next three days, we should leave Georgia and Alabama and America and Australia behind... and just be Michael and Maye: two tourists enjoying Canada's sights. What do you think?"

He looked at her beautiful almond-shaped eyes. "I think that's a great idea. It will give us some time to think about this properly and objectively."

She smiled and kissed him on the cheek and put her arm around him and rested her head on his shoulder still holding his hand. Her hair smelled wonderful.

"That sounds good. Let's not worry about the complications. We have three days to wander around and eat too much and drink too much."

He rested his head on hers and kissed the top of her head as though they had been a couple for years. This tender expression, so simple in its execution, made Maye squeeze his hand lovingly. She then moved forward and knelt down in front of him and, now holding both his hands, looked into his eyes. "Three days of being tourists," she said, "sounds so wonderful. I can't wait." She then paused and let go of his hands.

Cupping his face, she kissed him with a passion that surprised Mick. Maye was confident and was direct. He had been wondering how he would make the first move after all the clues she had given him, but that question was now moot. She was in charge, and he was happy to go along.

It wasn't long before their passionate kissing developed into a more anxious effort to bare all. Their hands were excitedly fumbling with each other's clothes, and the anticipation of sex in an anonymous hotel room with someone new was only heightening that excitement. It had been a long time for both of them...

* * *

"Well, that was a surprise," said Mick, his arm around Maye's shoulder as she rested her head in the crook of his neck and ran her finger through the hair on his chest. "My mum told me to watch out for fast women with loose morals... or was that loose women with fast morals? I can't remember."

"If there's one thing I have learned in DC," said Maye, "is that you must be ready to take any opportunity presented to you."

Mick listened as she spoke about working in the House of Representatives and the power plays that were *de rigueur* for that cauldron of hypocrisy. The 'puzzle palace' she called it, 'where dreams go to die and ethics are sacrificed on the altar of expediency or self-fulfillment.'

"It is hard to find good men or women," she said. "Most start out full of hope, but hope is soon lost to the churn and grind. If you speak up, you risk being sidelined. And then, if you're sidelined, you're never in a position to do any good at all. So you have to walk a fine line between being moral and being a sell-out if you have any hope of trying to make a difference. Just once I'd like to make a difference and be there for the people without the Party hacks trying to whip me into toeing the line."

Over a room-service dinner she related how so many bills, good bills, were introduced on the floor of the House and which should have passed debate, but which ended up getting killed in committee as the power players used them as bargaining chips for less-than-honorable ambitions. Ambitions that rarely served the citizens. As she spoke, Mick could tell that her motives for being in office were true, but her cynicism towards the system was growing. "Good men," she repeated, "or women... are hard to find."

She reached across the table, took Mick's hand and looked into his eyes. "I think you're a good man," she beamed, "from what I know about you. Jess loves you and has been shamefully touting your good name!"

"I'm not that good," he responded.

"I beg to differ," she cheekily replied.

He leaned across the table so his lips could meet hers and kissed her. "Well, I think you're pretty good, yourself!"

"Oh, I'm very good... especially when I'm bad!"

She stood up and moved towards him, opening up his bathrobe leaving him sitting at the table, exposed.

"Ooh. Yum!" she said, ogling him and fondling him. She then kneeled down before him and took his rapidly enlarging member in her hand and put it in her mouth.

He groaned and she smiled as she began to demonstrate an above average skill at this most pleasing expression of love—or lust. Mick closed his eyes and thought about how he couldn't wait to reciprocate.

"Oh, Maye!" he said in pleasured tones. She took his penis from her mouth and letting her tongue lick it from base to tip merely said, "Call me Congresswoman Young."

"Oh, Congresswoman Young... please poll your constituent!

She smiled and returned to the task at hand pushing her lips down as far they would go while her mouth took the fullness of this man's manhood. Pausing for just a moment she asked, "Do I have your vote, Sir?"

Mick, eyes still closed in pleasure, could not stop the words coming out of his mouth. "You can have anything you want at the moment!"

Again, she smiled and took him in her mouth while he ran his fingers through her soft hair.

Oh! Canada!

18

Fessin' Up

The two of them spent the night and the next morning in bed wrapped in each other's arms. Mick didn't want to admit to himself that this was more than just a physical attraction. Sure, she was beautiful and sensual, but now that he had learned that she was also an elected official, it was surprisingly even more exciting.

As they lay there, they could see that the day had turned out be very pleasant. When the sun was high they began to feel hungry and even though they would have been quite content to have spent the rest of the day in bed and merely order more room service, they decided to explore some of Vancouver's sights.

Mick tidied himself up and left through the Room 505 door and headed back to his own room to shower and change. They had arranged to meet away from the hotel a couple of blocks down the street amongst the crowd.

Maye had suggested a cafe near the seaplane terminal, and so they met there and ate and drank and watched the seaplanes come and go. The morning was a pleasure of sex. Now it was a pleasure of eating and really getting to know this woman, this representative of Georgia.

Mick watched her mesmerized by the seaplanes as they taxied in and out of the docks with their loads of tourists. She would be eating and talking but then would get distracted by a plane, and her voice would trail off for a few seconds.

"Tell me what it's like to fly Hercs," he said. Maye had been a C-130 Hercules pilot for almost seven years.

"I miss it every day. My time in the air force were some of the happiest in my life," she said. "I have such a deep love of the military and anyone who serves or has served in it."

"What made you want to join the air force?"

"My grandmother," she replied, surprising Mick. She put her fork down and wiped her mouth with a napkin before taking her glass of wine in her hand.

"Well, you know how my grandmother is Chinese?" Mick nodded. He remembered her saying that from their dinner in Dothan, "well, my grandfather was an American airman. Have you ever heard of the Flying Tigers?" she asked.

"Of course," replied Mick. "The American Volunteer Group. They flew for the Chinese during the war." (Maye was impressed... again.)

"After the Japanese surrendered, the civil war in China began between the nationalists and the communists. The communists gained a lot of territory, especially in the north. Some Flying Tigers pilots formed a company called China Air Transport. They'd fly supplies and arms for the nationalists from their base in Shanghai. My grandmother was sixteen and was working for them, washing their clothes. She had survived the massacre of Nanking and saw her mother raped and murdered by the Japs. When she was twelve she escaped with her older brother and younger brother and some catholic nuns by floating down the Yangtze to Shanghai where they could hide out for the next four years and survive the war.

"After the war she met some of the Americans who were flying their cargo planes from Shanghai and offered to wash their clothes for money to help feed herself and her brothers. Because she had learned some English from the nuns, she was useful for the Americans, and they hired her and looked after her. She says that if it wasn't for their generosity she and her brothers would have starved to death.

"Anyway, her older brother—my grand uncle—was forced to fight for the nationalists and he was never heard of again. She was seventeen and fell pregnant to one of the pilots, but he looked after her and her younger brother, and when the country fell he made sure that they were safe in Formosa when they evacuated. The baby she gave birth to was my mother, so my grandfather was a Flying Tiger. I'm very proud of that fact. He then moved the family to San Francisco and continued to fly for the US Government in Korea during the war and for the French in Indochina. Have you ever heard of Dien Bien Phu?"

Mick nodded and listened intently.

"Because my mother was Eurasian, she didn't really get accepted by the Chinese community in San Francisco. In fact, she was embarrassed about being half-Chinese and spent her whole life being as American as possible. In fact, she ended up marrying an American pilot friend who worked for her dad."

"My grandmother still held onto a lot of her old ways. She would tell me the stories of her childhood in Nanking and then when she was with the pilots in Shanghai and how she loved them all and would watch as they flew their old planes full of troops to fight the communists, including her older brother, and then bring back refugees or cotton or other materials to keep the economy going. She said that they were the bravest men she had ever seen, much braver than Chinese men. If you ever meet my grandmother, never mention the communists. She hates them. They stole her country and they stole her brother. China is not a subject we speak about in our family.

"So your dad was a pilot?"

"No, that was mom's first husband. He was killed in 1973 in South Vietnam. Mom re-married, this time to someone with no interest in flying. And *that's* my father. He was a good man but a boring and predictable one. He died of cancer six years ago. But it was those stories of brave men flying airplanes that made me want to join the air force, so I went to the Air Force Academy and became a Herc pilot. My grandmother was so proud... so were my mom and dad."

Mick wanted to know about her marriage and how it ended but wasn't sure how to brooch the topic. He didn't want to say too much.

Ben had told him those stories about her marriage in confidence. He decided to take a chance.

"Can I ask you about your marriage and what happened?" He waited tentatively.

She paused and her gaze stayed on one of the seaplanes as if she was wondering if she should discuss this chapter of her life. She decided that she would. After the intimacy they had already shared, what more could be hidden?

"I met him while we were at the academy in our last year. My first three years were very busy. I was doing a double major in political science and economics, and I was hating life. I was even doing a minor in Chinese because I figured it would be easy to learn with the help of my grandmother. But it was horrible and I hated it. I wanted to quit and just get out and then I met him. He was smart and handsome and he understood my workload, so while the other cadets were having fun and getting drunk, he'd be studying and I'd be studying. He was determined to be a fighter pilot while I was selected for cargo aircraft. He was pretty arrogant. Typical fighter pilot. I was young and he wanted to fly F16s. I was envious because I wanted to fly fighters but for whatever reason I was sent to Hercs. I don't regret that, though. I got to fly some incredible missions."

Mick was hanging on every word.

"After we both finished our training, we got married but had to spend a few years apart because we couldn't get stationed at the same base. I was posted to Dobbins in Georgia, and I really liked it there. We tried to make it work, or should I say that *I* tried to make it work. I knew he was screwing around on me, but I persevered with the marriage. A few years later I was offered a chance to attend the Defense language school in San Antonio on a two-year trial foreign language course, so I took it. I figured that he could get an instructors' posting there also and we could finally be married and in the same zip code. My minor in Chinese had come back to haunt me and they strongly encouraged me to do the full two-year course which they were trialing. I told him that the only way to save our marriage was if he took a two-year posting as an instructor at Randolph Air Force base at San Antonio.

"So, I started the Chinese-language course." She looked at Mick who raised his eyes and merely said "Chun jai". She laughed. So did the Chinese man sitting at the next table eating a meal with his wife. Mick had obviously said it too loudly and was a little embarrassed. He looked at the Chinese man who was also embarrassed and was now looking down at his noodle dish. Maye glanced over at him and back at Mick and smiled.

"Where did you learn that?" she asked. "You know it means 'silly boy', not 'silly girl'."

"I have a lot of friends who are Chinese, so I know how to swear and that's about it. But Mandarin is a hard language. You must have been under a lot of pressure."

Yes," she agreed, but seeing the Chinese couple at the next table she leaned in towards Mick and in a whisper said, "but it is the language of one of America's enemies and because my grandmother spoke it, and I knew enough of it to speak with her, I figured that it would be a good step for the future."

Mick nodded. It was going to be the Chinese century.

Maye suddenly went quite serious.

"Steven, I don't think I told you his name, well he blamed me for him not being a fighter pilot anymore. I tried to tell him that this was only a short-term posting. It was a two-year trial and so if he could just spend two years doing a nine-to-five flying job while I studied, then after that I would follow him wherever he wanted to go. I tried to convince him that he was *still* a fighter pilot, even if he was only flying trainers."

"Our marriage started to fall apart. I spent two months sleeping on the couch. We hardly said a word to each other. Some nights he wouldn't come home at all. That's when I met Ben who was flying Black Hawks. He just seemed to be a decent guy, even if he was a soldier," she joked. "Steven accused me of sleeping with him, which I wasn't, and things started to get violent. He would make sure that the bruises were on parts of my body that wouldn't be seen by anyone. He fractured my rib once and I had to get it seen to in San Antonio. There's no way I could go to the military medical center, so I went to the general hospital. I didn't have health insurance because the military looks after all that, so I had to pay for it myself."

Mick could feel his anger growing. He wanted to make this guy pay for hurting this wonderful woman.

"It was a very trying time in my life," she said. "I couldn't sleep. I couldn't concentrate. My grades were falling and it looked like I might even fail the course. I decided to see a therapist and that sort of helped.

"I guess I was happy to be around Ben. He seemed like a decent guy. Also, it was good to have a big guy like him in my circle of friends. I didn't trust men much at that time and I certainly wasn't going to be alone with Steven. Ben and I started spending more time together. Jess was still in DC, and he was living a bachelor life in San Antonio. I think he missed having female company. He noticed that something wasn't quite right and he offered me a place to stay. That's how he, Jess and I became friends. Jess came down to find out more about me and she and I hit it off. Sisterhood and all that."

The waitress came by and topped up their drinks.

"Steve knew I was staying at Ben's and one night he came around and scratched Ben's pick up with a key. That happened while Jess was staying. Ben found Steve and kicked his ass. That's when I got a restraining order on him with Ben and Jess's help. Steve's CO found out and he was removed from flight duty. We separated and the divorce was granted a year later after I gave the judge evidence of my psychological condition and the beatings. The air force really supported me well, but it wasn't long after that that I left full-time duty.

"One of my language instructors recommended me to a civilian company in DC and I worked there for a while until I was headhunted by a Taiwanese manufacturing company that was making sporting goods. I worked for them for two years flying around Asia to their factories and in the US and Canada. I'd help with their production and distribution. They said that they would pay me a higher salary if I did my MBA and so I got a lot of my economics and leadership training credited and finished it in about a year-and-a-half part time.

"I had no husband and no kids and had lots of time stuck in hotel rooms around the world doing assignments. When I got my master's I wanted to re-negotiate my contract as they had promised but they did the typical Chinese thing and reneged. I was furious. That, plus I didn't like the way they did business and how they treated their staff. They would speak Hokkien, you know, Taiwanese, if they wanted to talk about me behind my back. I guess they were too Chinese, and I was too American... so I left them. I had always been interested in politics since the academy and I had joined the Republican party in Georgia when I was posted to Dobbins a few years before. So now that I was out of the military, I decided to get more involved. I put my name up to run for a state office, but the party decided to put me up for a special-election for a federal district seat when the congressmen died in office. I then won the primary and then the district during the general election. I've been the representative for the last two years."

Mick had been listening intently and now was the time to ask questions. "Where's Steven now?"

"I don't really know. Someone said that he'd left the air force and wasn't doing too well. To be honest, I don't care where he is. Is that not very Christian of me?" she asked him.

The roar of the radial engines of the seaplanes and the raucous fighting between seagulls caught their attention, and Mick excused himself so he could visit the bathroom and also get some more drinks. Carrying two glasses of wine he returned to their table and saw Maye talking to the Chinese couple and pointing to a map. When he returned to the table the Chinese couple got up and with a lot of bowing of heads thanked Maye in Chinese and bowed and smiled at Mick. The little Chinese woman took Maye's hands in hers bowing profusely and with that they walked off to see the sights.

"Impressive," said Mick placing a glass before her and taking his seat.

"Don't be," replied Maye. "My Mandarin is so rusty I may have just given them directions to Seattle."

Maye took a sip. It was now her turn to learn about this man. She could still smell him on her skin.

19

I Come from a Land Down Under

"What about you?" said Maye. "I want to know about Michael O'Rourke from Down Under, but this time in more detail please!" Mick told her about how he was an only child and that his parents split up when he was young and how he thought it was his fault. How his father, about nine years later, had a heart attack while driving on a lonely highway with his dog and how the car he was driving crashed down the embankment on the side of the highway and how he was found a few days later by a truck driver sitting high enough to notice the car wreck. They found his body in the wreckage with the dog sitting next to it. His mother had severed all ties with his father and would tell him that he was a mean man who beat her. Now, as an adult, he wondered how true that actually was.

He told her of his mediocre grades; of his mother's various boyfriends, none of whom hung around much; and of being raised by a television where he learned about life and the United States through sitcoms. He told her of how he felt lost after leaving school and worked at various jobs without much direction, and how his good friend, a half-Chinese mate, got him a job in his father's restaurant where he waited tables.

After a while doing that, he spent time in Bali and Thailand and even China teaching English to kids for a while. He hiked around Europe and the US for a year before returning home to Australia. He had not found himself during all his travels, but it was while he was in the US he saw army helicopters at a local airshow and thought that they were impressive and dreamed of doing that. When he got home to Australia he thought he'd give it a try and was lucky enough to be selected for officer training, not so much for his grades but for his maturity, he was now twenty-three years old and had life experience. He was selected for flight training and the rest is history. "The good thing about the army," he said, "is that I didn't feel 'lost' anymore."

"I did take some time off from the army to do a business degree, which I paid for myself. I was able to get credits for my military training and also for my aviation training so was able to get a masters in just over a year.

"One of the projects we had to do was to come up with a product that we had to manufacture and then market and distribute. I came up with an idea for a combined helmet bag and carry bag for aviation. And so I went to Shenzhen in China to see if I could get it manufactured there. Long story short, I put my savings into it and it didn't work out and so then I was broke—not the millionaire I thought I was going to be. So I returned to the army where I am very happy and where I have stayed. I love it. It brought me to Alabama and to a dinner in Dothan where I met a pretty amazing woman."

Maye smiled and reached out and took Mick's hand in hers.

"I guess we all have sob stories in our past," she said looking into his eyes. He saw that she genuinely cared about his story and his lonely childhood and about being lost. "And I hope that you have found yourself now, because I'm glad I found you."

She stopped. This was getting a bit too serious a conversation. The question would linger until an answer was found: how involved would they become? He had a career on the other side of the world, and her career was busy and sensitive and high profile. This whole relationship was likely doomed to fail. She couldn't allow herself the luxury of expecting—or even hoping—that Mick may want to start a relationship with her. This realization saddened her, and she lowered her gaze and withdrew her hands.

Mick could see the sadness suddenly appear in her eyes. He could tell what she was thinking. It had been playing on his mind also for the last several days, and especially since yesterday when she revealed her real life in politics. Do they dare play with fire? Surely it could not end well. Her life and his were poles apart, a world apart, in fact.

"Hey!" he said, trying to bring the mood back up to where it was before. "You and I have three days in Vancouver..."

"And three nights!" she interjected with a cheeky smile.

"Right! And three nights. So, let's just enjoy ourselves. We can ponder more serious matters in a few days before we go back to our real lives. But for now, let's enjoy Vancouver."

And with that, they decided to explore the sights.

20

In the Cards

They did all the tourist attractions they could in one afternoon ending up in Chinatown. They went past a fortune teller and Maye dared Mick to have his fortune read.

Mick didn't believe in such nonsense, but it's amazing what a man will do for a beautiful woman. It was all for a laugh anyway.

They went into the little shop where a small Chinese woman sat in the corner watching a daytime soap. Mick and Maye hesitated at the door and the Chinese woman beckoned them in. She waved them towards her and motioned for them to sit at two chairs at a little table. The air was heavy with the smells of cooking and incense. It was cluttered with Chinese lamps and figurines of cats and dragons. Scrolls with *han* writing hung from the walls vying for space with ink paintings of the Great Wall and tigers and such. In the back room an old Chinese man glanced at them through a curtain of beads and, disinterested, returned to whatever he was doing.

"You want tea?" asked the old woman pointing to a white porcelain pot and some small cups.

"No, thank you," said Maye.

The old woman studied Maye carefully and, as if she was shortsighted, leaned in to look at her more closely.

"*Nǐ shì zhōngguó rén! Nǐ huì shuō pǔtōnghuà!*" she said suddenly, pointing at her accusingly.

Mick was startled by the old woman's sudden animation. He looked quizzically at Maye.

"Sometimes Chinese women can see my heritage," she said to Mick. "She told me that I was Chinese and that I could speak her language."

"How would she know that you could speak Mandarin?" he asked.

"She's just guessing," replied Maye and turned to her saying, "*Wǒ zhǐ huì shuō yīdiǎn pǔtōnghuà.*"

"We want a reading for this man," she said to the woman, insisting on speaking English. The little Chinese woman seemed put out by this. She wanted to speak to this American woman in her own tongue.

"Ok. Ok," said the little old woman. "I read your aura. I read your cards. I read your hands." With that she took Mick's hands and looked at his face, scrutinizing it closely. After a few seconds she turned his hands over and looked at his palms. Her eyes narrowed and she looked back at his face and started nodding.

She then took out a deck of cards. To Mick's surprise they were tarot cards.

"Tarot cards?" he said to Maye.

"I guess she's cross-disciplinary," she quipped.

The little old woman, who reminded Mick of Yoda from Star Wars, took the cards and spread them on the table, mixing them up. She then took Mick's hands and pushed them onto the mess of cards bidding him to do likewise.

"You touch every card," she demanded of him. "You mix them. Touch every card," she said.

Mick dutifully did as he was told, making sure that they were thoroughly mixed and that he touched them all. The old woman took his hands again. They were rough and dry and she was surprisingly forceful with her grip. The man in the back room pulled the bead curtain aside and glanced into the room and then let them fall back with a rattle as he disappeared out of sight.

"You choose six cards," she said. "You put them in a line," she said tapping the edge of the table closest to her. "Here! In a line! Even," tapping the table again with a bit more force. "You lay them with face down."

Mick picked his six cards and laid them in an even line on the edge of the table like a squad of soldiers, all face down. The old woman sat back and watched his face as he did this, every now and then glancing at Maye and frowning.

She pointed to the first card but was careful not to touch it. "You turn card," she ordered him. "This card, this is you."

Mick turned the card. It was a well-worn card with the edges no longer even and shiny, just like all the others in the mess of cards on the table. It showed a man in a suit of armor riding a horse near a river and holding a cup. The picture was upside down, but he was able to easily read the words which said 'Knight of Cups'. The little old woman nodded eagerly. She seemed happy that this card had been chosen. She then pointed to the next card.

"You turn this card. This card is your spirit."

He repeated the process. This time it was a picture of a man with a halo hanging from a tree by his ankle. The old woman nodded eagerly again.

"Now you turn next card. This is your love."

Mick turned the card. It was a young man holding a sword. It was upside down like the first card and said simply, 'Page of Swords'.

"Now next card. This is your love spirit. It is her spirit."

He turned the card revealing a picture of a man carrying swords away. It said seven of swords. The little woman's face did not change but she did glance again at Maye.

"Next card is your life together. Your future.'

Mick turned the card, and it showed a lightning bolt striking the top of a tower and knocking off a crown. Two figures, a man and a woman, could be seen falling from the tower. The woman's eyebrows raised slightly but she said, "Last card is the end of your life. How you will live."

Mick turned the final card. "The Hermit," he said as he looked at a white-bearded old man standing on a snow-capped mountain holding a lamp. "Hey, looks like I'm going to be hitting the slopes," he said looking at the picture and joking. Maye laughed.

"Yeah, old man," said Maye. "Nice beard." She looked at the woman. "So, what does this all mean?"

The woman's demeanor had not improved. She was not impressed that Maye would not speak with her in Mandarin, and she was being forced to speak in her broken English. She poured herself a cup of tea and slowly sipped it, as if to teach her a lesson. She then turned to Mick and spoke directly to him, ignoring Maye.

"You are kind man," she said in her fractured English taking his hands again. "You work with machines. Big machines. You drive big machines." She made a fist and moved it back and forward when she said that. She didn't make the movements of driving a car, but Mick noted she was unwittingly mimicking holding the controls of a helicopter. He laughed to himself.

"You miss being in the war," she said. "You want war. You want fight."

"No-one wants a war," he said to her puzzled.

"No," she replied, somewhat frustrated that she could not explain herself well enough. She thought for a moment trying to find just the right words.

"*Tā yuànyì wèi bǎohù tārén ér zhàn*," she said to Maye in Chinese, hoping she would translate.

Maye obliged her. "She said that you would want to fight to protect others."

The old woman nodded eagerly. Mick didn't believe in this type of stuff, but he had to admit to himself that he liked hearing those words from this old woman.

When she was satisfied that he understood what she meant, she continued.

"The woman you love," she said pointing to the androgynous figure of the Page of Swords, "has secret life."

Mick thought to himself, "Maye *does* have a secret life, I guess!" and glanced over at Maye. She could see what he was thinking and smiled a discreet smile.

"You will be with this woman, and you will have great change. Your life will be busy and difficult with this woman," she said pointing to the tower card. "It will be a big change."

Mick was making calculations of what his life would be like if he were to pursue Maye. It would be difficult, that's for sure! Was he now making the cards fit his hopes or was he just trying to find clarity? He glanced down at the last card, the Hermit. He found himself being a bit more serious and wondered how the card was interpreted. Would that mean that if he wasn't with Maye then he would be destined to be alone? To his own surprise, he found himself genuinely curious and asked the old woman what the last card meant.

"You will see clearly. You will not have others seeing for you," pointing to the lamp. "You will find your own path for your happiness."

He thought to himself, "well that wasn't so bad". Perhaps the old woman meant that he would decide for himself what path he would take: to be with Maye, or to not be with Maye. At least that's what he told himself.

21

Goodbye, Vancouver - We'll Miss You

Three fabulous days and three steamy nights had passed and Mick and Maye's attraction to each other only strengthened. Mick was tortured. He found himself thinking about possibilities with this woman.

He was incredibly happy with Maye. He just loved looking at her and he admired her strength and intelligence. He thought about her ex-husband and the beatings he gave her, and he just wanted to wrap his arms around her and protect her from that. (He also wanted to secretly kill her ex... or at least cause him some serious pain!)

But it was soon that they had to return to their individual realities and whatever their futures would hold. For him it seemed almost impossible. He would be in Alabama for the next eighteen months and then it was expected that he would return to Australia where he was slated to take command of one of the army's aviation schools as commanding officer and senior flying instructor. Did that mean that he would spend the next year-and-a-half in a bittersweet purgatory? Itching for Friday to arrive so he could speed out the gates of Fort Rucker and head to Atlanta to see her? Or steal away to DC for those weekends when Congress was in session? Was that his future? A day here? A night there? Would he have to share her with her constituents, and expect to do so without complaint?

Things did not seem too promising when looked at objectively. If he was smart, he would just tell her the truth. That he could easily fall in love with her (he didn't admit to himself that he was already halfway there), but that for the sake of her career and for his, it would be better to end things here and just have pleasant memories of their time in Vancouver. "We'll always have Vancouver," they could say to each other, trying to be blasé, but in reality, hiding their pain and regret.

It was time for her to drive back to Seattle to catch her flight to DC and for him to head to the airport here in Vancouver and fly to Atlanta... alone. And then drive to Alabama... alone. She had already started taking some calls from her staffers in her DC office but had fended them off telling them that she would deal with them when she was in the office the next day.

Mick had never felt uncomfortable being alone. That was how he was raised.

"Alone, but not lonely," he would say to those who were concerned for him, for there was always something to do.

But now, all he wanted was to do those things with her. Together. Not alone.

The flight back to Atlanta was lonely. So was the drive to Alabama.

22

Summoned

Back at the battalion, Mick found it hard to concentrate, although he did find himself appreciating the view of the Alabama countryside from five hundred feet up more so than previously. His mind wandered as they flew the training sorties, and at night, when they were training with their night vision devices, he would look up at the myriad of stars, so many more than could be seen without them.

His mind would wander back to the hotel room in Vancouver where they had lost themselves in each other's arms and slept (or didn't sleep) until 11 a.m. before emerging from their room to explore the sights. He would fantasize about her and what he would like to do with her; to her; let her do to him, when they were together next. He was enjoying being in Alabama at the moment, his home for the next year-and-a-half.

Neither of them had had the courage to make a firm decision about the future after they had returned from Vancouver and now, six weeks later, they had managed to steal a night here or a night there with each other, always away from Atlanta or Washington. They found a great little B and B in the sleepy town of Tuskegee. They chose Tuskegee because it took Mick about the same time to drive there on the Alabama state highways and back roads as it did for Maye to cruise down I-85. Of course, this was also the home of the famous Tuskegee airmen. On the one occasion Mick had flown to DC, they stayed out near Annapolis in Maryland, not far from the waters of the upper Chesapeake, and caught up with Ben and Jess and their families, both of whom had already adopted Mick as one of their own.

He was hoping for a text from her before today. They had come up with a secret code so that no-one could interpret their messages to each other. Perhaps there'll be one waiting for him when they landed.

At the end of the training sortie, Mick conducted his debrief to his student, a young Warrant Officer Grade One. He was in a good mood and gave the young trainee a good grade even though his handling of the aircraft was a bit ham-fisted. It had been noted amongst the students that 'that Aussie instructor is easy to fly with', especially lately.

After the debrief he grabbed his phone from his locker and saw that there was no text from Maye. He drove back to his condo at the end of the night's training at 3 a.m. and crawled into bed. He stretched out his arm across the empty mattress and wished that Maye was lying beside him.

He was awoken at 6 a.m. by his phone buzzing. With bleary eyes he fumbled for it hoping it wasn't the battalion operations officer wanting him to cover for a sick instructor. It was likely one of his friends from back home. It was 8 p.m. on Friday night in Queensland so it may have been one of his drunken mates getting an early start on the weekend and who had decided to give Mick a call.

Looking at the screen it took him a few seconds to register the message. It was from Maye. It said merely, "We need to talk. When can you come to Atlanta?"

This was not good.

23

Up I-85 to... Destiny

He called the battalion operations officer and the company commander to request some leave. He thought it might be a good idea to speak with Ben, also. A lot had been playing on his mind and Ben had always been a good sounding board. He checked with the operations officer and found that Ben's first training sortie was at eleven, so he decided to meet with him at ten, finding him in the crew room.

The crew room had a small kitchenette with the coffee machine making yet another pot of coffee, and the microwave buzzing as it cooked more popcorn, the staples of flying instructors.

Jess had been eager to find out what was happening between Maye and Mick now that things were getting more serious. After all, they had spent a lot of time together and had visited Ben and Jess's families in Maryland. Maye was not giving much away, and Ben didn't bother to ask Mick. After all, "...that's his business, not ours." Of course, this infuriated Jess. She kept needling Ben to find out more.

"Hey man," said Ben when he saw Mick. "I thought you were on night duty!"

"I am. I'm heading to Atlanta, but I needed to get some leave and I wanted to have a chat to you."

"Sure," his American friend said. "You wanna go outside?"

Mick nodded. Ben grabbed a couple of cans of soda from the fridge and they went out into the Alabama sunshine. It was barely 10 a.m.

but it was already eighty-five degrees. Summer was shaping up to be a scorcher this year and it was only the beginning of June. They sat at one of the tables that someone had donated to the company, while the sound of helicopters filled the air.

"So, you're heading to Atlanta?" said Ben, opening up a can of Coke. "Don't tell Jess. She'll go crazy and will call you or Maye to find out what's going on. Why Atlanta and not Tuskegee?"

"Maye texted me. She asked if I could come to Atlanta. She didn't say why and that she'd explain when I got there."

Ben looked serious. "That doesn't sound good, man." Ben knew that Mick was falling for Maye, even though he had his concerns. But Mick was a grown man, and it was not Ben's place to give him any more advice or to ask details, no matter how much Jess cajoled him. If he wanted to get his heart broken by Maye, that was his business, and now it sounded like that was about to happen.

Mick took a swig from his can. "I think she's going to tell me it's not going to work. Why else would she ask me to Atlanta? We were careful to keep it a secret, so if this is the end then there's no reason to hide anymore. I could just be the friend of a friend who's dropped by to say hello and then quietly return to Rucker, see out my posting, and then head home to Australia."

"Should I be sorry?" asked Ben.

"I don't think so," replied Mick. "I mean, we both knew it wasn't likely to work out. I guess it's time to pull this band-aid off, and do it quickly."

Mick looked at his watch and, seeing the time, downed his Coke in a few gulps.

"I'd better hit the road. You can tell Jess that it's over. That'll put her out of her misery."

"It'll sure put her out of mine," quipped Ben. "She's like a hound dog trying to tree a 'coon." Ben looked at his friend who would normally smile at such a quaint Americanism, but who was already getting into the 'breakup head space'. "Good luck, mite," he said, trying to be a bit more humorous, and trying on his Australian accent, though without much success. It did have the desired effect, however. Mick smiled.

"You almost got it, *mate*," said Mick, emphasizing the last word. "Keep trying!" And with that he was backing out of the parking lot and heading north for Interstate 85 which would take him to Atlanta to hear her beautiful lips deliver the sad news. He was determined to make it easy for her. He would promise that they would remain friends and he would mean it sincerely. She deserved that much.

24

Shoot the Hootch, Not the Messenger

Mick had always admired the antebellum mansions around Eufala, just on the border of Alabama and Georgia, which marked the halfway point on this drive. But today they didn't even register. In fact, when he hit Interstate 285, also called 'The Perimeter', that girdled Atlanta and delineated a type of socio-economic division, it dawned on him that he hadn't remembered any of the drive. It was as though he had been on autopilot since leaving Fort Rucker.

His GPS took him to the Galleria, a collection of malls and office buildings that straddle I-295 and I-75, heading to north-west Georgia.

He crossed the Chattahoochee River where Georgians liked to ride their inner tubes—or at least the modern, store-bought versions thereof—down the river's often fast-flowing reaches. 'Chute the 'Hooch', as they called it, hearkened back to simpler times. Not too many people would Chute the Hooch much these days.

After parking his car in the Galleria's big under-cover parking lot, he headed up to Maye's congressional district office. The four-hour drive from Alabama had given him time to process what was about to happen and he had resigned himself to the fact that their relationship was doomed before it had even had a chance to bloom.

Affixed to the glass front of the office was a big adhesive poster showing Maye smiling (God! She was so beautiful!) A sign above declared: 'Your representative in Congress—Miss Maye Young—Representative for the 11th District, Georgia.' He entered the office where a woman in her early fifties sat at reception. On the wall behind her was a large sign with the shape of an elephant and the words 'The Republican Party' in red, beneath which was a US flag and the flag of the state of Georgia. She looked up from her computer and smiled.

"Can ah help you?" she said with a broad southern accent.

"Um, I'm here to see Congresswoman Young," said Mick hesitantly. He wasn't expecting to have to speak to anyone but Maye.

"Are you Michael?" said the receptionist.

"Michael? Yes. Michael O'Rourke."

"Oh, the Congresswoman will be just a moment. She's expecting you. Please take a seat. Can ah get you some wahter, or a soda, p'haps?"

"No thanks, I'm fine," he replied, taking a seat on a soft fabric sofa adjacent to the receptionist's desk and a small conference room.

"What's your name?" asked Mick.

"My name's Carroll, Carroll Coffee... like the drink," she said, obviously well-rehearsed.

"I'm pleased to meet you, Carroll Coffee," said Mick and gave her a smile. "Please call me Mick! I'm only called Michael when I'm in trouble."

"Wayll, OK! Mick it is!"

On the wall opposite was a framed photo of Maye with the president, and he wondered if that was an asset or a liability, being photographed with him. The US President had certainly not endeared himself to much of the world, including back home in Australia. His thug-like diplomacy was not reserved just for America's competitors, he also used it with America's allies, including Australia. But the friendship between the two countries was much stronger and would survive a presidential term, or two... if he managed to get re-elected. But if the pundits were accurate, his shelf life as president might be as a single-term leader, such was his unpopularity at the moment.

Mick sat and waited. He could hear the muffled voices behind the door that was the entry to Maye's office. All through the reception area were images of Maye in various settings: with volunteers at a polling booth; with school kids at a science fair; a 'class photo' with other representatives on the steps of the Capitol Building. The more he saw her in these settings, the more unsettled he became.

He battled his emotions. Every photo showed her beautiful face. He felt ashamed that he found himself aroused by her in her fitted suits in these photos. But he also battled with the idea that if he had decided to be with her for the next year and a half, he would have had to have shared her with her constituents; with the party; with anyone who had a gripe and demanded to see their congresswoman.

There was a photo with the First Lady; another with former President George W Brash, and a number of others showing her with men and women who were either important, wanted to be important, or thought they were. There was a more recent one of her with President Troup and, it appeared to be, secret service agent Henry Lee, the hero of the assassination attempt. It was strange that she didn't mention him the night they met in Alabama. Agent Lee was all over the news. Mick was more impressed that Maye had met Agent Lee than her having met President Troup!

It was dizzying to see all these scenes and see her face smiling in each. The look on Carroll's face gave away that she wanted to say something but was hesitating. Finally, she mustered up the courage.

"Can ah ask you, are you Australian, 'cos ah jus' love your acceynt," said the receptionist, turning her chair to face him. Her sweater sported a small badge of a bulldog, the mascot of the University of Georgia.

"Yes, I am... and I love yours," said Mick with a smile. She looked confused.

"Oh, ah don't have an acceynt," she responded, a little dazed. Mick merely smiled and nodded as if to say, "Oh yes you do."

She smiled in realization. "Ah guess that to y'all, we *do* have an acceynt! That's so cute!"

"Well Carroll, I think your accent is cute!" said Mick, and she giggled even more.

"Oh, you hush!" Carroll said, waving the air at him, still giggling.

The door to Maye's office opened. It was bright inside. The windows faced south-east towards the Chattahoochee River and—past the carpet of green made by the pine trees speckled with glimpses of rooves and the blue haze of the Georgia heat—were the buildings of metropolitan Atlanta. The sun streamed in through the glass, lighting up the office's furniture. Maye stood next to the door, leaving a man in a grey charcoal suit and a woman in a no-nonsense black dress with bright red shoes and red belt, seated in the two chairs facing her desk, both peering at him.

Seeing Mick sitting on the sofa was such a relief. For a brief second, she leaned against the door and relaxed, her face lighting up. Then, realizing how she must appear, she stood erect and resumed her business-like composure. This was not lost on Carroll.

Maye closed her office door behind her and walked towards him, her face now not smiling. "Michael. Thanks for coming in. Would you mind stepping into the conference room," she said, glancing quickly at Carroll who was watching with keen interest. (Carroll was very adept at catching nuances in behavior).

Mick stood and walked into the adjoining room while Maye held the door open. He stood for a moment taking in the view of Atlanta. Who were those two in her office? Had they been discovered by the GOP?

"Great view!" he said, trying to keep the mood light. He wasn't going to try and hug her or show any affection. It would be easier that way... easier for her... easier for both of them.

"Yes," she replied, "it can be very distracting. I often find myself just day-dreaming, watching the cars drive by and looking towards the city." She paused, not knowing how to start. "I have something very serious to talk to you about," she said. "I'm not sure how you're going to take it."

25

Backroom Deals

Two Weeks Prior - GA GOP offices

"What do you have?" asked The Chairman as he came into the conference room.

The unidentified man spun his laptop around revealing an image showing Mick and Maye at a nondescript diner.

"This was taken in Alabama," said the unidentified man as The Chairman and committee members crowded to see. The meeting room held a long, polished table that could seat fifteen, and the gathered members of the Georgia GOP who were called to this meeting crowded around one end.

The unidentified man then showed an image of Mick and Maye at the large hangar at Moton airfield, near Tuskegee, holding hands.

"And this one is from DC, actually Maryland," he said, pressing the key again. Now they could be seen at a restaurant having a meal with an unidentified couple.

"What's his story?" asked one of the committeemen.

"He's Australian. Army officer. On exchange at Fort Rucker in Alabama."

"Australian?" said The Chairman. "What the hell? What do we know about him?"

The unidentified man with the computer was silent for a moment.

He shuffled and cleared his throat as if he was about to deliver bad news.

"Actually, we don't know anything about him. His name is Michael O'Rourke and he is a helicopter instructor in the Australian Army, currently stationed at Fort Rucker and living in a little town nearby called Dothan," he said. "Oh, and he's a major."

The Chairman looked up at the attractive brunette executive assistant that had brought him a bourbon rocks, placing it on the table in front of him.

"Wah, thank you, honey," he said in an unusually pleasant manner for such a usually gruff man. She smiled in return.

"Will you be needing anything else today, sir?" she asked him.

"I think that will be all for today, Elaine," said The Chairman. "You can go home now." He momentarily watched her leave as she pulled the door behind her. Elaine glanced back in at The Chairman before the door closed. She saw him looking at her and quickly closed the door, packed up her bags and started her journey home to her condo in Decatur, east of the city.

The other committee members were still entranced by this mystery man, and they talked amongst themselves, trying to foretell what this might mean to any campaign they had planned for the mid-term congressional elections later in the year. It had been relatively easy to get Maye elected. When she won the special election, it put her in a prime position such that when the general election was called, she was already the incumbent. She was smart. She was a woman. She was attractive. And she was a veteran. Rural Georgia was pro-Republican, but urban Georgia was notoriously Democrat. They had taken a chance and nominated her in an electorate that was part rural and part urban, and she had done well, winning the seat comfortably. And while Maye had not been some sort of *wunderkind*, she had demonstrated a ready appeal to the constituents, even if some of the other party members who had put in more time and who had expected to be nominated were upset. She was green and still had a lot to learn, but in the two years that she had represented the 11th District she had impressed everyone and was fast becoming a seasoned politician... and an asset to the Party.

Maye's only drawback was the fact that she was divorced and was childless. In twenty-first century America, that should not have made a difference. But in actuality it did... and especially in Georgia. The Party's spin doctors had tried to cast a different, more positive, light on her situation, but had failed miserably. All they had managed to do was insult mothers by making the inference that a childless woman, such as Maye, could work harder for her constituents because she could devote more time to them. What that brief campaign showed was that the spin doctors were completely out of touch with how the electorate thought. This was not the first time the Republican Party had failed to connect, and it was becoming a theme.

Now the Grand Old Party was facing what could be a difficult election campaign. Their record of candidates at the higher level was not impressive, to say the least. George W Brash had become president a decade prior, but was seen as lackluster at best, and a buffoon at worst. Susan Paulding from Alaska had been chosen as the running mate to Navy Vietnam veteran, Jack McDuffie. None of them were proving to be star material. Now, the current president, President Troup, with his oddly shaded complexion and wispy hair, was demonstrating a lack of worldliness and diplomacy, and had alienated many of America's allies and enraged its enemies. Regardless of his popularity amongst middle- and rural-America, he was despised around the world, and this could only hurt the country's long-term prospects now that China had risen and was taking its place as a world power. Having him re-elected would be a challenge and was the number one problem facing the GOP.

This was not lost on The Chairman. Even though he only controlled the goings-on of the Georgia Republicans, he was sensible enough to see that he had a candidate in Maye who had the potential to make up for the less-than-spectacular Republicans that had been put into the spotlight. If he could ensure Maye got a second term as the representative of the 11th District of Georgia, then he might be able to convince the Republican National Committee to endorse her as a running mate for whomever was going to be put up as presidential candidate if they decided to dump Troup. This had been alluded to him by senior members and became his focus. So far, she had been compliant and had done what was asked of her by the Party. And the Party was very pleased.

The Chairman had a six-, possibly ten- or even a fourteen-year plan, depending on how she fared, and it was centered on having Maye Young elected as Vice President of the United States of America... and no Australian Army major was going to cause the wheels to fall off this cart.

"I'm not too worried about this," said The Chairman "but we have to do our due diligence. We don't want our girl to be the target of a smear campaign."

"Let's have a talk with Maye." He looked at Robert Fulton, one of his political strategists in charge of communications, and a confidant. His trademark was a charcoal gray suit with a red tie, what he called his 'Republican-red' tie. "Bobby, take Rebecca and have a chat with Maye and then meet this guy. See if he fits our needs for the campaign."

Fulton nodded and looked at Rebecca Chatham, their communications adviser who met his eyes and nodded back.

"Go and see Maye and provide her with..." He paused, trying to find *les mots justes*, the right words. "Let's say, 'guidance', on what is expected. We need her to show us that she has the goods to get people off their asses and go and vote. Make sure she understands that she has to stick to our plan and that she's not to go off-script. No surprises, y'all hear me?"

He looked at the pictures on the screen once more and decided that that was enough for the day.

"Alright, that's all people. You know what to do. You can leave now, except Bobby, can you stay behind please?"

The unidentified man swooped up his computer and put it in his satchel and was out the door in one move. The others milled around momentarily, still trying to take in what this meant, and they drifted out of the conference room, talking amongst themselves. The Chairman stood up and walked through a side door in the conference room that led into his office. It was typically appointed for a man of his vintage. Wooden bookcases with glass doors housing various leather-bound books on torts and procedures. What appeared to be a Chesterfield was in the corner, not looking too comfortable. A sofa and some armchairs where many decisions were made by middle-aged and elderly men in many closed-door meetings. His desk was large and neat, probably organized by his EA Elaine, who had unfettered access to his office.

There were photos of him with President Troup, and also with former President Gerald W Brash, and other key members of GOP royalty. There were two showing him in hunting gear sporting a Remington over-under shotgun kneeling beside a fourteen-point buck that, it appeared, he had just shot. There was another, a family photo, of him and his wife and his two adult children. And another photo of one of his children holding a new-born. It looked like The Chairman was a grandfather.

He finished his bourbon and packed some papers into a bag.

"I need you to do me a favor," he said to Fulton who stood leaning on the backrest of one of the chairs in front of The Chairman's desk.

"I need you to get Sally-Anne out of the house and put her in this campaign." He paused to see Fulton's expression. Fulton did not flinch. He was inscrutable. But The Chairman also noticed that he did not respond.

"Is there a problem?" asked The Chairman, perhaps somewhat rhetorically.

His wife, who had kept her maiden name 'for professional reasons' as Sally-Anne Atkinson, had been an Atlanta socialite in her twenties when she and The Chairman, then just a young lawyer, met. Her family had made money during the big real-estate booms of the fifties in Florida and Georgia. The Chairman had known when an opportunity to become connected to the more 'well-to-do' families presented itself.

Sally-Anne was the only child of the Atlanta Atkinsons. Loved, but spoiled, she wanted for nothing growing up. She attended Pace Academy where her marks were more-or-less average, and later Agnes Scott all-female liberal arts college majoring in English literature and minoring in US history. It was while she was at Agnes Scott that she met The

Chairman and was married soon after her graduation. She became pregnant within months and so stayed at home as a full-time mom. Their second child was born three years later. It was only after they had grown enough to be able to look after themselves that Sally-Anne Atkinson decided to enroll in an educators' program so that she could get certification with the Georgia Professional Standards Commission to be a schoolteacher.

This did not come easily to her. She had squandered an expensive private-school education and her college years, and being a stay-at-home mom had limited her ability to get out and socialize and mix in more academic, or any other, circles. It weighed heavily on her and her self-esteem, but she persevered and she managed to pass and gained her certification. She then found herself doing an internship at her former school, Pace Academy. But even then, deep down, she found that the teenage girls at the academy were actually smarter than her, and she struggled with feelings of inadequacy and low self-worth. She could also feel her marriage slowly diluting. Sally-Anne went on to be a teacher at a middle school and had managed to climb to the dizzying heights of vice principal while her husband climbed the ladder of the legal profession and the Republican party in Georgia, such that now he was The Chairman of the state committee.

The Chairman had fallen out of love with his wife many years prior, but divorce was out of the question. Her family was too well connected, and he stood to gain much once her parents died. But as far as mixing in his circles, well Sally-Anne was way out her depth. Many of his friends were judges or state and federal congress members, and if their wives weren't doing something similar in their own fields, then they were bitchy and catty and looked down on Sally-Anne for being a 'mere middle-school teacher'. This, of course, reflected on The Chairman.

Or at least he thought it did. He would often find reasons for having Sally-Anne left off the guest list. Now his wife was becoming tired of not being included and demanded a more prominent role. The Chairman needed to find somewhere he could put his wife where she could feel important but not do too much damage. This campaign may be the perfect place to park her. Maye Young would undoubtedly keep her seat, provided she didn't do anything stupid and she could stick to the script. All The Chairman needed was for Maye to demonstrate that she could raise her profile. Maye would actually be doing all the hard work. Putting Sally-Anne there would not hurt Maye's chances and it would get his wife of his back. He needed Fulton to make this happen with Maye and her team.

"Do you think it's a good idea to put your wife on this campaign?" asked Fulton. "What do you wish her to do?"

"I don't care," said The Chairman. "She can stuff envelopes! I just need her to feel as though she's contributing. You know she won't damage Young's chances. She'll keep her district, so let's just put her there for the next five months. Get Young to babysit her. She can be the campaign coordinator or some other bullshit position. I don't care! We have the campaign strategy all worked out. We just need them to stick to it. My wife should have enough brains to do that."

Fulton didn't object. To do so would be futile. The Chairman grabbed his briefcase and together he and Fulton walked out into the car park.

"Listen, I don't give a damn about what she does for them, just so long as she feels that she's a part of the campaign."

With that, The Chairman got into his car. He wound down his window and said to Fulton, "Make sure Maye sticks to our campaign strategy. No surprises!" and drove out of the car park. His home was in the well-to-do suburb of Margaret Mitchell to the north-west. But The Chairman pulled out into traffic and headed east, towards Decatur.

Fulton had his tasks: park The Chairman's wife somewhere where she could feel important but not do any serious damage, and find out who this Australian guy was and what it meant to the campaign. It might be time to take this Aussie out of the picture if he proved to be a liability. It was time to talk with Maye.

26

The View of Atlanta

Mick didn't want to turn around. He didn't want to see her beautiful face, but he couldn't stand there all day looking at Atlanta from a distance. She said he may not like what she had to say… so he'd better just man up and take the bad news. He slowly turned and faced her. Yep! She was still gorgeous.

"I don't know how," she started, "but the Party found out about you and me. They've sent some of their people to discuss my future and the mid-terms."

"'To discuss my future.' That's what she said. I guess that's it for me," thought Mick. He smiled as best he could. Even though he had prepared for the breakup, somewhere, deep inside, he had hoped that that was not going to be the only option. But how could it not? He knew that her role as a congresswoman was the most important thing in this whole situation. A relationship for a year-and-a-half was only delaying the inevitable. In the meantime, she had to contest another election and she didn't need a distraction such as a boyfriend to hamper her chances. It was time to fall on his sword.

"What can I do to help? Shall I tell them that we won't be seeing each other anymore?" He looked at her, her eyebrows knotted. He wanted to reach out and take her in his arms but that was not a good idea, because he probably wouldn't let her go. No. It was time to make a manly departure.

"Maye, I mean it when I say that I'd like us to still be friends. I mean, if that's something that you want."

She walked towards him. Her eyes bore the sadness that Mick was feeling also. It appeared as though she was going to give him one last hug goodbye. She reached out her arms and took his hands in hers and looked into his eyes.

"Why do you want to break up with me?" she asked.

Mick was shocked. Was there something that he missed? The Party had sent their goons around to discuss her future. Surely that meant a future without him in it.

"Uhm..."

She smiled at him and drew him closer and kissed him softly on the lips.

"They want to meet you. I've told them what an amazing person you are and how I feel about you and they asked if they could speak with you."

Now Mick was very confused. Exactly what did this mean? He had played the scene over and over in his head on the drive up from Alabama. He had played out the breakup scene. He had played out the yelling and screaming scene. He had even played out the 'let's see if we can work this out' scene. But this was totally unexpected. He had no idea that he was to be speaking with the Republican Party!

He allowed himself to be a little happy at the idea of not breaking up with Maye. But as he held her and they embraced, he started to think about what he was going to say to these two party representatives. What was it that they expected? What had they hoped they would hear? Now Mick was coming back down to earth as he rapidly processed different scenarios.

Did they hope that he would marry her? To make her more acceptable to her constituents? She had told him about the bad press she had because she was unmarried and childless. How would marrying him help her? He had to return to Australia next year. Surely they could understand that he had duty back in Alabama in the meantime.

Now he was really confused. Exactly *what* did they expect to get by speaking with him? He gently pushed Maye away from him and held her shoulders so he could look at her.

"What do they want from me?" he asked. "What do they expect?"

"I'm not sure, but whatever happens, we can't keep this... us... a secret. If we want to keep seeing each other, then it has to be out in the open."

Mick's heart skipped a beat. She wanted to keep seeing him! Thank God! Maye reached up and put her hands on his, squeezing them.

"Just be yourself," she said, "and they'll love you as much as I do."

Wait a minute! Did she just say that she loved him? Mick allowed himself a smile. Maye then realized what she had just said. She closed her eyes and a small smile crept onto her lips. Her head bowed as if she had just resigned herself to accepting something as being true, even against her better judgment. She had said that she loved him. She didn't mean to say it... it just sort of jumped onto the phrase. She paused, took a deep breath and raised her head, her eyes still closed. She opened them to see Mick smiling. She decided to take control of this situation.

"Yeah, you heard me O'Rourke! I said it. No need to make a federal case out of it!" she said with a smile.

"I don't know about that, Representative Young," said Mick. "Those two suits in there" he said, his thumb pointing towards her office, "may wish to make a federal case out of this."

He gave her a kiss. Knowing that some sort of crazy Hollywood production was in his future, he puffed out his chest, lifted his chin and turning his head gave her some 'crazy eyes' and said, "Alright Mr. DeMille, I'm ready for my close-up."

And with that they walked out of the conference room and into Maye's office to meet the Grand Ol' Party of the Great State of Georgia.

27

The Audition

Maye led Mick by the hand to her office. Carroll noticed this immediately and froze, her long fingernails poised above her keyboard, her mouth agape. What was the congresswoman doing? Was this her boyfriend? Mick saw her expression and gave her a wink and a grin. Carroll's face suddenly beamed a huge smile.

The two GOP suits had turned their chairs to face the sofa that sat against the wall in Maye's office. They were ready to interview Maye and her 'man from nowhere'.

Maye sat down still holding Mick's hand as he sat next to her. His day had turned out better than he had hoped. She had said that she loved him.

It then dawned on him that those words brought with them a whole swag of problems. He had his posting in Alabama which meant that any relationship would need to be a long-distance one. Of course, Maye had to be in DC when Congress was sitting. And what about when his duty finished, and he had to head back to Australia? What then?

But those were questions for another time. Right now, he was on show, and he had to do the right thing for her. Maye began speaking with the two committee representatives as Carroll brought in four glasses of water and placed them on the coffee table. Maye looked at her and thanked her. Carroll was too interested in Mick to respond to her boss. She was looking at him, inanely smiling. Mick mouthed the words, 'Thanks Carroll' and raised his eyebrows, tilting his head slightly towards the man and the woman sitting opposite as if to say to her, 'Check out these two goons.' Carroll raised her eyebrows in response and, backing out of the office, shut the door, but not before mouthing the words, 'Good luck'. The man spoke.

"Hello Major. My name is..."

"Mick."

"I'm sorry?"

"My name is Mick, or Michael. You're not in the army so I don't expect you to call me by my army rank. My name is Mick or Michael. I answer to both. So, take your pick: Michael or Mick."

Maye looked down at the carpet and smiled to herself, gently squeezing his hand affectionately. The man also smiled, the ice having been broken, and continued.

"Um, Ok... Mick. My name is Robert Fulton, and this is my colleague, Rebecca Chatham. Allow me to explain why we're here."

"Let's see if I can save you some time," interjected Mick. "Your girl here," holding up Maye's hand "is up for re-election in November. She is unmarried and childless and that's not a good look, regardless of how good a representative she is. So, in order to avoid any bad press, you're here to see what my presence means for her, and how you might be able to spin the story to the GOP's advantage. Basically, you're assessing me to see if I will be an asset or a liability to Maye's campaign."

They squirmed a little. He had captured it in a nutshell. The truth, when said out loud, sounded harsh and unfeeling. Maye could see their embarrassment.

"Honey, I don't think that they are here to assess you, I think..."

"Oh no," said Fulton. "He is one hundred percent right. Your boyfriend is very astute," he said, looking at Maye. He then turned to Mick.

"I appreciate your candor, Mick. So, what do you think?"

Mick paused for a minute. Again, he had been given a shock by Maye's situation and needed some time to process it and project what these events would mean. Regulations would forbid him to get deeply involved in politics in Australia, but this wasn't Australia. It was a minor role in a minor election that would hardly be noticed outside the local area. He'd probably not even make the local paper. And what with his duties back at Fort Rucker, he would be a 'boyfriend *in absentia*'. Someone who Maye could claim was her partner but who was unable to be with her due to his military commitments. Americans would understand that. In fact, it would probably work in her favor.

"Mister Fulton. Miss Chatham. I think that the 11th District of Georgia would benefit greatly having Miss Maye Young serving another term as their representative in Washington... and I will assist in any way that I can."

Maye squeezed his hand again and Fulton and Chatham both smiled. Chatham beamed especially, her smile revealing perfect teeth, her lips a cherry red to match her belt and shoes. She now spoke.

"Mick, I'm sure you can appreciate, that we need to get people out there to vote. I'm sure it's the same in Australia."

"No. We have compulsory voting in Australia," he said. "We don't have to get people motivated to vote."

She was taken aback momentarily but continued.

"In any case, it is important to motivate people to get out and vote, so if we can get them interested in the campaign, it makes that task much easier."

"What do you need me to do?" Mick asked. This would be key.

"Firstly, we need to know your views on certain matters that make up the platform of the Republican party. It is important that we stay on message." She paused, as if trying to couch the next question carefully. Finally, she asked it. "What is your view on abortion?"

Mick stopped for a moment. He wasn't expecting them to be so direct but knew enough about American politics to give them what they wanted to hear. After a short pause he responded.

"America was founded on many rights, including the right to have a choice, a choice in one's own affairs." (He saw them wince a little). "That includes not having government interfere in their personal lives. (They liked that). "Another fundamental aspect of America is its belief that, unlike the views of its enemies, every life is important."

They were a bit confused. Was he pro-choice or was he pro-life? He seemed to take both sides.

"I'm not sure you've answered the question," she said.

"Yes I did. I gave you my views. But my primary view is that my view is not germane to any argument being made in US politics. For while I am a supporter of America, I am still a foreigner with no right to vote here and no view that can, or should, influence what each individual voter believes. Regardless of which way America leans, I will always be a supporter of this great country and its people and its inalienable right to have a viewpoint, even those that I do not share."

This left them a bit confused. They thought he said all the right things. He had taken a stand without taking a position, but had done so so articulately, even if it was a bit trite.

"What's your next question," said Mick, wishing to move this along. They scribbled some notes and Fulton spoke next.

"How about gun control? Do you believe in gun control?"

"I am an officer in the Australian Army. Gun control to me means a tight grouping by someone who is qualified to operate the weapon."

They were confused again.

"What do you mean 'tight grouping'?"

"The grouping of bullet holes in a target," he explained.

"So, then you support a person's right to own a weapon?"

"I gave you my opinion on gun control," he said.

This thrust and parry continued for a while longer. Mick could see that Fulton and Chatham were getting a little frustrated, perhaps a little disappointed that he was not the pushover they had hoped he would be. He could see their frustration and did not wish to cruel Maye's chances.

"Bob, Rebecca, let me just say this. I will never compromise my beliefs, but they are not at odds with your party. My belief is that this woman," he looked at Maye looking at him, "is one of the most remarkable women I have ever met. She has served her country in uniform, which is more than I can say for many others in her party," (this was a dig at them), "and she has worked hard at serving the people of her constituency and will continue to do so if given the opportunity. If my presence alongside her will help her win office for another term, I will gladly do so, because I am in love with her."

He could see Rebecca smile and, when he looked at Maye, she was beaming. He turned back to confront the two party suits.

"So, sign me up. I won't say anything that will embarrass her, or your party and I will appear by her side when duty permits me to." He turned to look at Maye and he could see her eyes moisten slightly. She took his head in her hands and leaned forward and kissed his lips, not caring what Fulton and Chatham thought.

The two committee members left Maye's office and told her that they will confer with the rest of the committee, and they would be in touch. It sounded ominous, not definite.

Mick and Maye said their goodbyes and stood for a moment in the reception area holding hands, looking at each other. Neither of them was completely sure that it was a successful meeting, but at least their feelings were now out in the open and they could be honest with each other. No more sneaking around in secret. Carroll sat at her desk, hardly able to contain herself. Her boss had a boyfriend! Her very own soap opera was about to come to her office and play out before her.

* * *

Fulton and Chatham took the elevator down to the parking lot. Fulton pulled out his cell phone and called The Chairman.

"It's me," he said. "We met him."

Chatham could not hear what The Chairman was saying. She pulled out a compact and began checking her lipstick. Fulton, his phone still at his ear, looked at her and said, "What do you think?"

Without looking up from her reflection she simply nodded and said, "Yep."

Fulton said just four words to the Chairman, "Yeah. We can use him."

28

Stay On Message!

The GAGOP had decided to let the fact that Maye had a boyfriend make its own way into the media while they assessed how the constituents responded. Of all the nine Republican congress members that were campaigning for re-election in Georgia, only the battles to be fought by Maye in the 11th, and Barry Candler in the 1st district on the Atlantic coast, held any concerns for the committee. Candler had a very strong opponent and so the campaign there would need some extra horsepower, whereas Maye's campaign in the 11th would need strict control on the message and quick responses to any perceived negatives, such as Maye and Mick not being married; Maye being childless, and so on. All the other districts were relatively safe, and they could stand to let their local branches run their own grass roots campaign in those seats. The urban districts would probably be held by the Democrats. Spending too much effort there was a waste of resources.

Mid-term elections for congress were notorious for having poor voter turnout, but the GAGOP was not too concerned about Maye losing her seat. She had the advantage of incumbency, and she was smart and pretty. Only a major scandal or some other unforeseen upheaval would unseat her.

What Maye didn't know was that she was being watched very closely not only by the GAGOP, but by the Republican National Committee. President Troup had not been a star performer during his time in office.

His approval rating at home, notwithstanding his support base, was very low and he was not held in high regard by world leaders. He was proving to be a liability and the RNC needed to be more responsive to middle America.

Maye, with her military background and her more worldly view, provided a good counterpoint for her relative youth. Her lack of experience in politics would be an issue in the short term, but so far she had handled herself with aplomb. Being a smart, attractive woman helped, but her service to the nation for virtually all her adult life was her trump card. She was the future, and many in the state committee had seen that and had brought her to the attention of the national committee.

As far at the GOP was concerned, this election was not about keeping her seat, she was expected to retain it easily. More importantly, it was about seeing what changes in voter behavior she could bring, so they agreed to let her have a loose rein to see what she would do. They would, however, ensure she kept to message. That was the most important thing they told her, "Do what you think you need to do to get the voters energized, but above all, STAY ON MESSAGE!"

In the meantime, the PR machine was ready to spin the story about her boyfriend. They were also ready to fluff him before he went in front of the cameras. It was five months until the mid-term elections.

29

Maye's Campaign Strategy

Maye's staff were eager, although not very well organized. It was made up mainly of those that could afford to give her time, so it was a grab-bag of retirees and housewives with kids at school.

Her key salaried support staff did their best to light a fire under the volunteers. It was hard to discipline them if that became necessary. Instead, what this needed was leadership in the true sense of the word, as well as management. They had a little under five months to run an effective campaign, and while that may sound like a long time, in politics it is the blink of an eye.

Maye met with her campaign manager, a middle-aged woman by the name of Sally-Anne Atkinson who had worked on the periphery of one other district race, but not with Maye. She had been assigned by the state committee and Maye suspected that she had been put there not so much for what she was able to do, but rather to keep her out of the way.

Maye and Sally-Anne sat in the conference room with Bob Fulton to discuss the campaign. They had been there for over twenty pointless minutes. Bob discussed the goings-on in the state committee and the new position holders. The Atlanta skyline was disappearing in the heat haze, but a storm was forecast to hit soon. One of those big, Georgia thunderstorms.

Maye wanted to move things along so asked Sally-Anne what the strategy was going to be for her campaign.

"Wey'll, what we first need to do is get a new portrait of you and some photos of you with the voters and we'll get a new flyer printed and mailed out. Then every house will have your picture. We can get about thirty volunteers to do a door knock and have them hand out flyers and speak directly with residents. We'll get the coroplast posters onto as many lawns as possible and have each county organize a town hall meeting."

Maye looked at Sally-Anne who was busy studying her notes, none of which seemed to be very organized. Bob sat beside her watching on. He could see that Maye did not look too enthusiastic about Sally-Anne's plan for the campaign. It was old-fashioned and lacked an understanding of modern marketing.

"You know, Maye," Bob began "we're not worried that you'll lose your seat, so this campaign will be more-or-less just a means of keeping you in the public's eye."

She gave him a look of frustration. "I thought this was supposed to be a campaign to get the voters enthusiastic," she said. "This plan could do with a little more imagination." Sally-Anne looked wounded. "If we want to get voters enthusiastic about voting, and getting them out to vote," said Maye, "then we need to have an enthusiastic campaign, don't you think?"

She thanked Sally-Anne for her time and told her to check with Carroll at reception to see when she could program a time to book a new portrait. She told her that she'd make herself available for photos when she was out in the district and help her wherever she could. With that, she stood and walked them to the door.

"Can I talk to you about another matter," she said to Bob, holding his arm.

"Um, sure," he replied, and Sally-Anne took the cue to wait in reception for them to finish their chat. Maye closed the door and they both sat down. The clouds had started to roll in fast, and large dark shadows were falling on the pine trees nearby. The Atlanta skyline was still bathed in brilliant sunshine.

"I'll work with Sally-Anne, but I'm also going to do my own thing...

run my own activities and town halls. We need to market this election better and her big ideas are straight out of the Nixon-era. We need to adapt or die."

Fulton could see her frustration and nodded.

"Like I said, we're confident you'll hold this seat," he assured her. "You do whatever you need to provided you stay on message. Just let the committee know what you need. In the meantime, keep Sally-Anne around. She's The Chairman's wife and wants to help, and so does The Chairman. Make her feel a part of this."

Maye nodded and they stood. Fulton opened the door and Maye caught Sally-Anne's eye.

"I'm very excited to be working with you, Sally-Anne," she said. Fulton nodded his approval.

"I've got some great ideas we can include with your campaign, and it will be a fun time. We'll get the message out there! Thanks for dropping by and see you soon."

Sally-Anne smiled, feeling validated and useful. The two left and Maye went into her office. Looking out at the now darkening trees and buildings below, she took out her cell phone and called Mick.

"Hey, it's me. When will you get here?"

A thunderclap sounded and rain started pelting the window, the trees below began to sway. The storm had hit the 11th District.

30

The Planning Session

As they lay in bed listening to the rain, they spoke about the campaign and the old-fashioned ideas that Sally-Anne had.

"I know I'll most likely hold the seat unless they find some dirt on me..." she said to him. But before she could finish her sentence, he butted in.

"If they knew what you let me do to you just then, it would be a scandal! For a few bucks, I'll keep my mouth shut," he offered.

"Quiet, you... or you'll end up like that guy in Tucson!" she quipped and flicked his nipple.

"But honestly, I'd like to really push this campaign and see where it could go. What do you think? Where should we put our efforts?"

They batted around some ideas and Mick got the impression that he was going to be instrumental in this, more so than he expected. Every time Maye discussed an event or an interview or other such campaign commitment, it was always "If they ask you this", or "you would be good at that". He wasn't sure how much time he could give her, but he would do whatever he could. From his place in Dothan to her place in Cherokee County was more than a four-hour drive, so the next few months were going to be hectic.

They came up with an idea to open her campaign by climbing Kennesaw Mountain on the anniversary of the civil war battle there and holding a press conference but decided that it would be too hard to try and get the National Parks Service's permission... plus Kennesaw Mountain was like a sacred site to a lot of Georgians. Better to be a bit more subtle.

"How energetic do you feel?" he asked her.

"Are you ready to go again," she said, reaching down to see if he was erect.

"No," he replied grabbing her and holding her close so she couldn't use her hands.

"What do you have in mind, Major?" she asked, now looking into his eyes as he continued to pull her close.

"What about a reverse Sherman?"

A reverse Sherman? What the hell was that? She gave him a puzzled look.

"So, Sherman marched from Chattanooga to Atlanta, right?"

She was embarrassed to admit that she didn't really know much about the Atlanta campaign of the Civil War. He saw her expression and threw her a bone.

"Well," he said, "Sherman's Army went from Tennessee down to Atlanta pushing the Confederates back to Kennesaw Mountain, right?"

"Hey... you're telling this story!" she said, intrigued.

"Well, his army advanced south-east along where I-75 is today, from Adairsville through Cartersville to Kennesaw Mountain."

Maye was duly impressed. "So, if I do a Reverse Sherman, I'm traveling up I-75?"

"Exactly!" said Mick.

"And what *exactly* am I doing as I travel up I-75?"

"Well, you're not going up I-75 itself, more paralleling it. And you're gathering support and news coverage!"

She didn't look too convinced. It seemed a lot of effort for an election where she was confident that she wouldn't lose her seat in Congress.

"What you're talking about is retail politics," she said. "That's not as effective as people would have you think," she told him. "Direct contact with voters doesn't always translate to votes."

"I think that a politician's job is to listen to the people. What better way of doing that but by walking amongst them? Don't do town hall events, do a march! You're young and fit. The other candidates won't do anything like that."

She still wasn't convinced. All the campaign tactics from the good ones she had experienced during her first election, to the not-so-good ones that Sally-Anne Atkinson had offered for this election, had avoided a lot of personal contact. Instead, it was more TV advertisements and interviews and online engagement. Door-to-door was left to the volunteers.

Mick told her of what was done back in Australia. There, voting was compulsory, so it wasn't necessary to get people to vote. The important thing was to convince them to vote for you by making them understand that you were one of them. He thought it could work. After all, what did they have to lose?

"We've got a break in training, and I think I can get two weeks away from Rucker. What do you say?" he said, giving her a squeeze. "I'm game if you are."

She looked at him. Having him on the campaign for two solid weeks sounded great, but it could also backfire. In the conservative South, having a boyfriend accompany a congresswoman may not translate very well. So, what were the counter arguments? Well, she was young and in a safe district so why not be the face of twenty-first century conservative politics in Georgia? Anyway, it sounded like a good way to get some exercise. What the hell! She was in!

"Let's do it. Do you want to plan it? You'll have to let Sally-Anne be part of it. She's an idiot but I reckon you can win her over. You certainly won over Carroll. She loves you."

"I had to get her to love me," he joked. "Otherwise, she wouldn't let me take advantage of some of the spaces in your calendar. But now, I want to take advantage of another one of your spaces," and with that he disappeared beneath the sheets. Just like Sherman's Army, he headed south, but instead of burning the countryside, he kissed her. First her neck, then her breasts, then the inside of her elbows and her hands, then her stomach, and... well you get the idea.

31

Gathering the Team

Maye and Mick, along with Sally-Anne and two other staffers, met for dinner and drinks at a restaurant bar in Buckhead, not far from The Perimeter. They had proposed the idea of the 'Reverse Sherman' march, but someone pointed out that is sounded like a sexual position. Robert Early, one of the staffers, a smart, young black law student who had taken a break from his full-time law studies at the University of Georgia to work with Maye, suggested that they call it 'The March to Tennessee'.

Even though Tennessee was on the other side of the state line, it also formed the northern border of the 14th district which abutted Maye's 11th district. Besides, they didn't intend to actually go all the way to Tennessee. But 'The March to Tennessee' had a better ring to it, so it was settled upon.

Mick had met Rob a couple of times before and had taken an instant liking to him. He was about 5'11" with a slim, athletic build. Not too big and beefy; more on the slight side, like a runner. He wore his hair cropped and short, which accentuated his receding hairline giving him a larger than normal forehead. Oddly enough, it suited his face. His eyes were bright and happy, and he reminded Mick of a young Will Smith, although he did wear a silly-looking half goatee under his chin.

Pam Spalding was from a high-profile Atlanta legal family. She had decided not to follow in the family footsteps and, instead of studying law, was studying communications, although half-way through her studies she saw the need to be across both disciplines, so decided to major in both. Pretty and bespectacled, her quiet demeanor belied a bright personality and a sharp mind. She had impressed Maye at a GOP fundraiser and offered her a part-time job in her campaign to help with building her social media branding. Now she was a key member of what was a very young inner circle that constituted Maye's team.

Of course, Maye's receptionist, Carroll, was also a part of the team, and while she did not really have any specific skills that could contribute directly, her wide-ranging knowledge of the machinations of Maye's office, and of the personalities that came and went—plus the fact that she was the gatekeeper to her office and the guardian of her diary—made her indispensable.

"What about if we use a Confederate flag in our campaign," suggested Mick. "It would stamp you as being a Southerner, and it is such a striking flag."

The others seemed to all shake their heads in unison.

"That would not be very politically correct," said Pam. "The Confederate flag is now associated with racism." The others nodded. "It's one of the reasons the Georgia state flag was changed... because it contained the Confederate flag."

"That's ridiculous," countered Mick. "The civil war was about state's rights, not just about slavery."

"People don't see it that way," said Rob. "To many, it's a symbol that is too sensitive to be used. And to those that agree with you, well they're usually too timid to rock the boat."

Mick thought about it for a moment.

"What do you think?" he asked Rob. "I mean, you're black. Do you think it's a symbol of racism?"

Rob smiled. Most people preferred the term 'African-American', but to Rob, who hated political correctness and the self-loathing it brought with it—Hell! He was in the GOP, for cryin' out loud!—black was a perfectly acceptable term. After all, he'd never been to Africa, so why call him African?

"I don't think so," he said. "If we can't accept our history, we'll never make any progress forward."

"Nicely put," said Mick. "Honey, what do you think?"

"I think it might be a bit too sensitive. I like the idea, but perhaps we should play it safe first... to see how things pan out."

"OK," he replied. "Hey mate," he said to Rob, "C'mon, let's get another round of drinks."

Mick and Rob waited at the bar. A couple was being served before them: a Japanese-looking guy with an American girlfriend who couldn't keep their hands off each other, even at the bar.

"So, Rob, what do you think about this election?" Mick asked of him.

"We are quietly confident," said Rob, understating the GAGOP's intention. "But you never know what will happen to change the voters' minds. I mean, look at President Troup. Everyone thought that he would lose, especially after that scandal about how he said he could get any woman he wanted. But he was voted in as president... so who knows? It's funny how his approval rating went up when someone tried to shoot him. But provided Maye doesn't trip over herself, and she continues to do what she's doing, then she should be fine," said Rob. "Of course, we could shoot her if her numbers drop," he joked.

He paused for a moment wondering whether he should say to Mick what was on his mind. The bar area was starting to fill up and soon the restaurant would too. Mick could see that he was thinking something.

"What?" he asked. "It looks like you want to say something," he said. Rob just smiled, a little embarrassed perhaps, and looked down at his shoes.

"C'mon! Spill!" demanded Mick, slapping him on the back. Rob enjoyed the easy familiarity he had with his boss' boyfriend even after only a couple of meetings. He felt comfortable speaking with him, as though he didn't have to prove anything. Lately, he had felt that he had to; like he had to show that he was more than 'that token black kid' or 'that college student' or 'the brother that's gone to the Republicans and turned his back on his own kind.' With Mick he could just be the guy that works for his girlfriend and helps her run things. No labels.

"Well man," he said. "I like Maye. She's great. She's got great young ideas and she's smart and she connects with people. But being a congresswoman, man. Hell! It's hard work. But since she's been seeing you, man, she's always in a great mood! I've always liked working for her, but these days, I look forward to seeing her. She's so positive and upbeat."

Their drinks arrived and they headed back to the team. Japan guy was sitting in a booth two tables down, his American girlfriend nuzzling his neck. Two very loud and obnoxious white guys were yelling at the TV as they watched some college football. The Arizona Wildcats versus Texas Tech Red Raiders game was being shown, and even though they were several hundred miles away from either college, it seemed that they had a vested interest in this game.

As they were placing the drinks on the table, Rob merely said to Mick, "That's between you and I, though!"

Mick just smiled at him and slapped him on the back.

"What's between you and him?" asked Maye of Rob with a smile on her face. She had seen how the two of them had hit it off so readily, and was happy that two important men in her life were getting along so well. Mick went behind Maye and put her hands on her shoulders and kissed the top of her head.

"That is between bro's!" he said. And Rob, sitting opposite, put out his fist for a fist bump. Mick obliged and then grabbed the drinks tray and took it back to the bar.

As he returned, he saw Japan guy and American girl kissing passionately. 'Get a room!' he thought to himself as he watched them. As he did, he saw the two college guys looking over towards their table at Maye, Rob, Pam and Sally-Anne. They were smiling and saying something to each other. One of them, the bigger of the two, then saw Mick looking at them and just stared at him, daring him to come over. Mick thought better and went back to their table. As he did, he heard one of them saying, just loud enough so that Mick could hear, "That's right. Just keep walking, asshole." And then both of them started to laugh before giving each other a high five.

"Idiots!" thought Mick to himself.

The evening was supposed to be about campaign planning, and while they did come up with some ideas nothing concrete was decided upon. Sally-Anne contributed very little. She seemed very much out of her depth.

Pam had suggested continuous video posts. She had seen that because most of the other congressional representatives and senators were much older, they had not really taken to social media as much as their younger staff would have liked. Sure, there were the obligatory posts, but there was no imagination in any of them!

"You really need to capture the attention of voters," she said, "by being unique and original. Some of the campaign commercials that are being released are creepy, or inappropriate, or just plain stupid," she complained.

"What we need is to make it simple, yet effective... but above all, honest. Show the people what a good person you are... but in a way that captures their imagination," said Pam. "You're young, so use young methods to appeal to a younger audience."

Sally-Anne listened intently. While Pam and Rob had been batting around ideas, she had been sipping her drink and taking it all in. Their ideas were definitely from a knowledge that she did not possess, and she was learning a great deal.

Mick held Maye's hand under the table and would give her leg a squeeze every now and then. To be daring, Maye leaned forward as if to hear better, but what she was really doing was putting her hand in Mick's crotch and squeezing it hard. Mick groaned, slightly in pain, and picked up his glass and gulped his beer. It hurt a bit but he liked it. It was definitely arousing him. He could not wait to get her back to her apartment tonight and then spend the weekend with her at her house at Lake Allatoona.

After an hour or so, Rob and Pam decided to go for a dance. Maye excused herself to visit the bathroom leaving Sally-Anne and Mick alone.

"So, Sally-Anne, how are you feeling about things?" asked Mick. "Are you happy to be on Maye's team? Got some good ideas to get voters out there?"

She took the straw from her mouth.

"To be honest, I'm quite new at this," she said. "I was put with Maye to sort of 'learn the ropes', so I hope she doesn't think that I will be coming up with some award-winning campaign," she admitted.

"That's fine," said Mick. "Hey! I'm new at this, too! I've never been part of a political campaign, either... and to be honest, Maye is only my fourth real girlfriend! So we'll both find out what we're doing at the same time!"

He pushed his glass against hers and they clinked.

"Here's to first timers learning together!" he said, and they both took a drink. Sally-Anne felt somewhat relieved at his words. "What do you do when you're not planning election campaigns," he asked her.

"Until recently I was a deputy principal at a middle school," she said. "We had five hundred kids, grades 6 through 8, and we were always under-staffed. I thought that job was hard, but looking back now, that was a walk in the park compared to this."

Maye returned to the table and soon after, so did Rob and Pam. The two college guys were as obnoxious as ever. One of them said loudly, 'mud shark' and laughed. Mick suddenly sensed a change in the mood at the table, but didn't know why. It seemed they were eager to leave.

"Sally-Anne, are you going back to the office?" asked Maye. Sally-Anne said that she was. "Can you give me a lift? We came here in Mick's car, and I need mine for tomorrow. If you can take me back to the office, I can pick up my car and that will save us some time."

"Sure," replied Sally-Anne, happy to be of some service to Maye.

"Can I bum a ride?" asked Pam. "My car's there, too." Sally-Anne said yes. She was trying to endear herself to her new, albeit much younger, colleagues and would have happily driven them both to Savannah and back if they had asked.

"I guess we're calling it a night," said Maye. "Honey, I'll meet you back at the apartment?" she said to Mick. He nodded and gave her a kiss, then he and Rob headed to the parking garage to get their cars.

"Are you right to drive? You haven't had too much to drink, have you?" Rob asked Mick.

"I'm fine, mate," he said. "Just a couple of beers. I have to stay on the straight and narrow now that I'm dating such a superstar of the Republican Party!" he said.

Suddenly Pam started a chant, "Two more years! Two more years!" and the others joined in, laughing at how funny they were.

* * *

Mick and Rob walked through the multi-level parking lot. The air was muggy and warm, even after midnight. In Buckhead, the bars closed at 2 a.m. so everyone was locked away trying to keep cool and to keep drunk. The bars were packed, but the streets not so much.

They had spoken a bit more about Maye and the campaign and the need to come up with some good ideas. As they walked through the rows of cars, they could hear the slow squealing of tires on painted floors. Their own voices echoed in the cavernous parking level.

"So that pretty blond thing must be a mud shark," came an ominous voice from the shadows.

About five cars away, standing near the ticket machine, were the two college guys who were watching football in the bar.

Rob tried to ignore them and started fumbling for the parking ticket.

"I didn't know mud sharks swam in Buckhead, did you?" asked the taller of the idiots to his shorter idiot friend."

"Nope," he replied, "neither did I."

Mick was still unsure what they were talking about, but could tell they wanted trouble. They started towards them, menacingly.

One of them looked around, checking for witnesses and cameras.

The big one went straight for Rob and king hit him, sending him to the ground. In a quick move, he bent down and picked him up in a headlock, preventing him from getting to his feet or breathing.

The other approached Mick. In his hand was a knife. Rob was clawing at big college guy, trying to breathe. Gasping, he saw Mick, his hands up like he was trying to surrender, backing away fast. Knife guy started laughing. He had the upper hand and feigned a rush towards him. Mick backed up and turned, moving away quickly, leaving the two attackers dragging Rob to a darker part of the parking lot.

Knife guy laughed harder and turned to join his bigger friend who was dragging Rob—still struggling for breath— into the shadows.

"You're not going anywhere, nigger!" said the bigger one as he continued to drag him behind some cars and out of view.

Knife guy stood and watched his bigger friend choking the last of Rob's breath. Rob clawed at hit assailant, but he was quickly fading. A few more seconds of this and he would pass out.

A voice boomed from behind, "Hey, mate!"

Knife guy wheeled around to see Mick, shirtless. He moved towards Mick, knife ready to slash and stab. It was then that he saw that Mick had wrapped his shirt around his hand tightly. But what he did not see was the chunk of concrete in Mick's other hand.

The bigger one yelled to his knife-wielding friend to "get him!" Knife guy moved towards Mick, jabbing with his knife, aiming to keep him at arm's length and to do some damage.

Mick easily deflected the knife with his shirt. He felt the blade come through the cloth and cut his hand, but now he was close enough to bring the concrete down on the side of his attacker's head.

Knife guy dropped the knife and grabbed at his head, dazed.

Mick took one step back and kicked him in the crotch. Knife guy fell to his knees and Mick kicked the knife away. Knife guy, knelt grabbing his pants, blood oozing from his head.

Mick grabbed him by the hair pulling his head back and stood hard on one of his ankles. Knife guy cried out in pain again, clawing at Mick, his ankle bent sickeningly under the weight of his captor.

Looking at the bigger of the two college guys, still holding Rob in a headlock, Mick said to him, "Call him nigger again."

Rob's attacker, trying to process the suddenly changed situation, paused and released his choke hold long enough for Rob to gulp some air. He realized his only chance was to keep Rob as his hostage.

"I said, call him a nigger again," Mick said calmly.

Big guy didn't move and didn't say a word. He wasn't sure what to do. His shorter friend was screaming in pain. Mick stood down harder on his ankle and pulled back on his hair. He then turned his head slightly to talk to his captive, all the while keeping an eye on big guy who still had Rob.

"Would you mind keeping quiet, little girl. The grown-ups are talking. Now," he said quietly and deliberately, looking straight at big guy, "I-said-call-him-a-nigger, again."

Big guy still didn't move. He didn't know what to do.

"OK," said Mick, and raised the concrete block and brought it down hard on knife guy's head again. He screamed in pain.

"I can do this all night," said Mick "but I don't think your friend would like it too much, do you?"

Knife guy was sobbing uncontrollably crying out "Stop! Stop!" Blood covered half his face, and if his ankle wasn't broken, it sure was not going to be working quite right anytime soon.

The big guy let Rob go and he fell to the ground breathing hard, clutching his throat with one hand. He struggled away while his attacker stood motionless, looking at Mick whose hand was raised, ready to strike again.

"OK. Let him go!" said the college guy.

"Oh, I don't think so," Mick replied calmly as Rob joined him, breathing hard and holding his throat. "Someone needs to be taught a lesson in manners." Knife guy was sobbing, waiting for another blow.

Just then, out of the corner of his eye, Mick saw some movement amongst the cars. It was Japan man and America girl. They were moving towards them, both with a look of determination, ready to intervene. The girl looked just as menacing as the man, when suddenly the girl pulled at her partner's arm, stopping him. Japan man stopped. America girl said something, and he nodded.

"Is everything alright?" called out America girl.

Rob stood up and raised his hand to signal that everything was fine.

The taller of the two attackers ran off leaving his friend to fend for himself.

"Yes. Thanks. We're just going to call the cops and sort out this guy who tried to attack us," called out Rob.

The couple, who had seemed so determined to get involved, suddenly turned and disappeared into the darkness. Mick pushed knife guy to the ground and knelt down, putting his weight on his throat and then pushing a hand onto his face against his nose and mouth.

"If you stay still, I'll let you breathe," said Mick.

Knife guy struggled, trying to throw him off. Mick pushed down harder on his throat and with his free hand he smashed down on the guy's crotch as hard as he could with a clenched fist, and then pushed his hand down on his face again, covering his mouth and nostrils.

"I said stay still and I will let you breathe."

He stopped struggling and Mick released his grip on his nostrils. He looked up at Rob who was now watching what his boss' boyfriend was doing.

"Grab his wallet," he said. Rob stood there, bewildered.

Mick nodded towards knife guy's waist.

"Give us your wallet," said Mick to knife guy. He twisted his body and fished out his wallet from his back pocket. Rob took it.

"Get his license," said Mick. Rob took out knife guy's license and held it for Mick to read. Mick shook his head and looked down at his captive.

"What's your name, age and address," he said to the guy lying beneath him. Mick took some of the weight off his hand and knee.

"John Wilcox. 23. 1642 Hunter's Run, Stone Mountain," he said. Obviously in a lot of pain. Mick looked up at Rob who was reading the license.

"Is that correct, mate?" Rob read it and nodded. Mick then turned to his captive again.

"Well, John Wilcox, 23 of Hunter's Run, Stone Mountain. It seems your friend didn't really care much about you, did he? Now I'm going to let you go but if I am visited by any of your friends or the police or anyone else who has taken offense to me or my friend, then you'd better hope that they kill us because I will pay a visit to 1642 Hunter's Run in Stone Mountain and I will come inside and I will finish what I started, and then I will take some gasoline and I will burn your house to the ground. Do you understand me, John Wilcox, 23 of Hunter's Run, Stone Mountain?"

Wilcox nodded, terrified. Mick let him get up and Rob gave him back his wallet. He limped away in pain, his shirt and face covered in blood.

"Are you going to be alright to drive home," he asked Rob, calmly, as if nothing had happened.

"Hey man, thanks. I thought that asshole was going to kill me."

"The world is full of arseholes," said Mick. "They just need to be put in their place. Besides, no-one fucks with a mate of mine... unless it's a really hot chick!" he said jokingly. It did the trick. Rob started laughing, the adrenalin still causing him to shake, and went to give Mick a hug.

"Hey! Hey! None of this hugging, shit!" said Mick. "Besides, I'm not wearing a shirt. That's just creepy. How about a hearty handshake instead, mate?"

They shook hands. Rob's eyes beaming with gratitude.

"Do me a favor," asked Mick as he picked up his shirt and went to put it on. His hand was bleeding, and his shirt was torn where the blade had cut it. "Don't tell Maye about this. She's got enough going on without her worrying about you and I."

"Were you serious about burning that guy's house down?" asked Rob, the whole terrifying event starting to sink in.

"Nah! I'm a lover, not a fighter," replied Mick.

"You could have fooled me!" said Rob and they headed for their cars. In the shadows Japan guy and America girl watched, ready to call the cops like good citizens. The danger passed, they got in their car and drove away.

32

The Battle at Kennesaw Mountain

They began their campaign with a media release and a video for online release. Maye had five thousand followers on Twitter, and about the same on Instagram, and her Facebook page had about seven thousand likes. For a first-time congresswoman, those statistics were pretty good. Her relative youth, good looks, and the fact she was a smart and accomplished woman certainly helped when it came to social media. She knew that of the prospective voter base, females would be more inclined to follow her online than males, and this had played on her mind. It was a strength for the female vote, but it left a weakness for the male vote. Now that Mick was with her, it may prove a good way to gather more interest from male constituents if they could work in some activities that would appeal to that demographic. She wondered how best to take advantage of his involvement and whether it was appropriate to do so. He might not appreciate being a stalking horse. She needn't have worried. He turned out to be more adept at campaigning than anyone could imagine.

It was Mick's aim to raise her profile and to energize people in the 11th to be as excited about her as he was. He had been doing a lot of thinking of late, wondering what the future would hold. She was almost certain to retain her seat and therefore would spend the next two years commuting between Georgia and DC. He would have to return to Australia half-way through her next term at the end of next year. Even if he remained in the US for as long as possible before he had to take up his promotion and posting, he would still only be able to remain until the middle of January, just after the next Congress returned from the Christmas break and commenced the new session. That was just seventeen months! Seventeen months of commuting between southern Alabama and Georgia.

But that was future Mick's problem. Right now, it was all about Maye and putting her in a good light. They had passed Dobbins Air Force Base where Maye had once worked as a C-130 Hercules pilot. A Herc took off as they passed the base with its big WWII-era B-29 Superfortress bomber, now on display as a 'gate guard'.

Soon they were not far from the entrance to the Kennesaw Mountain National Battlefield Park. The park and its mountain—more a large hill—rose about eight hundred feet above suburbia. The mountain itself and the areas immediately at its base, were the scene of a courageous defense by Confederate troops and one of the last hold-outs before the Union Army was able to enter Atlanta. Now it was the site of a national park and symbolic to all true Atlantans who were not embarrassed to proclaim their southern heritage. And thus, it was the perfect site to commence their 'great march north-west.'

The state committee called in a favor from one of its members, and Maye's team had a huge Winnebago RV for their mobile campaign office. Adorning it was a large image of Maye's face smiling, asking people to re-elect her as the 11th's voice in Washington. Maye and Mick were going to walk the entire route from Kennesaw Mountain right up to Adairsville in the north-western part of the district on the way to Chattanooga, a distance of about fifty miles.

The state committee, upon hearing of the plan, had tried to dissuade her until The Chairman stepped in and told her to do as she saw fit. Mick had made sure that Sally-Anne was feeling valued, although her ideas still had all the hallmarks of a campaign from the last century. She was running around constantly on the phone, with a voice that sounded as though she was almost begging people to be interested.

At Kennesaw Mountain, Maye's volunteers had helped muster the few media that had bothered to turn up. There was a reporter from the *Atlanta Journal-Constitution* newspaper and two crews from local TV: WAGA's FOX 5 and WGPB, the Public Broadcasting Service affiliate. It was a rather poor turnout and Maye couldn't help but wonder if Sally-Anne was definitely out of her depth.

She kept apologizing for the meager interest, but Mick calmed her down telling her that this was just day one on a two-week quest and that there would be plenty of opportunities to get more coverage. "It's not a sprint, it's a marathon," he would say. Mick's reassurance helped her hold back her tears.

They readied for the press conference. The volunteers wore red T-shirts sporting the campaign slogan: *'Old Values, Young Candidate'*, a reference to Maye's conservative values and her relative youth... as well as her name. The alternative slogan: "Candidate Young, the young candidate" didn't make the cut, nor a dozen other variations. In the meantime, Mick took The Chairman's wife aside.

"Are you going to be alright," Mick asked Sally-Anne who was rummaging around in her handbag looking for a Kleenex.

"Oh, I'll be fine," she said, finally finding one and blowing her nose. "I just wanted Maye to be happy with the coverage... and looking at the number of people who actually turned up... Hell! We could hold the event in an elevator and still have room for more media!"

"Don't worry about it. Maye's happy you're here... and we've still got two weeks to go. As Maye and I are walking, you can be doing your thing in the RV drumming up more interest. We'll be fine. You watch!"

She smiled and wiped her nose and left to see how Maye was doing in front of the two cameras and three reporters. In her mind she had pictured a dozen or more.

Mick headed to the RV to get a drink and to pick up two flags that they were going to be carrying. He then hopped off the RV and headed over towards the media conference. Sally-Anne was standing near Maye who was handling herself with aplomb. She spoke articulately and with passion, trying to enthuse Georgians in her district to get out and vote and show Washington that people in the South were not to be taken for granted.

As she spoke, Sally-Anne watched and listened, standing behind the crew from FOX 5 News. When she saw Mick approaching from the RV her heart leaped into her mouth. Without thinking she said just one word, slowly and loud enough so that everyone could hear it: "FAAAAHHHHHCK!"

Definitely not something that a genteel lady from the South would say!

33

A Rebel Yell

After Sally-Anne's surprising profanity, the whole throng turned to her, then turned to see what she was looking at.

There was Mick, about to sidle up to Maye, holding two large flags: the Stars and Stripes on one shoulder and a Confederate flag over the other. He looked at the faces, aghast, all staring back at him. He looked at them and merely said, "What?"

"You can't wave that flag," whispered Sally-Anne loudly enough that everyone could hear.

Mick looked at the red flag with its star-studded blue saltire resting against his shoulder.

"Why not?" he said. His face looked serious and quizzical, as if he was not sure what all the fuss was about, even though he most certainly did.

The two TV cameras were trained on him. The reporter from the AJC, who was doubling as cameraman, began taking photos and bumbling with his cell phone which doubled as his recorder. He was wishing he had a photographer with him. The FOX 5 reporter jostled with the PBS reporter to get a good position so she could thrust the microphone under Mick's chin. The two cameramen were a bit more restrained and adjusted their cameras, keeping out of each other's way.

"Is there a reason you are carrying that flag?" asked the PBS reporter who seemed very taken aback. The FOX 5 reporter held her microphone steady, and the AJC reporter shoved his phone between the two, ready to capture every word. Maye grabbed his upper arm trying to pull him away subtly. Meanwhile, the others were at a loss for what to do.

"The reason I am carrying this flag is that it is a great symbol of what we stand for," he said.

"He's Australian," said Maye interjecting and trying to put her face into shot, "so he's not fully aware of what this flag means," she said. She hoped that would be enough, but the reporters could smell a story... and this one was being handed to them on a platter.

"Oh, Maye, don't sell me short. I may be Australian, but I'm not stupid!"

"That flag is a symbol of slavery in the United States," said the reporter from PBS. "Were you aware of that?" she said smugly.

"What's your name?" asked Mick of the reporter. The FOX 5 cameraman filmed the exchange while the PBS cameraman merely kept his camera trained on Mick.

"Heather Taliaferro," she replied.

"Well, Heather, I don't know anything about this flag being a symbol of slavery," he said looking at it.

"Well, it is, and it is probably inappropriate that you should be waving it as part of a campaign. It is divisive in this country," she said, the smugness dripping from her words.

"What school did you go to, Heather?" asked Mick.

"Penn State," she replied. "That's in Pennsylvania," she added, with an air of superiority.

"So, you're a Yankee? (The FOX 5 cameraman snickered). Well, Heather, first of all, this is not the flag of the Confederate States of America. It is the flag of the Army of Virginia, and it is a battle flag which means it was carried into battle by soldiers who were fighting for their state and what they believed to be their rights. The flag of the Confederacy was not this flag, it was the stars and bars."

The reporter, stunned momentarily, tried to talk over him, as reporters are want to do. "You may not understand the offense that this flag..."

Mick then looked at the FOX 5 crew and the reporter from the AJC.

"This flag does not symbolize slavery. I am completely aware of what it has come to mean, but we are taking back the original meaning. It is a rallying point for a fight. The political correctness that has gripped this nation has weakened it. What was a nation of rugged individualists has become cowed and weak under the disapproving finger of left-wing liberals who want everyone to be friends and go around and hug trees. *They* are the new bullies because *they* control the media. Well, I've got a wakeup call for the permanently offended: the US has enemies, and they don't care about political correctness, or holding hands and hugging trees. They want to hurt the US and its economy, and until America can 'sack up' and learn to be great once more, then they will win.

"This flag," and he pointed to the 'offending' standard, "is a battle flag. It is not a flag that promotes slavery. It is not a flag for white supremacists. It is not a flag for extremists. It is a flag around which those who want to fight for their rights can rally.

"And before you go, let me give you a little lesson in your own history, Heather," he said looking at her.

"When Sherman marched the Union army from Tennessee to Atlanta, and on to the sea, his soldiers raped and pillaged and burned all the way down to the coast. But if that wasn't enough, he had them burn the farms and salt the earth and destroy and devastate any semblance of industry in Georgia. He burnt Atlanta to the ground. Does that sound like something you want to celebrate as being honorable? The Confederate soldiers did their best to defend their land. They rallied around their battle flags, and they fought for Georgia against the northern aggression and the rape of their women and lands.

"We are marching north towards Tennessee following in the footsteps of those brave soldiers that fought then. We will carry the flag of the United States as a symbol of freedom and free speech, and alongside it we will hold the flag of the Army of Virginia as a symbol that we're up for a fight against political correctness and left-wing namby-pambies who have castrated this once-great nation. We hope that those that agree will give us a honk as they see us on the road."

He then looked squarely into the FOX 5 camera.

"Maye Young is your representative for the 11th Congressional District of Georgia and she's up for a fight, and will fight for Georgia and the South, and fight against bullying by big government, and wokeism."

And with that, and with both flags over his shoulders, Mick turned on his heels and began the march. Maye walked beside him. They had taken only the first steps on their long march and her boyfriend may have just torpedoed her campaign.

She was trying to gather the words that she wanted to say to him or, more precisely, yell at him.

34

⚭

Every Journey Begins with One Step

As Maye caught up with Mick, he handed her the Stars and Stripes.

"It'd be better if you were seen holding this flag," said Mick. "I'll hold the rebel flag."

Maye was not quite sure where to begin. Had her boyfriend just derailed her campaign? Her seat in Congress? Was this the end of her political career?

"What did you just do?" she said incredulously. "I think you just ruined my chances of re-election!"

Mick kept walking and Maye stayed in step. They were heading north-west on Old 41 Highway. They didn't look back. If they had, they would have seen the cameras being rapidly packed up and the reporters racing for their cars. They had a great story, so now it was time to file it.

Maye started to forecast what was likely to happen and what she would need to do. She could see it now: *'Racist Republican's Campaign Launch'*, or *'Out of touch with the New South'*, or *'Young has old ideas.'* How was she going to control the damage?

The reporter from PBS recovered from her dressing down and tried to contact The Chairman at GAGOP committee headquarters to get a quote. He wasn't available so instead she was directed to Rebecca

Chatham, the communications adviser, who happened to be with Robert Fulton at the time.

"Were you aware that Maye Young was using the Confederate flag for her campaign?" asked the reporter. "Did the Republican Party encourage her to do this?"

Chatham listened in shock. She covered the handpiece and whispered to Fulton, 'They're using a Confederate flag in their campaign."

Fulton mouthed the word "Fuck!" and immediately scrambled for his cell phone. Chatham returned to the reporter's question.

"Who is using the flag did you say?" she asked, trying to buy time.

"It is one of Representative Young's campaign staff. He sounded Australian," replied the reporter.

Chatham covered the handpiece again and whispered to Fulton, "It's O'Rourke. He's got the flag!"

"Oh, I think that must be an error," she said, returning to the call from the reporter. "Mr. O'Rourke is from Australia and is not familiar with what is appropriate here in Georgia. I'm sure it was an innocent mistake. We at the Republican party do not endorse the use of any symbol of racial divide," she said. "We are a diverse organization and do not encourage symbols of white supremacy."

"So you're saying that the Confederate flag is a symbol of white supremacy?" asked the reporter in a dismissive tone, as if she had already got the quote she wanted and did not need Chatham to clarify it.

"That's not what I said," Chatham replied, immediately regretting the statement. "I said we do not encourage such symbols."

The reporter continued leading Chatham on. For a seasoned professional like Chatham, it was unusual that she could be goaded so easily.

"If the state Republican committee didn't authorize the use of the Confederate flag—or, what did you call it? A symbol of white supremacy—in Young's re-election campaign, would you say that she had decided to move away from Republican campaign strategy? Has she gone rogue? Will the Republican Party comment on such symbols of, as you say, white supremacy?"

This was getting out of hand quickly and Chatham shut her down saying that they'll be in touch with a statement. But the reporter had got everything she wanted. She then dialed again. This time to her producer. She told him what was going on.

"Stay with them," he said to his reporter, "and keep the cameras on them. Get as much footage as you can. I have a great idea." The producer then made some quick phone calls. It was time to create a story!

* * *

As the media left, Rob Early raced off to catch up to Mick and Maye. Pam, who had been recording everything on a digital camera, also took some stills of the two walking away.

Sally-Anne, stunned, spoke to the FOX 5 reporter.

"That was an interesting interview," she said to the FOX 5 team, trying to gauge their reaction.

"It's about time we got some honesty," said the cameraman, packing up his camera.

Sally-Anne asked him what his opinion was.

"I liked it," he said. "He said what most of us have been thinking for a long time. We're sick and tired of political correctness. It's too bad *he's* not running for Congress. I'd vote for him."

The reporter, a black woman looking very polished in a maroon skirt and blouse with perfect hair, listened to the cameraman. She said to him, and to Sally-Anne, "I'm glad that bitch at PBS got schooled. That footage is gold dust. We can run with that no problems," she said beaming. The cameraman smiled back in return, nodding. That's why he had filmed it... to give PBS a taste of their own medicine.

"So you don't think that he did the wrong thing using that flag? You don't see it as a slavery thing?" she asked.

"I don't see it that way," said the reporter. "The Georgia flag had it for decades and it was only recently that it became an issue. Besides, this is the New South. Racism happens everywhere and that flag doesn't have to be used as its symbol. I liked what he said, that it is a battle flag. We can run with that. Our viewers will love it. Georgians will love it."

Sally-Anne, almost in tears, hugged the reporter who was caught completely off guard.

Embarrassed, she released the poor woman, who was amused by this unexpected emotion, and turned to watch Maye and Mick walking up Highway 41. What she saw was another shock.

"Well, I'll be," she said. The FOX 5 crew turned to see what had caught her attention. What they saw was the representative of the 11th District, Maye Young, carrying the Stars and Stripes. Her boyfriend had his arm around her shoulder. But instead of him carrying the rebel flag, his other arm was around the shoulder of someone else, and *that* someone was carrying the rebel flag.

Rob Early, Maye's handsome, young black campaign worker, had raced after them and was now marching beside them... proudly carrying the rebel flag.

The reporter from the *Atlanta Journal Constitution* had managed to get his camera out and snapped a few images. The news tonight and the paper tomorrow would probably spell the end of Maye's campaign.

35

Just a Mom and a
Schoolteacher

As Rebecca Chatham was talking to the reporter from PBS, trying to pour water on the flames she had inadvertently fanned, Rob Fulton was trying to contact Sally-Anne to find out exactly what was going on at the launch.

"Come on. Answer the Goddam' phone!" he urged. Rebecca was still trying to convince the reporter who had called for another quote that it was a mistake on the part of the Australian who did not know any better, and that his views did not represent the views of the Republican Party. Sally-Anne answered.

"Hello? Sally-Anne here," she said.

"Sally-Anne! What the fuck is going on there?" he yelled down the phone. His voice was loud, and Rebecca frowned at him, signaling him to keep it down.

"I would suggest you keep a civil tongue in your head, Robert!" she said. "Now, what do you want?"

He tried to calm down and said, through clenched teeth, "I would like to inquire as to how the campaign launch is going. I understand that there may be a problem," he uttered gratingly, trying not to scream at her.

"Oh, there's no problem here," she said to him. "It's going fine."

"Well then," he said, again trying not to erupt like Mount Saint Helens, "we are fielding a phone call from a reporter saying that the flag of the Confederacy was being used in the launch. Is that true?

"It's not the flag of the Confederacy," she responded. "It's the flag of the Army of Virginia... or something like that. I can't remember exactly what Mick said. He was very good."

Fulton's head dropped and he cupped his forehead with his hand. Any flag that is not the American flag or the Georgia state flag was a problem during this campaign... especially any flag that could be perceived as a racist symbol.

"You tell them to get rid of that Goddamned flag," he ordered her.

"Robert, I don't believe that you should be telling me what to do. I am in charge of this campaign, am I not?" she replied defiantly.

She was enraged that this man should be telling her what to do. For too long she had felt not in control of her life. Her husband did not respect her or their marriage—she knew that for a fact—and her husband's colleagues did not either. Certainly, Rob Fulton did not. Her kids loved her but did not take her seriously. She was just 'Mom', and whenever they had a real problem, they would go to their father. Even some of the teachers at the middle school where she had worked before this campaign had shown little respect for her position as vice principal.

Now, after years of being treated like a doormat, Mick and Maye and Rob and Pam were treating her as an equal. She may not be able to provide the service that Maye needed, but right now she could provide something different: interference.

"Yes, Sally-Anne," said a seething Fulton through clenched teeth, "you are in charge of Miss Young's campaign, so I would suggest that you strongly urge her to re-consider using any flag that is not the American flag... and definitely do not let that motherfucking Australian in front of any camera or microphone!"

Fulton was regretting letting Mick be a part of this campaign. So was Chatham, still trying to swat the reporter's questions. He had rapidly turned into a liability, and it was only Day One! This did not bode well for the rest of the campaign. Mid-terms were usually safe elections. Maye should not lose her seat unless something big happens to change the mind of the voters. Well, guess what? Walking down the road in Georgia carrying a Confederate flag, in this day and age, *was* something big. Fulton could see the 11th District changing hands and go from a relatively safe Republican seat to a Democratic seat. And it would be due to the advice he had given The Chairman about using Mick as part of the campaign. He returned to his call with The Chairman's wife.

"Well, Robert," she said as condescendingly as possible, "I think Mr. O'Rourke is doing a fine job, and I think he is an asset to this campaign. I don't think taking him out of it would be a good idea."

This infuriated Fulton. How dare this housewife tell him who was an asset and who was not. What did she know about politics? She was just a mom and a schoolteacher. Her opinion meant nothing. Did she not know who he was? It was time to put her back in her place.

"Sally-Anne, you are there to do what the committee wants you to do, do you understand? You are there to follow orders, my orders. Can you get that through your skull? And right now, I am ordering you to get O'Rourke away from any media and get that fucking flag down! Do you understand me?"

There was silence. Sally-Anne was the first to speak.

"May I speak with my husband, please?" she said quietly. Fulton took a deep breath, half regretting losing his temper at his boss' wife. In as calm a voice as possible, he replied.

"I'm sorry, Sally-Anne, The Chairman is not in today." He was getting frustrated with her. "And if you think that passive-aggressive threat is going to work on me, you've got another think coming," he said. "You can go and squeal as much as you want to your husband, but he is going to see it my way. So, take that housewife intimidation and stick it where the sun don't shine," he fumed. He was ready to do battle with this woman. How dare she try and make him cower.

"So he's not at the office at the moment?" asked Sally-Anne, making sure her voice was measured and calm. Fulton was still fuming but calmed his voice down.

"No, he is not. But trust me when I say I will give him a full brief when he returns and get him to call you straight away." (His smugness could be heard on the other end).

"Oh, you needn't worry," replied Sally-Anne. "I can speak to him. I think I know where he might be."

36

The Spirit of '76

The FOX 5 team caught up with Maye, Mick and Rob. The sound guy drove while the reporter hung out of the front passenger seat and the cameraman filmed from the rear.

As they came abeam the trio, Maye looked a bit sheepish. This was not how she had intended her campaign launch to go. She had expected a large throng of media and some scripted and rehearsed lines, and perhaps some questions about Mick before they commenced their walk towards Adairsville in neighboring Bartow County.

Now, her Australian boyfriend had stirred a hornets' nest with this flag stunt. The PBS reporter was indignant during the conference. Maye could see it during the interview. Now, the FOX 5 team was following her and Mick and Rob. This was turning into a circus! There was nowhere for them to go, however. They were on foot. Their support vehicle, the Winnebago, was to be driven by Pam and Sally-Anne. A quick look behind her saw the Winnebago in the parking lot of the Kennesaw Mountain Battleground Park, getting steadily smaller. Any hope of hiding inside it was out of the question. Instead, she would have to try and sort this out herself.

To her surprise, the reporter was not so much concerned with her. Instead, she had trained her microphone onto Rob, holding the rebel flag. The sight of a black man with a rebel flag was front-page stuff. She leaned out further and began the questioning.

"Why are you carrying that flag?" she asked him. The cameraman had half his body hanging out of the station-wagon to get a dramatic image of the reporter leaning out of the car. He then trained his camera onto Rob, panning upwards to get the full effect of the flag against the blue, Georgia sky.

"I believe Maye Young is a tough representative for Georgia and she's willing to fight for her district and this state. This flag represents her willingness to fight and I'm rallying around this flag to help her in any battle she takes on just as the Confederate soldiers rallied around it. That is how much I believe in her," he said passionately. "I'm ready to fight, too!"

Mick put his arm around him and brought him in for a man hug, a huge smile on his face.

"Good on you, mate!" he said.

The reporter wanted to get a black perspective on this.

"But aren't you concerned that this flag represents the South's fight for the right to keep slaves? And that you are minimizing the gains that have been made by the black community?"

Rob then demonstrated how smart he actually was.

"The gains made over the last one hundred and sixty years cannot be minimized by a flag. Regardless of what you think this flag represents, the fact remains that it is a battle flag for soldiers, not a political flag for slavery. Miss Young wore a uniform in the United States Air Force to protect people like you and me who never did wear a uniform. Mr. O'Rourke here wore the uniform of the Australian Army and fought alongside Americans in Iraq and in Afghanistan.

"These two people represent all that is good in our armed forces and Miss Young represents all that is good in what we hope our politicians should be. If she asked me to fight alongside her, I would. But she didn't. I saw the caliber of this woman and I volunteered to stand alongside her. If my display of loyalty to her and to her cause is merely holding this flag, then I will gladly do it, and do so proudly."

As remarkable as that sentiment was, he was about to offer his *pièce de résistance*. It would become the soundbite of the campaign.

"I am a proud American, and I am a proud Georgian. This flag is my battle flag against wokeism."

While not having the same impact as Rosa Parks, this speech by Rob Early, college student of Atlanta, Georgia; staffer of the representative of the 11th US Congressional District of the state of Georgia, would follow him for his career. His words would always be met with deep admiration as a statement of healing and forgiveness, and one that did more than most to unite an America becoming more and more divided.

The FOX 5 cameraman smiled. Maye saw his grin and the cameraman gave her a thumbs-up. She wasn't sure what that meant. Did it mean he supported their cause, or did it mean he had just caught award-winning material that would cement his career? But Sally-Anne, if she had seen that, would know exactly what that thumbs-up meant.

Back at the Kennesaw Mountain Battleground Park, standing behind the Winnebago, Sally-Anne Atkinson was in the process of calling her husband's cell phone.

<h1 style="text-align:center">37</h1>

❦

Decadence in Decatur

The Chairman leaned on one elbow while he spoke on his phone. He listened intently, swearing intermittently.

On the other end was Bobby Fulton describing what was happening at Kennesaw Mountain, how Maye's campaign launch had become a disaster because of 'that Goddamned Australian.' The Chairman was told how WGPB had already started stirring the pot and that they wanted to talk to him to get a statement about the GOP's use of the Confederate battle flag and its symbolism for white supremacy.

"God Dammit!" cried The Chairman. "What about my Goddamned wife!" he yelled. "What the hell was she doing while all this was going on?" He listened to Fulton's description and opinion of what they should do next, and what they should do with The Chairman's wife. She had been placed on that campaign so that she could stay out of the way. Now she was right in the middle of the disaster. How much of it was her doing?

"OK. OK," said The Chairman into the phone. "I'll look after my wife. In the meantime, get onto the *Journal* and see if we can kill the story. I'll get onto FOX. They owe me a favor. As for PBS, those assholes will run this story for days! We'll need to come up with some statements quickly.

"Send someone out... No! *You* go out there! Get your butt out to Kennesaw and sort this crap out. I don't care if you have to drag that asshole back here hogtied to the hood of your Chevy, but get O'Rourke away from Young. He's poison!"

The Chairman stood up and paused for a moment, thinking. How was he going to kill this story? He could get it stopped at FOX. They were always sympathetic. Same at the *Atlanta Journal Constitution*. But the PBS station was another matter. They were always hostile to the conservatives.

He could picture it now on tonight's news and online. The party's golden girl, air force veteran Maye Young, with a Confederate flag. This was not going to be a good look.

His phone rang. He saw that it was his wife. His thoughts immediately turned to how he was going to deal with her. She was going to be sorry that she didn't stop this. He was going to bring her whole world crashing down around her ears. How dare she treat him like that! He answered...

"What the hell are you doing out there!" he yelled at her as he felt an arm around his leg.

Sally-Anne heard her husband yelling and could picture him turning red, that vein on his forehead getting larger.

"Where are you?" she asked him.

"I'm at the committee offices," he said angrily. As soon as he did, he immediately regretted it. There was silence for a moment.

"No you're not," she said. "I'm looking at your car right now," she lied.

The Chairman raced over to the window and looked out, searching for his wife's car.

"How is Elaine?" she asked him. "Is she on her knees for you right now?"

The Chairman turned to look at his naked executive assistant, lying on her bed, looking back at him quizzically, wondering why the old man had a shocked look on his face.

"I... ah..." he stuttered. He looked out of the window again. Sally-Anne had him right where she wanted him.

After all those years of being the devoted mother and wife. After all those years of being ignored and made to feel less-than-adequate. After all those years of turning a blind eye to her husband's dalliances, this was the moment that she had longed for. Of course she wasn't looking at The Chairman's car. How could she? She was at Kennesaw Mountain. And if her husband had thought about it for a moment, he would have known that. But he panicked. He was not where he was supposed to be, and he was not thinking ahead. A small bluff had revealed his deceit.

"Now look," he said, ready to bargain. "I can explain. It's not as it appears to be," he tried vainly to say.

"Oh, I know exactly what it appears to be... and what it actually is," replied Sally-Anne. "You've been fucking your EA just like you were fucking that legal counsel three years ago, and that intern before that. I know all about what you get up to," she said. "That intern was eighteen years old. For God's sake, our daughter was five years older than that little bitch when you were sleeping with her," said Sally-Anne.

"Now, that's not true," The Chairman said unconvincingly.

"Oh it is," replied Sally-Anne. "You don't think I would let you get away with that without having lots of proof," she told him. "You thought I was so stupid. You thought I couldn't tell you were sleeping around. I could smell it on you!"

The Chairman couldn't think straight. What was happening? What was she going to do with this information?

"For someone who thinks he's so smart, you didn't cover your tracks very well," she told him. "I have plenty of proof ready to go to whomever would like it. That lawyer you were doing it with. I've had her in my pocket since you stopped seeing her. She doesn't want her husband or her law partners to know she was cheating with a wrinkled old fool like you!"

The Chairman thought about the enemies he had made during his rise to where he was now. This scandal could ruin his reputation.

He would have to make a deal. His reputation was critical, as was staying in the marriage until Sally-Anne's parents kicked the bucket.

"I am going to make you sorry that you have been doing this to me. I am going to bring your whole world and your insignificant little interests crashing down around your ears! How dare you treat me like that," she proclaimed. (It's funny how she used the same expressions as her husband. They had obviously been with each other for too long).

The Chairman sat down in an armchair, his head resting in his hand with his phone to his ear. Elaine got up and covered herself with a towel. She could tell that it was his wife and that they had been discovered. She was now out of a job and out of a sugar daddy. She would probably have to start looking for a new job and a new condo. There was no way she could afford to stay in this one in Decatur anymore. Time to move outside The Perimeter.

She looked at The Chairman sitting naked. His pot belly even more rounded as he slumped, defeated.

"OK. What do you want?" he asked into the cell phone.

38

Acrimony in Acworth

FOX 5 had gone, but not before wishing them luck.

The AJC reporter had driven up ahead, parked his car and then walked with them asking more questions and taking photos. Rob had done them proud with his interview. The newspaper, like the FOX 5 reporter, was more interested in why a black man was carrying a rebel flag.

Sally-Anne and Pam were now driving the Winnebago past them about a mile, then doubling back and passing them again in the opposite direction. It was impossible to drive at the same speed they were walking. At the end of the day, another of Maye's staffers would drive out to meet them and bring Rob, Pam and Sally-Anne back to the district offices near Cobb Galleria. It was about forty-five miles to Adairsville, and they had set aside a week to do this, so about six miles a day was easily achievable.

Mick had come up with the idea, but it was Rob who had suggested that they follow US Highway 41 which was the closest route to that taken by the withdrawing Confederate Army during Sherman's march through Georgia. Besides, staying on I-75 would be difficult for their support vehicle and illegal for them as pedestrians. If they stayed on Highway 41, not only was it accessible for their team, but it also allowed them to meet Georgians and listen to them, or to answer questions from reporters. This proved to be a very wise decision, but not at first.

They had been walking about two hours, stopping as often as they could to talk to people and tell them their cause. They had crossed Cobb Parkway and were walking along the Old Highway 41 through historic Acworth towards Allatoona when some young men in sedans drove by and yelled out 'racists' and threw milkshakes at the trio. This happened not once, but three times. The last time they caught much of the sticky mess. The PBS cameraman from WGPB had been filming them almost continuously for the last hour and he caught it all. The reporter tried to get an interview as they were cleaning themselves.

The WGPB team got a few audio grabs and some footage of the group wiping strawberry milkshake from their red T-shirts and left in a hurry. Pam and Sally-Anne arrived and parked in the parking lot of a strip mall and the trio boarded the 'Bago and washed up and changed their T-shirts.

Back out on the streets they continued on their way. Their flags drew some attention as they walked through Acworth. People would come up to them and ask them what they were doing. Some asked why they had the slavery flag. Others told them that it was good to see the Confederate flag flying. It was certainly a mix of reactions. Quite a few told them to take that flag down and that it was inappropriate.

By about 2 p.m. it was ninety degrees, and so the team decided to call it a day and do a postmortem on how the morning went. Maye was very concerned about what the Republican committee would say when the story aired on the evening news, on YouTube and in tomorrow's AJC. She had deliberately refrained from looking at what was already posted online, but now was the time to do exactly that. Even though there were many positive comments about the flag, there were also several negative ones.

So far, nothing on FOX 5's site, but what was posted on the WGPB site was a disaster. The video showed Mick holding the rebel flag, but his speech was not aired.

An image of Maye then cut immediately to a close-up of the flag with the disapproving voiceover using terms like 'racially divisive' and 'ultra conservative'. Then there was an image of a woman holding a small child yelling abuse at them, shouting 'Racists!" and 'We don't want that flag here! This is the twenty-first century!'

"When did that happen?" asked Pam incredulously.

"It didn't," replied Maye. "They've staged that. We haven't had any protests like that."

The scene cut to a group of white twenty-somethings leaning from a car and hurling cups, and then it cut to Maye and Mick, with Maye stained with milkshake. There was no sign of Rob holding the rebel flag or being hit with milkshake, too. The report was not complimentary in the least. Worse would come after they had a chance to really edit it.

The team sat at the table in the RV and cooled down in the air conditioning

"I think that we should quit this idea here," said Maye "and go back to more conventional campaigning. This will blow over if we don't give them any more material. I should be able to leave this as a blip on the radar. I'm just worried that the images of me and the Confederate flag will keep surfacing."

Mick corrected her. "Honey, don't call it the Confederate flag otherwise they'll..."

"Oh, just stop it!" Maye snapped. "OK, we get it. You know a lot about our history. You know lots of trivia. You're smart. We get it. What you don't know about is how the political machine works here.

"This," she said, pointing to the computer screen and the WGPB images, "will haunt me for the entire campaign. This was a bad idea. You should have told me that you were going to use that flag. We had already told you that it was too controversial, but you went ahead and did it anyway."

Mick stood there and took her spray of anger. The others were silent and let her vent. She looked down at the screen, pausing momentarily and then looked back at Mick.

"You have no idea what this will do to my reputation with the GOP. I'll look like some sort of amateur. If I don't lose my seat, I'll definitely lose my reputation," she proclaimed.

"Until today I didn't have any serious Democrat competition. But if they see this, and decide to field a strong candidate, then that's it for me! Bye, Bye, Maye. Don't let the door hit you in the ass on your way out of the Capitol Building."

Mick spoke. "Whatever happens, I'll be there to support you. We can..."

"Oh, you'll be there to support me, will you? You are an Australian! You have a career in the army back in Australia! You will be gone next year... gone back home... and I will be left here with my career in ruins. Just a joke at Democrat parties for a while... and then forgotten about within a year."

The others were silent. Mick also. Just then was a hard banging on the door of the RV. Pam went to open it.

Barging into the RV, pushing Pam out of the way, was Robert Fulton, looking furious.

39

Full On

Fulton had his cell phone in his hand, and he stood there momentarily. Pam stood behind him, looking like she wanted to shrink and hide in one of the cupboards.

Pointing his cell phone at the group he raged. "What the fuck are you people doing? Are you single-handedly trying to bring down the GOP in this state? Have you seen what's on PBS?"

He walked menacingly towards them. His large frame accentuated by the confined space within the RV. And even though he was angry, and it was close to one hundred degrees outside, his charcoal-gray suit and Republican-red tie still looked immaculate.

"All you had to do was just stick to the plan. Mail outs. Some TV interviews. Visit some little league games. But Oh No! You had to be wiseasses and pull out that fucking flag! Are y'all brain dead? For Christ's sake, we changed the Goddamned state flag because it had the Confederate flag on it!"

Maye tried to speak. She wanted to explain that what PBS showed had been taken out of context and that some of it was manufactured.

"Listen, Bobby, I..."

"Oh no! I haven't finished yet!" he said, glaring at her. "Who do you think you are? You are nobody! Do you think that just because you're in Congress that you're someone special? We put you there!" he yelled, banging his chest. "I put you there!" he yelled, banging his chest again.

"Do you honestly think that you were the best candidate for the 11th District? For any district? I had a stack of files a foot high of people who were better candidates than you. But the committee decided to give it to a woman. To give it to a...," he raised his hands and did some air quotes, "'veteran!' Shit! My fifteen-year-old moron of a son could have done a better job than you at being a candidate. Even he knows that you cannot win by getting rednecks on side by pulling that flag stunt. This fucking state may be full of rednecks, but guess what? They don't vote!"

He paused. Sally-Anne had her phone in her hand and gripped it tightly on the table, her knuckles clenched around it, white with fear. She was silent. She had seen Fulton in a rage once before, something that was very rare. He was usually very quiet and measured. The 'Silent Assassin' some had called him. He was scary now, but he was scarier when he wasn't yelling. That's when you knew your time was up and you were finished.

"And you!" he barked, pointing his phone gripped in a tight fist at Sally-Anne. "Why didn't you stop them? Surely even a housewife like you would know that carrying a Confederate flag was a bad idea. Even the middle-school kids you teach know that."

Mick stepped forward, angry. He hadn't warmed to Fulton even from the outset. He wasn't going to let this cardboard cutout lecture his girlfriend or her staff in that way. Fulton saw him move towards him.

"Ah! And as for you! Just because you're fucking her doesn't mean you have a say in what goes on."

Mick was incensed and moved forward to hit him, but Maye and Rob jumped in front of him and grabbed him, stopping him from taking a swing.

"Let him do it!" yelled Fulton. "I'd love to have him arrested. That would solve all my problems. Come on, tough guy. Do it. Let's see how smart you are, motherfucker!"

Mick thought again. Rob looked at him and shook his head. Maye held onto him also. Hitting Fulton would certainly make him feel better, but it would mean the end for Maye... and for him also. He'd be sent back to Australia once his chain-of-command found out. And then there were the lawyers that Fulton and his cronies had, just waiting for things like this. Winning an assault case like this would be a walk in the park, and a nice little earner for them.

Fulton smiled an evil smile, full of contempt for him.

"That's right, asshole. Go and hide behind the skirt of a woman. Let her fight your battles for you, you worthless piece of shit."

Sally-Anne stood up trembling and walked towards Fulton as if she wanted to escape the Winnebago, but he was blocking the door. How he despised her. She was not up to the job of being the wife of The Chairman. No wonder he was sleeping with his EA. He needed someone who was more of 'a player'. Someone who could charm, and who could hold her own with the Georgia elite. She wasn't up to it. She was a liability... just a housewife. Now she was about to run away and cry.

"Here," she said to him, handing him her phone.

He looked at her and then down at her phone. He took it roughly and examined it for a few seconds. In shock, he looked at her.

"You have been relieved of your duties with the committee," she said. "Thank you for your service to the Georgia GOP."

She stood there and stared him down. The others looked on, confused. Not ten seconds ago they were being abused by Fulton. Now the RV was eerily quiet. No-one said a word, no-one except Sally-Anne.

"Thank you for your service, Bobby," she said as if she was addressing a seventh grader. Taking her phone she added, "Please leave now."

Fulton was at a loss. He entered the RV yelling. Now he left—silent.

Sally-Anne turned to the group. Dumbfounded, they sat there looking at her.

"Not bad for a housewife, huh?" she said.

Maye stood up and launched herself at her and gave her a big hug. Sally-Anne was slightly stunned, her arms not knowing where to go, until she brought them around Maye's body and hugged her back.

"No time for soppiness now," she said, gently releasing herself from Maye's embrace. "We have some work to do."

She turned to Pam and handed her her phone.

"Download this and let's do some editing. We need to get our message out there if PBS is going to play dirty."

Pam looked at the phone. On it was a video of Fulton in his rage yelling abuse and calling Georgians 'rednecks'. Sally-Anne had been recording the whole thing. The party girl from Paces was about to be a key player in Maye's campaign for re-election.

Just then, Mick's phone buzzed. It was a message from Ben back in Alabama. It simply said, 'Mickey, you need to call the ASLO. I think it's serious.'

40

The ASLO

The ASLO was the Australian Liaison Officer at Fort Rucker. He was a lieutenant colonel sent there to oversee the Australian exchange personnel, and to be the go-between for the US Army and the Australian Army for anything related to army aviation. His other duties included being the Australian representative at functions, both official and social. Mick knew that if the ASLO was calling him, then it probably wasn't a social call.

He stepped outside into the heat while Sally-Anne, Pam, Rob and Maye reviewed the footage that Sally-Anne had taken. He punched in the number for the ASLO.

"Lieutenant Colonel Barton," answered the man at the other end of the line. It was strange to hear an Australian accent again.

"G'day Sir, Major O'Rourke here," said Mick, bracing himself for whatever was coming. He had a feeling this was going to be a one-way conversation.

"Mate!" said Lieutenant Colonel Barton, but not in the way that friends greet each other. It was more of a 'what-the-hell-are-you-doing-that-requires-me-to-call-you' sort of tone.

"I just got off the phone with Brigadier Parkes, the Australian Defence Attaché at the embassy in Washington. He told me that the ambassador had been contacted by the media about you and said that some Australian Army officer was getting involved in some election campaign in Georgia. The ambassador was not impressed, and Brigadier Parkes was ropeable. Please tell me that there's a good explanation for this that's not going to cause me any heartache and paperwork."

Lieutenant Colonel Barton was a very easy-going senior officer, and Mick and he got on very well. Mick had been to his place on a number of occasions when his wife had held barbecues for the 'Aussie orphans', as she called the single Australians posted to Fort Rucker. For Lieutenant Colonel Barton to receive a message from the defense attaché at the Australian Embassy meant that the media was going to make Mick a part of the story. There was no other reason for them to single him out and call the embassy. It looked like this was the beginning of a whole world of hurt for Mick which would, no-doubt, end with him being recalled to Australia, sooner rather than later.

"Um," said Mick as he thought of the best way to tell his local boss that the story was true. And that he was in the center of a political campaign which had taken a significant turn. Like a kangaroo in the headlights of a car, he did not know which way to hop, and just waited for the impact.

"I don't think I like where this is going," said Lieutenant Colonel Barton, hearing Mick's hesitation. "I'm thinking that it's true, then," he said, sounding defeated.

"Well, Sir," began Mick. "It's a bit more complicated than you might expect." He could almost hear the colonel's head slump in despair through the phone.

Mick looked at the people walking by in Acworth, oblivious to the dramas unfolding in the RV parked in the strip mall, or with him, as he stood in the broiling sun. How he wished his life could be simple right now. Just this morning he had woken up next to Maye and the day was full of hope. Now it had become very complicated... and it was only 4 p.m! What was the evening news going to show?

"Look. Mick. I'm going to have to let Brigadier Parkes talk to you. I think you know where this is going to go. Expect his call in a few minutes. I guess I'll be seeing you in Rucker in a day or two. Good Luck." And with that, he hung up.

Mick stood and waited a few minutes. He could imagine Lieutenant Colonel Barton calling the brigadier... and the brigadier yelling... and the brigadier picking up the phone and dialing Mick's number. Sure enough, his phone rang.

"Michael O'Rourke here," he said, trying to keep his voice as steady as possible.

"This is Brigadier Parkes, DA at the embassy." His voice was firm. There was definitely no room for niceties in this conversation. He explained that the ambassador had received a phone call from the Public Broadcasting Service explaining that an Australian Army officer was involved in politics and had been seen with a Confederate flag. The brigadier was aware of the divisiveness of this symbol. Mick did not think it appropriate to correct him on the nuances of the flags.

"You must be aware that serving army officers are not allowed to get involved in politics. It is in contravention of the Defence Act. You will have to cease any activities immediately and return to Fort Rucker while we decide what happens next."

Mick sort of expected that this would be the outcome of this conversation, so it was not a total surprise.

"What do you think that will be," he asked the brigadier.

"I'm not sure. Probably an early RTA. Possibly a charge will be conferred," the brigadier replied.

His heart sank as the words 'RTA'—Return to Australia—and 'charge' were uttered. Two outcomes he had not really considered as he lay in bed in Maye's arms this morning. The next words that the senior officer would say were, however, the most shocking.

"The ambassador will be calling the Minister for Defence in about an hour." Mick looked at his watch. It was now 5 a.m. in Canberra. By 7 a.m., the CA—the Chief of Army— and probably his boss, the CDF—the Chief of the Defence Force—would be informed. His career now looked like it was on a precipice.

"Don't be surprised if you get a call from the Chief's office asking for an explanation so the CA can brief the CDF, and then the minister. I would expect that you will be charged for political activities being undertaken by a defense member, as well as a Section 60: Prejudicial Conduct Bringing Discredit to the Australian Defence Force."

The Australian Defence Force was very risk averse when it came to bad press. The PR *apparatchiks* held way too much power and worked hard to keep the message clean so that the Minister for Defence was not embarrassed. This situation could very well embarrass the minister, so the PR teams would be looking to spin this just as Bobby Fulton had wanted to with Maye's campaign. All defense personnel in Australia in the army, navy or air force, were banned from participating in political activities, except for voting.

Mick knew that the brigadier was wrong.

"Sir," he said "the Defence Act only refers to political activities in Australia and it only applies to Australian politics. I am not committing any offense against the Act."

The brigadier became suddenly incensed.

"Don't you be smart with me, Major!" he boomed. "You are to cease involvement immediately and return to Fort Rucker. You are to report to the ASLO no later than Friday, 0800. By then I will have a decision from ADF HQ on what is to happen to you. Do you understand me?"

"Yes, Sir," replied Mick, crestfallen. The phone went silent.

He looked at his watch as he thought about his career. Time of death, 3.45 p.m.

41

For FOX' Sake!

Pam tapped away at the keyboard and, with the help of Rob, created a YouTube video with a couple of cutaways featuring Maye. Mick walked in to see them enthusiastically making suggestions. Sally-Anne had a big smile on her face, feeling happy to be able to make a valuable contribution. She saw Mick and grabbed her phone and took him outside.

"I need to video you!" she said, and took him by the hand placing him in front of the big sign on the side of the RV showing Maye's smiling face. She told him what he had to do but gave him free rein to say what he wanted. He seemed a bit subdued, but she got what she needed.

"Are you OK?" she asked him.

"I'm fine," he assured her, unconvincingly.

She grabbed his arm and squeezed it. Her eyes looked earnest. "Michael, you believed in me. I believe in you... but not now. I don't believe that you're fine. Tell me what it is."

He told her about the phone call and that he had to report back at Fort Rucker in three days. She asked him was there anything she could do.

"Yes," he said. "Don't tell Maye."

* * *

The clip that Pam put together was a little rough, but it gave the right impression for what they wanted. Now, they would wait to see what FOX 5 would air on their evening news bulletin. They would be ready to counter it.

Pam uploaded it to Maye's website and then to YouTube. Then they texted everyone they knew and pleaded with them to view it, comment and then share it. Each one of them came up with a great idea on how to get more and more people to view it. Sally-Anne convinced her former colleague at her middle school to perhaps send it out to the PTA, which was completely against the rules... but who cares? Mick contacted Ben and Jess and their circle back in Alabama as well as his mates back in Australia. Rob contacted his friends from university, and Pam had a wide circle also. Of course, each one of Maye's staffers, that were not with them in Acworth, had also been called.

Soon it was time to watch the five o'clock news programs, especially FOX 5. FOX 5 had a reputation for being sensationalists so this would be right up their alley. Only Sally-Anne thought that they might go easy on them. Of course, PBS would continue to crucify them.

While they waited for the bulletin to start, they checked their 'watched' count on YouTube. At first, they had a spike in views, but that could be put down to their friends all watching it at the same time... then it slowed right down. Even though the clip was startling, it was not getting the traction they had hoped.

Soon, the commercials ended, and FOX 5 started its bulletin. They all sat to watch the TV in the RV and crossed their fingers. The two co-anchors appeared: a down to earth black guy and a blond woman sat behind their desk with the screen behind them showing the station logo. After the dramatic musical introduction, a quick precis of the main news items: Some show dogs stolen from a car at a gas station at Roswell; a man injured in a fall at the MARTA train station at Five Points; and police finally capture a serial rapist near Underwood Hills.

"But first, a Georgia member of the US Congress has caused a stir by using the Confederate Flag as part of her re-election campaign. Congresswoman Maye Young, the representative of the 11th district which includes Marietta and all of Bartow and Cherokee counties, stunned locals today

when she began her election campaign at Kennesaw Mountain before commencing her march towards Tennessee carrying the divisive flag. Congresswoman Maye is walking in the footsteps of General Sherman's advance through Georgia to the sea during the American Civil War. Kelly Lowndes reports."

The scene dissolved to Lowndes standing in front of Kennesaw Mountain.

"Thanks Michael," she said. *"Popular representative for Georgia, air force veteran Miss Maye Young, representing the 11th district, commenced her re-election campaign today here at Kennesaw Mountain surprising everyone with the use of the controversial rebel flag. Determined to raise awareness of her campaign, she is walking from Kennesaw Mountain Battlefield Park to Adairsville in north-west Bartow County spreading the news to anyone who would hear about what she stands for.*

"The flag that has caused all the fuss was carried by her boyfriend, Australian Army officer Michael O'Rourke, who educated all of us about the flag and what it means for the campaign."

The scene cut to Mick explaining what the flag represented and then cut to Maye, holding the American flag, and answering questions to Kelly Lowndes as she hung out of the window of the station wagon. The team in the RV looked at each other and smiled. So far, the story was not bad. In fact, it was quite positive.

"The use of the flag was highlighted by a member of Miss Young's team, student of law at the University of Georgia working as Miss Maye's campaign coordinator for this year's mid-term elections, Mr. Robert Early."

Now the scene cut to Rob, marching proudly with the flagpole resting on his shoulder, the flag flapping gently as he walked. His piece to camera looked terrific; a black man carrying the rebel flag was a very powerful image, but it was what he said that was so striking.

All over Atlanta, viewers saw a handsome, young black man proudly carrying what some say is a symbol of oppression. His words resonated beautifully:

"These two people represent all that is good in our armed forces and Miss Young represents all that is good in what we hope our politicians

should be. If she asked me to fight alongside her, I would. But she didn't. I saw the caliber of this woman and I volunteered to stand alongside her.

"If my display of loyalty to her and to her cause is holding this flag, then I will gladly do it, and do so proudly.

"I am a proud American, and I am a proud Georgian. This flag is my battle flag."

As if choreographed, Maye, Mick, Sally-Anne and Pam all turned and looked at Rob approvingly. His words were the most powerful statement of all those delivered; and his face and that flag were the most powerful images of all those captured so far.

The two anchors were now on screen. The distinguished looking black man sat looking at the monitor, his chin resting thoughtfully on his fingers as he processed what he had just seen.

"That was quite remarkable," he said to his co-anchor, obviously impressed by Rob's sentiment.

The next half of the interview was dedicated to Mick giving the WGPB reporter a dressing down with the banner headline: *A History Lesson.* FOX 5 took great delight in showing Mick, with his Australian accent, giving the WGPB reporter a lesson in history and making her look like a fool.

Maye turned and looked at her team. The FOX 5 news article was good. No! It was great. It was complimentary and upbeat. Best of all, it was not divisive. Maye came out in a positive light and looked fantastic in the hot Georgia sun. Mick looked like a know-it-all but his Aussie accent made him and his history lesson a curiosity. But the real hero was Rob Early. For the first time since the interview at Kennesaw Mountain this morning, Maye smiled a genuine smile. If the *AJC* article tomorrow was good, then they were in business. So far, the online story was fair and balanced, and any mention of the flag was neutral, not negative. Only WGPB seemed to be taking offense.

As they broke out the bottles of Coke to celebrate, Sally-Anne, in private, sent a simple text to her husband The Chairman saying just two words: 'Very good.'

42

The Confederates Have
Invaded

Pam, Rob and Sally-Anne caught a lift back to Atlanta with another of Maye's staffers while Mick and Maye remained with the RV at a nearby campground overnight. They had agreed they would meet again the following day at 9 a.m., ready for the next five or so miles, but tonight they were going to enjoy the campground on the bank of Lake Allatoona, the lake on which Maye had her house less than three miles away, in fact.

The YouTube video slowly ticked over more views during the evening. It certainly wasn't going viral, but after the day's events, that didn't seem to concern them. They had survived what could have been a devastating setback. Now it was time to turn off the computer to discuss what to do the following day. But what they didn't see on YouTube was the evening's high traffic period. What they didn't see was the explosion of views and the positive responses, all helped by FOX 5's news coverage and online story.

As they crawled into the surprisingly comfortable bed of the RV, tired and a little sunburned, Maye turned serious.

"Honey, you can't pull surprises like that. We need to be more measured in what we do on this campaign. Conservatives don't like surprises, especially the ones in power. Please check with me before you do anything... um... unusual."

Mick understood. He had taken a gamble and it had backfired, at first. Had it not been for Rob's gesture and Sally-Anne's influence, the whole campaign may have derailed after the first day. As it stood, a good report from FOX 5 had saved them. If the *Atlanta Journal Constitution's* story tomorrow was positive, then they may be OK. So far, their online story didn't indicate that it would be negative.

"I'm sorry," he replied, holding her close. "I just thought we needed to shake things up a little. I'll toe the line from now on. Speaking of toes... I think I need to go down and check to make sure yours are all OK. I may be delayed on my journey, however... but don't be too concerned. I'll let you know when I arrive.

With that he went beneath the sheets and slid his hands under her T-shirt, pulling it up so he could kiss her breasts and stomach. His hands then slid down and his fingers took the elastic of her panties and he slowly pulled them down. Maye obliged by lifting her pelvis... one of the sexiest things a woman can do for a man... and she lay back and let her man from Down Under do what he loved to do to her down under.

As the Georgia night brought welcome rest to Mick and Maye, in cyberspace, ones and zeros sped around the world's networks as the number of views of their video clicked over. Sky News in Australia, with its almost two million subscribers, picked up the story. As dawn broke in Australia on the other side of the world, the story of their campaign that was bucking convention—and the Australian know-it-all that was in the thick of it—was being viewed by hundreds of thousands.

The Australian Prime Minister and the Minister for Defence were briefed on the situation and watched the video, their staff going into overdrive...

* * *

It was already 9:15 a.m. and no sign of the others. They had agreed not to look at anything online or on TV until they were all together and before they headed into Acworth. It was there that Mick and

Maye would recommence their march to Tennessee... or at least to Adairsville, as far north as they could go in the 11th District before they went into Calhoun County, which was in the 14th District held by Morris Turner. That's where they intended on stopping, and then start the next phase of their campaign. But right now, they had to wait for Rob and the others.

It was going to be another hot day, so the pair stayed inside the RV making breakfast and staying out of the heat, which had already climbed to eighty degrees.

By 9:30 a.m. there was still no sign of them, so Maye took out her phone to call them. Just then, Rob's Ford appeared at the top of the gravel lane of the RV park. They stepped out into the heat. The cicadas were already making their shrill ruckus in the woods surrounding the park. They noticed a number of residents looking at them and figured it was their garish RV with big images of Maye smiling that was attracting the attention.

As Rob's car pulled up, some of the park's residents began to wander over also. Pam got out of the car even before it has come to a complete stop. She had the AJC in her hand.

"Have you seen it?" she said excitedly, holding it up? "It's really good!"

She handed it to Maye, and she unfolded it. There, on the front page, was an incredible image taken by the reporter. It showed Maye, Mick and Rob walking up the road at Kennesaw Mountain; Maye carrying the Stars and Stripes and Rob carrying the rebel flag. Between them was Mick with his arms around both. The symbolism was exquisite and completely unstaged. Above it was the headline: *Young views heal wounds*.

Maye and Mick read the opening paragraph:

Miss Maye Young, congressional representative for the 11th District of Georgia, launched her re-election campaign yesterday with the use of the controversial Confederate flag as the symbol of her willingness to fight political correctness and for the causes which she believes in.

"Ending a sentence in a preposition," said Mick. "Hmmm" he moaned disapprovingly. He continued reading.

With her was her boyfriend, Australian Army officer Major Michael O'Rourke, and one of her campaign managers, Mr. Robert Early, who held aloft the Confederate flag proclaiming he was a proud American and proud Georgian and that he was ready to fight for Miss Young in this campaign.

Mick patted Rob on the back when he read that.

In an unusual campaign tactic, Miss Young's campaign is making the journey from Kennesaw Mountain towards Tennessee on foot in a defiant march in the opposite direction to General Sherman's Union troops as she gets out and meets her constituents to sell her message.

Sally-Anne chimed in. "This is a good story, and that picture is wonderful. That is Pulitzer Prize winning stuff," she said pointing to the picture of the trio which had been given a vignette border to make it look antique.

"But that's not all," said Pam again, excitedly. She was beaming. "Have you seen YouTube? The clip has gone viral! We've had a quarter of a million views in twelve hours!" She clapped her hands and started bouncing up and down. "We're going to break the internet!" she squealed.

Maye smiled. "Calm down, Pam," she said. "We still have a lot to do and a long way to go."

It was Rob's turn to add his contained excitement. "I think you'd better follow us back into Acworth," he said. "A crowd is forming there, and they want to see you both," he told them. "A 'good ol' boy' even recognized me and shook my hand and told me that he was 'a proud Georgian, too'. Everyone is waving Confederate flags!"

"They're not Confederate flags. They're... oh never mind," said Mick. He was too happy to be a pedant today.

Mick and Maye got into the RV with Sally-Anne while Rob and Pam drove in front, taking them from the calm of the RV park back into town. As they left the park, some of the visitors waved at them and their garish RV with the big pictures of Maye on the side, and gave them a thumbs up and applauded, yelling support.

"Go get 'em, girl!" shouted one fellow.

"You've got my vote," yelled another, "but I don't live in Georgia," he added, being smart.

As Mick drove them to Acworth, Maye looked at the front page of the paper with Sally-Anne, admiring the imagery.

"That's such a beautiful picture," said Sally-Anne. "It really captures the scene nicely. I think you'll be surprised when we get to Acworth," she said. "I think you really hit a nerve with people. There are a lot of people who are looking for politicians to have guts, and deciding to use the Confederate flag took guts."

Maye was silent for a few moments as she looked at the picture. She then looked through the windscreen as they approached Old Highway 41 into Acworth and to her boyfriend driving the RV. The man who, even though he came from the other side of the planet, did the unthinkable and, in less than twenty-four hours, had changed the whole complexion of what was going to be a vanilla re-election in a safe Republican district into some sort of crusade against political correctness.

"It was his idea," she confided in Sally-Anne. "The whole 'March to Tennessee' and the Confederate flag. It was all his idea."

"He's quite something, isn't he?" said Sally-Anne, looking at Mick waving at people on the sidewalk who saw the RV and were getting excited. She then looked at Maye who was staring at him. Her look belied whatever she was feeling. She couldn't tell if it was pride, or pain.

Sleepy little Acworth had not seen such an influx of people on a weekday. There were scores, if not hundreds, of cars parked everywhere; every parking lot was full. On the sidewalk were at least 300 people carrying signs and flags showing their support for Maye and her team. Rob had become an overnight celebrity and was being slapped on the back by white folks and black folks, also. Several young ladies, both black and white, went out of their way to hug him. Maye even saw one girl slide a piece of paper into his pocket, no doubt her phone number, or a proposition.

Maye was inundated with people wishing to shake her hand and wish her well. Mick, also, became the center of attention with people telling him that they loved what he said to 'that PBS bitch.' Some wanted autographs from them both. To sign their flags or the posters that they had created.

There were more reporters there with their camera and sound men and the AJC had sent another reporter and a dedicated photographer also. The GAGOP sent Rebecca Chatham who stood not far from the members of the media in a tight, beige dress with white jacket. Her cleavage was just low enough to attract attention, but not so low that it seemed too obvious. She had a good body, and she knew it. The dress was well chosen, albeit not necessarily for a board room... but for today, when she needed to get people on side, it was the right choice. She had been schmoozing the media, especially the men. Rebecca often rubbed the female reporters up the wrong way. She didn't know why.

The crowd ebbed and flowed, and Mick and Maye did their best to greet as many as possible. How they were going to get on their way for the march seemed an impossibility at the moment.

Rebecca Chatham made her way to them and yelled above the crowd's clamor.

"You guys have done great," she said trying to be authentic. "I've come to help you with the rest of the campaign. I'm replacing Bobby," she yelled.

Maye was busy signing autographs but managed to yell back, "Where did he go?"

Rebecca was being jostled somewhat and scowled at some fans.

"He's been re-assigned to another role and has left the committee in Atlanta," she said. "I have organized a bus to meet us here at ten o'clock. You can continue on your journey and do more stops to meet more people. We don't have to stop at Adairsville. You can do Kingston, White and Rydal and then we can go into Cherokee County and do Canton down to Woodstock and back to Kennesaw and Marietta and Smyrna. Those last stops will be the most important. We can get you in front of a lot more people the closer we get to 285."

Mick heard this and immediately disagreed with her suggestions, but after Maye's talk with him in bed last night and him agreeing to toe the line, he didn't feel it was his place to say anything. Sure, traveling by bus would allow them to cover more territory faster. And sure, the closer they got to The Perimeter—I-285—and Atlanta's suburbs, they would have a larger audience, but that was not in keeping with the idea of the 'March to Tennessee'. The march may be an election stunt, but that's what the campaign needed. He kept his mouth shut and continued to sign autographs.

Maye nodded her head at Rebecca, shaking hands and being slapped on the back (which hurt, somewhat). She looked past the crowd. Sally-Anne and Pam were marshaling the media to a position where the RV could be seen in the background, as well as a locomotive that stood on permanent display on the side of the road with the word 'Acworth' painted on its side, a local landmark that signified the importance of the rail line for what was once a tiny hamlet but was now a bedroom community for Atlanta. She was also yelling something at Rob who was busy on the phone to God-knows-who.

What Sally-Anne was doing was textbook coordination. She had proven herself to be more valuable than expected and, with her new power over her husband—The Chairman—she had become critical to Maye's campaign and her longevity within the GAGOP. Having enough foresight to film Bobby Fulton's meltdown and putting that on YouTube certainly galvanized the public and forced the GOP to apologize to the public for the behavior of one of their 'unstable' public relations contractors.

"The views expressed by Mr. Fulton are not the views of the Republican Party of Georgia and we apologize if this contractor caused offense," The Chairman said in interview. "His behavior was reprehensible, and his contract has been terminated," he said, throwing Bobby Fulton completely under the bus. The YouTube video of him was starting to overtake Maye's other videos, and even thought it was laced with profanity and insulted Georgians, it had the desired effect: the comments were one hundred percent in support of Maye.

But even more telling was the clip about Georgians and their love of the Confederate battle flag. That was a risk, but it sure paid off. The crowds that had gathered to support Maye waving rebel flags were testament to that. When they saw Rob Early, everyone wanted a picture with him and the flag.

Rebecca Chatham waited for Maye to respond as she worked the crowd. She had the bus standing by and was ready to replace Sally-Anne and take full control of PR. In her opinion it was time to get professional with this lot.

"I don't think so, Rebecca," shouted Maye. "We'll stick with our 'March to Tennessee' idea. Sally-Anne has got this under control. You can head back to Atlanta."

Rebecca was stunned! She could not believe that she had been replaced by a housewife. Her! How was it that a political operative with twelve years' experience with the GOP could be replaced by a schoolteacher housewife? Her! Maye could see Rebecca glaring at Sally-Anne. She was frozen to the spot, though still being jostled by the crowd.

"Thanks, Rebecca," said Maye. "When you get back to Atlanta, tell The Chairman that we're thrilled to have Sally-Anne with us and that we thank him for assigning such a valuable asset to our little campaign." And with that she let the crowd draw them towards where the media was setting up. (Sally-Anne witnessed this, and her eyes glistened.)

As the sound guys were putting remote mikes on Mick and Maye, and the cameramen were getting their white balances, Sally-Anne came over and spoke with them both. She had fed the reporters some questions they could ask and was about to prep Mick and Maye. Sally-Anne was really getting into the groove.

"I have asked Rob to get the staff to pre-position themselves with some Republican banners at obvious points along Old Highway 41 at Emerson, Cartersville and Cassville. We're going to encourage people to take a drive out and join us. This is what you need to say..."

She explained the plan and also some key words to say and what tags to use. She would be better prepared by tomorrow after she had a chance to get some posters and signage made and to have Pam create a new campaign page about the 'March to Tennessee' on Maye's website.

The cameras rolled and Mick and Maye were filmed by six separate news agencies. Pam rounded up the local newspaper representatives who were eager to get to speak with them, but who were a little intimidated by the major players. She got the Cobb County local newspaper, *The Bright Side* and the *Marietta Daily Journal* to get some alone time with them both. Once they were done, she would get up to Cartersville and see the *Daily Tribune* and coordinate with them a news feed via Twitter so that they could re-tweet it to their subscribers. Sally-Anne had instructed her to form relationships with all the local papers and make their editors feel special; that they were getting news straight from the candidate's team and not having to take second-hand stories that had been syndicated from the larger news agencies. Both Pam and Sally-Anne knew that even though Maye was probably going to keep her seat, if the percentage of voters that cast a vote was high, then *that* would be the measure of success. Motivating the voters of the 11th District to take time out of their day to go to a polling booth was the aim of the whole campaign.

This was grassroots campaigning. Showing up in areas that rarely saw candidates because there were not enough votes there. Mick had suggested this as part of his 'Reverse Sherman' march idea. Sherman had destroyed Georgia's industry and livelihood and had demoralized the community. Maye was going to re-invigorate it by showing her commitment to rural Georgia as well as suburban Atlanta.

43

〰

Acworth to Emerson

The walk from Acworth to Emerson was only about six and a half miles, but it took them four hours to complete. Such was the eagerness of locals to meet the new celebrity couple. Many of them came along for the walk and soon the Acworth Police Department was providing a squad car to escort them. When they reached the boundary with Emerson, the Emerson PD, which consisted entirely of two cars and three police officers—one of them the Chief of Police—took over. It was the most excitement they had had in... well, ever!

All-in-all it was a very civilized event, with the crowd behaving itself, and its many members—sporting their flags and posters—keeping good spirits, even in the Georgia heat.

Sally-Anne had organized for lots of bottled water to be delivered up and down the crowd, along with sunscreen. She had a bus brought up from Atlanta for some of the less-abled walkers. Then, at the end of that march, the bus shuttled people back to Acworth where required. All of Maye's team were suitably impressed with her foresight and organizational ability for the day's events. She said it wasn't much different than organizing a middle-school event and that she had plenty of contacts. Sally-Anne was turning out to be their secret weapon.

When they got to sleepy little Emerson, Maye gave an impromptu campaign speech to those who had walked with them from Acworth, as well as to the people of Emerson, who seemed to have emerged from

167

everywhere. There was not a huge crowd there, maybe three or four hundred, but what *was* there was another FOX 5 crew and a couple of the other stations. Interestingly, WGPB was nowhere to be seen.

Sally-Anne organized for the *Daily Tribune* to have a private interview and suggested to the editor that for tomorrow's leg to Cartersville that anyone in Emerson who could spare the time should join them on the march... and the same for those in Cartersville. She would organize some more buses as shuttles to get them back to their start points.

Overnight, Maye's staff grew, with paid staffers joining them to help, and volunteers suddenly appearing, enthralled by the spectacle and the commentary on the news, online, and in the papers. Sally-Anne was in her element organizing them all: getting port-a-potties strategically placed along the route; water distribution; food vendors; extra trash cans and working closely with the police. She made sure that the county commissioners and city councilors—whatever their political allegiance—had a positive encounter with their congresswoman, and great photo opportunities to help with their own re-election. In particular, she ensured that even Democrat diehards were given 'good press', a gesture that was not lost on many. The messaging was positive and upbeat. Mick came up with another idea that the GOP would have immediately quashed had they heard it.

Maye's staff had been paying attention to the prospective candidates for the 11th District. Of course, there was the Democrat who was a social worker, and two independents that seemed serious, and one who was not. There was also a special interest candidate who also professed to be a Democrat but seemed to be centered on mainly LBGT issues and nothing else. Of all the prospective candidates, Harman Douglas, the 48-year-old social worker, had the most potential. It was unlikely he would win; the seat was too conservative, but stranger things had happened. Maye called him to chat and discussed how he could raise his profile. Mick listened intently, hoping his idea would not backfire.

Maye mounted a flat-bed truck that had been used by the state Republican committee for just this purpose, and which had been pre-positioned there for when Maye and the crowd arrived in Cartersville.

Then she did the unexpected. She introduced Harman Douglas, a Democrat competitor for the 11th District. Many in the crowd booed him but, to his credit, he kept smiling and waving to the hostile crowd like a seasoned professional. Maye bade them to stop their jeering and to calm down. She took the microphone.

"Mr. Douglas is representing the Democratic Party of Georgia for the 11th Congressional District here in our great state," she said. The crowd booed louder, and someone threw a scrunched-up piece of paper at him.

"Please show this man some respect," said Maye. "Because one of the things upon which we pride ourselves in this country is the right to free speech, and the right to assembly. You may not agree with Mr. Douglas, but you must respect his decision to run for office in our great democracy," she implored them. This quietened them down and they listened intently.

"Being a politician, or any representative, is not easy. And to make the decision to run for public office is also not easy. Many sacrifices must be made: time with family; time with friends; special events like birthdays and little league games. And guess what? No-one is ever one hundred per cent happy with you. In fact, you will have more detractors than cheerleaders.

"Mr. Douglas is a social worker. He works with broken families and tries to help kids in abusive situations... to find them protection. Can you imagine what he would see and hear about? Can you imagine how heartbreaking that would be? You may not believe in what he stands for, and you may not believe in his policies, but there is no reason that you cannot believe in him and that his motivations are true.

"Mr. Douglas represents the sort of people we want in public office: good men and women who are prepared to make the sacrifice to serve their constituents just as those in uniform serve their country or their communities. Please, if you believe in me, then believe in him also... and if you are deciding where to cast your vote, I hope you cast it with me... but if you do not, and you decide to vote Democrat, then I believe that the people of the 11th District will be well-served by this man."

Maye turned to Harman and held out her hand.

"Sir, thank you for standing up for what you believe in, and I wish you all the best in the election." He was so taken with Maye's gesture that his eyes watered, and he reached out and embraced her. The crowd cheered and a few women were seen wiping tears from their eyes. As Douglas stepped down off the podium, he was met with smiles and people wanting to shake his hand or slap him on the back and to wish him luck.

Off to the side Sally-Anne, too, was smiling. She turned to Mick and shook her head.

"Do you have any more good ideas?" she asked him. "They seem to be working well."

"You're doing all the hard work," he replied. "I'm just Maye's handbag." He cast his hand over the crowd, mobbing Maye and Harman Douglas. It was unheard of to see two opposing candidates appear to actually like each other and want each other to do well. In the time of partisan politics, this sort of respect between candidates was never seen, and the crowd was lapping it up. So were the reporters.

* * *

That evening, FOX 5 led again with the story of 'The Miracle in Cartersville' where political rivals shared the podium.

The Chairman was with Rebecca and his new deputy watching the coverage. They had already seen the reports online and he was furious. Why was Maye giving airtime to a Democrat candidate for her own seat? And what the hell was Sally-Anne doing?

"Oh this is Goddamned terrible!" he yelled at no-one in particular, but more so at the TV. "What the fuck is she doing?"

The anchors interrogated the reporter at the scene, the same attractive black woman that covered the event yesterday, and she sang the praises of the 'Young team with young ideas.' She reported that the Young team wanted as many Georgians to join them on their 'March to Tennessee' and to bring as many people as they could, with a special emphasis on those who were aged or infirm, and a special shout out to veterans and historians and school kids and anyone who wants a change in politics.

The scene cut back to the studio and both anchors remarked how it was wonderful to see Republicans and Democrats on the same side for a change.

The Chairman turned off the TV, his face looking like he needed to go to the bathroom urgently.

"Republicans and Democrats are *not* on the same side. What in Hades are they doing up there, giving oxygen to the Democrat candidate!?"

Rebecca spoke. "We can bring her back to Atlanta tomorrow," she suggested. "We can set up a major media event..."

"Did you see that crowd?" The Chairman demanded, pointing to the now blank TV. They have all the media they want. Bringing her back here won't help anyone. If she's getting all the media, we just need to get her to change her message... and to stop letting the Goddamned competition get his face on TV!"

The Chairman pointed to his new deputy, Kyle Lanier, just in from the national committee. "You!" he said, "Get up to Cartersville tomorrow morning before they start their next leg. Separate her from the others and have a word to her in private. Tell her that if she doesn't start sticking to script and if she doesn't stop consorting with the Democrat, then we'll pull our endorsement from her."

The others looked at The Chairman. As much as they didn't agree with her campaign strategy, they couldn't deny that it was somewhat popular. Pulling her from the campaign now would not be a good look. The Chairman saw their concerned faces and challenged them, his palms turned towards them.

"What? Do you think that that would be a bad idea? Do you think that taking her off the campaign now is a bad idea?" He slammed his fist on the conference table. "Well, I don't give a damn!"

"We can win that seat easily with anyone. Anyone! I have a dozen potential candidates who wanted to run, but we had to leave it for a woman and a veteran. I'm sick and tired of this political correctness bullshit! Our job is to win! Not to court the Democrats or the liberals or anyone else. We can keep that seat with or without that stupid bitch, so it's better to get rid of her now!"

He looked at Lanier with a meanness that was unnerving. "Get her back on the reservation!" he demanded.

* * *

By 8 a.m., Cartersville was virtually in gridlock. Cars and pick-ups, sporting rebel and national flags were making their way through the streets while hundreds waited to join the day's walk. News crews were making their way through the crowd speaking with excited 'Youngsters', the name the fans of Congresswoman Maye Young had decided to call themselves.

Three buses pulled up and out came one hundred and forty men, and some women, dressed in period costume: Confederate soldiers with some Union soldiers for good measure. They milled around in groups and added spectacle to the already colorful tableau, posing for photos with the marchers.

Next came two buses of veterans, some from the Vietnam era in their seventies and eighties. Others from more recent wars in Iraq and Afghanistan. Most of them carried flags, a mix of rebel flags and national flags. The biggest ones were attached to the wheelchairs that some veterans needed, especially the older ones, alongside the MIA/ POW black and white flags, keeping the memory of those missing in action and those who were prisoners of war.

A couple of Australian flags were seen in the crowd and Mick headed over to say g'day to them. Sure enough, it was a couple of Aussies who were living in Atlanta who brought their American friends along.

The food vendors were doing a roaring trade, especially when the Cartersville High School kids turned up. Two hundred hungry adolescents who were excited not so much about the politics, but more so about missing a day of school.

A bunch of Harley-Davidsons roared past, with rebel flags and Stars and Stripes and a few sporting the old Georgia state flag, their riders wearing leathers with a bald eagle emblazoned on it. It was the US Military Vets Motorcycle Club of Georgia, the Cartersville Chapter as well as the Atlanta Chapter. They doubled back and parked alongside the sidewalk in formation ready to escort the march.

When Lanier got there, Sally-Anne immediately recognized him and even though he tried to avoid her, she was soon cornering him.

"What has my husband got you doing?" she demanded, pulling him away. He tried to deny that he was there for any other purpose than to offer his help, and that he just wanted to speak with Maye.

"You don't need to speak with her. She's speaking with her fans... now you head back to Atlanta and tell my husband that I will be contacting him later with another request." She led him by his upper arm back towards where he had come from. "You go on, now, you hear?"

He didn't know what to do. The crowd was swelling by the minute. He had never seen anything like it. He stood and watched them all; people of all types from mothers with young children in strollers, high school kids to veterans to moms and dads to the elderly, all being interviewed by the media.

"Just as the Arab Spring brought people to protest and force a change, so too has this grass-roots movement of resistance to political correctness and political partisanship," spruiked one reporter to camera.

Lanier had seen enough. There was nothing he needed to do here. The Chairman had completely misinterpreted the impact that this campaign was having in such a short time, so he headed back to Atlanta as Sally-Anne had advised. He'd been on political campaigns before but why was this one so different? The answer was pretty easy: Maye was smart and beautiful; Mick was exotic; Rob and the rebel flag were inspiring; and bipartisanship and an unusual campaign stunt had inspired a population that was becoming cynical with politics and political correctness. This 'March to Tennessee' had no more than two more days before they reached Adairsville and the district boundary, but it demonstrated a new way of politicking.

Lanier knew that if The Chairman was smart, he would encourage this campaign tactic to go on, not to stop it. Whatever Maye was doing was working... and it needed to continue to work.

His phone rang while he was heading south to Atlanta. He recognized the number as being one of the senior leaders of the Republican National Committee. What The Chairman of the Georgia GOP didn't know was that the national committee was taking an interest in this campaign in the Georgia 11th. Lanier may have been tasked by The Chairman to try and 'get Maye back on the reservation', but he was also a scout for the national committee, and he knew firsthand that there were Republicans much higher up the food chain than The Chairman who were watching the 'March to Tennessee' with great interest, and he was about to report to them about it.

44

Across the Lake

In an office in Parliament House in Canberra, Australia's capital, the Minister for Defence, Brian Kingston, had been given an update on what was happening in the US concerning this 'Australian Army officer that had captured the imagination of Georgians.' His dressing down of the TV reporter had gone viral and had not impressed the Chief of the Australian Defence Force. The position of CDF is a revolving appointment and at the moment it was an admiral from the Royal Australian Navy, and this admiral was not impressed for a special reason. It was not because Mick's actions were embarrassing. Quite the opposite. The reaction had been overwhelmingly positive. It was because it had now become an issue with which he had to deal, and which was distracting him from issues that *he* considered were more important. But unfortunately, because it was important to the Minister for Defence, it therefore had to be important to the CDF.

The Minister for Defence, or MinDef as his title was often referred to, had read the brief from the Australian Embassy in Washington. He knew that Major O'Rourke was to report back to Fort Rucker in two days. So he had contacted the CDF at Russell Offices, the headquarters of the Australian Defence Force, and demanded that he come and see him in his offices at Parliament House immediately. (He liked bossing around the men and women in uniform.)

The CDF and the Chiefs of each of the armed services were very familiar with the machinations that went on in MinDef's office, and none of them liked being summoned there. Parliament House was on the south side of Lake Burley Griffin, the man-made lake that divided Canberra into north and south. Parliament House stood on the south side of the lake, while ADF Headquarters in Russell Offices stood on the north, with a bridge connecting the two. The military leaders would often deride the decisions that were made 'across the lake' in the same way that politicians and public servants would do likewise, but in the other direction.

And so it was that on this cold, winter's day in August, the most senior military officer in Australia, the Chief of the Defence Force, was making the trek 'across the lake' to visit MinDef in order to talk about a lowly army major and his girlfriend who were walking along an old highway in Georgia, on the other side of the planet.

Admiral Forrest was ushered into MinDef's office by a staffer and sat down across the desk from Minister Kingston.

Admiral Forrest despised him and his staffers. In his eyes they were all power-hungry game players who claimed to serve the Australian people but who seemed to serve their own needs and that of their political parties. How he missed being at sea working with true professionals.

The minister looked up from his brief provided to him by a department at Russell Offices, also a bunch of public servants with no experience in wearing a uniform. Time to put on his game face!

"Does he have any connections to the Republican Party," the minister asked the CDF.

"We don't think so, Minister," replied Admiral Forrest. "The Australian Liaison Officer at Fort Rucker made inquiries and it appears that his only association is a romantic one with Miss Young. She's a member of the US House of Representatives representing Georgia, I am told."

MinDef flicked through the papers. His computer screen was frozen on a YouTube video showing the army major and the congresswoman on a podium. In the background, some of the crowd were holding posters saying, 'Good Day Mate!' and 'Maye and Mick!' with a love heart around the two names.

MinDef's communications adviser sat nearby. She had already given the minister her opinion before the CDF had arrived.

"The Prime Minister has been given a heads up," said Minister Kingston, "but he wants Major O'Rourke removed from any part he is playing in US politics, even at this level. It is not a good look for us and if the Democrats win government—and they have a good chance if Troup keeps on treading on his dick around the world—then they may not appreciate any Australian involvement in their affairs."

Admiral Forrest nodded. "Yes, Minister," he said. "That shouldn't be too hard. We'll get him back to Fort Rucker and then recall him back to Australia."

The Minister let the YouTube video play.

"He certainly is popular," he said, not taking his eyes off the screen. "Isn't it forbidden in the Act for a defence member to get involved in politics while still serving?" he asked.

"Yes, Minister... but only in Australia. He's not involved in Australian politics, so that part of the Defence Act doesn't apply," replied Admiral Forrest.

"That's too bad. We could have charged him over this," said the Minister, probably a little jealous that Mick seemed to be more popular than he was.

"We can still charge him under Section 60 of the Defence Force Discipline Act."

The Minister gave the CDF a puzzled look.

"Prejudicial conduct bringing disrepute onto the ADF," explained Admiral Forrest.

The Minister smiled. "Good." He continued to watch as women came up and kissed Mick. He was like a rock star... at least in whatever little town in Georgia this was filmed.

"Get him back to Australia and put him somewhere where he won't cause any more trouble. If he objects, charge him for this retrospectively."

Forrest wasn't too convinced that that would be possible, or even necessary. Kingston was yet another civilian who was in charge, but these politicians came and went, and he would be gone in the next election if the opinion polls were any indication. The minister's party was 'on the nose' with the Australian public. In other words, it was beginning to 'stink with the voters' like three-day-old fish. When the time came for Australians to go to the voting booths, the Prime Minister would probably lose his seat, and so would the members of his cabinet. And that time was going to be soon, so Australia-US relations were important now more than ever.

President Troup had offended most of America's friends and angered its enemies. Australia had always been a stalwart ally of the US, but Troup was not admired in Australia, so the Australian Parliament had to tread a clever course to not offend the US, but to also be seen to be standing up to Troup when he tried to run roughshod over its ally down under.

Admiral Forrest drove back across the lake to Russell Offices and headed back to his office. He sat at his desk and looked at the spectacular view of Lake Burley Griffin across to Parliament House and the Brindabella Ranges in the background. They had dustings of snow on them. He picked up the phone and called the Chief of Army, Lieutenant General Nick Braddon.

"Nick, it's the Chief. Can you come up and see me please? It's about O'Rourke."

45

Lieutenant General Braddon

Lieutenant General Braddon, the Chief of Army, got on well with Admiral Forrest. They had done some staff courses and joint tactics courses together, and when Admiral Forrest was Chief of Navy, he and General Braddon were nearly always at the same events.

Admiral Forrest was now a four-star officer while Lieutenant General Braddon was still a three-star officer… however only two months before, they were both three-star officers until Forrest, then a Vice Admiral, was appointed to the top role as Chief of the Defence Force, along with a promotion to Admiral. So, only two months before, Lieutenant General Braddon would call him 'mate'. Now military protocol required he address him as 'Sir.'

The army's chief sat down while the CDF made them both a coffee. The CDF had his favorite coffee machine and loved making his brews for him and his visitors. Every Australian uniformed visitor in the country was subordinate to him, but he still liked making any one of them a coffee if they were in his office for a chat.

"MinDef's gunning for O'Rourke," he told the general. "I told him he was being recalled to Australia. I think he wants to have him charged if he puts up a fuss."

The Chief of Army took the cup from the admiral who sat down at his desk. Reclining back in his chair he looked at his army colleague sipping his coffee. "What do you think?" he asked, gauging his reaction.

Lieutenant General Braddon shrugged his shoulders. "It's a bit of a stretch. He's become incredibly popular with the public here because of what he's doing in the States. The media love him! My comms team is getting inundated with requests for interviews with him virtually every hour along with a comment from us. I've told them to issue a holding statement to all of them, but they'll just get their US correspondents to track him down and interview him directly. We need to see how this plays out with the minister and having him recalled."

The admiral thought about this. Surely the minister's staffers were aware that Mick was popular at home; that he was some type of 'local boy makes good', not to mention the romantic story attached to the hype. And all this in the space of three days!

"If we bring him home, then to the public we'll look like a pack of bastards. If we don't bring him home, then the minister will have our arses. Either way we're screwed!" said the CDF. The general nodded and took another sip. (The CDF made great coffee!) The admiral's gaze drifted to Parliament House on the other side of Lake Burley Griffin.

"Bloody O'Rourke!" said the admiral. "What a fucking circus!"

The general thought for a moment and put down his coffee cup with an idea.

"Boss," he said, "I can give him a call directly. Just me to him. Let him know what the situation is back here. He probably has no idea what hype he is causing here and all the media interest because of his affair with Congresswoman Young. If I tell him that his relationship and his involvement in her campaign is causing a lot of trouble between the ADF and the minister, he may voluntarily step out of the limelight... and then the news cycle will find another story."

The admiral nodded. "That's a good idea, Nick. Getting a call directly from the Chief of Army might do the trick. Hell, if you think it would help, I'll even give him a call!"

"From what I understand from his chain-of-command," continued the general, "he's a very smart and reasonable man. That's why he's over there as a major. It's normally a captain's exchange... but he's slated to take over the Aviation School as its CO so we made an exception in his case. Perhaps if he thinks that he'll lose his command, then he may see reason."

"That's good," the admiral agreed, "but make sure that you don't threaten him. This has to be his decision. If he wants his career to go the way he expects it to, then he'll come to his senses... but it has to be up to him. Then our hands will be clean."

The general nodded and got up to leave. At the door he paused and looked around at the office and its trappings and its 'million-dollar' view across the lake to Parliament House. The general dropped the formality for a moment.

"How's the job treating you, Brian?" said the career soldier to the CDF with genuine concern.

The admiral was about to sign some papers but looked up and shook his head. "I remember when Air Marshall Ainslie took this office as Chief, he looked his age. Three years later and he looked like he had aged a decade. I've only been in this role for two months and it already feels like two years." He looked towards Parliament House, the giant Australian flag looking magnificent as it waved in the stiffening breeze with the snow-capped Brindabellas in the background.

"But it's those fools over there," he said, pointing his pen towards the seat of power, "that are causing more heartache than anyone else. You can smell the fear over there. They know they will lose the next election... and then we'll have to put up with another moron in the seat."

He looked back at the Chief of Army who was donning his slouch hat, about to leave. "I appreciate you taking time to speak with him directly. I think that will help. Thanks Nick," he said to him, more as a mate than as his boss. The general snapped to attention and saluted.

"No worries, Sir!" And went downstairs to make a phone call to Georgia.

46

⧉

This is the Chief

The Chief of Army contacted the Australian Defence Attaché and got Major O'Rourke's number. As it rang, he then remembered the time difference. It would be four in the morning about now. He was about to hang up and wait a few hours, but he heard a voice on the other end.

"Hello? Mick here," came the response. Mick actually sounded awake, but a little groggy.

"Mick, it's the Chief here," said Lieutenant General Braddon.

"Chief who?" replied Mick.

"Chief of Army," said the general. "Lieutenant General Braddon."

Mick suddenly sat bolt upright.

"Sir! Sorry Sir. I didn't recognize your voice!" he said, getting up and walking to the other end of the RV. He opened the door so he could step outside. The pre-dawn air of Georgia was warm, and he sat on the small step at the entrance, closing the door behind him. The RV park was silent. A few bats could be seen flittering looking for insects, but otherwise it was just Mick sitting in his underwear, talking to the Chief of Army.

"Mate," said the chief, as informally as possible, "I wanted to give you a call to say G'day and ask how things are going."

At first, Mick thought that was a nice gesture by the general. It was a very Australian thing, but it was also a sign of a good leader. However, it rapidly dawned on him that that was quite unlikely. Mick was merely a major, one of many in the Australian Army, and while Lieutenant General Braddon was definitely his superior, he was not his *direct* superior. In fact, Lieutenant General Braddon had never said a word to Mick, nor had he even met him. Now, he was calling (at 4 a.m. no less) to say 'G'day' and to 'see how things were going.'

"Sir," he said, "forgive me but I suspect that this is not a social call. Is there something with which I can help you?" He braced himself for whatever was coming next, but he suspected he already knew what it would be.

"I am not sure you're aware, but you've become quite a celebrity here," said the general. "Your relationship with Miss Young is generating a lot of interest with the media and the public. You've become somewhat of a celebrity!"

Mick tried to mull over what this meant to the chief. His mother had called him and told him that they saw him on the news, and a few cheeky texts from his mates back home, but other than that, he actually had little inkling of what was happening back in Australia. He had no idea that he was on the front page of all the papers and online, also. He was the subject of all the news broadcasts, and each Australian network had a relationship with one of the US networks and would run the interviews that had been recorded by the American news agencies.

He knew immediately that if he was of interest to the media back in Australia, then that would be a headache to the Chief of Army.

"I'm assuming that that's not appreciated at Army HQ, is it Sir?" he said, resting his head in his hand as he looked down at his feet on the pea gravel. The hum of the air conditioner, in fact of all the air conditioners on all the RVs, were the only sounds he could hear, besides the crickets.

"No, mate," said the chief, "not really." He made a concerted effort to remain as informal as possible. There was no need to start pulling rank and ordering Mick to remove himself from the public's eye.

Mick quickly deduced why the Chief of Army was being so friendly. He was sure he had already been in front of the CDF, possibly even the Minister for Defence, in what was probably not a friendly visit. He had to play this one well. He didn't know what the machinations in Parliament were back home. As far as he knew, he had been seen on TV a couple of times. But now that the Chief of Army was calling him directly, it started to dawn on him how serious this was back in Australia, and how if he was recalled home that it would have a cascading effect. His relationship with Maye would unlikely survive a half-a-world's separation as well as their two very demanding jobs. His presence in the campaign, while not crucial to Maye's re-election, was proving to be somewhat valuable, so an early return to Australia would take some of the wind out of the sails. And what about his posting as commanding officer of the army's aviation school? That might be taken away, which meant that there was no need to promote him. He would lose his command and lose his promotion. All these things were now suddenly becoming clear.

"I would have thought that this was positive PR, Sir," he said, grasping at straws.

"Well, the view from the minister is that this is an extension of your involvement in politics, which is against the Defence Act, even though you're not actually in Australia." The chief paused to let that sink in. He then gave him this piece of advice.

"Mick, if you don't pull out, the minister wants me to charge you under Section 60. That will have an impact on any future postings or promotions. He will force my hand... regardless of my opinion on whether it is right or not. You could probably fight it, but at what cost? And you would need to be back here in Australia to fight it anyway."

The chief heard silence on the other end of the line.

"Can I have a day or two to think about it, Sir? I still have a week's leave" he asked the chief. "I'm supposed to be back at Fort Rucker on Friday. Can I give you my decision then?"

This caught the general by surprise. He didn't think that Major O'Rourke had any option but to pull out of the campaign and continue with his posting at Fort Rucker. His only other option, which he didn't think would be one to be entertained, was to stay involved with the campaign until being forced to return to Australia to front the charge.

As far as the chief was concerned, the choice was clear. But he gave the now confused major some breathing space to make up his own mind and to come to his senses.

"Sure. But only 'til Friday. You still have your duty to the army and to your students at Fort Rucker. I'm sure the battalion there will want you to continue instructing with them until your posting is over. If we had to bring you home, that would be an embarrassment not only for you, but for the Australian Army also."

Mick told him that he would contact him via email on Friday, Saturday Australia time, and then crept back into the RV and back into bed with Maye.

"Who was that?" she asked him sleepily.

"Just my Alabama girlfriend," replied Mick, snuggling up to her. "She wants to know when I'm coming back to 'Bama," he joked.

"Tell her she can have you after I've finished with you," she replied jokingly, her words groggy as she tried to get back to sleep. "You're too valuable to my re-election. Too many people love you here... including me."

And with that, she nodded off to sleep. Mick, on the other hand, was wide awake and would be until the sun came up.

47

❧

The Caravan

The next day the crowd had grown larger. Shuttling people to and from Atlanta, and to and from Adairsville, was working wonders. And whenever the TV crews filmed the crowd, it seemed as though everyone was bright and happy.

The Civil War re-enactors were a hit. Even companies from Tennessee came down to join the fun. At one stage there were over three hundred soldiers in Federal and Confederate uniforms, all marching and carrying US flags and rebel flags along with over six hundred citizens of all shapes and sizes at any one time also marching along Old Highway 41.

The news helicopters circled, and the TV vans drove by slowly with cameramen hanging out or their drones buzzing just above the marchers.

Mick and Maye led, as always, with people being shuttled ahead of the march so they could walk at the head of the column for a few hundred yards and get a chance to meet the two celebrities and maybe get some photos with them. The column was incredibly slow, such that it was more like an amble than a march. This was just as well because many people were elderly or were pushing strollers. Some took the opportunity to get into fancy dress, but they soon regretted that as the Georgia sun started to take its toll.

A number of celebrities, and wannabe celebrities, suddenly turned up out of the blue. The Real Housewives of Atlanta reality TV stars made a nuisance of themselves trying to extend their fifteen minutes of fame, and Jamie Foxx came out to say hello, as did Alyson Hannigan along with some athletes from the Atlanta Braves. Elton John even stopped by with his son (but not his husband! Was there trouble in paradise?) These 'shooting stars', as Mick called them, only served to swell the numbers even more and by afternoon, over fifteen hundred people were marching towards Tennessee.

By the time they reached their stop at sleepy little Cassville, Sally-Anne and the team had a well-oiled system in place. Buses were doing continuous shuttles, and anyone could hop on or hop off at any time to participate. The TV stations were lapping it up and were providing details on where to get onto buses so that people could drive out; join the march and then get a ride back to their cars and head home. A great outing that cost next to nothing, and the chance to meet some new celebrities, and some old ones, also.

Mick was not his usual self. The conversation with the Chief of Army had been playing on his mind.

Sally-Anne could tell during one of her many visits to the head of the march and asked Mick what was the matter. She suspected it was what he had told her two days before, about being in trouble with his army.

Later, after nightfall, and when the crowd had dispersed and the last of the buses had left for the evening, the team sat around the bar at a hotel not far from Cassville to bask in the glow of another great day. Morris Turner from the 14th District, which was between Maye's district and the Tennessee border, was desperate for her to hand over the march to him where their respective districts met at the county line. Sally-Anne had told him that they had a plan for when they got to Adairsville, and she would get back to him tomorrow.

Sally-Anne managed to find some time to speak with Mick alone while Maye talked with Rob and Pam about some ideas for the next day.

"Are you staying or going?" asked Sally-Anne as they both headed to the bar to get another round.

"Looks like I'll be going," he replied sullenly. "But not 'til the day after tomorrow. I'll tell Maye tomorrow night and we should hit Adairsville by Friday. I'll have to head back to Alabama then."

"She'll be devastated," said Sally-Anne. "Will you be breaking up? That will be hard on her, and for this campaign."

Mick shook his head. "No, we won't be breaking up, but I won't be able to be a part of her campaign. The army won't stand for that. I can visit on weekends and provide moral support, but my time in the spotlight is over. The Maye and Mick show will become the Maye show. Anyway, that's the way it should be. She's the candidate... I'm just the handbag," he said, trying to be funny, but not really succeeding.

"Is there anything I can do?" asked Sally-Anne. She would miss him as much as Maye would. He had had faith in her from the start, even when she didn't have faith in herself.

As the barman placed the drinks on the tray, Mick joked, "If you can convince the president to tell my prime minister to back off, then that would be good." He picked up the tray and returned to the group. Maye looked up at him and smiled that beautiful smile. An Asian businessman sat reading the AJC over in the corner. He must have been a bit annoyed for he kept looking over towards their table.

Mick sat down and forced a smile, but his mind was elsewhere. He looked towards the businessman.

"Who's that?" asked Maye, seeing her boyfriend looking at the businessman.

"Um, I don't know," replied Mick, a little shocked that Maye had caught him. "I was just looking at the front page of the paper. Just then, the businessman tossed the paper on the table and got up and left through the door that went outside to the courtyard. Mick immediately went for the abandoned *Atlanta Journal Constitution* and brought it back to the table so they could all see the front-page story. For the third day in a row, Mick and Maye had featured as the lead story.

Flicking through the paper, Mick saw what he was looking for and took out the page. Getting up, he looked around and went out the door that led to the courtyard.

48

The Little Blue Bird

The Chairman was with the head of the Republican National Congressional Committee, Representative Cooper Camden from Wyoming. Also at their table were their two girlfriends who were giggling about something infantile. They were in a little out-of-the-way restaurant near Chamblee in the city's north-east, not far from Elaine's apartment. One advantage of having his wife on the campaign was that he could spend all his time with his girlfriend. Of course, the topic of conversation was the campaign, and the unforeseen enthusiasm it had generated. This had not gone unnoticed by the RNCC, and the national committee in general

The Chairman told Cooper that Maye had not heeded the campaign advice and that she was a wildcard. He recommended that after these mid-terms they should find a new candidate for the 11th District who was more compliant.

"She's generating interest, but I reckon that it's a flash in the pan," said The Chairman. "Her relationship is putting her on the covers of women's magazines, but once that ends, she'll just be another candidate."

At the next table a young college-aged couple was engrossed in their phones. The Chairman nodded his head toward them.

"It's all those kids with their phones," he complained. "That's what's generating interest, but it won't translate into contributions." He then looked at his girlfriend and the girl Cooper brought with him from Washington (on separate flights, of course). They were both looking at their phones and comparing the vapid content.

Cooper smiled and took a sip from his bourbon.

"I don't think you have a complete grasp on what's happening," he said to him. "Young has been a solid performer for a first-timer. She's been voting the way we want her to, and she's had some good ideas, also. There were a couple of times she voted against the party, but she hasn't been trying to pork barrel like some of the other members. I tell you, she has been no trouble to the Whip, and she's been helpful for other members, especially other first-timers. She's pretty popular with her peers."

The Chairman looked annoyed, like he wanted to punish the petulant schoolgirl. Cooper could see he wasn't convinced and leaned in towards him. The Chairman leaned in also.

"There is talk of putting her up as a nominee for VP in two years," he said, then leaned back and nodded his head. The Chairman was shocked. This couldn't be. There were plenty of more experienced potential candidates who had three or four terms under their belts. Why her?

"You have to be kidding!" he exclaimed. Cooper merely shrugged off The Chairman's surprise.

"Look what she's doing," he said. "She's got people following her in the Georgia summer up the Goddamn highway! She's the fucking Pied Piper! Her and her Australian boyfriend are making politics sexy! And you know what? It's palatable celebrity. It's not celebrity for the sake of being famous. They're both veterans. They're both attractive. She's a woman. She's smart. She's got good ideas. She's a hard worker. She represents a new and young Republican Party. I tell you, if we want people to look at us again as a viable choice, especially after Troup screws it up for us... and he will... then we need to have a rock star on the ticket. And she's it!"

The Chairman took that in for a moment. He wanted to rein her in but now he's being told that she might well be the Golden Child.

He then pondered the future with her as a vice-presidential candidate. What that would mean for Georgia and for the GAGOP. This could actually be a good thing and, dare he say it, good for him.

"What about Greene?" he asked. Vice President Jasper Greene was a popular nomination, and with Troup's flamboyance and arrogance, he provided a sensible foil. Insiders knew that the relationship between President Troup and Vice President Greene was only cordial. The VP would try to dissuade the president from some of his more outlandish schemes, or would not support the president's brash plans as vehemently as Troup wanted, preferring to be more measured and sensible... and Troup hated that. As far as he was concerned, he needed a VP that was one hundred percent on board with him, and Greene was not.

"Greene may end up being the presidential nominee," whispered Cooper.

The Chairman wasn't totally convinced. Troup was the incumbent. If they dumped him as the nominee, they lost that massive advantage.

The girls giggled about something inane, and Elaine put her hand on The Chairman's thigh, running it up towards his crotch. It seemed that even though Sally-Anne knew of her husband's infidelity, she had decided to let him continue the affair provided that he was at her beck and call for the campaign. Elaine had had her stay of execution, but she knew she had to keep her 'sugar daddy' happy, and get as much as she could from him before this all ended. If she had to put up with having an overweight, more-than-middle-aged man pawing at her and demeaning her, then that was what she would do until she was in a position to move on. Besides, she had her own boyfriend on the side if she needed real satisfaction.

Cooper's mistress did likewise and snuggled into him. He endured it for a few seconds and then asked her to move away. He always tried to be careful not to be seen to be intimate with her and, even though he was away from his wife back in Wyoming, away from DC, and in a small restaurant in Atlanta's suburbs, it still paid to be careful.

The couple at the next table got up, paid their bill and left. Cooper waited for them to leave and then gave The Chairman some advice.

"The campaign is going well, so you have to keep feeding that story. I know you've been getting FOX to spin it well. We can see that up north. And the *Journal Constitution* has been pretty good, too. Whatever contacts you have, make sure they stay on your side. Do whatever you need to but keep them happy and keep the press positive."

A waiter walked past to bus the table next to them.

"Oh, and try to get them to feature the Australian a bit more. It seems he's a bit of a sex symbol with the soccer moms. They all want to be Young and have him in their beds."

The Chairman grimaced. Cooper saw it immediately.

"What!?" Cooper demanded.

"I was on the phone to my wife this afternoon..." Elaine heard the words 'my wife' and took her hand off The Chairman's crotch and sat back to sulk. "...it seems he has to return to Alabama and leave the campaign."

Cooper closed his eyes and exhaled noisily. This was not what he wanted to hear. He wanted to keep those two together and in the public eye for as long as possible, at least until O'Rourke was due to go back to Australia. By then, Maye would have scored a few touchdowns, and would be able to run without him. In fact, it would add an air of excitement to a campaign: 'Who can win the heart of the most eligible bachelorette in the world?' But for now, he needed the Australian by her side during this campaign.

"How can we keep him here?" he asked The Chairman, as if it was a simple problem with an easy fix. As far as he was concerned, Mick was merely a commodity—something to be bought and sold—and now he had to find a way to acquire it.

"My wife wants him to stay on also," said the Chairman. "She made a suggestion but it's totally unacceptable."

Cooper didn't want to hear about what was acceptable and what wasn't. He shrugged at The Chairman showing him his palms as if to say, "What is it?"

The Chairman looked sheepish, almost embarrassed to even say it.

He took a deep breath, "She wants Troup to speak with the Prime Minister of Australia and get him to ask that he stay on."

"Out of the question," replied Cooper. "There's no way he'd agree to that. The media would have a field day. We've got enough problems with him and the House wanting to impeach him. This little side show in Georgia with your girl and her Australian boyfriend is a great distraction for the news cycle while those assholes in the..." He stopped mid-sentence. He just had the germ of a fantastic idea.

"What?" asked The Chairman.

"We might not be able to get him to call the Australian Prime Minister... but we can get him to put out a few of his ridiculous tweets and see what happens in Australia. The Deputy Ambassador over there will be able to give me some advice on how that will play out Down Under. He's been there a few years. We were both freshmen representatives together."

The Chairman was intrigued. But how would he get Troup to tweet this? He needn't have worried; Cooper told him how.

"His media adviser writes a lot of his tweets. John Dawson. He writes them so it sounds like its Troup's words... which is harder than it sounds," joked Cooper. "To write like an illiterate buffoon is not easy," he said as he grabbed his cell phone and flicked through his contacts. Another couple was brought in to sit at the next table. The girls were now deeply engrossed in their own conversation, sipping their cocktails through straws which they pinched with perfectly manicured nails.

"John, it's Cooper" he said down the line. "I'm down at Atlanta and I'm... yes, he's here with me." Cooper then put his hand over the phone and said to The Chairman, "John says 'Hi'." (In fact, Dawson had not. He could not stand The Chairman and actually said to Cooper, "Tell that asshole to fuck off!")

"Listen, we need a favor. That Australian Army officer that's with Maye Young down here in... Yes, that's him. Well, we need him to stay with the campaign, but he probably has to report for duty back in Alabama soon. Can you get the president to tweet out a few messages to try and convince his government to let him stay here in Georgia?"

Cooper listened for a few moments and responded as necessary.

"I don't know the details. Perhaps we can convince them that his continued presence with Young is a good thing for US-Australian relations. Say something about whatever is important to the Aussies at the moment. Beer exports or whatever the fuck they do down there."

He listened some more and saw The Chairman pull out his cell phone and start texting someone.

"What? China? That's their concern also? OK! That sounds like a good angle. Can you do it?" A pause while he grabbed a mouthful of bourbon. "That's great! I owe you one." He hung up from his call and looked at The Chairman.

"That should do it," he said. "Now, about this campaign, we need to get your wife off it and give them some real horsepower; give them a full campaign team and plenty of money. The RNCC can cough up about ten million now and once we start telling people she's going to be the candidate, I reckon the bucks will start flowing in... but give Young a blank check to do whatever she wants to for her campaign."

The Chairman was still texting and said without looking up, "Actually, a lot of her campaign stuff came from O'Rourke. He has been coming up with ideas about how to win the voters, according to my wife. She thinks he is the best asset to have on the campaign right... Oh no!"

Cooper looked at him. The Chairman was looking at his phone, shocked, and then at the table next to him, then back to his phone, and at Elaine.

"What is it?" Cooper demanded. The Chairman held out his phone to show him the image on the screen. There, in glorious Technicolor, was an image of Cooper and The Chairman with their girlfriends at that very restaurant. It appeared, judging by the angle, to have been taken from the table next to them. Probably by that young couple that was there a few minutes earlier. Sally-Anne had probably put them up to this, which means that she had been having him followed! That bitch!

"God dammit!" said Cooper. "What is she going to do with that? Is she trying to blackmail us? Fer Chrissake, we're going to try and get Troup to keep the Australian here. What more does she want?"

"I don't know what she's up to. But she did want to stay on this campaign. I guess she just wants to make sure that she will be," said The Chairman, terribly embarrassed. Elaine saw the picture and showed Cooper's girlfriend, and they were also not impressed.

"Well, I guess she is going to be right in the middle of this whole crap shoot, isn't she! We sure as hell can't get rid of her now," blasted Cooper at The Chairman. John Dawson was right. This guy was an asshole.

* * *

Just as Jenny Deakin was about to turn in, she checked her phone once more. Ever since she was promoted to Head of Communications in the Prime Minister's office about three months ago, she had been doing some long hours, and today was no exception. She had been working since before 6 a.m. and now it was midnight, and she was only now just crawling into bed. This was the fourth day in a row, and she didn't know how long it could go on. At least she didn't have to be anywhere before 9 a.m. tomorrow... so she was looking forward to a nice rest.

She checked the PM's tweets that had been scheduled and they had all gone out at the appropriate times. A quick flick through and...

"Oh, Shit!" she cried out loud, even though she was the only person in the room. President Troup had called out the PM on the subject of that army major who has been on the news, and who was the topic of a conversation between the PM and the Minister for Defence that very day.

The little blue bird that tweets said, *"Great to see Major Mickey O'Rorke (sic) of the #Australian Army campaigning in Georgia for what America needs. A strong economy and control of China, especially in the South Pacific. We could do with more men like him and I look forward to him being here for the next couple of years. Thank you Australia for being a great friend to the US #allies #bff."*

She leaped out of bed and called her boyfriend who was still at work in MinDef's office.

"What are you doing up?" he asked her." Terry Reid, Communications Adviser to the Minister for Defence—and Jenny's boyfriend—was still sorting out some mess that those 'dickheads in Defence' as he called the senior leadership in the army, navy and air force, had caused (for there was no love lost between them). The two had been keeping their relationship as secret as possible. There was no reason why the incestuous cauldron of Parliament House needed another couple about whom to gossip. What's more, because both of them were communications advisers for two high-profile parliamentarians, well the Opposition would have a field day.

"Troup has tweeted about O'Rourke!" she exclaimed, as she thumbed through the comments. They were, for the most part, very complimentary about him and about Australia.

"Oh, you've gotta be kidding me!" replied Reid, grabbing for his phone and opening up the app." Got it!" he said as he found the tweet. He began reading the comments. "The minister wants him back here and if he doesn't fall into line, he wants him to be charged," he said to his girlfriend.

"You've got to stop him," she urged, her voice slightly panicky. It had been a long week and she didn't need another headache. "Once the PM sees this, he won't want anything to upset the Yanks. He'll want O'Rourke to be right in the middle of this," she told him. "He has to stay in the States and be a part of this campaign!"

Neither Reid nor Deakin had any real idea of what it meant to be in the military, just like most party-political advisers or public servants. Their view was that if they wanted something to happen in any of the armed services, then it would just happen without question. This arrogance on their part would manifest itself downstream into significant administrative activity by defence force officers who would put in late nights and weekends to get the information, or the brief or the report or whatever finished so that it could be on the minister's desk by such and such a time. Their efforts would go un-noticed and un-thanked. Thus, the divide between those in uniform and those across the lake, especially the public servants, would never really be filled in. But that is the nature of the beast in a democracy. The politicians and their advisers give instructions and expect results and have no idea, and even less care, about the ramifications of their decisions.

"I'm calling the PM," said Reid. "I'll call you back."

About twenty minutes later, on orders from the PM—but on Reid's advice—he found himself calling the Minister for Defence, the Minister for Veterans and Defence Personnel, the Minister for Foreign Affairs, the Chief of the Defence Force and Chief of Army and telling them that they had a meeting with the PM at 6 a.m. in his office. This was at Reid's urging. It was important to get ahead of the news cycle on this one. It was now 12.40 a.m. The 6 a.m. news would be all over this and would be working on the story now... and the PM needed to be available for interviews by 7 a.m.

<h1 style="text-align:center">49</h1>

Bring Your Hat, Don't Bring Your Coffee Mug

The four ministers and the Chief of the Defence Force and Chief of Army sat in the PM's office at 6 a.m. on that Saturday morning. The Minister for Defence and the Minister for Foreign Affairs complained about O'Rourke; this solitary army officer that was causing them so many problems. They asked the two defense chiefs why they couldn't control their people. The two chiefs calmly listened to their whining, both of them despising these two politicians in silence.

"What the hell is he doing over there anyway!" exclaimed Kingston, the Minister for Defence, trying to demonstrate his potency to his party colleagues by giving the two career military men a dressing down. "Why can't you just order this troublemaker to return to duty. Have you lost control of all discipline within the army?" he demanded, trying to embarrass the senior soldier. The Chief of Army, Lieutenant General Braddon, spoke up.

"Minister, Major O'Rourke has done nothing wrong. He has violated no defense rules and has committed no crimes either against Australian law or US law. If anything, he has been a great ambassador for our country and for the army."

The minister was ready to explode. How dare this tin soldier speak to him like that!

"He is a thorn in our side." Kingston said fiery. "He is the reason we are here before 6 a.m. so we can get fucked over by the media all day," he seethed. "He needs to have his arse handed to him on a plate! If you can't do it, maybe I should find someone who can," he threatened them.

"Go easy, Minister," said Henry O'Malley, the Minister for Veterans and Defence Personnel. "O'Rourke probably has no idea what is happening here. He appears to be doing this for his girlfriend and he's making the ADF look good."

The Minister for Defence glared at the junior minister. Both the CDF and the Chief of Army appreciated the support. O'Malley was a popular minister and was a former naval officer, so he understood the life of a man or woman in uniform. The senior leadership in the Department of Defence worked well with him and his staff more so than they did for their boss, the Minister for Defence. And even though he was the minister in charge, Kingston had been a lawyer before he was elected to office and had no inkling of what it took to wear a uniform. He was owed a favor by the PM and that's why he got the highly sought-after defense portfolio. That news was not taken well at ADF HQ. Since his appointment, he had managed to rub every senior officer and senior public servant in the department the wrong way.

"Where are we with O'Rourke," demanded the PM to all of them as he entered his office, but primarily at his Minister for Defence.

There was a moment of silence. The Chief of the Defence Force, Admiral Forrest, decided to speak up.

"Sir, the Minister for Defence has taken ownership on this topic and has demonstrated his leadership," said Forrest.

"Good!" said the PM. "What's the plan?"

Admiral Forrest continued, "Upon advice from the Minister for Defence, we are recalling him to Australia and charging him under Section 60, Prejudicial Conduct, for bringing disrepute onto the Australian Defence Force, namely for becoming a public face in the political campaign."

The PM looked as though he was about to burst a blood vessel. Before he could say anything, Lieutenant General Braddon chimed in.

"Yes, Prime Minister, the Minister for Defence was very specific about taking action and removing Major O'Rourke from the public's eye and punishing him accordingly. We'll be notifying him today and ordering him home as soon as possible."

Prime Minister Mitchell turned his gaze to his Defence Minister. Kingston was ready to take the credit that the two service chiefs had thrown his way. Maybe he underestimated them. Then, he could see the expression on the PM's face and could tell that he was not pleased.

"Are you an imbecile?" he asked him. "What do you think would happen if I took a person who has gained more of a following in four days than you have in your whole bloody career, and who has served his country in uniform, including in war, and bring him back home and then publicly humiliate him by charging him? And what sort of message do you think that sends to the Americans? That we are so angry that someone would be involved in their democratic process, and in a positive way, that we will charge him and destroy his career?"

The Minister for Defence shot both the admiral and the general an icy stare. He had just been stitched up by these two men and humiliated in front of the PM and his colleagues. The two career military men had read the situation better than MinDef and had set him up for a fall. Neither of them met his gaze. Both were paying attention to the PM with expressionless faces.

"No. He needs to stay over there and remain involved with this campaign. When is he due to return to Australia?" he asked.

"Sir," said the general, "he is posted to Fort Rucker in Alabama until the end of next year. Miss Young's election campaign will be over this November where she may or may not retain her seat."

"But she's contesting in Georgia, isn't she?" asked the PM. The general confirmed that to be the case.

"Can we get him a posting to Georgia?" he asked the general.

"I'd have to look at that, Sir," he responded. "He's a pilot so opportunities there are limited. Fort Benning is in Columbus and the Special Operations guys are at Savannah. Both are in Georgia.

"I don't care how you do it, get him posted to somewhere in that state where he can be a part of this campaign. We need to keep the Americans on side and involved. Agreed?"

The three ministers nodded in agreement. Only the two men in uniform were not falling into step.

"What?" said the Prime Minister looking at them, a little annoyed. The CDF spoke up.

"Prime Minister, Major O'Rourke is a member of the ADF on duty. He is not a diplomat. He is not a member of the Department of Foreign Affairs and Trade. He is not even a defense attaché. He is a pilot. What you are asking of him is outside his area of responsibility and it is not fair to burden him with this task. He should be allowed to do his primary role."

The ministers fell silent. The PM was now *very* annoyed, this time at the Chief of the Defence Force. The Minister for Defence was relieved that the heat was off him.

"Listen to me, Admiral," said the PM threateningly. "We need to keep the US here in the South Pacific. You know better than most the dangers of Chinese influence in our region. Keeping the US involved here is paramount to our security. We also need to keep things sensible until the submarine deal is finalized with the Americans. If Major O'Rourke keeps Australia in the forefront of the minds of the US Congress and the president, then *that* is his new duty. Do you understand?"

The admiral and general had been given their orders. As much as they disagreed with the PM, they were obliged to obey. One of their own would now be a pawn in international strategy, whether he liked it or not. They got up to head back across the lake leaving the PM with the members of his cabinet to discuss their messaging. The Minister for Defence got up to walk them out. When they got to the door of the PM's office, Kingston pulled the two senior uniformed officers aside. He looked furious and said in a soft and threatening tone, "You two tried to throw me under the bus. Both of you will pay for this." And with that he returned to his seat with the three other parliamentarians.

The CDF and Chief of Army walked out of the outer office into the hallway.

"Arsehole," said the CDF.

"Yep," replied the Chief of Army.

50

At the Border

By the time the 'March to Tennessee' had reached Adairsville, things had grown beyond all proportions. The excitement had become self-generating, and now that they had funding from the national committee, the possibilities were endless.

The tweet from Troup had certainly helped and the Australian LO at Fort Rucker had been in touch a few times to let Mick know that the media from Australia was trying to get a hold of him. Other agencies had tried through the Republican party in Georgia and the locally-based Australian correspondents from the various networks back home had made their way to Atlanta to try and get a story. Mick had managed to fend them off which they did not appreciate. They were forced to show footage taken by American affiliates.

Sally-Anne invited any Republican from any district in the state to come up for a chance to be in the front of the march. This act not only endeared her to her fellow Republicans representing Georgia, but it also endeared her to the RNCC and the National Committee as a whole. It was a smart move by Sally-Anne. Maye was seen as a 'team player'. Her graciousness towards her prime Democrat competitor continued and she mentioned him and his candidacy often.

Even though the Republican senior leadership rankled at this generosity at first, the public lapped it up. Maye's popularity soared and the Republican senior leadership had to admit that whatever she was doing, it was certainly working. And not only in Georgia, but all over the country. Average citizens not only followed the Mick and Maye relationship, but they also expressed how they wished that Maye was their representative. Even some districts that were swing seats were won over by Maye Young. This was of particular interest to the Republican leaders. If she could do this in the mid-terms, what would happen if the stakes were higher?

At Adairsville, the rally took on the look of a mini–Republican National Convention. Red T-shirts and hats and pictures of elephants were everywhere. Civil war re-enactors were everywhere. They were in great demand for photos and were considered 'the cool kids' in the march, a novelty to them. Sally-Anne had had as many retirement homes emptied as possible with many aged citizens in wheelchairs with young Republican volunteers in their red T-shirts assigned to look after them.

So it was with veterans also. If a veteran in a wheelchair was there, then his helper was a veteran. They were encouraged to wear their caps and their decorations and demonstrate that they were proud to have served.

What had been experienced was a new birth—a renaissance—of middle America which had felt that it had been left behind by the power brokers in New York and California. That was why President Troup had been elected. What the liberal camps had failed to take into account was the feeling of abandonment of middle America. It was that sense of abandonment that had handed the presidency to the Republicans.

But where Troup had managed to endear himself to conservatives and right wingers, Maye had managed to do the same, but also to a large section of the liberal-leaning conservatives, and even some Democrats.

Now they were in Adairsville, the final destination of their 'March to Tennessee'. Rebel flags were everywhere with signs saying what Rob Early said five days before in Kennessaw Mountain: 'This is my battle flag'. (This was Sally-Anne's idea and she had them made up and distributed amongst the crowd). Lifting up the rebel flag was now seen as something of which to be proud, all across the state. The rebel flag flew proudly alongside the Stars and Stripes and the confidence of the people grew. Amid speeches and thanks, they handed over the march to Morris Turner, the representative for the 14th District. He would try and keep the momentum going through his electorate and keep the march going up to the Tennessee border.

But everyone wanted a piece of the M&M show. Maye was being mobbed with women wanting a selfie with her. She looked over at Mick, just as popular, being mobbed or pulled aside by someone who wanted to speak with him. He looked engrossed in a conversation with a Chinese man wearing a Mick and Maye T-shirt until she was virtually pulled aside for yet another picture.

That night, after the march was over and the crowds had gone, and the only people left were Mick and Maye and her staff, they decided to have some quiet drinks in a Hampton Inn at Adairsville. The staff were excited to have them there and to get selfies with the 'Double "M"s' as they had been dubbed.

Mick needed to let them all know that he had to report back to duty at Fort Rucker but that he would be back as often as he could to help Maye and the team out. They had all become very close and he would miss them all dearly.

Maye was devastated. She knew that he would have to return to duty, but somewhere deep down she had hoped that he would find a way to stay.

"When do you have to go back," she said, her eyes starting to react to the melancholy. This news had really sullied the evening, and what was supposed to be a celebratory drink to mark the end of the march, became a wake.

"Tomorrow, first thing," he said. "I have to report at the ASLO's office by 1600. He gave me an extra day to say goodbye."

They tried to keep the mood light-hearted but that evening, as the staff turned in and Mick and Maye went to bed, there was a foreboding in the campaign. Mick had proven to be extremely popular in his own right, but when he and Maye were together, they were electric. Everyone wanted a snap of the couple. That would now not be possible.

51

Beautiful Forever

They crawled into the soft hotel bed, exhausted and a little sun struck. It had been a great week and they had succeeded in rousing the electorate beyond their wildest dreams. To have the RNCC send down campaign workers and give them a blank check for their campaigning was unheard of. Maye suspected that she was being singled out, and she even considered, albeit briefly, that maybe they had other things in store for her. Perhaps a more senior role in the party's congressional organization.

She had been watching Mick all day. Of course, she knew that having him on the entire campaign would not be possible, but the march and the craziness of the whole week had made that a distant thought. His announcement tonight brought it all to the fore. She held him tight and kissed him, looking into his eyes.

"Who was that man you were talking to today?" she asked him. "The Asian-looking fellow."

"No-one," replied Mick. "Just a well-wisher." He didn't sound overly convincing, and Maye was going to question him further about this mysterious man when he interjected.

"He and I had a talk about you and how to get the Chinese vote."

This caught Maye by surprise. Why was Mick interested in attracting Chinese voters?

"There's about a five percent demographic in Georgia that identifies as Asian, mainly Chinese," he said, "Well, I was discussing this with him, and he suggested that you find some way of connecting with Chinese-Americans by using your name. When I told him your full name, he became very excited."

"I know what my name means if you say it in Chinese," said Maye. "It means 'beautiful forever'.

"If you knew that, why haven't you been using it?" Mick asked her.

"Firstly, don't you think it's a bit arrogant for me to call myself beautiful?"

He kissed her on her forehead. "I think you are."

She hugged him but continued in a serious tone. "I don't want to be thought of as Chinese, or part Chinese, or *whatever* Chinese. I'm an American, and China is our competitor. My platform needs to be anti-China, and pro-American jobs."

Mick was taken aback at her vehement opposition to any association with the up-and-coming superpower.

"I think the hysteria around China is a bit exaggerated," he said. "In any case, if you wanted to tap into that market, I don't think too many people would either know, or care. Besides, you'd get the Asian vote. There are a lot of Chinese and Koreans out there!"

She thought about that for a moment. It was odd that Mick had suddenly become conscious of the Asian demographic as a voter base, but so far all his instincts had been correct. He seemed to have great ideas, and they had all worked.

"How do you come up with these ideas?" asked Maye.

"I just figure what I'd like to see in a candidate, and I try the things that seemed to work back home in Australia," he replied.

"What about the Chinese angle?" she asked.

"We have a lot of Chinese back in Australia," he said. "Especially in the universities now. I had to deal a lot with them when I was doing my studies. Also, one of my good mates is half-Chinese."

He paused for a minute, deciding if he should reveal some of his past.

"You know," he said, "I spent some time in China teaching English."

Maye sat up on one elbow and faced him.

"What!? You never told me that!"

"It was while I was traveling. I wasn't very good, so I left after a few months."

Maye laid back down and thought for a moment or two.

"OK," said Maye, "talk to Sally-Anne and we'll give it a try and see what reaction we get." She then hugged him tighter. "But right now, I just want to hold you. If I have to lose you tomorrow, I need to get as much of you as I can in the time we have left."

52

The Reprieve

Around midnight, Mick's phone rang. Late night phone calls were proving to be a problem. If it wasn't some of his mates calling to tell him he was looking good as his girlfriend's handbag, it was media trying to get an interview. They didn't seem to have any shame in calling at all hours of the day or night... especially night!

"G'day Mick, it's the CA," he heard on the phone. He immediately became alert and got out of bed to find a quiet place to talk so as not to awaken Maye. He went into the bathroom and closed the door so he could talk to the Chief of Army quietly.

"Sir," he said, "go ahead."

"Mick, I understand that you are to report to the Australian LO at Fort Rucker. Is that right?"

"Yes, Sir," he replied. "It's 11 p.m. here and I'm heading back to Alabama around breakfast time."

"OK. Change of plans," said the Chief of Army. "You have been re-assigned." Mick was now completely awake. What exactly did he mean when he said 're-assigned'? Did this mean that he was going to lose his command? And with that, lose his promotion to lieutenant colonel?

"You are now to be posted against a new APN effective immediately," said the chief.

This was not good. An APN was an Army Position Number and it meant that his role would change. Bye Bye promotion! Worse still, it meant he wouldn't be finishing his time at Fort Rucker. He braced himself for the bad news.

"What will be my role, Sir?" he asked with disappointment.

"You are to be assigned to Project Land 420."

What?! Mick was stunned. Project Land 420 was a project to acquire more armored vehicles. But he was a pilot! Was this some sort of punishment?

"Um, OK Sir. I don't know anything about tanks, though. Is the position in Canberra, or at the School of Armour?" he asked.

"Neither," replied Lieutenant General Braddon. "Your duty will keep you in the States. Your APN is more for convenience than actual technical duty. We have acknowledged that your situation is unique, so we have created a position for you called 'Australian Defence Industry Liaison Officer'. Your role will be to meet with the various companies that provide defense equipment to Australia and see where the friction points are and report that back to ADF HQ."

Mick had to digest this. What the chief was saying was that the Australian Army was making a fake position for him so he could remain in the US. How could that be? More importantly, why would they do that?

The chief explained what had transpired that morning in the Prime Minister's office and how he and the CDF had been ordered to find a way of him staying involved in the campaign, and to keep Australia firmly in the eye of the US government and the American public.

The subject of the PM came up and the importance of maintaining good relations with the US. The chief gave him advice on how best to handle this new role but that his main job was, to his regret, to be the face of Australia during this campaign. Unfortunately, he would not be going back to flying duties in Alabama but would see out his posting in his new role.

"Also, I have some bad news for you," he said. Mick braced himself a second time. The first news was good... so this must be the other shoe dropping.

"We'd like you to transfer from Aviation Corps to Armoured

Corps," said the chief hesitantly. He knew that pilots jealously guarded their role within Aviation Corps in the army.

"May I ask if that's totally necessary?" inquired Mick.

The chief hesitated. He couldn't believe that he was saying this. "We'd like you to be able to wear emu plumes in your slouch hat."

Mick was stunned. Why the hell would the Chief of Army want Mick to wear emu plumes, feathers from Australia's large flightless bird, in his uniform hat? It was a part of the uniform, but only if you were in Armoured Corps. Surely this could not be the reason for the transfer from aviation to armoured? The chief could hear the silence and thought it wise to explain.

"It wasn't my idea, mate," said the chief, still calling Mick 'mate' like they were drinking buddies. "It was the PM's communications adviser's big idea. She thought it would look good on TV... very cavalier. The PM thought it was a good idea, but I tried to explain that that was not a good enough reason to ask you to transfer..."

Before the chief could finish his explanation, Mick interrupted. "I'll do it, Sir. No problem."

The Chief of Army was shocked. "I thought you would have put up more of a fight," he said.

"I get what they're trying to do," Mick said. He had a knack for the impactful, and he could see the artistic logic, even if it wasn't military logic. "They want maximum impact, so if it means having a part of my uniform as a talking point, then that would be maximum impact for virtually no effort." In Mick's mind, it could only help Maye's campaign... and besides, he didn't care if he was wearing damn feathers in his hat! So long as he was still in an Australian Army uniform, then that was fine!

The chief was impressed. He immediately knew he had the right person for the job.

"When I told them that you would be the Defence Industry Liaison Officer, the 'DILO', they wanted to change the title to Army DILO and pronounce it 'Armadillo'... but I put a quick stop to that," he said with a chuckle.

"Yeah," said Mick, "being called the Armadillo would lead to a lot of jokes about roadkill over here," he said. "Good call, Boss!" The Chief of Army appreciated that his major was feeling relaxed enough about this stupid situation that he would refer to him as 'boss'. It made his job much easier knowing he didn't have to be breaking bad news. In fact, he was over the moon that Major O'Rourke had warmed to the idea so readily and that he was happy to be a part of the PM's ridiculous scheming. But the chief had more serious things to consider about this predicament that he needed to let his officer know about.

"If I can offer you one piece of advice, Mick," said the chief, "There are a lot of people here who want you to keep Australia in the spotlight with the Americans, especially President Troup. If you can keep doing what you're doing, we'll be OK. I'll fly top cover for you back here and try and keep the PM and his comms people off your back, but I can't help you over there. Your first point of call if you need anything will be Brigadier Parkes at the embassy. If he can't sort it out, then he'll get onto me straight away. Alright?"

"Yes, Sir," said Mick, still trying to process it. For a few seconds the line fell silent. Mick could only guess what the CA was going through back in Canberra.

"Good luck, mate," said the chief. "You're going to need it." And with that, he was gone.

After the talk, Mick was feeling quite elated. He crawled back into bed and cuddled up to Maye. This would not be the last night that he would feel her in his arms, after all.

"Everything OK?" she asked sleepily.

"Everything is more than OK," he replied. "I'm staying with you on your campaign indefinitely."

Maye was suddenly awake and rolled over, sitting upright. Mick explained to her the conversation he had just had with the CA and how he had a new position that would allow him scope to remain with Maye almost throughout the whole of her campaign. And all he had to do was to look good, change the badges on his uniform, wear some feathers in his hat... and not screw up.

"Well, Major," she said excitedly at the prospect of having him for the campaign, "you have been a great ambassador for your country and a great campaign tactician. I think it is time that you were shown the appreciation of a grateful nation and a grateful party." And with that she threw her leg over him and pushed her pelvis onto his to get him excited...

53

The Devils Went Down to Georgia

As far as the march was concerned it was not over. While it had all but died with Morris Turner when he tried to take the torch through his own district, Mick and Maye were determined to show her electorate that she was interested in its entirety, not just the parts serviced by Interstate 75 and Old Highway 40.

They decided to continue their own march by turning east from Adairsville and headed eastwards through Cherokee County and then continued their journey before turning south towards Woodstock, on the outer suburbs of Atlanta, which formed the southern part of the district. Everywhere she went she made speeches, and so did Mick. The Australian Embassy in DC FedExed new accoutrements for his uniform, and so now he was wearing the badges of the Royal Australian Armoured Corps, and the striking emu plumes in his slouch hat.

As much as the Chief of Army would have hated to admit, it did have the desired effect that the PM's communications adviser was seeking. Mick knew that it would also, and so he wasn't averse to making the change. He kind of knew that his flying career in the army was most likely over. It had probably died during the meeting the Chief of Army had with the Prime Minister... but at the moment he was happy to be helping his girlfriend. Not in his wildest dreams did he ever think that he would be walking through Georgia with an American girlfriend, try-ing to help her make an impact with the Republican Party and with the US Congress! "But 'such is life' as Ned Kelly said", he thought to himself.

The march had continued deep into Cherokee County to Waleska and south through the county seat at Canton down to Woodstock. It took them eight more days and their followership had dwindled only slightly, likely due to the inconvenience of not having an interstate highway nearby. But the people in Cherokee county appreciated the in-terest, and residents made special efforts to come out to join Mick and Maye for their new march through Georgia.

Woodstock had once been a sleepy stopover on the L&N railway line but was now an up-and-coming suburb of Atlanta. This is where they had their end-of-march rally. It had been two weeks, and the enthusi-asm had died down only a little, but the followers were still markedly proud enough to continue to wave the rebel flag. In fact, throughout Georgia, more and more rebel flags were being seen as a fight against political correctness, and a return to confidence and individualism that had made America so great.

President Troup had been elected on the slogan of 'Let's make US great once more!' and Maye's campaign had not only been successful, but it had also reinforced Troup's message and he was tweeting his ap-proval. Actually, it was Dawson who was doing most of the tweeting about Maye as master of the president's account. Troup really didn't give a damn about Maye or her re-election, but Dawson knew what the GOP was planning for Maye and the presidential elections, and so was only happy to help facilitate the messaging. In Australia, the PM and his comms adviser were ecstatic that Major O'Rourke was 'on the pres-ident's radar'. If only they knew that President Troup had no interest in Mick, and that it was a senior *apparatchik* of the Republican Party who was 'subbing' for the president on social media.

Major Michael O'Rourke. A great ambassador for his country. #goaustralia #mayeyoung

At Woodstock, after the crowds had dispersed and only the die-hards remained, Mick and Maye were asked to meet with some senior members of the Party, including The Chairman. Maye thought it best that Sally-Anne was not a part of this meeting. There was no need for her to sit at the same table as her husband, although she *had* proven herself invaluable. Interestingly, they had specifically asked to have Mick there.

They met at a little restaurant that used to be the old rail freight depot on the now defunct railroad, but which had now been gentrified and made into a trendy eatery. The staff was playing various country and country rock songs that befitted the ambience, perhaps a little too loud, so they found a table that was in a quiet corner for their 'chat'. The Chairman, as well as Cooper Camden, from the National Republican Congressional Committee sat on one side; Maye and Mick sat opposite. Two chairs were left vacant.

Of course, Maye knew Cooper from Congress. He was the person who led all the Republican representatives in the House and ensured that they all toed the line. If she and Mick hadn't been doing so well, she would have been nervous about him being there. But he was in very good spirits and seemed relaxed and genuinely happy to see her, and to meet Mick.

Camden started. "We're very impressed with what you've done, Maye. Your campaign tactics are very unorthodox, but dammit, they're working!" he conceded.

"Mick actually deserves the credit, Cooper," she replied. "He came up with most of the good ideas, but it was Sally-Anne who should be praised. She was the one who coordinated them. Without her, we would not have been able to do it. You should be very proud of your wife. Thank you for putting her on our team."

Her comments were directed at The Chairman. Both he and Camden grimaced a little and shifted a little uncomfortably in their seats. They both knew that Maye was playing cat and mouse with them.

"Well, notwithstanding her input, you're extremely popular here and even outside Georgia's borders. Hell, we're getting good press in Australia and Britain," responded Camden.

Two silver-haired men in suits appeared next to the table. Maye immediately recognized the taller of the two as Preston Webster. Webster was head of the Nebraska Republican Party and was general counsel of the national committee. The other man, shorter and bespectacled, was the Senate Republican Conference Chairman, Senator Dawson Terrell, Camden's equivalent in the Senate. Together Cooper Camden and Dawson Terrell controlled all the Republicans in Congress, in both the House and the Senate respectively. Their presence here in the 11th District was no trifling matter.

"Hello Maye," said Terrell, "and this must be our wonder from Down Under." He turned to Mick and thrust out his hand. "Hello, Mick, I'm Dawson, and this is Preston."

Mick took his hand and shook it, and then Preston's.

"G'day Dawson, Preston. How are you?"

"Oh, we're fine. In fact, we're more than fine. It is a real honor to meet you," said Preston Webster.

"Are you guys with the Georgia GOP?" asked Mick innocently as they sat down at the table. He had no idea who these two people were. They smiled and shook their heads. Maye grabbed his arm and leaned in.

"Senator Dawson Terrell is the head of the Republicans in the Senate, and Preston Webster is chief counsel for the RNC," she informed him. She didn't realize it, but she was squeezing his arm tightly, her nails leaving marks. Mick tried not to wince in pain.

"What are so many heavy hitters doing here in Georgia?" inquired Mick, realizing that this was no ordinary campaign meeting. "I'm sure you're here to give my girl a big pat on the back," he added, trying to keep the mood light.

It was then that they decided to reveal the purpose of their visit. It seemed that not only had the 'Mick and Maye' fairytale captured the imagination of the American public over the last two weeks, but it had also been the topic of many conversations within the Party, including in senior leadership circles in DC.

"It is no secret that President Troup is very popular here at home, especially amongst those middle Americans who feel that their America is slowly slipping away from them. But it is also no secret that he has not been a popular leader with a large cross section of less sympathetic voters, nor is he popular abroad," said Webster quietly. "We need to always have a succession plan... and that's why we're talking to you."

Every man at that table looked at Maye for her reaction. Her gorgeous eyes hardly batted and she looked up at the ceiling, contemplating what she had just heard, and what they were inferring.

"We are eager for the good will you and your remarkably astute boyfriend have generated—not only amongst Georgians, but with people all over the country—to be carried through to the next election in 2020," he added.

Mick and Maye sat there in silence, taking in those words.

"Maye," said Webster, "we're looking at putting you up for nomination as VP candidate in 2020."

This came from out of nowhere. A second-term congresswoman (if she kept her seat in the mid-term elections) in her early thirties being asked to be vice president of the US. It was too incredible to believe.

Mick's head spun. He wasn't sure if he should be happy for Maye or not. What would this mean for them as a couple? Only three weeks ago, he had been sneaking around with a congresswoman in cheap hotels in Alabama so that their relationship could stay a secret. Now the relationship was being used as a tool for Maye's re-election... and possibly for the next presidential campaign as President Troup's running mate.

The king-makers—or in this case the queen-makers—at the table saw Maye's hesitation as she pondered what this would mean. They were eager to keep the momentum going. Camden piped up.

"You know, Mick was largely responsible for the seismic shifts in the campaign," he hastened to add to his colleagues. "He made the Confederate flag trendy again, almost single-handedly. Mick, if you were to be asked what was needed in a vice-presidential campaign, what would your advice be?"

This was very smart on the part of Camden. By getting Mick's input he was forcing buy-in from him and, by association, Maye. She turned her head and looked at her boyfriend. Her head was swimming, too. She needed to hear an opinion from someone she could trust. The Chairman, Webster and Terrell waited intently.

"Well," started Mick. "I guess the key thing is to be authentic with Americans, but still play fair. I think the world is tired of partisan politics. If people were genuinely concerned about the welfare of the constituents, then they would look for ways to cooperate rather than to segregate into fractious factions."

"Interesting, but maybe a little naive," exhorted The Chairman, subtly chiding at Mick.

"Perhaps," suggested the Australian, "but if I was a voter here, and I found a candidate that gave credit to whomever had a good idea, even if it was from the opposition, then I'd be more inclined to vote for that person. It tells me that that he—or she—is open to ideas from all, and beholden to none. It seemed to work for us on the march," he added. Maye gave his leg a rub, showing her approval.

"I wouldn't be so quick to deride Mick's opinion," rejoined Terrell to The Chairman. "Our polling has shown that his view is not that uncommon, by both Republicans and Democrats," he said.

The Chairman was not impressed. How dare this foreigner make him look bad.

The screeching of a fiddle came over the loudspeakers as the Charlie Daniels Band was heard playing the opening stanzas of *The devil went down to Georgia*. The staff cheered their delight. The song had the same impact in Georgia as *Sweet Home Alabama* had in the next state.

"Let me tell you, Maye," said Terrell, "At first it seemed that you were giving too much airtime to the Democrats. I mean, what the hell were you thinking bringing up your opponent? But those sorts of stunts are working, and The Chairman of the Party is happy. So, the RNC is very happy. And that's one of the reasons why we're here." He smiled and added, "We like being happy at the RNC... and Maye, if you agree to run for Veep, well that would make us all *very* happy."

'The devil went down to Georgia, he was lookin' for a soul to steal' sang the staff.

"What does the president think?" asked Maye. "And what about Vice President Greene? Why isn't he running again?"

Both Maye and Mick could see the pained expression on their faces as they exchanged quick glances at each other. It suddenly became clear that this meeting was a secret meeting, and that neither the president nor the vice president was aware of the Party's intention for the next election.

"Oh," said Maye. "They don't know that you're here."

"Well," replied Camden, "we are sure that you can appreciate the delicacy of this situation. Ideally, we would like you to finish your campaign for re-election for your district. We're sure that you will do very well and will get enough exposure and support to carry your nomination as the Republican choice for vice president when the time comes. Leave the rest to us."

Maye considered this for a few moments. Mick was a bit confused about the internal machinations of the Party and the primaries.

"Exactly what does that mean?" he asked.

"What it means is that the Party wants to hedge its bets," Maye said looking at their faces for a reaction. Cooper raised his eyebrows slightly. She totally understood what was being asked. She then turned to her boyfriend and explained.

"The Party could endorse me publicly as the next candidate, but they would get the president and vice president offside. The president and the VP both probably expect to get full party support at the next election running on the same ticket: Troup and Greene. But the current administration is not as attractive as it could be. So, the problem is what choice do you make? For the next election, run with Troup and Greene and keep their advantage of being in office, or dump them for two other candidates but run the risk of losing the advantage of President Troup being the incumbent."

Maye then looked at the two men from the national committee, accusingly. "The next best thing is to keep President Troup in that position, but encourage him to dump Vice President Greene and put someone else on the ticket... such as a woman from Georgia."

Each of them looked somewhat sheepish.

"That's about right, isn't it? You want me to win the mid-terms, and then throw my hat into the ring as a VP contender but to make it look like it's my idea, and not the Party's, and get the president to think that choosing me was his decision. You get what you want, but if it doesn't work out and we lose, then it was the president's poor choice of me as a candidate and the GOP is blameless."

Mick, angry, felt obliged to speak.

"Why don't you just have the balls to come out and endorse her when the time is right and say outright that she's the Party's choice?" he asked. "If you think Troup can win with Maye as his VP, then put your full support behind her and him!"

Their silence spoke volumes and he realized how naïve he was being. He shook his head.

The staff were singing and playing 'air fiddles'. *Johnny, rosin up your bow and play your fiddle hard. 'Cause Hell's broke loose in Georgia, and the devil deals the cards.*
And if you win, you get this shiny fiddle made of gold, but if you lose, the devil gets your soul.

"That's what I fucking hate about politics! You're all pricks with no balls."

Cooper piped up.

"That might be the case, but it's the reality. Maye understands that and ultimately the decision is hers. Of course, we would like you to be part of her campaign. You have a knack for it. Together, I think you can do it."

Mick took Maye's hand in his and looked at her, and she at him. This was that moment in a person's life where things will completely change. Did she stay on the currently safe path and remain a representative, or did she throw her hat into the ring for a vice-presidential campaign and risk alienating others in the party and possibly failing miserably but all the while keeping the Party bosses from being the bad guys? He merely said to her seven words, "Whatever you choose, one hundred percent support."

He played 'Fire on the Mountain' run boys, run. The devil's in the house of the rising sun. The chicken in the bread pan pickin' out dough. Granny will your dog bite? No, child, no!

54

The Shakedown

The Chairman and Camden said goodbye to their RNC colleagues. They were discussing Maye's potential candidacy, and how to get more support for her within the Party when Sally-Anne suddenly appeared. The Chairman saw her and seethed.

"I guess you can be happy now," he said. "Your girl has been tapped on the shoulder."

Sally-Anne was uncertain exactly what that meant. She hadn't seen Terrell or Webster, nor would she know who they were if she had. And she certainly had no idea that Maye had been approached to run for VP in 2020. Her concern at the moment was the mid-term election.

Cooper, obviously annoyed at Sally-Anne, got into his car and drove off without saying goodbye. Cooper had always been pleasant to Sally-Anne, so him being so rude was very much out of character.

"What was that about?" she asked her husband.

"Your dirty trick worked," he rasped. "You know, we were working on the tweet when you sent that picture. It was unnecessary."

"What picture?" she asked.

"Oh, come off it," demanded The Chairman. "You know very well what picture."

"I honestly don't," she replied.

"I thought we had an agreement," he said. "You would excuse my extra-curricular activities, and I would keep them out of your social cir-cle."

"What picture!?" she asserted. "I don't know what you're talking about."

The Chairman pulled out his phone in frustration. He brought the picture up on his phone and thrust it in front of her face. Sally-Anne pulled her head back from this obvious act of aggression and took her husband's phone.

"Who's that with Cooper?" she asked, ignoring the fact that Elaine was with her husband.

"Oh, come off it, Sally-Anne. You got what you wanted. Why don't you go inside and see your girl. She has some news for you. But if you pull a stunt like that again, I'll make sure that we destroy her campaign before we get anywhere near the polls."

Sally-Anne stood there wondering who was that with Cooper? What news did Maye have? What campaign was he talking about? The mid-term campaign had been in full swing for over two weeks.

She shrugged it off and walked into the restaurant. The cool of the air conditioning was very much welcome. In the corner of the restaurant were Mick and Maye, holding hands. A couple of customers were getting selfies with them and asking them to sign their menus, which they obligingly did.

When they saw her, they told her to sit down. Maye explained that they just had a meeting with some RNC heavyweights, including her husband. That's why she wasn't a part of the meeting.

"We have some big news." She paused to look into Sally-Anne's eyes. "How would you like to be part of a vice-presidential campaign?"

She wasn't sure exactly what Maye meant. Who's campaign? Certainly not Troup's and Greene's re-election campaign.

They could see her confusion. Mick leaned away and thrust out his hands presenting Maye to her and then sang 'Hail to the Vice-Chief, she's been chosen for the nation'.

Sally-Anne paused for a second, and then the penny dropped for her. Maye was going to be a vice-presidential candidate. That's what her husband meant when he said that she had been 'tapped on the shoulder.' She launched herself at the two of them and hugged them both, squealing for joy. Had she thought about what was about to happen, she may have paused a little longer to ponder what it was going to mean. But right now, she was just ecstatic for two people to whom she had become so attached during the last two weeks marching across the 11th District.

"If you win, you will be the first female vice-president of the United States!" She then turned to Mick and, forgetting that they were just boyfriend and girlfriend added, "and you will be the Second Gentleman of the United States!"

"Woah there! Settle down, Tiger!" said Mick. "I'm Maye's boyfriend, and I'm an Australian. That's not really a possibility. Maybe the Second Boyfriend of the United States: SBOTUS!" he joked.

As far as Sally-Anne was concerned, she had married them off. She could imagine the two of them on the campaign trail: a strong-willed, smart, gorgeous, young, woman and her handsome—and exotic—soldier husband. It would be a very potent package to present to the American people. A modern-day John and Jackie just as she had been portraying them for the last two weeks in the little fishpond of the 11th District. Now the fish have been released into the ocean.

"Let's not get ahead of ourselves," said Maye, trying to bring them all back down to earth. I still have to win the mid-terms and stay in Congress.

But they all knew that that problem was merely academic. Her popularity was beyond reproach, and she was enjoying figures in the high sixties with one poll even having her as high as seventy-three percent. Depending on how the RNC was going to handle this, she still had to campaign for her district accordingly.

55

The Walk to the Finish

The next three months of the campaign were not as hectic as the first two weeks. They were more of a grind. A type of war of attrition, but they had the upper hand. The Democrats never really had a chance, but Maye never lost an opportunity to talk up her opponent and make him feel important. But even he knew that a divorced social worker with a beard could not compete with the young and vibrant and beautiful Republican candidate. The fact that she was smart and capable didn't even seem to figure in the polls.

The Democrats even knew they could not make a fuss about the rebel flag. One of them tried that and the reaction from the public had been venomous and strong. It seemed that the rebel flag was here to stay!

The retail politics remained a crowd pleaser. Instead of Maye featuring in TV advertisements and online with some kooky commercials, they instead told the voters at which mall or sporting event that she could be seen, and it was there that her staff set up facilities so that she was able to listen to the opinions and concerns of the voters. Most of them were things that were not in her purview and were strictly county or state matters, but there were definitely concerns in which a federal representative could become involved.

On Mick's advice, and after the first few of such events, she featured in an election advertisement that was totally out of the box.

"Hi. I'm Representative Maye Young. Don't come whining to me if you have problem... unless you have a solution.

"So go off and complain to your friends if all you want is to be heard, but if you want something done, come to me with a problem and a solution... and together we'll work to get it accomplished.

I'm Maye Young, and I approved this message. If you don't like it, you know where to go. To the voting booth!"

The public loved it, especially members of the old guard. They liked seeing a woman being strong and politically incorrect and telling it like it was.

Maye Young was the elixir of youth and would keep the Republican Party's image youthful and appealing. But it was her boyfriend, the thunder from Down Under—as the media was now calling him—who was being the textbook partner. Just interesting enough to be a useful commodity when Maye was otherwise engaged, and who could be trusted to tout his girlfriend's virtues as a candidate for the district and for the country and its resurgence.

Mick became sought after as a speaker, which meant that the campaign could spread its resources. And each time he spoke, the GAGOP had a handler for him, and each time he received a glowing report back to the committee.

Mick was given some token tasks to do as the 'Australian Defence Industry Liaison Officer' and he visited various armories and production lines and met with executives and workers. It was not difficult. All he had to do was listen to their issues and predict where problems would arise in the supply chain. The real work in liaising with American defense suppliers was already being done by experts far more qualified than him. Mick was just a figurehead. It was fun, but he did miss flying.

President Troup had not been informed of the Party's intention to put Maye forward as his VP. That would happen after the mid-terms and before the campaigning for the general elections in two years. In the meantime, the campaign continued, and Mick's popularity was growing (much to the delight of the Australian Prime Minister and his staff).

The national committee decided he needed an assistant for the rest of the campaign. Even though this was just a district election, it had taken on national interest. All eyes were on the Georgia 11th! So, to help Mick he would be given an executive assistant. Maye, after all, had Pam and Rob and Sally-Anne and Carroll, as well as some more team members who had been assigned, including make-up and wardrobe assistants. The Party seemed to be very keen to help her in any way and it was obvious to those on the inside that this level of support was a precursor to the Party's greater intentions.

Mick asked if he could choose the person, and Maye was happy for him to do so. Her only stipulation was that it wasn't some 'size four bimbo with big boobs and no brains'. Mick laughed and said, "you know I don't like big boobs".

The man that Mick chose was a shortish guy by the name of Jesús Emmanuel. He was a Latino of Mexican heritage. He was ex-army, a paratrooper who had served in the 82nd Airborne Division - the 'All Americans'. Jesús said that he would call himself the 81st Airborne, the 'All Mexicans'. Mick liked him from the moment he met him.

"If I hire you, you have two jobs to do," he told Jesús. "You must make sure that I'm never drinking alone... so you have to join me. And second, teach me Spanish."

"Hooah!" he responded without thinking.

"Hooah, indeed! Welcome aboard." And that was the story of how Jesús Emmanuel came to be Mick's shadow, and his new Spanish language coach.

"*¿Cuando empiezo?*" said Jesús.

"What does that mean?" asked Mick.

"When do I start," he replied.

"You just did! Nicely played," laughed Mick. "You and I are going to get along just fine," he said, shaking Jesús's hand.

"*Bueno!*"

There was method in Mick's madness. He was definitely playing the long game.

56

A Contender

"I really think it's time you courted the Chinese vote," said Mick out of the blue. Maye looked at him across the breakfast table as she read the AJC. There wasn't much about the mid-terms. Instead, the main story was on President Troup's latest *faux pas* with the Canadian Prime Minister, and how Chicago's O'Hare Airport was the victim of a computer cyber-attack throwing air travel into chaos. The Russians or the Chinese were the prime suspects.

"I don't think that's a good idea at the moment," replied Maye holding up the paper and showing him the story about the cyber-attack.

"Perhaps," he thought, "but when the announcement comes, you'll need to get that five percent of the vote. Troup can't deal with China. It will be left to you to calm things."

Maye looked at him quizzically. Mick was getting a bit ahead of himself. If the candidacy for the VP does happen, that campaign is a year away.

Maye's phone chirped. It was from @the real Daniel Troup.

"Listen to this, '*Chinese hackers have hit Chicago airport. Time to take the fight to them. #Troup2020*'. He's trying to get some traction before the election," said Maye.

* * *

The weekend before the mid-terms saw Mick and Maye doing the rounds in the district. They pumped the flesh and kissed babies and covered as much territory as they could in the three days. On the Tuesday of the election, the GAGOP and the RNC were watching closely, as was the rest of Atlanta, and Georgia, and much of the country.

As far as the Party was concerned, Maye was auditioning for the American people. The result of the election and voter turnout would be her 'call back', or not.

It was no surprise that the exit polls were predominantly in Maye's favor, and the evening news led with that story even before the polls had closed.

The following day the count had been completed. Maye, of course, retained her seat. That was expected. What wasn't expected was the turn out. The percentage of voters within the 11th District that had made the effort to vote was over seventy percent of the adult population, and Maye returned sixty-two percent of the vote for her! The Democrats were notably silent about that, except for Harman Douglas, the leading Democrat candidate. He was interviewed and thanked Maye for a clean and positive campaign, and that he felt that the district was in good hands, even if he didn't agree with the policies of the Republican Party.

This display of mutual admiration was not lost on the pundits. Maye's clean campaign; her ability to articulate ideas clearly; her attractiveness; her relationship with the exotic Australian, were all winning her acclaim in Georgia, and elsewhere in the country. Each of these factors, relevant to her candidature or otherwise, only helped her cause... and the RNC—in closed conversations—was delighted.

The Party leadership now got down to her VP campaign. They felt that it could now start in earnest. Maye would need to be trained, and Troup convinced that she was his best chance at re-election. Vice President Jasper Greene had been a strong representative and a great foil for Troup's bluster, but nevertheless, he would be tapped on the shoulder and told to get his resumé ready. As good as he was, Troup needed to be re-elected, and Maye Young was better at getting voters to the booths. Greene was to be given his marching orders. Such is the character of politics, and those that want power.

57

The Superbowl Upset

Since her landslide re-election Maye enjoyed a honeymoon period.

The following week, when Congress was in session, she was the darling of the Party. The mid-term elections had been dismal for the Republicans, not helped by President Troup's unstable leadership. Many members of the GOP had lost their seats, including a few seats considered 'red and safe'. Maye, on the other hand, had delivered a landslide vote with a landslide voter turnout, not to mention good publicity from both sides of the politically-polarized media. Even a few Democrats sneaked into her office in DC to congratulate her on her campaign. Of all campaigns of all candidates across the country, her campaign had generated better coverage and better media commentary, and her results were testament to her campaign acumen.

Thanksgiving was spent back in Georgia with a special celebration the day before with Ben and Jess in Atlanta before they flew to Baltimore to be with their families there, leaving Mick and Maye to enjoy the holiday alone in Maye's house on Lake Allatoona.

But the joint session of congress in late November had proved forbidding. President Troup's demands for an increase in funds to upgrade the country's southern border with more manpower, military involvement and special legislation meant that the appropriations bill was stalled in the senate after the Democrats threatened a filibuster. They thought that stalling the passing of that bill by threat of holding the floor and debating it would force the president's hand. But Troup was not going to blink first. The resultant to-ing and fro-ing between the parties and the president ended in an impasse when President Troup called their bluff and decided not to sign *any* bill that permitted the government to operate until he got his funding for southern border security. That included signing *any* approval for *any* money for *any* government agency.

Without money, the government would have to shut down and stop work until an agreement was reached. It was a game of 'chicken' between the executive and the legislature, but it was the government workers who were the losers.

Maye was caught up in the fray during the multitude of meetings and sittings that were held during December but, without an agreement, the government was forced to close its doors just four days before Christmas and send all employees home with no pay. If a civil servant was going to work, he or she would be doing so as a volunteer.

And even when the newly elected or re-elected senators and members arrived and took their positions in the new Congress in early January, the situation could still not be resolved. The shutdown continued well into January.

The US looked like a basket case around the world, and its president a petulant schoolboy. Panicked Republicans held closed-door meetings. Many wanted the future to include a new candidate for president. The senior leaders were already including Maye and her high approval ratings in their campaign plans to help Troup's low approval number, but when the polls leading up to the Superbowl came back, the Republican's downhill slide was cemented.

In the sixth week of the shutdown, and after the appalling losses in the mid-terms in November, the Republican party, at the end of January 2019, had an approval rating of just thirty-eight percent. With those numbers, the next election would be a bloodbath. Panic set in within the Party and representatives and senators were increasingly nervous. The RNC was holding meeting after meeting to come up with a viable game plan as Troup was being crucified in the media.

In Georgia, on February third, Mick sat down to watch the Superbowl while Maye sat with him, explaining the rules of American football. Her phone buzzed and she answered.

As Maye's team, the San Francisco '49ers, battled the Seattle Seahawks for NFL's ultimate prize, the ultimate prize of American politics suddenly came up for grabs. Maye hung up the phone as the '49ers scored a touchdown.

"You'll never believe this," she said to Mick. "They want me to run against Troup for the Oval Office!"

58

Shrimp and Grits and Iowa

Even though Maye was now in high demand, not only in her district, but elsewhere, she still had to be made into a viable candidate. The plans of the Republicans for her to run were still a closely guarded secret while they assessed how Troup might recover from the debacle of the government shutdown, which finally ended after four grueling and embarrassing weeks.

By the end of May, the Republicans' approval rating had increased from the thirty-eight percent in February to forty-three percent. Troup's approval continued to wallow around the low forties also.

By mid-June, it was time. With trade tensions with China at an all-time low, not helped by Troup's arrogance, Maye took the opportunity to announce her candidature for the 2020 election.

The announcement was met with division within the GOP, and anger by those who discovered that factions within the party had been secretly planning this for months. Maye was both cheered and heckled by members of her own party but, to her credit, weathered the detractors, and graciously thanked the supporters. With Troup's performance bringing down the Republican name, the rock star that Maye had become seemed to be the logical choice.

Other Republicans had hinted that they would run also, but the RNC made it clear that any more candidates who nominated would be 'discouraged' as far as the Party was able. Ideally, they wanted the presidential primaries next year to make the decision as to who would be the Party's nominee and do that from just two candidates. They said that that way 'was the purest example of democracy in action.'

The RNC, along with her congressional duties, had Maye on a very busy schedule, which had meant long periods away from Mick. But he had been put to good use by the Party and was becoming a highly sought-after speaker, especially at military and veterans' events.

Troup, of course, was furious from the moment he heard Maye was intending to run. The Twittersphere almost cracked with his constant tweets denigrating Maye's candidature and the Republican party leadership. He seemed to take great delight in referring to Mick as 'that foreigner' and questioning Maye's background and nationality. It was ironic, seeing as how his wife, the First Lady, was from Slovakia and had only attained citizenship a few years before.

The RNC organized her registration as a candidate through the Federal Electoral Commission, and they dispensed with any exploratory committee normally convened to see if a potential candidate had support. It was obvious that she did, not only within Georgia, but also with a wider audience. What's more, through the GAGOP, they commenced her training. While she may have been a smart, young professional, she did not have a background in law, economics or international policy that would be needed. Her degree in political science and her MBA were good, but definitely not enough. If she was to be presented to the American people, she not only had to be pretty and young, she had to be intelligent and worldly. An area where the Republicans had faltered often.

Professors and policy experts would coach her as often as her schedule would allow and she would put in ten hours a day for her constituents and another four hours of coaching per night. The pace was relentless, and she and Mick would often go for days without seeing each other.

Back in Australia, the government had been re-elected in a surprise result in an election that was expected to topple the incumbent, Prime Minister Mitchell. Mick's involvement in US affairs was said to have been a factor in keeping the Prime Minister in office, and the citizens of Mick's home state of Queensland voted overwhelmingly to keep the PM's government in office, which ended up being the deciding factor. It had helped that Maye and him had sent private video messages of thanks back to the PM and to the CDF for allowing him to remain in the US 'for love'. Somehow, these private video messages had been leaked to the media, and it didn't take a rocket scientist to deduce that it was the PM's communications advisers behind the leak. But it had the desired effect. The public continued its hunger for more of 'Mick and Maye' and the PM's approval rating rose on the back of his 'facilitation of their relationship'.

But now that Maye was running for the White House, the Australian government had to make a decision on how best to handle this new development. By letting Mick assist with Maye's re-election as a member of the House of Representatives, well that was easy. Troup would have no problem with that. But now that she was going to be campaigning for the White House as a candidate for president, it came down to 'which horse do we bet on?' Troup, who would most likely win the nomination, and then possibly remain in office if he won the election, or Young—who was popular—but an unknown and an outsider to win the nomination.

In the end it was a visit by the head of the RNC to the Australian Ambassador that helped the PM decide. The head of the RNC urged Australia's representative to convince the PM to let Mick remain involved. "We'd remember your assistance in this matter," were his words to the ambassador, "and we'd make sure we'd demonstrate our appreciation." This was enough to make the PM decide to leave Mick where he was. But he also knew that he had to remain neutral in any commentary on the US election. "We remain a staunch ally of the United States, regardless of whomever is in the Oval Office", was the key message. Secretly, they were hoping for Maye to beat Troup. The PM thought it would be easier to deal with her if she won office.

* * *

Mick, now with some certainty in what was expected of him by his government for the foreseeable future—even though he knew he was merely a commodity for the PM—was creating new opportunities to keep his girlfriend in the public eye. The RNC had appointed a campaign committee for them both, but Mick and Maye kept a tight rein on them. After all, wasn't their 'out-of-the-box' campaign for the midterms successful?

At a small restaurant in Decatur, Mick and Sally-Anne discussed strategy away from the appointed campaign committee members.

"We have to get California and New York on our side," said Sally-Anne. "They will tend towards the Democrats, and they have the largest number of electoral college votes," she said. "We'll probably win Texas, but the fruit loops in California and the liberals in New York can tend to be problematic."

"First-things-first," said Mick. "We'll need to ensure we win the primaries and caucuses to make sure Maye's on the ticket, then we can concentrate on getting electoral college votes," he said. He had been studying American politics hard and applying his own sensibilities, and it seemed to be working.

He knew that the campaign would have to be run in two distinct phases. The first phase would be to get the nomination to run for president by having registered members of the Republican Party vote for the best Republican candidate. This would happen at the party primary elections and caucuses, known collectively as 'the primaries'. At the primaries, members vote for a delegate to represent their choice of candidate, and that delegate would then travel to the Republican National Convention. The candidate with the greatest number of delegates at the convention is the winner and will then be the nominee for the presidential election.

The person chosen to represent the Republican Party would enter the second phase, and that was to run against the candidates from the other political parties at the general election for president. Because the Republican and Democratic Parties were the largest political parties in the United States, the general election invariably came down to a two-horse race: the person chosen by the Republican Party versus the person chosen by the Democratic Party.

The problem Maye was facing was that it was unusual to challenge a sitting president who could nominate for a second term. A president in office had a huge advantage over any other candidate. It would be hard to convince people to dump a sitting president in favor of an unknown. Furthermore, President Troup would not be impressed that the Party was not backing him for a second term... and that could have ramifications. So going to the primaries as a challenger was going to be a difficult task... and that was just the beginning.

"I think we need to get to Iowa for their caucuses," he said. He knew Iowa was the first state to hold its primaries and was the focus of nation-wide attention. "We'll get a lot of free coverage and a good head of steam if we can do well there. But Troup is popular in the Midwest. I mean, that's his voter base," he said. "If we can soften his support, then they will desert him and flock to Maye. But we have to do it subtly and without making Troup look foolish. He'll do that himself," he said.

"What do you have in mind?" asked Sally-Anne, taking a fork-full of shrimp and grits.

"Our 'March to Tennessee' did well, didn't it?" he asked rhetorically. Sally-Anne nodded as she wiped her mouth with a napkin.

"Well," Mick continued pensively, "Let's repeat it, but let's do it as a road trip ending up in Iowa for their state fair. The other candidates will try to do the same thing, so we'll need to be different. If we can do the state fair in August, and do it well, then we'll probably do well during their primaries next February."

He grabbed a pen and a paper placemat and drew a rough sketch of the US. His army training was obvious as he devised a battle plan.

"Here's what I think," said Mick. "We do a road trip through the Atlantic and Midwest states and get a following like we did here in Georgia and weaken Troup's hold on them ending up in Iowa in August. After that, it will be a question of getting to each of the states well ahead of the primaries, starting with the Iowa caucuses in February.

"The advantage we'll have over Troup, besides the fact that Maye is the better choice, is that Troup won't have the freedom to just pack up and go to each state to campaign. His duties in the White House will hobble him somewhat. That allows us to be more agile and responsive.

Sally-Anne was impressed. It seemed simple enough, but the actuality and the logistics would be huge.

"Will we be able to get enough money to do that?" she said. "That's a big campaign. Troup will demand funding from the Party for his re-election. That will mean Republican money will be split"

Her lunch companion smiled. "That's the problem with American elections," said Mick. "You need to have deep pockets, or backers with deep pockets. What I suggest is that we use as many weapons as we can to get the media to do the big-ticket things for free, namely publicity. We'll also use as much disruptive technology and ideas as we can."

Sally-Anne grimaced slightly. The thought of technology concerned her. Mick could see that concern in her pained expression.

"Don't worry," he assured her. "Your strength lies in conventional co-ordination. We can get others to do the digital disruption. Pam and Rob can help oversee that.

She looked relieved. It was funny that when Mick came up with these ideas, she felt confident that it would fall into place. He was able to not only encourage her, he also made her feel that she was capable of things that just a few months earlier she would never have dreamed.

Just then Jesús showed up.

"*¡Hola amigo! ¿Qué onda?* said Mick, greeting Jesús and asking him what was happening.

Jesús smiled at his Australian boss. "*Nada, jefe,*" he responded and sat down as Mick offered him a seat. After six months, his Spanish was coming along nicely. Sally-Anne looked impressed... again. Mick saw her expression.

"And here is how we try and get into California and Florida," he told her placing his hand on Jesús's shoulder. "Jesús will be our savior, no pun intended."

"If we can reach enough Latinos in and around LA to get southern California to tip, and Maye gets her hometown of San Francisco, we might be able to turn the state," said Mick. "As for Florida, I'm not Jewish, but we have enough Cubans and Dominicans and Puerto Ricans down there that getting them onside with the Republicans would be, quite possibly, a game changer. If I need to wear a yarmulke while I'm speaking Spanish, then I'll do that."

Jesús laughed. "*Estas muy loco, jefe.*" Sally-Anne couldn't speak Spanish, but she knew enough to agree with Jesús: Mick *was* indeed, very crazy.

"You are very committed to Maye," said Sally-Anne, her brow furrowed.

"I think she'll be a great candidate for president," he said, "and while I'm her boyfriend and still in the US, I'll do my best to help her realize that goal."

But in the short term, they had to come up with a campaign plan and get the campaign committee to endorse it. Jesús craned his neck as he looked around the restaurant.

"*¿Dónde está el baño?*" he asked searching for the bathroom. Mick pointed with his pen.

"*Está allí,*" he said and continued eating. Sally-Anne took a drink.

"How are you going to learn Spanish so quickly, although I'm quite impressed at how much you know," she said.

"Spanish isn't that much different to French," he responded, "and I speak enough French to get by. The key thing is to connect. We have to connect with as many people as possible. Troup is not going to like it, but we have to keep this a contest between the Democrats and the Republicans, not the Republicans and the Republicans. We can't afford to win based on just turning the Republican vote from Troup to Maye. We'd just end up splitting the conservative vote and handing the election to the Democrats. What we need to do is get enough Republicans to turn from Troup to us, and enough Democrats to turn from whomever the Democratic nominee will be, to us. That's how we'll get the votes."

"Another thing is that we have to empathize with the electorate. Our big weakness is that Maye has no kids, but that can also be a selling point... but it's a hard sell," said Mick, considering how it would play out.

"What do you suggest?" asked Sally-Anne.

"We need to make Maye attractive to as many interest groups as possible: Republicans that are on the fence; swing voters, Asians, Latinos, veterans. And to start, we'll target moderate Democrats in Georgia by using Harman Douglas," said Mick.

Sally-Anne was a bit shocked. Harman Douglas was the Democratic candidate for the 11th District who was defeated resoundingly by Maye.

"The Republicans haven't cornered the market on good ideas," he said. "There are just as many Democrats who want to see the best for the country as the Republicans do, they just see it from the left."

"If we get Harman to join Maye's team as a special adviser on social affairs, including child welfare and schooling, along with your knowledge on schooling, then we can show the electorate that while we don't... I mean while *Maye* doesn't have kids, she is serious about families, child welfare and education. She'll be putting people with the right background and the right qualifications on her campaign team, even if they aren't Republicans."

"That's brilliant!" exclaimed Sally-Anne. "A bi-partisan campaign committee."

"No, not bi-partisan appointments... merit-based appointments. If you have the right qualifications, you get the job. Not if you're a minority or a female or a Democrat or a Republican. You are chosen based on merit."

Sally-Anne smiled. It had been a long time since common sense prevailed in politics.

"Harman seemed a decent bloke," Mick continued. "It's important that he understands that he doesn't have to become a Republican and he is free to vote Democrat or any way his heart desires, provided his number one concern is the people he is there to represent and defend. Everything else is secondary."

Jesús returned and saw Sally-Anne with a wry grin on her face.

"*¿De qué has estado hablando?*" he asked them, inquiring about what they had been discussing.

A couple of diners recognized Mick and sidled up to him for his autograph. This would be an interesting campaign.

59

The Falling One Star

During Maye's next session in Congress, Mick went with her to Washington and paid a visit to the Australian Embassy. The ambassador, who would never have given him the time of day less than a year ago, was now extremely pleased to welcome the major. The Australian Military Defence Attaché—the DA—was cordial, while all the other staffers seemed to be somewhat starstruck, especially the female staff, by the minor celebrity who had come to see them.

After the official niceties were over, the DA asked to see Mick in private. They went into his office and Brigadier Parkes closed the door.

"How's fame treating you?" he asked, pouring them both a coffee.

Mick took the mug. He would have preferred a Coke. Outside, the early Washington summer was bright and hot.

"It has its ups and downs, Sir," replied Mick. "I do miss my flying, though," he added.

"We both know that your appointment as Australian Defence Liaison Officer is a sham position. Before you, such a position did not exist and after you, it will cease to exist again."

Mick looked at the brigadier. He was not angry, nor was he being friendly. He was, well, neutral. Matter-of-fact. That was always dangerous when a senior officer was neither friendly nor angry. It was hard to figure out where one stood.

"I know, Sir," said Mick. "But I was ordered to do it so I, well, do it."

"As a good soldier would," said the senior officer. "But what is your intention? What do you want to do with your career?"

Mick was confused. Why was a one-star general interested in *his* career.

"To be honest, I have not given it much thought in the short term, Sir," he said. "As you are aware, I'm rather busy at the moment. It seems that the PM is leaning on the Chief of Army for me to continue in this, um, role."

The brigadier now looked serious and leaned forward so he could emphasize what he was about to say.

"The Chief of Army is getting phone calls almost daily from the PM's staff, wanting updates on the situation with you. The CA is getting tired of fending them off. He contacted me to try and gauge what you thought would be the end-state of all..." he thumped a copy of the *Washington Post* on his desk, "this!" On the front page was a picture of Maye with the tag *'Georgia's Rebel'*.

Mick was angered by the senior officer's attitude and the disrespect he had just shown for his girlfriend, but he remained calm. Brigadier Parkes was rapidly becoming one of his least favorite officers. Now it seemed that he was being pressured by the Chief of Army who was, in turn, being pressured by the Prime Minister's office which was, no doubt, only concerned about how his involvement might be of benefit to the PM's opinion polls. It also seemed that no-one was really concerned about how his relationship actually was with Maye. All they saw was the product that could be bartered, and all they could think about was 'what's in this for us?' They had turned it into a 'clockwork orange'.

"If you have nothing further, Sir, I'll be heading off. I have a lunch date with my partner up on the hill," said Mick, trying to say it in such a way that it didn't sound like an arrogant quip from a political insider, but with enough contempt that it would show that the brigadier was, definitely, a spectator.

Mick was not in uniform so was not supposed to salute the more senior officer, but he snapped to attention, the equivalent of a salute. The brigadier would normally return the compliment, but instead, he chose to ignore it. Quite an insult within the military.

"Major," he said, "what do you wish me to say to the Chief of Army?" There was plenty of passive aggressiveness in his tone and his treatment of Mick. Using a person's rank in the Australian Defence Force was like calling a son or daughter by their full name. It meant business! Just as Mick was about to respond, he saw the ambassador and one of his staffers, paused in the corridor.

"Mister Ambassador?" said Mick. The brigadier was momentarily taken aback.

"Major O'Rourke. Yes? What can I do for you?" he said warmly.

"Will you be speaking with the PM anytime soon?" Mick asked him.

The ambassador nodded. "Actually," he replied, "I will be calling him this evening around ten o'clock. Why is that?"

"Would you mind passing on a message from me to him and his PR staff? Please stop bothering the Chief of Army looking for information about my intentions. If the PM's office wants information on my love life, they are to ask me directly. I do not communicate with the Chief of Army about personal matters, and my relationship with Congresswoman Young is a personal matter, so the Chief of Army will have no information of any use to them."

The ambassador was lost for words for a moment but agreed to Mick's request.

Mick turned to the brigadier and, trying to mask his contempt, replied, "I hope that will sort out your problem sufficiently, Sir," he offered. "The CA should not be bothered any more by the PM's office about my love life. And I hope I shan't be either."

He dropped off his visitor's pass at the front desk and went outside into the Washington sunshine. He was about to call an Uber when a car pulled up and offered him a ride to the Capitol Building. It was the FBI. They wanted to have a chat.

60

Los Federales

The Chevy Suburban was a bit of a cliché, but at least it was spacious and cool. Although, Mick didn't appreciate the weaving in and out of traffic that the driver was doing.

Assistant Special Agent-in-Charge Gus Gilmer introduced himself and pointed to the driver as Special Agent McDuffie.

"We'll only take a few minutes of your time, Major," Gilmer said. Mick was not sure if he should be concerned. They were heading north-west, towards Du Pont Circle, not south-east, towards the Capitol Building. He wasn't a citizen of this country, and if these two men were not federal agents as they claimed to be, he could be in big trouble.

"What do you want," asked Mick, trying not to sound concerned.

"I'm not sure if you're aware of our areas of responsibility," said Agent Gilmer, "but we are responsible for domestic security. It is our responsibility to ensure that anyone who has any influence with figures of importance, is vetted. Especially those from outside the United States."

Mick started to take in his surroundings. The Suburban had obviously been fitted out with special features. The glass was bullet resistant, and if the tint was any darker, it would be opaque.

Gilmer had a short-cropped hair cut and friendly eyes, although he had not smiled yet, so who could really tell. He wore a dark-blue suit with white socks and spit-polished shoes. McDuffie, on the other hand, was dressed in a long-sleeved shirt and pants only. He looked like he was on his way to a sports bar. Mick leaned forward and gave McDuffie the once over. He could see a bulge on his right ankle where a holster probably was. Gilmer also sported a holstered weapon that revealed itself as his jacket front fell away when he turned to face him.

Mick was satisfied that these two were legitimate agents and assumed that they were telling the truth about being FBI. Gilmer had flashed a badge, but Mick wouldn't know an FBI badge from a boy scout badge. McDuffie continued to swerve in and out of traffic making the ride rather uncomfortable. Mick turned to Gilmer who was holding onto the handle above the window to steady himself. Mick did likewise as the car tilted left and right against its suspension.

"OK," said Mick. "Shoot. What do you want to know?"

"We have some concerns about your involvement with Miss Young," said Gilmer. "Of course, we could be way off track, but it would be good to know exactly what your intentions are."

Mick could not help but roll his eyes. 'Are you fucking kidding me?' he asked himself. That's twice in twenty minutes he had been asked that same question. First, by the defense attaché, now it was the FBI! The SUV swerved again as McDuffie continued his impression of a bad Nascar racer. Mick decided enough was enough.

"Oi! Special Agent McDickhead! Pull the fucking car over!"

McDuffiee looked into the rear-view mirror at Gilmer. Gilmer merely nodded, and McDuffie pulled up at the curb coming to a stop. He turned around, arm over the back of his seat and glared at Mick.

"Thank fuck for that. Where did you learn to drive? At the fair?" he remonstrated. He then turned to Gilmer.

"Listen, I am dating Miss Young. That's about it. I am also helping her, where I can, to campaign... just as any good boyfriend would do. I have no political intentions. I just want to help my girlfriend in her job."

He went to open the car door and decided to give them one further blast. His mood had soured since his conversation with the brigadier, and now *this* stupidity by the FBI. It was like some dumb movie, but if it had been a movie, he would have walked out on it. Unfortunately, it was his life now.

"Next time, if you want to talk, then just come to me and talk. I'll tell you anything you want to know that I know. But if you don't have the decency to do that, and you think you need to intimidate me, then don't bother. Just take your badges and fuck off."

He went to get out and Gilmer leaned towards the open door.

"We'll be in touch, Major O'Rourke. We have lots of questions... for *you* in particular," he said menacingly. Mick shut the door. Although the glass was tinted dark, he could still make out McDuffie in the driver's seat. McDuffie gave him the bird as he drove away. His first meeting with the FBI was not as smooth as it could be, and he didn't care for another.

He was now past Du Pont Circle, further from the Capitol than when he had left the Australian Embassy. He decided to catch an Uber. He punched in his details and, to his surprise, an Uber was only a few hundred yards away. It arrived less than thirty seconds later. At least something was going right.

The sedan pulled up and Mick got into the front passenger seat. He wondered which country would be represented by its driver. He was not surprised to see an Asian driving, but he *was* surprised by his broad American accent. The driver smiled and asked him if he had a preference for the route. Mick just said, 'the fastest possible' and started to relax.

"How's your day been going," asked the driver. The Uber app said his name was Tim.

"A bit crazy," said Mick. "How 'bout yours?" he responded.

"Pretty good. You sound like you're English," said Tim.

"Australian," responded Mick. Tim then became a little animated. He had an Australian guy in his car who was on his way to the Capitol Building. Didn't he see his face on the news the other night? He looked at Mick, then back to the road, then back at Mick again.

"Are you that Aussie guy that's dating the Senator from Georgia?" he asked, looking at Mick very closely. This made Mick uncomfortable. He wanted his driver to be looking at the road, not at him. Unconsciously, he grabbed the seat and the door.

"If I said 'Yes', would you keep your eyes on the road?" he asked.

Tim slammed on the brakes. "Sorry, man," he said. "You must think I'm a lousy driver."

Mick smiled. "Nope. I've already had one bad driver today. He had no excuse. You're just excited."

"I sure am," said Tim. "I haven't had a celebrity in my car before," he said.

"I'm hardly a celebrity," responded Mick. "And she's not a Senator, she's a Representative... but yes, we're dating."

"This is so cool," said Tim. "I can't wait to tell my wife. She loves the two of you. She's been following you both since she saw you doing the Kenny Mountain thing," he said.

Mick thought that was rather strange that a local story had made it to Washington DC... but who knows if they had seen it on the internet or elsewhere? "Kennesaw Mountain... and thank you. I'll tell Representative Young she has fans here in DC."

"How can we donate to Miss Young's campaign," Tim offered. "Can I send you my email address so you can send me the details," he asked as they stopped at a traffic light.

Before Mick could suggest he go onto the campaign committee website, Tim had his phone out and was ready to take down his details. He saw that Mick hesitated.

"Sorry. That was a bit creepy. You don't know me from Adam. I'm just some dipshit Uber driver and I sound like some stalker. Sorry, Mick—I hope you don't mind me calling you that—but you and Maye have really touched my wife and I. If we lived in Georgia, we'd vote for her." Tim went to put his phone away and apologized again.

"You could go onto the campaign website, but send me your contact details and I'll send you and your wife a personal email," he offered.

Tim's eyes lit up and he scrambled to get his phone out before the lights turned green.

"707-132-5657," said Mick.

Tim punched it into his phone and sent him a text with his email address. Mick's phone buzzed notifying him. "My wife will be so thrilled," he said as they started up again. "Let us know how we can contribute."

Soon Mick was shaking his hand and saying goodbye as he was dropped off near the Capitol Reflecting Pool, but not before Tim got a selfie with Mick. Mick then waved him goodbye and headed up the steps. He was still thinking about the embassy and the FBI to really take in the sight of one of the most recognized buildings in the world, but it dawned on him how the trajectory of his life had changed so much since meeting that attractive girl at that dinner party in Alabama.

How many other guys could say that they told the PM to back off, and the FBI to fuck off in one day?

'Such is life!'

61

Georgetown

Maye took him to the member's dining room. It was nothing but a glorified bistro, but he didn't care. Maye was still very popular and even though her candidacy had ruffled feathers, she still had a lot of supporters eager to wish her luck and support.

If that wasn't enough, even a Democrat came over and told her that she thought that her appointment of a Democrat to her staff was a wonderful gesture.

"He was the obvious choice and the best man for the job," she told her Democrat fan. "The kids in Georgia deserve the best."

The two of them were then left alone to eat in peace, but many waved in passing obliging her to respond in kind.

"I had two very odd encounters today," Mick told his girlfriend. "One at the embassy and one on my way to Du Pont Circle."

"Why were you going to Du Pont Circle," she asked, confused.

"Oh, I wasn't," he said. "The FBI took me there." He then recounted his conversations with the brigadier and the ambassador, and then with the FBI agents.

Maye was concerned about the FBI agents. What did they want? Why hadn't they contacted her? Did Mick have anything that she needed to know about?

He assured her that they were just fishing, or doing their job, or justifying their existence, or whatever. In any case, he told them where to go. His main concern was not the FBI, but the Australian Army. He had been given a lot of leeway to stay on Maye's campaign not because they believed in her, but because Australian government was hedging its bets in the long term—and feathering its nest in the short term—with some good PR that drifted from the US onto Australian TVs.

Maye was still concerned about the FBI but put them out of her mind. She'd have a chat to the Attorney-General's staff later and tell them to be decent about things and be open and come and see them in a civilized manner, not using some sort of Hollywood drive-by pick up.

But what also interested Maye were the questions posed to Mick: what *were* his intentions?

They had both tried to avoid the serious conversation for some time now, but with the mid-terms over, and the new session of Congress now underway—and the campaign for the White House building up steam—what was to become of their relationship? If they were to be serious, then the hard conversation would need to be had.

Maye suggested that they postpone it until that night. A nice dinner and some wine and then a serious talk. Mick was not sure where this would lead, and he felt that it was all to come down to him and his decision. In any case, Maye needed to know before she really started the campaign run.

They finished their meal with the uncomfortable expectation of a serious discussion to come. Mick didn't feel like having dessert.

* * *

At Maye's apartment on Prospect Street, not far from the Key Bridge, they had finished their dinner and were drinking a nice red from a Virginia vineyard. They sat near the window and watched the cars pass on the street below. Mick thought he heard his phone buzz but checking it it showed nothing. He fiddled with it, trying to delay the inevitable.

"Are you as uncomfortable as I am?" asked Maye, knowing that 'the conversation' that dare not speak its name was about to be had.

"A little," replied Mick, trying to sound a bit upbeat. Maye looked over at her boyfriend, this man from the other side of the globe, who had done so much to help her get to where she was: a serious contender for the Republican nomination. If it had not been for him and his support and his 'out of the box' ideas, she would be just another representative from Georgia. And while being a representative from Georgia sounded impressive, who could name the representative from the 11th District from ten years ago? Very few people, that's for sure. So, regardless of what people thought about her position, it was just one of hundreds, and one that would be forgotten in a few years' time... unless... unless she was elected to the White House. She daren't think about that possibility, though. She didn't want to jinx it.

In any case, it was this Australian man who had been instrumental in getting her to this situation, and if he would stay by her side, she knew it would only increase her chances. Besides, she loved him and wanted him to be with her forever.

She put down her wine glass and stood up. In the darkness of the apartment with just a couple of candles for light... and the glow from the streetlights casting shapes on the ceiling, she looked down at her boyfriend sitting on the chair near the window.

Maye hitched up her skirt and slid her panties down, letting them fall around her ankles. She kicked them off and watched Mick's face, slightly shocked. This was obviously *not* what he had expected was about to occur. Maye then undid her blouse and let if fall to the floor, then her bra. She stood in front of her boyfriend with just a short skirt on. In one deft move, she undid the button that held it together, slid the zipper down slightly and let the skirt fall to the floor. And that is where she stood: naked, bare, vulnerable. The congresswoman stood naked in front of her boyfriend in a darkened room in Washington. Not four hours earlier she had been voting on bills in the House.

She knelt down and unzipped Mick's pants and pulled them off. It didn't take more than a few seconds for him to show his excitement. She stepped forward and straddled him, letting him slide inside her. She lowered her full weight onto him and, cupping his head in her hands, kissed him passionately while gyrating her hips slowly and rhythmi-cally.

"I thought I needed to thank you for everything you have done for me over the last twelve months," she whispered in his ear. She then straightened her back and placed her nipple in his mouth and pulled his head gently into her chest. While he sucked on her nipple and ran his hands over her back and waist, she kissed the top of his head smelling his hair. He had been busy all day and had not showered, but she delighted in his smell. The more she took in his scent, the more aroused she became.

In the dim light of the apartment in Prospect Street, Georgetown, Miss Maye Leigh Young, member of the 116th United States Congress; Representative of the 11th Congressional District of Georgia, and potential Republican presidential nominee, straddled her boyfriend naked until he climaxed inside her. At that moment, Major Michael O'Rourke of the Australian Army, assigned for duty with the US Army in Alabama, posted to the other side of the planet from his home in Australia, designated commanding officer of the Australian Army's Aviation School, did not want to be anywhere else in the world, nor with anyone else in the world. At that moment, he would give it all up to stay with her.

62

The Conversation That Dare Not Speak Its Name

As they lay in the darkened room, staring up at the light cast from the streetlamps onto the ceiling, they remarked about where their lives had taken them. Mick told Maye how happy he was to have come into her orbit, even though everything seemed to be getting so complicated. He told her how he often missed the simpler days of being a pilot back in Australia.

He told her about the late-night sorties as they flew through the outback on some exercise. The crew would be silent as they would all be exhausted from the day's flying, the rhythmic thump of the helicopter's rotors and the vibration of the engines would somehow combine to form a sort of relaxing, mechanical blanket that soothed them.

He would describe the myriad of stars that could be seen in the Australian desert, so many more than could be seen from the cities and so many more than could be seen in the Northern Hemisphere. He described how when he wore night vision goggles, the black sky became a dark green with millions of light green flecks, the stars that only appeared to those who wore the goggles. And how you could see flashes of shooting stars, too small for the naked eye but brilliantly bright through the NVGs. Below them, not a light could be seen. There was no-one for hundreds of miles in any direction. How he missed those early days of his flying career, and the stark and lonely Australian landscape.

Maye listened. She did not know how this evening would turn out. They had enjoyed each other's bodies with passion, but now were pensive and somber as they talked about their pasts. She liked hearing about Australia and would like to visit one day, but for her, her life had gone where she had not expected. But listening to how he described flying, she knew that this conversation was not going to go the way she had hoped. She could tell that he was about to break the bad news to her that he had decided to pursue his career in the army and return to Australia. She stared at the ceiling.

"You miss it, don't you?" she said. It was asked rhetorically, although Mick felt obliged to answer.

"Of course. I'm sure you miss flying too, don't you?" he asked with genuine curiosity.

"I miss being in the air force," she responded. "I miss the camaraderie and the adventure. And I will miss you, too."

Mick got up on one elbow and looked at her, puzzled. "Where are you going?" he asked.

She turned to look at him. "I'm just waiting for you to tell me that you're going back to Australia. Back to the army."

Mick smiled and lay his head back down on the pillow. "I'm doing nothing of the sort," he said. I intend to stay with you for as long as I can."

And with that, she turned and embraced him. They held each other tightly and kissed as though their very existence on this planet relied upon it.

In about eighteen months, the next president of the United States would be inaugurated. They had that long to make sure that it was going to be Maye. Mick knew that for the time being, he was protected and had the freedom to be involved, provided he didn't embarrass his government... but how long would that last? He knew his promotion and posting as commanding officer was not going to happen. Even if he did return to Australia, it would be given to someone else, and he'd be out of the running for it. He may get promoted, but he wouldn't have a unit to command and would probably end up in a headquarters staff job, somewhere in Canberra. But at the moment he didn't really care.

Now it was time to come up with some good campaigning to counter what would be negative messaging from President Troup.

63

Sixteen Months is a Short Time in Politics

By the end of June, they had come up with a plan of how the rest of the year would be spent on the campaign trail finishing up with the presidential primaries the following February. It was sixteen months until the presidential election.

Many detractors from within the Republican Party criticized Maye for potentially splitting the conservative vote and for pandering to the Democrats. She pointed out that partisan politics was why the American people were cynical and becoming more and more divided. It was while she was sitting in her office pondering the latest insult from within her own party that she came up with the perfect slogan for her campaign.

Though the GOP had provided her with reports and recommendations from communications advisers and focus groups, the ideas that Mick and she had come up with had proven popular and successful. So why not go with her gut?

Excitedly, she called her boyfriend.

"I have the perfect slogan for the campaign," she said down the phone.

"Hit me with it, spunky!" he cheekily replied.

"Well, you know how you remarked that the country seems to be divided more than ever?"

Mick agreed with her. How it seemed that no-one was happy, and that everyone seemed to be perpetually offended about something. And that this once great nation had lost its confidence such that the United States did not seem... well... united any more.

"That division got me thinking, and so did all the jag-offs in the party that are giving me a hard time by saying I'm dividing the party," she continued. "So I was wondering how we can get this country, and all its states and territories and people and groups and minorities and majorities united once more... and it just came to me in a flash: 'Uniting these Great States'."

She paused allowing it to sink in. After a few seconds with Mick not saying a word, she began to wonder if perhaps it was not such a great slogan. Then her boyfriend broke the interminable silence.

"I... love... it!"

They began discussing it excitedly, building upon it and capitalizing upon it.

'*Maye Young: Uniting these Great States.*'

* * *

Mick had started sending back reports to the Chief of Army and to the prime minister through the defense attaché and through the ambassador. He called it 'feeding the beast', but now that those two egos were being stroked, things seemed a bit more optimistic. The PM was happy that they still had a player in the game, even if President Troup was none-too-pleased, and the Chief of Army was happy because he could concentrate on more serious matters like running the Australian Army, instead of pandering to the PM's staffers who wanted Lieutenant General Braddon to tell them every time Major O'Rourke blew his nose. The chief was also happy that Mick's public appearances, especially when he wore his uniform, replete with emu plumes, were actually turning out to be good PR for his army. A fact that was not lost on many of the American senior officers that paid him office calls when they were in

Australia, or the US Ambassador who, all of a sudden, becoming more 'chummy' with him. It didn't hurt for them to hedge their bets.

But now the time had come to really hammer home the campaign.

Maye had a number of commitments that would see her so busy that she would have little time to campaign herself. She had her Washington commitments that had her reviewing bills and amendments and the general daily churn of being a member of Congress. And of course, she had her district responsibilities back in Georgia, and then her 'homework' with the members of the GOP that were her support and training team, preparing her for the arduous journey to November the following year and the presidential election. In between, it would be appearances and debates and interviews.

Her trump card however, was Mick. Not only had he come up with some great campaign tactics, but he had also proven to be very popular with current and former military personnel. Maye had made sure she joined both the American Legion and the Veterans of Foreign Wars, both of which she was eligible for through her service. This was not lost on both organizations back in Georgia and now it would be pivotal to her campaign. The fact that Mick was popular with both—as Maye's partner and as a veteran in his own right—meant that he had been warmly welcomed at both organizations, even if he was not eligible to join.

During the 'March to Tennessee', Legion Riders on their Harley's had ridden formations of honor for the march and were a hit with the kids. And so it was another of Mick's campaign ideas that they were about to commence on a new type of road trip. Up the East Coast through the safe Republican state of South Carolina to hard-to-predict North Carolina. Virginia would be a hard sell, but Pennsylvania could be tipped in favor of the Republicans and in favor of Maye with its twenty electoral college votes.

Even though they were concentrating on the primaries, it didn't hurt to wave the flag early and get an idea of how the public felt about Maye. He would use the road trip to gather as much information and experiences that could be turned into an understanding of what were the important issues that Maye and he needed to know. But he was a pragmatist, also. As much as he would like to spend time in the states with big populations, the smaller states did not often receive the attention they craved. Maye would do better in the big states, but Mick could be useful in the smaller states.

It was a waste of time going any further north of Pennsylvania; those states were too blue and pro-Democrat. It was imperative to soften President Troup's popularity in the safe Republican states and convince any constituencies that might 'jump ship' from the Democrat camp to come to the Republican cause. So from Pennsylvania it would be a quick detour to friendly territory into West Virginia's rust belt and its abandoned factories and abandoned dreams, and then westward-ho to Ohio.

Michigan was up for grabs. It had definite Democratic leanings but the death of American manufacturing, especially in the auto industry, had left many in the state disillusioned and disenfranchised, just as it had in West Virginia. But unlike West Virginia, Detroit would be difficult. Was it possible to win Michigan over? Mick had nothing to lose, so he put it on the list. From Michigan it was into Indiana and Kentucky bypassing Illinois altogether. Like New England and New York, Chicago was too blue, and it would be a waste of valuable time. Instead, it was through Tennessee, Arkansas and Missouri ending up in Iowa for the State Fair at the end of August.

Mick drew his plan on a map of the US showing which states voted for Troup at the last presidentials. He and Jesús were at a Mexican chain restaurant, not far from Maye's office in Marietta, Georgia. Even though Jesús had protested that no self-respecting Mexican would be seen dead in such a place, they had a special deal on tap beer, so he relented. They had just finished their meal and another intensive Spanish language lesson when Mick pushed his diagram to Jesús for him to see.

"What do you think?" asked Mick to Jesús. His body man ignored him and didn't even bother to look up from his phone.

"*En Español, jefe,*" he merely said, telling his boss to ask him in Spanish.

"*Ah Mierda,*" he swore. "*¿Qué piensas?*" He said, asking him what he thought... and then, "*¿Es así como lo dices?*" asking him if that was how one said it.

"*Si,*" Jesús replied, and looked at the map. "Have you thought about going from post to post; Legion and VFW? They could host you in every key town. I mean, you've already been invited to a few in Georgia... why not make them your steppingstones as you travel to Iowa," Jesús suggested, giving his boss a break and speaking in English. "Also, one of their programs is the 'Get out the Vote' program. They want people to be more aware of what their politicians are doing. Could be a good source of free publicity, *jefe!*"

Mick considered that for a second and realized that it was perfect. He connected well with veterans, and with plenty of Vietnam Veterans still charging around the country, they would help with the gray vote; and with more recent and current veterans of service in uniform also swelling the ranks of the VFW and American Legion... and sometimes in both, they were a ready source of helpers and boosters. President Troup had never served in uniform having been a businessman all his life, so this was yet another way to differentiate Maye's campaign from his.

Mick turned to his mate and said in his best possible Spanish: "*¡Tu idea es excelente!* Let's call it: 'Uniting these Great States: The Search for the Real America'.*"

Together they spit-balled some more ideas and then called Rob Early and Sally-Anne Atkinson and arranged to meet with them to discuss it along with Maye. They would then sell it to the campaign committee.

As Mick and Jesús prepared to call it a night, they passed a TV showing a repeat of the Superbowl from February, the day Maye was told of the Party's wish for her to contest.

"What team do you follow, *jefe?*" asked Jesús.

"I don't have an NFL team, mate," he replied. Jesús looked at him and paused.

"Why not make that part of your trip," he suggested. "You're searching for the right football team to follow. They'll be having their summer training sessions. Could be good publicity."

Mick smiled. His bodyman was hitting home runs with his suggestions, or perhaps he should say 'scoring touchdowns'. Go from VFW/Legion post to post; search for the right football team; these were the things that would connect with middle-America—specifically males—and would cross race, age and demographic boundaries at the same time. This would be a good campaign... and a fun one, too!

The road trip would commence the following week, the first week of July, and finish in Iowa in mid-August. They would try and organize special events on special regional celebrations. Sally-Anne would be instrumental in orchestrating these events and would rely heavily on volunteers in each location. She and Pam and Rob would travel ahead where necessary to commence the coordination.

It would be a lean team and so they had to be smart. They could not rely on paying people to help out now that Troup knew that a big slice of Republican campaign funding was going to Maye's campaign. Volunteers and good will would be the key.

64

The Lean Team

The plan was met with positive responses. Sally-Anne trusted Mick's judgment, and Jesús was proving to be an asset. Rob and Pam would be on the road with them, also. Meanwhile, the campaign team that the GAGOP had put together with the blessing and funding of the RNC, would remain with Maye and continue selling her by more conventional means.

Mick's '*The Search for the Real America*' would be a sideshow while the main attraction was 'getting ready in the wings'; they were the support band before the main act, whose responsibility was to get the crowed worked up and enthusiastic.

As much as their little group was a veritable United Nations, they would still have a hard sell. Maye, with her Asian heritage and air force background; Mick, the Australian army officer who was proving popular with many different groups; Sally-Anne, the Atlanta socialite and soccer mom turned campaign strategist (who had her husband over a barrel... a useful ace up her sleeve); Rob, the smart and handsome black college student whose maturity belied his age; Pam, who could be mistaken for a ditzy college co-ed but who was a whiz at social media; and Jesús, the Mexican-born, former US Army paratrooper. This 'rag-tag bunch of misfits' as Mick had branded them, was going up against the full campaign weight of President Troup, and his deep pockets, in what some had predicted would be an internecine battle within the

Party's ranks that would end up with both camps battered and bleeding and leaving the Republican Party the ultimate loser. The more optimistic saw it as a great opportunity to rid the party of a president who rode into power on the strength of a disillusioned electorate—against all odds, mind you—but who had, so far, not achieved anything of note, except alienating so many within, and outside, the United States. He still had a devoted following, but many of those followers were feeling a bit disillusioned. The promises that he said he would deliver still seemed far off, if they were even conceivable in the first place. Would they still be promises yet to be realized in two years when it came time to head to the polls?

Mick called the group together for his 'round table'. "No idea is stupid," he would say and none of them felt that they couldn't make a suggestion. The result was a wide range of campaign strategies from which to choose, some more likely to be effective than others.

"Not only is '*The Search for the Real America*' key to this year," he said, "we have to buy time for Maye to get completely up to speed in time for the debates and for other preparations. She'll need to be on the campaign trail in earnest later this year in the lead up to the primaries next year.

"What we need to do is some mis-direction. We need to be the story for the next several weeks. We are Maye's team, and we will be representing Maye. She will be doing her preparations and will inject into the road trip at opportune times... but we have to be as big a story as she is.

"It is vital that we draw President Troup out and let him step on his own dick. Maye can then remain 'Miss Clean'. And it is vital that we use soft diplomacy if we want to convince Troup supporters that Maye is a better choice for them."

"What do you suggest is the way we make our story bigger than her and bigger than Troup?" asked Pam.

Mick looked at each member of the team and smiled. He then pointed to each member deliberately and said, "Black; brown; white; American; Australian; female; veterans; wealthy background; not-so-wealthy background." It was almost improper the way he said it, but all he was doing was stating the obvious, but it also epitomized the '*Uniting these Great States*' theme of Maye's campaign.

"We are a diverse bunch, not by design, but by capability and what we have to offer. *That* is what we need to capitalize upon. Our little United Nations here is a great story. We'll offer ourselves up to the PR girl in the campaign team and see what she can come up with to enhance the *Uniting these Great States* message. I'm sure she'll be able to concoct some good ideas," he offered.

He thought for a moment. "It's too bad we don't have a film crew coming with us," he said. "We could capture everything and could turn it into a documentary." He looked at Pam. "Why don't you make the campaign team think that that's a good idea, too. See what they suggest."

* * *

As the weeks passed and the preparations for Mick's '*The Search for the Real America*' were underway, the situation eased somewhat, but definitely not enough. Even though donations were coming in, when the team filed their returns to the Federal Electoral Commission, they compared their numbers to that of Troup. The president came from a wealthy family that had made its money in real estate and so he had the advantage of significant investment income streams, and political favorites with deep pockets. In comparison, Maye's numbers were good, but insignificant in comparison.

Maye put her beautiful Lake Allatoona house on the market, buying, instead, a condo closer to her campaign office in Marietta, and sinking the rest into her campaign. Mick had advised her not to do that. Her house was beautiful and if she was not successful, then at least she would find solace in that home. Her response was that if she wasn't prepared to risk it all, then she wasn't serious about the White House.

But it was obvious that Maye's team had to be smart and prudent with this campaign. They would have to rely upon free sources of good publicity to get her face on to small screens and not-so-small screens.

This was definitely the time for digital disruption alongside conventional courses of action. The *Search for the Real America* was key. The road trip had to help Maye not only connect with voters, but had to gently persuade them to believe in her and move away from Troup.

Sally-Anne and Jesús had the job of coordinating the stops at each VFW and Legion post. Mick gave them specific instructions to find every significant ceremony each post was holding that coincided with their schedule or, if there wasn't one, suggest that if one were to be arranged, that Mick would attend.

To help with accommodation costs, the Winnebago was pressed into action as a residence for Mick and Jesús and Rob, while Sally-Anne and Pam would stay in hotels. When compared to other campaigns that had the attendant luxury buses for the candidate and his team, and a convoy of cars for the supporting staff, the Maye Young campaign was really doing it on the cheap. It consisted of five persons, a Winnebago and a Ford station wagon.

Try as hard as they might, the money coming in did not cover the outgoings enough to allow them to have a war chest and the SRA—as 'the Search for the Real America' road trip had become called—threatened to wither on the vine. A crowdfunding account had been raised and it was generating some revenue, but not to the same level as Troup and his business associates would muster. They had been keeping the dire financial situation away from Maye as much as they could, but eventually they had to admit that they were experiencing difficulties in gaining enough finance for this venture that would take them through half of the contiguous United States for nearly two months. If they couldn't find the money, they would have to drastically change their plans.

* * *

Three days later, Pam, who had been doggedly maintaining the campaign's social media presence, was posting to the various platforms when she was messaged by a sportswear company eager to assist. They specifically wanted Mick to be a part of the negotiations and asked if she would give them a call.

Pam was aware of the dire straits they were in financially, and in an effort to be the problem solver, elected to call them without conferring with the other members of the team. She was glad she did. The sportswear company confided in her that they had been following Maye's mid-term campaign and were impressed in how she handled herself and how her boyfriend did likewise. They were eager to provide assistance in the hope that Mick would do some interviews with them about the campaign. In return, they would pay a six-figure sum. It was imperative that it remained secret because the interviews would only be made public if Maye won the election.

Almost bursting with pride, Pam took Mick aside and told him of this opportunity.

"I think this could be the answer to our money problems," said Pam. "You are great in front of the camera, so that's why they want you."

"It sounds like they want me or Maye to endorse their sportswear," he queried. "Did they say that?"

"No," Pam assured him. "They want to interview you and then air the interviews if Maye gets elected. They want to be seen as the first supporters. If Maye doesn't get elected, then their interviews won't be seen. It sounds like they're hedging their bets.

"Plus," she continued, "they want to raise a YouTube channel and do a range of interviews of sports personalities to raise their profile. You will be their first interview." She was almost giddy with excitement. This was the sort of stuff she loved, digital disruption, and to think that she could help a company raise its YouTube channel by supplying Mick was making her overjoyed.

Mick thought about it. They specifically asked that this be kept secret. He guessed that that was logical. What's more, if they did try and corner him into a product endorsement, he was smart enough to back out of a tight corner. And while he was a bit uneasy about not discussing this with Maye and the other members of the team, he didn't think that there was any issue with it, provided that the payment was declared with the Federal Election Commission as a donation.

He called them, and they arranged for a meeting. Maye was back in

Washington as Congress was in session, and the rest of the team had been given a few days off by Maye in appreciation for their hard work anyway, so he agreed to meet with them and do the interview. They arranged for his flights to San Francisco to meet with the principals of the company, and to speak with one of their YouTube composers who was raising the new channel for the organization.

Picked up in a car from his hotel, he was dropped off in the financial district, not far from the TransAmerica Tower. There he was met by two suited men who took him to a coffee shop on the ground floor of the building for a quick coffee and a chat before going upstairs to do the interview. One of the suited men introduced himself as Paul Putnam, Marketing Director. The other was introduced to him as David Schley, Chief Financial Officer of the company. Putnam was tall and confident. A typical PR person. Schley on the other hand, was a smaller, weedy type who had a nervous expression and kept looking around as if he didn't want to be photographed. They gave him two envelopes: one was a list of the questions they were going to ask him in front of the camera.

"We want you to feel at ease," said Putnam. "These are the questions we want to discuss. Take some time to read them and consider your answers.

"We'll do the interview upstairs and you are free to stop it at any time if you don't like the direction it is heading.

This made Mick feel a little easier. Provided the interviewer stuck to these questions, there was nothing in them that could embarrass Maye or himself. Schley then held up another envelope.

"And this is for your campaign," he said. "Open it."

Mick obliged. In it was a check for one million dollars. Mick's eyes widened. He could see the response to his reaction in the faces of Putnam and Schley. He then tried to return to a poker face, but it was too late. Now he knew why Schley seemed nervous.

"That is very generous," said Mick. "I was under the impression that it was going to be a six-figure sum. This exceeds our expectations."

"Well," said Schley nervously, "we think that Maye may de-throne

Troup. The Democrats can't seem to get their act together, so we're putting our money on who we think has the best chance to beat him."

Mick knew that Maye was a superior candidate, hell a superior person, compared to the president, but to hear it from two businessmen on the other side of the country, and to have them show their confidence with a seven-figure donation, made him feel supremely confident.

And just like that, the search for Maye's middle America—the real America—was back on track.

* * *

While he was in San Francisco, he paid a visit to Maye's mother in Oakland, just across the bay. Welcomed like a prodigal son, he was taken into their home. Besides a few obvious Chinese trinkets, there was nothing to show that Maye's mother or grandmother had any connection to China, except in their appearance. There wasn't even the aroma of Asian cooking, which always got his mouth watering. Deep down he was hoping that he might be served some Chinese delicacies, but it did not seem to be a house that devoted much effort to Chinese culture or food.

Maye's grandmother was old and frail, approaching ninety-two, but still spritely in her mind even if her body was failing her. And Maye's mother was enthralled by her daughter's new beau, and went out of her way to make him feel a part of the family. Her Eurasian heritage had blessed her with stunning good looks, still evident now in her seventies, but looking as though she was in her fifties. Maye had certainly inherited her exotic beauty.

As they sat and chatted, the TV on, but the sound turned down, a story about President Troup was televised. The bottom third caption said 'US-China relations on the mend' and images of Troup with his advisers and then images of manufacturing in China were shown. Though their conversation had been cordial and civilized, and Maye's mother and grandmother on their best behavior, suddenly the older woman began yelling at the TV in Chinese.

"*Nǐ bèipànle wǒmen de jiārén!*" she cried out, pointing at the TV where

Troup and his secret service agents, including Agent Lee, were seen at a function at the Chinese Embassy.

"I'm sorry," said Maye's mother to Mick. "Sometimes she gets very animated when it comes to politics. She's not a big fan of the president."

Mick saw Maye's grandmother almost ready to throw her cane at the TV. "What was she yelling?"he asked.

"'You betrayed us', or 'you betrayed our family', or something like that. I don't speak Mandarin very well. I guess she's angry because Troup's not taking a harder line against China."

Mick sat back, bemused by the old woman. She, in the meantime, had completely forgotten that they had company, and was pointing her cane at the TV and muttering angrily at the image of Troup and Lee and some other official.

65

The Little Blue Bird is Pooping

The step-off for the road trip was fast approaching. Pam and Sally-Anne had ensured that Cheryl Macon, the campaign's official PR head, was feeding the media monster.

It was hard to gauge what impact the road trip was having on Georgians. The *Atlanta Journal Constitution* barely mentioned it except for an article or two. Fox News did one segment and discussed the impact that the two-horse race would have on the Republican Party, but aside from that, none of the other news outlets seemed the least bit interested.

President Troup, as expected, had begun tweeting his displeasure at the 'turncoat' from within his own party. Maye was singled out as a candidate who was too young and that could not be trusted to understand business the way that he did. As was their plan, Maye did not respond in kind. Instead, her tweets merely said things like: *"Thank you Mr. Troup for letting people know your thoughts about me as your competitor for the nation's highest office,'* or *'Mr. Troup's comment, right or wrong, demonstrates what is great about this nation - the right to hold an opinion'. #Young2020. #Young-Candidate/Old-Fashioned Values.* She was also careful not to use his title but referred to him as 'Mister'. No need to reinforce the fact that he was the president, at least for now.

But as expected, he was churning out excrement courtesy of his

Twitter account, and the little blue bird was trying to crap all over the campaign, but not once landing on the desired target.

Maye's dignified responses may have been driving the president crazy, but it was also having the desired effect with the electorate. Troup was looking more like a baby who had thrown a tantrum and had tossed all his toys out of the crib, while Maye was holding the moral high ground firmly, but still with grace and dignity.

In the meantime, the GAGOP's campaign team was starting to pay dividends. They had also been hard at work creating campaign collateral such as logos, flyers, posters and the like... the usual paraphernalia. But they had been quite inventive about it. Upon Mick's suggestion, a lot of the 'candid' images showed the varied background of Maye's inner team. It was unintentional, that they should be so diverse, but it was absolute gold dust for the PR team and the subtle messaging.

As head of the PR Team, Cheryl Macon was virtually salivating at the thought of capitalizing on it: interviews and videos with Rob and with Jesús and with Sally-Anne and Pam—and of course, Mick and Maye. She was able to use the images of Rob with the rebel flag, some of which were absolutely stunning— "Annie Liebovitz stunning," she would say. She also dug up images of Maye when she was in uniform in the air force, and also when she was flying C-130 transports, along with images of Mick flying Chinooks in Afghanistan, and Jesús on the ground also in Afghanistan. She organized for some portraits to be taken of Sally-Anne and Pam and Rob.

"My idea," she told them all, "is to make the team's diversity central to your minor campaign," she said proudly. Sally-Anne and Rob and Pam tried to hide their smirk at 'Cheryl's idea'. This had already been worked out in their round table but, as Mick said, it was important for the campaign team to feel that these were their ideas if they were to keep the GAGOP on side.

"I've organized for a camera team to accompany you and they'll film as much as they can which we can use for social media," Cheryl proudly proclaimed.

"Keep all the footage," said Mick. "Make sure that the team captures it as though they were filming a movie. We can use it to make a documentary and release it prior to the primaries."

Cheryl smiled. She had been told that Mick had some good instincts about campaign imagery, and this was definitely the case. The whole team had marveled at some of his ideas, some of which they had agreed to with some skepticism... but so far they had all virtually worked. They wondered what other things he had up his sleeve.

66

One Small Step

It was the first day of July when the team commenced the '*Search for the Real America*'.

The camera team organized by Cheryl headed off first after filming the low-key farewell from Maye's offices in Marietta. They had stage-managed the departure with Mick shown kissing Maye goodbye and hugging her until Rob and Jesús dragged him away. It was cheesy and fake, but the viewers would lap this up.

They did a detour to Stone Mountain so they could get some footage of the Winnebago passing the huge engraving of the Confederate generals and President Davis carved into the side of the monolith. All this was 'B'-roll footage, and Mick and the camera team knew that these sorts of detours would be a necessary evil on this road trip. There were other landmarks in Atlanta they could have used, but he thought it important to highlight the history of the South. "No reason why cancel culture should affect us and our message," he said to the team.

Between each vehicle they had a UHF radio. As they finished at Stone Mountain, Sally-Anne, who was now riding with the film crew, contacted the other vehicles and told them to follow her to Snellville, about six miles away.

Mick and Jesús in the Winnebago followed Pam and Rob in the Ford, and in front was Sally-Anne and the film crew. As they drove, well-wishers honked at them and gave them the thumbs up. Even though they had not received as much coverage as they had hoped, there were enough people in Georgia who recognized Maye's smiling face on the side of the RV and the Stars and Stripes and rebel flags.

As they approached Snellville, they followed the film crew into a driveway off Highway 78. Mick and Jesús immediately recognized it by its flagpole. It was an American Legion post. Mick was not sure why they were there. Their first stop was supposed to be Gainesville, about eighty miles away from Maye's office, not Snellville, an outer suburb of Atlanta. But once they got into the post's parking lot, they saw the reason. There, in their American Legion colors, were ten Legion Riders on their Harley-Davidsons.

Mick and Jesús got out of the RV and went over. The Legion Riders saw Mick and came over to meet him. They greeted him and Jesús as brothers, as fellow soldiers. The commander called Mick 'Major O'Rourke' and Mick had to rein him in and tell him that he was 'Mick. Just plain Mick'. The commander acquiesced and called him by his first name, and they stood around and 'jawed off' about their respective times in uniform in those days when they were 'ten-foot tall and bullet proof', as they would say. While this was happening, Sally-Anne and Pam raced around with the film crew, and gathered candid imagery, both still and video. Within minutes, Pam had images posted online onto their Instagram and Facebook and Twitter accounts. Her intention, and one that would prove critical during the whole road trip, was 'real time' updates.

The commander of the Legion Riders explained to Mick and Jesús what was happening.

"We've organized to escort your campaign convoy," he said, looking at the three vehicles that made up this campaign convoy with a bit of a smile, "to the county line past Buford, where we will hand you over to the Gainesville Chapter who will escort you the rest of the way to Gainesville," he explained.

"Whose idea was this?" asked Mick, delighted.

The commander pointed to Sally-Anne who just shrugged her shoulders and said, "It was Jesús' idea. I just thought these boys would add some color and character."

Pam's phone started chirping its notifications as followers 'liked' what they saw. Pam held up her phone. "It's starting," she said as her phone continued to chime its notifications.

Mick, absolutely thrilled at this wonderful gesture, turned to the Legion Riders' commander, and in true military fashion requested instructions.

"Commander, we're ready for your convoy orders," he said with a military voice. This deferment of authority was received with great appreciation by the American Legion, and though they may not have realized it, they unconsciously 'braced up' and took on a serious and professional demeanor, just as soldiers do when orders are about to be given. To the film crew and Sally-Anne, Pam and Rob, who had never been associated with soldiers before, this instinctive response by these ex-military men was novel and somewhat comforting. What they saw were professionals taking charge and working together.

The commander called them all in and gave them their orders. The riders would ride point and tail-end charlie of the convoy, that is to say, 'front and back'. Right hand lane. Lights on. Maintain the speed limit. Stop when separated to allow the convoy to rejoin. They then discussed the routes and the procedure for laager (or stopping at the end of the route). The film crew was permitted freedom of movement and captured this orders group. So did Pam. It would be posted by the time the convoy would leave the Legion post and shared between the VFW and Legion posts.

Jesús looked at Mick at the end of the convoy orders and said, "Now this is more like it, boss!" Mick smiled and gave him a fist bump. They both appreciated the no-nonsense military ways of professional soldiers, even if these soldiers were sporting beards and pot bellies and a few more gray hairs than they would have liked. But once a soldier...

They then returned to their cars; the film crew set up near where the driveway entered busy Highway 78 ready to film the departure of the campaign convoy with its American Legion motorcycle escorts. They didn't realize it at the time, but this little ceremony would be repeated the full length of the 'Search for the Real America' road trip and would get bigger and more ceremonial. Jesús' idea, and Sally-Anne's eye for the spectacle and drama, had combined to create a unique signature for their journey.

Past Buford, on I-985, the American Legion Riders Chapter of Snellville met their counterparts from Gainesville, and conducted a handover/takeover on the county line. This was captured on video and then the convoy re-commenced with the Gainesville Riders taking them to Gainesville. Yet again, Pam and the film crew captured a short video and posted it to social media. The Legion Riders shared it amongst their legion brothers and with the other legion posts in Georgia and South Carolina and beyond.

At Gainesville they were welcome to park their RV at the Legion Post while the others checked into a hotel nearby. That afternoon Mick and Jesús attended a legion meeting as guests and Mick discussed Maye's candidature to a mixed audience of Troup supporters and those that supported Maye. There was also a smattering of Democrats supporters there who politely listened. Mick was able to mix easily with them all, including the Vietnam-era veterans, and by the end of the night he had them eating out of his hands.

Later in the evening he went to talk to the post commander.

"Us staying in Gainesville is no accident," he told the commander. "We know you have a memorial to Vietnam Veterans here," he said. "Jesús and I would like to hold a vigil tonight at the memorial and see in the dawn there," he told him. "No media. No fanfare. We just want to honor the fallen," he told him sincerely.

The post commander was a veteran of the First Gulf War with almost twenty years in the army himself. Now he was the local president of the Gainesville Chamber of Commerce, and the owner of a print shop. He thought it was a great idea. He then called the other members of the legion who were at the bar and told them of Mick's idea. They all offered to participate.

Mick contacted Sally-Anne, Pam and Rob and the film crew and told them that he and Jesús were going to stay at the legion post that night, and that the rest of them could have the night off. He made no mention of the vigil.

* * *

When night fell, Mick and Jesús parked their RV near the Vietnam Veterans' Memorial park. Mick took first watch and stood in front of the low stone wall that had upon it carved the names of the local citizens who lost their lives in Vietnam. All except for a few were army soldiers, the rest were marines.

Mick had intended to do the first watch for an hour and a half and had expected to be alone. What he didn't expect were the several American Legion members and Veterans of Foreign Wars members who had decided to join in. The result was Mick's lone vigil was held accompanied by around twenty others. Holding candles, they stood in silence. The older ones who had actually served in Vietnam, now well into their seventies, were encouraged to sit. Some of the more stubborn ones tried to remain standing for as long as they could, only to realize that though the enemy had not succeeded in taking their youth in the rice paddies and jungles of Vietnam, time inevitably had. Some of the Vietnam veterans were so distraught that their bodies would no longer allow them to stand in silence for ninety minutes, that they began to weep as they were forced to sit down on nearby benches. They were consoled by their comrades.

By around 9 p.m., the word had spread via the legion and VFW network, and more and more members arrived to participate. Some wives came also with food and drink.

As each sentry on the picket left the vigil, another took his place. This continued into the morning when the temperature dropped to near freezing, but still the former soldiers came, and still they stood.

A few of the wives who came out took photographs and videos but other than that, no media was invited. This was a solemn ceremony... not a publicity stunt.

The next day, the legion post held a ceremony at the memorial park and Mick and Jesús attended in uniform. The campaign team buzzed around taking photographs and video, but for Mick and Jesús this was not about photo opportunities. Like the night before, this was about honoring American servicemen and women. Sally-Anne, Pam and Rob could sympathize... but they certainly could not empathize.

The ceremony over, the team headed to their next port of call: Augusta, home of the University of Georgia, again escorted by Gainesville Legion Riders as they cruised down the Athens Highway to where they would be handed over to the next riders, a joint group from Jefferson and Statham. Even though Statham was not on the route, the word had passed around the American Legion posts about what they had done the night before. Suddenly, all the Legion Riders on the route wanted to participate. What had been a novel idea in Atlanta was now becoming a 'thing', and Sally-Anne could not be happier. It was providing a wealth of content for Pam to post on social media and the campaign social media accounts continued to get more and more likes and followers.

At Athens, they checked in with the local VFW post who were more than happy to welcome them and allow them to use their facility. Sally-Anne and Pam and Rob had not experienced the Legion Post at Gainesville, but upon Jesús' suggestion they stayed with him and Mick while the VFW members showed them their hospitality. Jesús was a member of the Atlanta chapter, and he recognized a couple of the Athens boys.

"Hey, Jesús!" said Tom Tucker, a member of the local post looking over towards Rob. "Who's that black kid over there?"

Jesús wasn't sure where this was going. Was this going to be the start of an uncomfortable situation? With hesitation, and with a certain defensiveness, he told him.

"That's Robert Early. He's one of our campaign workers, and he's a good..." Before Jesús could finish, Tom launched towards Rob.

"Hey guys!" he shouted to his fellow veterans, "This is that kid that carried the flag!"

When Tom reached him, he reached out to shake Rob's hand. Rob was taken aback by this, not knowing why this strange bearded white guy wanted to shake his hand. Suddenly, the other VFW members were crowding around him, slapping him on the back. It seemed that Rob's gesture the year before still resonated. One of the guys pulled out a book with newspaper clippings and printouts from the internet. The photo of Rob with the rebel flag had been printed and placed into the book. For the rest of the evening, Rob was a minor celebrity and the VFW veterans jostled to have their pictures taken with Rob the Rebel (as he had been nicknamed) and Mick and Jesús. Sally-Anne and Pam stood back and watched with glee. This was social media gold... and completely unscripted.

67

Going Viral

Before they left Georgia, they stopped in at Rob's alma mater, the University of Georgia. The Bulldogs, the college's football team, was having a spring training session and they sat in the bleachers with hundreds of other fans, to watch the training.

Some of the fans recognized the group and started to mob them looking for autographs and the like. One of the assistant coaches noticed the activity in the stands and went to investigate. He also recognized the group and invited them down to the sideline to watch with the other players waiting their turn to run onto the field.

A reporter from *Georgia,* the magazine of the University of Georgia, was covering the spring training and upon seeing the group took the opportunity to get some imagery and some interviews. Of course, Pam and Sally-Anne helped to stage-manage the situation and made sure their camera team got in on the action, and soon Rob was being featured flanked by two burly linebackers, or with 'Uga' the bulldog, the team's mascot, as the *Georgia* photographer posed them in various situations trying to get 'just the right shot'.

Jesús told the magazine's reporter—actually a journalism major in her senior year—that one of the reasons they were there was not only so Rob could show them around the school of which he was so proud, but because Mick wanted to learn more about American football so he could choose a team to root for. This, of course, was somewhat of a lie.

Mick knew exactly how American football worked, Maye had helped him with the rules during the Superbowl when she was given the news that she'd be supported for a tilt at the presidency. American football was somewhat similar to rugby league which he played back in Australia for a local suburban team on the weekends, but in the words of Jesús, "Why spoil a story with facts?" Pam captured this conversation on video and posted it to the platforms asking followers which team Mick should support in the NFL. Almost immediately, opinions started flooding in. Once Pam saw that they had hit a nerve with this question, she started posting images of Mick and Rob with the Bulldogs, or Mick being 'schooled' in the intricacies of American football by the head coach.

Every time someone suggested a team, Pam would ask why, and that would generate a whole tirade of responses for and against.

The 'Search for the Real America' was hitting a chord with veterans, motorcycle enthusiasts, football fans and more... and their social media followership, on all platforms, increased exponentially, particularly on YouTube where Mick's Australian accent could be heard, and him studiously listening to the rules of gridiron football as being explained to him by the coaches of the UGA Bulldogs.

The people of 'real America' were becoming very interested in this trip, and money was accruing rapidly through their crowdfunding platform... and it had only begun two days prior!

* * *

The next day they were getting ready to hit the road, waiting for their escort, but not before Sally-Anne was banging on the door of the RV.

"Have you seen the AJC?" she blurted excitedly, climbing the steps of the RV with Pam close behind. Slamming down the paper on the dining table of the RV was the *Atlanta Journal Constitution* paper. Rob, with his slim build and button-down conservative shirt and dockers, was pictured with the two huge, black, UGA linebackers in full uniform, and superimposed in the background was the rebel flag. Below it was a great image of Mick looking pensive as the coach is seen explaining something, their gaze looking towards something the coach was pointing out. The headline read: 'Searching for the Real America'.

"And Pam has some exciting news, too! Tell 'em, Pam," she squealed.

"Well, it seems that overnight we had a lot of interest from veterans and football fans," she said. "The VFW and Legion guys have shared it on their network, and it has gone viral among them. They have some great shots of you and Jesús at Gainesville..."

"Why didn't you tell us that you were going to do that vigil?" interjected Sally-Anne, a little put out.

"That was a private event for soldiers only," said Jesús, putting the matter to rest. "What else, Pam?"

She continued. "The VFW and American Legion are squabbling over who gets to escort us to Charleston.

"And then there's the football fans," she continued with a smile. "So far, we have three formal invitations from NFL teams to come and see their teams in practice: the Titans in Tennessee, the Pittsburgh Steelers and the Green Bay Packers."

Mick looked at Jesús. His suggestions, both of them, were paying significant dividends. It was the same with Rob. He was able to inject himself just at the right time to create situations that bamboozled the 'permanently offended' left wing liberals, although he had brought some criticism from black liberals, but he had predicted that from the moment he picked up the rebel flag, and he was ready for the criticisms. He was a brilliant tactician and, coupled with his articulate expression and good looks, the media loved him.

Between the three of them, they were hitting home runs and Sally-Anne and Pam were doing wonders getting the messaging out there. Sally-Anne's phone chimed.

"It's been doing that since 5 a.m!" she said proudly. She looked at her phone. A sudden expression of shock quickly turned into a smile.

"And, it seems that my husband approves!" She held up the phone so they could all see it. There was a text from The Chairman: 'GOP very happy with media coverage. Keep it up!'

Outside, the rumble of Harley Davidsons broke their reverie. They pulled the curtains of the RV aside to see about ten VFW riders... and more turning into the VFW car park, Stars and Stripes and battle flags flying. Their escort to commence their journey to Charleston in South Carolina was here!

68

Firing the Shots at Fort Sumter

Arriving at Charleston they had been handed from Legion or VFW post to the next post, like a baton in a relay. Along Interstates 20 and 26; through Augusta and into South Carolina; through Columbus and down to Charleston, the Winnebago and two station wagons—the meager convoy of candidate Maye Young—was swollen with scores of veterans on their motorcycles.

Each post had contacted the next ahead of time and had given them directions (provided by Mick and Jesús) on how to conduct the handover. They were to pull over on the side of the freeway at a spot already identified by the riders who were to take command of the next leg. At that site, the commander of the outgoing escort formally handed over responsibility for escort to the incoming escort commander. This was captured by the camera crew and, when they were underway again, Pam would take the footage of the process and add some simple sub-titles to it along with the badges of the VFW and American Legion, and where they were going to be next, and then post it. Upon Mick's suggestion, he told her to post the message: 'Bring a Battle Flag and have it signed by Rob Early—the soldier fighting against PC thuggery.'

The sharing of social media posts created its own microcosm such that when they got to just outside Orangeburg, halfway from Columbus in South Carolina to the coast and Charleston, the handover-takeover had taken on a definite ceremonial flavor.

A large Stars and Stripes was provided by the VFW to the American Legion for the ceremony. The VFW did not have any formal riders' group in that part of the state, so the American Legion Riders were to provide the escort with some VFW members riding in company. Also presented was a large rebel battle flag and the state flag of South Carolina. All three were to be in the vanguard of the forward escort, riding in accordance with flag etiquette: the Stars and Stripes in the middle, the South Carolina flag on the right, and the battle flag on the left.

As a measure of respect for Mick, an Australian flag was also obtained, and it would ride behind the three flags. The VFW and American Legion had combined and coordinated their escort duties and had created a ceremonial handover-takeover with their bikes arranged like horses with their riders standing at attention in front of each. With the handover of the convoy and the handover of the flags, the commander would hand the Stars and Stripes to the Ensign Riders—a new title they had created—and then the command would be given to 'mount up', whereupon they would ride in a pre-determined order and formation.

"How did they come up with that?" Sally-Anne remarked incredulously as they watched the new ceremony.

Jesús was taken by the raw emotion of it, and he struggled to hold back a tear. "That's just what soldiers do," he said.

While Mick and Jesús were deeply touched the others watched with respectful deference. But Sally-Anne, Pam and the camera crew saw great media opportunities and they buzzed around to get 'postworthy imagery' again. When they were back on the road, Pam did her magic in the back of the RV with Sally-Anne and the camera crew cameraman providing input while Rob drove one of the cars and the camera crew soundman the other.

Over the next twenty-four hours, the whole of the VFW and American Legion network shared and re-shared the imagery; they commented and gave it 'likes' and 'thumbs up' and however else they could show their appreciation, support and good wishes. It did not take long for it to spread past the VFW and Legion networks and the network of followers that Pam and Sally-Anne had been painstakingly gathering.

They pulled into the American Legion post on James Island in Charleston to spend the night so they could be ready to head to Fort Sumter, the famous American Civil War battle site, the following morning. That afternoon and into the evening the American Legion post hosted an informal cook-out in honor of the Maye Young 'Search for the Real America' convoy and invited VFW and Legion members from throughout the city. Again, Rob was the center of attention and, just as Mick had asked, a number of battle flags were presented to him to autograph, as well as a few prints of the *Atlanta Journal Constitution* image that had so captured the spirit of the 'March to Tennessee', back during the campaign for the mid-terms.

The local FOX affiliate sent a news crew to interview Mick and the team along with the *Post and Courier*, Charleston's daily newspaper. Sally-Anne decided that it would be good to commence the foray into the Latino constituency, something that the Republican Party had never really been able to crack. She had contacted *El Informador* and suggested they come and do a story on a key member of Maye's team, Jesús. In the end, Jesús turned the interview around and made it about Mick and his desire to bring Latinos into the Maye Young tent as part of the greater America. Sally-Anne had coached Jesús before the interview (Sally-Anne had become quite the PR professional in the last few months) but Jesús went 'off the reservation' and marshaled the interview where he thought it was best. To both his and Sally-Anne's delight, the reporter was excited by this access to whom she saw as the famous 'Meek', the candidate's boyfriend, who was taking time to learn Spanish, and her interview was extremely positive. They hoped that the final published product would be just as positive.

The cook-out turned into a reminiscing and tall-tale telling event where veterans—comrades—relived old times when the world was theirs for the taking. For many, the years had been unkind, physically and emotionally, which was not helped with alcohol. And they were seeing their beloved America dividing and fracturing. But at the moment they were amongst comrades in arms, who would always have each other's backs. And maybe Maye Young would be just the tonic that their America needed.

* * *

The next morning, Mick, Jesús and Rob—who had stayed in the RV that night after the last of the veterans had departed—awoke with sore heads to the sounds of activity outside the Winnebago.

In the parking lot, and on the sidewalk, were hundreds of people with signs of support and flags, many of them battle flags, who were waiting for them to emerge from the RV. Even though they tried to remain quiet, three hundred people in a parking lot could hardly be expected to. When they saw the curtain pulled and the three faces peering out through squinting eyes, they started cheering. The boys had no choice but to begin their day.

The '*Search for the Real America*' would, today, continue with a tour of Fort Sumter and Sally-Anne had offered the local mayor the opportunity to be a part of it. A history buff, he offered to conduct the tour of his city and this famous Civil War battle site. He was a Democrat, so artfully dodged any situations where partisanship would be an issue and focused on his pride for his city. Mick helped him out and made sure that there was no talk of party politics. He kept purely on the historical importance of this site where the opening shots of the Civil War were fired, and highlighted how South Carolina's sons fired the shots that were heard around the world. This delighted the proud South Carolinians, and the mayor especially. He even pulled Mick aside at the end of the event and thanked him for not making it a Democrat/Republican issue.

After Charleston, and with their now expected veterans' escort of riders, and the handover-takeover ceremonies on the side of the interstates, they found that along the route, signs and spectators could be seen with Stars and Stripes and battle flags waiting for the convoy to pass. The convoy headed north to North Carolina and to Roanoke Island and nearby Kittyhawk.

* * *

In a room in Washington, Cooper Camden, Chairman of the Republican National Congressional Committee, sat with other senior leaders of his committee as well as from the Republican Senate Committee to discuss the 'Search for the Real America' convoy and the remarkable impact it was having on social media and conventional media. They had all agreed that so far Maye Young's boyfriend had not put a foot wrong, and that the press had been extremely positive. Even the young black kid was doing wonders, and any image of him with the battle flag was making quite a splash. One of the members mentioned that the South Carolina Hispanic paper had written a great article about Mick and his assistant "Jesus" (mispronouncing the name).

"This guy is keeping everyone happy. He's even got the damn Democrats leaning towards him!" said Cooper, pointing to the paper with a picture of the Mayor of Charleston with Mick, touring Fort Sumter. "If we can leverage off him and turn some of the more conservative blacks and Hispanics towards us, we can get some mileage out of this."

He looked at the other members in the room as he thought about this whole concept. President Troup had not tweeted about this for a few days, but now that it was starting to jump from social media networks to traditional media, he was likely to react, and react in a negative way, which would look bad for the Party. This would be a problem that they needed to contain.

"We need to get Maye in here. She needs to inject herself more into this road trip," said Cooper. "We need to get her face out there so that we have a counterpoint when Troup starts firing off," he said. Cooper looked at the expressions on the faces of the other members of the committee. Some showed concern, others frustration, at the thought of the battle ahead with Troup. The president was a liability, they all knew that, but the thought of having an internal struggle within the Republican presidential race would be pounced upon by the media which, with the exception of FOX, always leaned to the left in general, and against Troup in particular. The time had finally come to kill off the president's chances at re-election.

As the paper sat in the middle of the table with Mick at Fort Sumter, inside the RNC meeting room, the first shots of what could be an internal party civil war were about to be fired.

What Happened at Roanoke?

On Roanoke Island's Fort Raleigh, the site of one of America's oldest settlements which held one of the nation's most famous mysteries, the campaign entourage attended the tour. This was mainly for Mick's benefit, and for the imagery it would generate that would feed the media monsters.

Mick was genuinely interested, and so Sally-Anne and the camera team were going to great lengths to capture his pensive expressions as Christine, the local archaeologist, who was also a ranger with the US Parks Service, explained the settlement, and told the story of the mystery of the colonists who, in 1585, disappeared without a trace from the fledgling colony.

They jockeyed for the right angles and patiently awaited the right expression—which Mick would oblige, knowing that that was what they were waiting for—and, after they had gathered what they thought was enough footage, they found a quiet corner of the amphitheater in the shade of some trees to have a quick look at what they had captured through a small, hand-held monitor.

Sally-Anne was ecstatic. The shots were terrific and there were plenty of dramatic expressions just right for TV and for future advertising, as well as frames that were suitable to have stills pulled from for use in print. Sally-Anne was eager to show Mick and from her vantage point scoured the settlement's buildings and grounds looking for him and Christine, the Parks Service Ranger. The small crowd that had followed Christine had moved on, and the ranger could be seen talking to some schoolkids near one of the colonial building re-creations. In the distance, near a copse of trees was Mick, speaking with two men, one looking like he had just stepped out of a board room. She lifted her camera and zoomed in on the trio to see if she could recognize them. She could not, but snapped off a couple of photos, never-the-less.

She watched with interest. If she did not know any better, they looked like they were from the Party, but what were they doing in North Carolina? Sally-Anne could see that the conversation was getting more animated, and Mick stormed off again. She immediately went to intercept him.

"Who were they?" she said breathlessly trying to keep up with his quick pace.

"FBI," replied Mick curtly.

Sally-Anne froze. That was not the response she expected. She thought for a second, and then raced after Mick who was heading for the RV.

"What does the FBI want with you?" she blurted, trying to hide the concern she suddenly felt.

"I don't know. They seem to have a bee in their bonnet about me being a threat to the country."

Sally-Anne froze again as she tried to take in this revelation. It was something she had not considered at all... that Mick could be a threat to the United States. But now that it had been mentioned, there were some concerns.

Though she was not a professional political strategist or communications adviser, she had been around them enough and had attended enough functions and gatherings of powerful people in the GOP that she had a good idea of the internal machinations of the political world. She knew quite well how desperate people could be to gain power and just as desperate they could be to keep it. If the FBI was looking into Mick, it could mean one of two things: that President Troup had his dirty hand in this and wanted to foil the campaign of another Republican Party candidate or, the less likely, that Major Michael O'Rourke of the Australian Army, who was now the boyfriend of a presidential candidate, was a legitimate threat to the United States.

She watched Mick disappear into the car park where the RV was, her mind trying to wrap itself around this puzzle. While she had only known Mick for a few months, he, at no time, seemed anything but genuine. His efforts to help Maye were one hundred percent in support of her and her campaign. Not only had he been a loyal and dutiful boyfriend to Maye, but he had also shown compassion to everyone on the team, including her... especially during the difficult opening stanzas of the campaign where she didn't know what she was doing. Now that the campaign was gathering momentum, he had let her have her head and she was reveling in the process and making gains. She was an important player in this whole affair and Mick was genuinely interested in what her opinions were, and respected them and any decisions she made, which was more than she could say about her husband.

No, there was no way that Mick could be a threat to the US. To the contrary. This had President Troup's dirty fingerprints all over it. It appeared that Troup had his cronies in the Department of Justice set the dogs of the FBI onto Mick, probably to scare him off. This meant that Troup was scared, and so he should be. As the road trip picked up steam, she had been amazed at the number of people who had expressed their dissatisfaction with his presidency, and many of those dissatisfied constituents even admitted that they were Republicans! His approval ratings were in the mid-thirties on a good day and there was widespread dissatisfaction with his ham-fisted diplomacy from every corner of the media.

She headed for the RV where she found Mick sitting inside with a Coke, gazing out to the car park and looking angry. She could not but feel for him. He was in an odd situation, and one that probably would not get better for him. If Maye was to get the nomination, both she and Mick would be the target of some nasty vitriol from Troup, and that is what it seemed was about to occur. If Maye won the presidency, and she immediately put that out of her mind lest she jinx it, what was to become of him? And what if she did not win? Would their relationship survive? And while it seemed that he was currently the darling of the public, the public had a habit of turning on its darlings. Especially when they became the targets of smear campaigns by nefarious minds. That sort of stuff was what the media lived for. No, Sally-Anne had been too close to these sorts of shenanigans for most of her adult life.

Mick had believed in her, and she in him. She was not sure what had happened today at Roanoke, but she wasn't about to let Troup and his lackeys throw dirt on Mick and Maye's campaign.

70

Allentown and Fake News

As the entourage kept traveling north, it made its way to Allentown in Pennsylvania. The heady days of steel manufacturing had long passed, and the inhabitants of this town yearned for the time when the factories were busy, and the shops were full. Now all their jobs had gone overseas to India or China, and they desperately clung to the hopes that any politician would give them.

When the bikers rode into town, flags flying, leading the small convoy with the RV following behind, it generated a lot of excitement amongst the townsfolk who were in desperate need of exactly that. Mick and the team headed to the American Legion Hall where they were welcomed as minor celebrities. Pennsylvania had always leaned to the left, so it was very surprising to have so many people declare their affinity for Maye and her campaign. They seemed to be disappointed with their current president who had promised so much but had delivered so little. For all his bluster there was very little to show for it, at least in the streets of this town. But the real surprise was what led the evening news. There was a picture of Mick talking to the two FBI agents at Fort Raleigh with the headline 'Troup scared". The anchorwoman reported that the FBI was being accused of interfering in the campaign, and that the candidate's boyfriend, Major Michael O'Rourke, was being harassed by federal agents by order of the president.

In the American Legion Hall the crowd grew quiet as they listened to the report on the news. It helped to have the headline 'Troup scared' on the screen throughout the whole bulletin, which brought cheers from the crowd.

After the bulletin the crowd slapped each other on the back. Mick looked over at Sally-Anne and smiled. He knew that this was her handiwork. A reporter from the *Morning Call*, the local newspaper, asked Mick for his opinion on the news bulletin.

"Well, there's not much I can really say about that," he said, "but if it's true, then it's quite childish."

Mick answered a few more questions for the reporter: the usual sort of fluff; nothing too extreme nor controversial, but just enough to keep his reputation as a decent man—and honorable army officer—intact. It also helped to paint him as the loyal and helpful boyfriend to someone who was becoming a very popular political candidate. He had nothing to do with this new story.

What Mick did not know was that Sally-Anne had inadvertently played right into the hands of the Party. They had been looking for a way to embarrass Troup, and now their hands were clean. By Sally-Anne leaking the photograph and the story to the media, it had gathered its own resonance within the echo chamber that was the media, and was now ticking up its own momentum. The faceless men of the Republican Party, who either backed Maye, or the fence sitters who were undecided about her as a candidate but who knew that Troup would be a liability, were happy. They could now sit back and watch. Provided the Democrats did not win, things would work out in their favor. And the Democrats did not have a viable candidate as yet, even though they had a number of prospects who were jockeying for their place in the media spotlight and trying to endear themselves to the Democratic party's power brokers and rank and file. All this was leading up to Iowa, but at this stage Mick's road trip seemed to be the most interesting campaign story and, like the news article, was building momentum.

During the interview with the *Morning Call*, the reporter's phone notified her of a tweet. And, like a good millennial, she immediately reached for her phone, even though she was in the middle of an interview. Her face indicated that it was important as she beamed a huge smile.

"No FBI agents were sent to harass O'Rourke from the oval office. I am guessing they are actors and this is just more fake news."

Holding up the phone to Mick, she showed him the tweet which was from the president. Even though he was renowned for tweeting every insignificant thought that came into his head, the news story had really thrown the fox into the henhouse. The reporter held the microphone to her mouth ready to ask a question. This would be her chance to have a scoop.

"President Troup has just tweeted that he had nothing to do with sending the FBI to harass you. He says that he would not be surprised if they were paid actors. Did you hire actors to play FBI agents and is this part of your campaign tactics?"

This question was a complete surprise to Mick. Not thirty minutes earlier he was completely oblivious to anyone knowing that the FBI had approached him at Roanoke. Now, all of a sudden, it was likely to be a lead story, courtesy of Troup and his incessant tweeting. Mick was at a loss to explain this.

"The two men in that picture were not known to me until they approached me in Washington a number of weeks ago," said Mick. "They indicated that they worked for the government. I won't say what agency they belonged to, but they are not actors, and I did not have anything to do with them approaching me."

Mick collected his thoughts for a second and continued.

"I would be very surprised if the president would send federal agents to harass me. But I will say this, I was not impressed when they introduced themselves to me and made claims about what they wished I would do. I am not easily intimidated, and they certainly did not intimidate me. As for whether they are FBI or not, I have no comment, but I certainly had nothing to do with them appearing on this campaign."

He thought that would be the end of it, but decided to leave a coda.

"If they are FBI agents, and I am not saying that they are, then the FBI needs to get better agents. These guys were like Laurel and Hardy."

* * *

That evening, the two men in question were called to the J. Edgar Hoover building, FBI Headquarters, in Washington DC. Their meeting with the bureau's Chief of Staff, Peter Murray, was not a pleasant one. Indeed, the conversation was more or less one way, at least at first.

Murray, originally from Georgia, educated them—by demonstration—in the various ways that a Southerner might swear and cuss. The bureau had been made to look incompetent, not only by the ham-fisted way that Gilmer and McDuffie had gone about their job, but also by the president and his tweet. Needless to say, Mick was not popular with the bureau that evening, and particularly so with agents Gilmer and Mc-Duffie, who endured Murray's tirade in silence as he demanded to know why the two agents had such a 'bug up their asses' (his words) about the 'Goddamn Australian.'

Once the chief of staff had managed to calm down slightly, Gilmer pulled out some photos from his jacket pocket and placed them in front of Murray with determination... perhaps even a little bit of showman-ship, as if to say, "Now it's my turn." Murray looked at them.

"What am I looking at?" he asked. The photos showed Mick in various locations. In each photo was the same Asian man, either nearby in the crowd, or in the background.

"This is why we have a bug up our asses," said Gilmer. "This isn't the first time we've seen O'Rourke and this guy in the same place. We spotted them together in Cassville, which is just..."

"I know where Cassville is," said Murray pensively as he looked more closely at the picture. "Any ideas who he is?"

"No. But we've seen him shadowing O'Rourke," replied Gilmer.

Murray looked more closely at the figure. He didn't appear like a stalker or any of the other crazies that seem to get attracted to celebrities, and O'Rourke was becoming quite a celebrity. He looked fit, relatively young, with neat hair and clothes. This man was deserving of more attention.

"FIS, d'ya think?" asked Murray, looking up at Gilmer and McDuffie.

The two agents didn't know if he was from a foreign intelligence service, but that was their guess.

"We don't know who O'Rourke associates with. He could already have a relationship with the Chinese. We've looked at his social media contacts and there seems to be a higher-than-average number of Chinese friends there. Some of his pictures show him as a young man before his army days waiting tables in a Chinese restaurant and his good friend looks like he has some Asian heritage. He got out of the army for a while and spent time in China. It's quite possible, based on what we've seen, that there is a connection. All signs point to him being quite cozy with the Chinese," he said laying down a printout of a copy of Mick's passport with a couple of visas for the People's Republic of China, and multiple entry stamps showing he had been a visitor to the communist state on several occasions.

This revelation stopped Murray in his tracks and McDuffie allowed himself a wry smile. Not one minute before, both he and his partner were being berated by the FBI's chief of staff. Now the tables had turned, and he was decidedly very interested in what the two of them had been tracking.

Murray picked up the phone and his secretary responded. Even though it was late into the evening, she spent almost as many hours in the office as her boss.

"Helen, get me Dave Rogerson at Homeland Security. He'll be at home now." He hung up and awaited the call back and looked at the two agents standing before him pointing to the mysterious Asian man in the photos speaking with O'Rourke.

"We'll see if we can identify him and whether or not he's been flagged. Do you have a better picture with his face? This one probably won't work with the facial recognition programs."

Gilmer threw down another half dozen images of the man, any of which would have been more than suitable for the software to match the face with a passport photograph. The phone rang and Murray picked it up.

"Hello Dave? It's Pete Murray at the Bureau. I have a request and we need to keep it on the QT. It's to do with Major Michael O'Rourke." He paused and Gilmer and McDuffie heard the head of Homeland Security respond on the other end of the line.

"Yes," replied Murray, "the Australian guy. We have some concerns about him."

71

The Red States

The American Legion and the VFW network had ensured that each new location would have somewhere for Mick's party to hold a rally, as well as an instant crowd of supporters accompanied by the spectacle of a biker escort waving American and rebel flags. The media in each location lapped it up, and crowds seem to just appear along the interstates, or hanging signs of support on the overpasses, and wherever the VFW or Legion halls were that the RV and entourage would end up.

The veterans and legion members took it upon themselves to provide security for Mick and his crew. Each night after the hall meetings and barbecues, Mick's team would head to a local hotel except for Mick and Jesús who would spend the night in the RV. They would chat to the veterans about their time in uniform until the small hours of the morning, whereupon Mick and Jesús would turn in, but the veterans would mill around the parking lot smoking and drinking and laughing and telling lies to each other and making sure that no one got close to the RV who was not supposed to be there.

Not only did this generate a lot of interest within the ranks of the two organizations, it also generated interest with serving members of the armed forces, and Mick was being invited to various military bases as he passed through on the way to Iowa.

At each major city they would hold the road trip ceremony where they would sell their support car at a dealership and generate a selling price higher than that which they paid. It seemed that people were expecting that the value of the car would increase if Maye was elected and that this car had been driven by the boyfriend of the president (who might become the First Gentleman, they opined). Mick had become quite a commodity, and with each publicity event his value as a commodity only grew. This was not lost on the GOP, nor the president.

Mick's plan was to tour those states that were Red States, safe Republican states, and those states that could be swung. He knew that those were the states that did not get much exposure to the candidates during a presidential campaign. They had very few votes in them. The candidates preferred California, Texas and New York.

The advantage of going to safe Republican states was that the welcome would always be warm, and the press would normally be sympathetic. It also meant that any stories that surfaced online would normally be positive and enthusiastic. The smaller newspapers would have their stories picked up by the larger newspapers who didn't have representatives there. That was always good exposure for the small papers and one of the reasons why their editors and senior reporters—often the same person—were targeted for special treatment.

Mick was like the pathfinder, and Maye was the invasion force.

And that is exactly what he did. Much of the media interest centered on him, but he was eager to put his team in the spotlight as often as possible to take advantage of their wide-ranging appeal. But he was very clever about it. He knew that the diversity in his entourage would be of moderate interest to the conservative voters but would be particularly interesting to the more liberal voters. He would talk up the 'capability and merit-based appointments of his team' to the conservatives, and to the liberals he would sell the team as the product of 'diverse inclusiveness'. He just had to figure which was the right button to push for which particular audience.

And of course, there was the issue of the rebel flag. That did not seem to want to go away. Even though many of the states through which they were traveling were northern states, there was enough sympathy, interest, novelty and backlash against political correctness that carrying the rebel flag proved to be advantageous. The road trip weaved and wended its way through the Midwest. And even though it was only a short drive to Des Moines in Iowa, they continued westward to Arizona, Utah, Wyoming and through the north through Idaho coming back down through the Dakotas. These states certainly did not receive much attention in previous campaigns, yet they were devoutly loyal to the conservative side of politics. As far as Mick was concerned, they deserved as much attention as the larger states. He especially enjoyed those states. The people seemed more open and friendly and no nonsense. Rugged individualism was still alive and well and lived in the Black Hills and the Big Sky Country and elsewhere in this part of America.

They had been on the road for over seven weeks. Going through the Midwest in the middle of summer often proved trying. Utah and Arizona in summer was especially punishing. But they also experienced some of the wonders that made America so great and so beautiful.

The Grand Canyon, the Painted Desert, the Rockies, big sky country in Wyoming and Montana, Mount Rushmore and the Black Hills, and through the cornfields of the Midwest; they all offered up wonderful experiences that the four of them and their camera crews reveled in. They were able to get some spectacular footage, which was exploited wonderfully by Sally-Anne and Pam, as well as the more 'fun' events like the *Search for the Real America* at the 'World's Largest Fishing Fly' in Utah, or the 'World's Largest Ball of Twine' in Kansas. Their social media following continued to grow, and Pam organized for various interactions between Maye and Mick who were both working hard for her campaign but separated by thousands of miles. She would post their Skype calls, those that were appropriate that is, so that people could see not only what they were trying to achieve individually on the campaign, but also trying to overcome the tyranny of separation by distance as their relationship continued to grow.

By the time they got to Des Moines, they were exhausted, but they had raised Maye's profile and they had raised hundreds of thousands of dollars. In fact, at last estimate, it was more like $1.5 million just on the road alone. Their crowdfunding was ten times that amount!

Sally-Anne had managed to even get merchandise for the road trip and had it constantly resupplied at every major town. When Mick asked her how she was able to fund this, she just told him to not worry his pretty little head. What Mick did not know was that funding was coming from the Republican Party. It was in their best interest for this circus, albeit a very popular and well organized one, to continue. And with each passing day the support for Maye and her candidacy increased amongst the members of the Republican Party, and so did the Party's ratings in the polls.

For a party to dump a sitting president in favor of another candidate during a presidential campaign had only occurred once before, and so it was always going to be a difficult prospect to get support from within the Party for this to happen again. But Maye's greatest advantage was the president himself. Troup never disappointed in stumbling over his own words and his own actions. And with every embarrassing gaffe, and every insulting comment, more and more Republicans switched their allegiance to Maye and outwardly and openly supported her candidature, risking the wrath of the president.

In the meantime, the Democrats fumbled around with their candidates. As was often the case, in the absence of a popular choice, there arose a free-for-all in potential candidates vying for positive coverage, popularity, and the support of the party. And this was no exception.

The usual suspects emerged. Previous presidential hopefuls were dusted off and pushed back into the spotlight. A few state governors threw their hats into the ring; a multimillionaire who made his fortune in technology, and a candidate who traveled predominantly on her green credentials but who did not want to be a member of the Green Party of the United States.

There was one, however, who seemed to be leading the pack. Joe Baldwin had been vice president under Jefferson and had been a senator for six terms prior to that. He seemed to be leading the race of Democrat potentials. It was expected he would draw a big crowd at the fair.

They all began arriving for the Iowa State fair around the same time as Mick and his entourage. The fair organizers were now well versed in this, and they had marquees and stages available for the political candidates to spruik their messages.

Since the fifties they had set aside a day for candidates. The local paper, *The Des Moines Register* hosted the *Political Soapbox* and gave every candidate twenty minutes to speak and to answer questions from the crowd in a pavilion on the Grand Concourse of the fair where Iowans, interstate visitors, and the media, could get an idea of what each candidate stood for.

This year was a little bit different. With Maye as a candidate: smart, young, beautiful and female, and with Mick's cross-country road trip generating so much interest, there was a much more palpable interest in the campaign by fairgoers. What was unusual about this year was that there was a sitting Republican president, so having a Republican campaigning who was not the president was highly unusual. As such, the twenty or so would-be candidates who would be speaking at the *Political Soapbox* all came from the Democratic Party, although there were a couple from minor parties, and one was an independent. What made it even more unusual was that Mick wasn't the candidate. Maye was! But the interest in this campaign had become so intriguing that the organizers from *The Register*, and from the State Fair organizing committee, were more than happy to have the Australian boyfriend of the young Republican woman who was trying to take the president's place speak. It was one for the history books, and the importance of the occasion was not lost on the organizers who advertised it as widely as possible. Anything to bring more people through the gates.

72

¿Está todo bien?

The VFW and American Legion supporters had encouraged as many members as they could to attend in uniform. It gave the crowd a distinctly military flavor, even if some of the uniforms were a little tighter than the last time they were worn. Regardless, it was not lost on the conservative Iowans who had a deep appreciation for their servicemen and women.

Sally-Anne hovered around Mick as she got him ready for his big presentation to the growing crowd. He was to deliver his speech in uniform, which was not the original intention, but the remarkably strong military presence dictated a change of plans. "Are you ready," she asked.

"No!" replied Mick, with a tinge of frustration. It had been a long fourteen months, and he wasn't afraid to admit that he was particularly nervous. Even though he had spoken literally scores of times, this was really the beginning of the campaign. To paraphrase Churchill, the phony war was over; the Battle for Maye was about to begin.

Sally-Anne saw Mick reviewing some notes.

"Do you want me to read that?" she asked.

"No, that's fine. I think I have them all," Mick responded.

Sally-Anne furrowed her brow. She took the notes and began going over them.

Mick tried to grab them, but Sally-Anne was too quick. She turned away so she could read them. Each page contained a jolt, and she darted from one page's heading or bullet point to the next, to the next. Mick protested, but he soon realized that that was futile.

Shocked at what she had read, she confronted Mick. "Where did these come from?"

He could see the pain on her face. The notes contained the five key messages that would form Maye's platform. They would not make the Republican Party happy. In fact, they could risk the whole campaign.

"Maye and I discussed them, and we feel that this set of messages will give her the best chance of winning. But more importantly, it's what she believes in."

Sally-Anne tried to digest that. Politics in America was so scripted and wound up so tightly with lobbyists and corporations with deep pockets, that any free will or free thought was not only frowned upon, it was actively quashed. If the Republican Party opposed any of these ideas, then all their efforts would be for naught, and Maye's campaign could be seriously damaged. Perhaps irrevocably. They could lose their support base within the GOP and everything they had worked for would evaporate. Presidential candidate Maye Young would be relegated to a cocktail party joke, the candidate that didn't even get to the starting gate.

"This could kill our chances," Sally-Anne implored. "This comes straight out of the Democrat's playbook," she cried. "If we make this the basis of Maye's platform, we could lose our base constituency."

Sally-Anne looked at Mick, the worry clearly evident on her face. She looked around the RV, where posters, press clippings, merchandise for Maye had accumulated over the last three months since she announced her intention to run for the presidency, and fourteen months since Sally-Anne had joined her team. Almost two months of hard slogging on the road to Iowa and five months on the campaign trail before that with the mid-terms.

She was so distraught that everything had taken on an air of negativity, and she suddenly hated everything about this campaign. All the interminable shaking of hands, and smiling, and inane comments, and interviews, and motel rooms, and fast food, and constipation, all to end up in Iowa—in the middle of fucking nowhere—only to have the campaign die an agonizing death surrounded by pigs and cows and fatties wearing sweatpants and gorging themselves on fried food and candy floss. She didn't want to hate it. She had come to love it all… but now, like a lover that wants to end the relationship, she hated it. It had not only stolen her time, it had stolen her hope.

Mick looked at Sally-Anne with sad eyes. She had come to this campaign a washed-up socialite, cast aside by her husband who no longer needed her or her connections to get ahead.

"What do you want from all this?" asked Mick, casting his hand around the RV and pointing to the posters and press clippings. "What do you hope to get out of all the hard work you have done?"

"I want Maye to win!" she extolled.

"Do you disagree with what's on those pieces of paper?" asked Mick. His voice was quiet and measured, in the same way a father quietly reproaches a misbehaving child, by showing disappointment, not anger.

"Of course I don't," she said. "But if we say these things publicly, then we'll have no chance of keeping the backing of the Party. We need the Party to support Maye's candidacy." Her voice was high, almost cracking. She was on the verge of becoming quite emotional.

"Michael. We have to be in the game to be able to make a difference," she said. "I've seen plenty of good people—decent people—who wanted to make a difference. To get into public office to do good. You know what happened to them? Most of them didn't get into the starting lineup. They didn't get endorsed and they were not allowed to play in the game. They didn't end upon the bench. Hell, they weren't even given a ticket to watch the game from the bleachers. They were left out in the parking lot where they couldn't see the game. All they could do was listen to the crowd cheer and wishing they were a part of it all."

Mick slowly walked towards Sally-Anne. The still Iowa air seemed heavy with the sounds of the crowd and music and generators, and the wafting smell of barbeque and candy floss. It filled the silence in the RV as the two stood in front of each other.

Sally-Anne's eyes shimmered as she began to tear up. She had been a part of a team that had turned something small into something big. For the first time in her sixty or more years of being on this planet, she had felt that she had purpose, real purpose. But it was all predicated on the chance that Maye would be endorsed as the Republican's candidate for the presidency. The rug could be pulled out from everything if they took a wrong turn, and as far as she was concerned, Mick's speech would be exactly that: a wrong turn.

Mick reached out and embraced her. It had been so long since she had had a man hold her that she immediately began to cry. Fourteen months. Fourteen long, emotional months, starting with her finally coming to terms with her husband's infidelity, and then her finding her place as a vital member of a movement, a movement that was turning into a revolution. She may have lost her marriage (she had lost that years ago), but she had found herself with this Australian, and with the handsome and smart young black college student, Rob; the beautiful and canny Pam; the devoted and loyal Jesús. Gosh, even the camera teams had become good friends. This campaign had been the time of her life and she wanted it to continue until the election in fifteen months. She had found herself, finally, thanks to these young people, and she wanted to know where it would lead. Where Maye's campaign would go. Now they were in Iowa, and it could end right here, even before the primaries.

She felt Mick's embrace loosen. He held her at arm's length and looked at her. She looked down, embarrassed that she was weeping. He gently cupped her head in his hands and made her look into his eyes. They were warm and inviting, no longer disappointed. He had seen her sadness and concern, and he smiled.

"You have been a Godsend throughout this whole journey," he said to her soothingly, "but you have to trust us on this. You have to stand by what you believe in, and if you believe in what's on those pieces of paper, you will stand by me when I say them on stage for Maye. It's what she wants to represent."

He wiped the tear that was slowly drifting down her cheek. "Trust us on this," he said. "Trust me on this."

At that moment, the door of the RV opened and Jesús appeared. Surprised at seeing Mick holding Sally-Anne, he kept a poker face.

"*Jefe, es hora,*" he said, letting him know it was time. He saw Sally-Anne was teary. "*¿Esta todo bien?*" he said, asking if everything was alright.

"*Si,*" replied Mick, "*Ella esta cansada. Ha sido un largo viaje.*" His Spanish had been improving every day, but his acting had not. Even though he had tried to convince Jesús that Sally-Anne was merely tired because the journey had been a long one, he had not succeeded. Jesús could tell it was more.

Jesús put his hand on her shoulder. "Sally-Anne," he said, "everything will be OK. Mick has got this!"

And with that they left the RV.

Sally-Anne stood there, alone and completely deflated. Her role with the team, with the campaign, had revitalized her and had given her back her feeling of self-worth. Not for many years had she felt valued and important, and now it could very well slip away. She knew how the Republican Party worked. It was probably the same for the Democrats. If this was going to be Maye's platform, then there was certainly no chance of her getting to the White House. Her campaign was about to come to a crashing halt within the hour.

Her phone buzzed. She pulled it out and read the text. Excitedly, she raced out of the RV and to her car.

73

Gimme Five!

Mick and Jesús headed for the Grand Concourse, past the kids' rides and the petting zoo, and past the crowds eating various 'meats on a stick', and the ubiquitous pork chops.

There were plenty of supporters there with political T-shirts. Some of the more well-organized candidates had their teams padding the crowds and giving away merchandise, most of it Democrat blue. With Maye the only Republican candidate trying to win votes here, there were very few red T-shirts to be seen.

What there were, however, were lots of military uniforms. With Mick being in his, the emu plumes standing proud on his slouch hat, he soon gathered a following as people began to recognize him. It wasn't long before he had a crowd walking with him and surrounding him, many of them in uniform, and almost all reaching out to shake his hand or to pat him, or Jesús, on the back.

When the crowd got so large that they were unable to move, Jesús swung into action and got as many uniformed men as he could to form a vanguard, a sort of offensive line to protect the quarterback, and they headed to the pavilion. With a formation of men in uniform trailing a tail of well-wishers, it was quite a spectacle.

Soon they were at the marquee pavilion opposite the grandstand where the candidates would participate in the *Political Soapbox*. There were more political boosters, and a throng of reporters, from the traditional media, independent media and lots of vloggers. The curious stood back and watched, gnawing on pork chops, the signature 'street meat' of the Iowa State Fair.

A few of the Democrat hopefuls led the bill and mounted the stage to deliver their messages. All of them, without fail, talked about gun control and making the wealthy pay more and the minorities being given more support. In a conservative state like Iowa, and a predominantly rural one, that did not go over too well.

Jesús came up to Mick and looked him up and down. Mick was signing autographs and shaking hands.

"How are we looking," asked Mick, still signing autographs.

"*Eres próximo, jefe*," replied Jesús, letting Mick know he was up next. He handed Mick his slouch hat. Mick made his apologies to those who had autograph books thrust at him and followed Jesús towards the stage. One of the editors from the *Des Moines Register* was acting as emcee for the political soapbox. Mick waited at the base of the steps for his cue.

The emcee gave his introduction and motioned for Mick to come up onto the stage. Mounting the steps, he was met with an enthusiastic round of applause and cheering, especially from those in uniform.

He began his speech by thanking everyone and telling them how wonderful it was to visit the Midwest as an Australian. The warmth of the people reminded him of the warmth of those back home. The crowd cheered their appreciation. He then continued by stating that he was there merely to represent his girlfriend, Maye. This went down even better. He apologized for her not being there but that she was busy working in Washington trying to convince the old fogies in Congress where the nation needed to go.

"Maye has some fantastic ideas for America," he continued. He deliberately did not call her Congresswoman Young, or Representative Young. By referring to her by her Christian name, it reinforced his relationship with her and also humanized her to the audience as someone who could be their friend. "Her ideas will take the country in the right direction for the rest of the twenty-first century and make it greater than it already is," he proclaimed.

"Now what I'm about to say may cause you to raise your eyebrows," he said seriously, "but I ask you to hear me out 'til the end, and *then* make up your mind. It is very important to keep an open mind for the next five minutes."

The media that was there immediately trained their cameras onto Mick. They could sense a story was about to unfold.

"Miss Maye Young's platform is based on five key foundations. Now hear me out before you make up your mind, but her plan will hedge the bets of America's future to make it great again. It will hedge its future." Mick paused for effect. "It will *hedge* America's future," he said with emphasis.

With the sound of the fair as the backdrop, Mick went on to describe how Maye's policies were the Hedge for the future and that the 'H' in hedge stood for 'health care' and how universal health care was the mark of an advanced society. This was met with very mixed reactions. Not really the forte of any Republican platform.

In the audience a man in his thirties pulled two phones from his pocket. He madly dialed numbers on both and spoke into one urgently while holding the other towards one of the big PA speakers as Mick explained why universal health care was good for the country, and the economy.

Next was 'E', for economy. Mick explained simply, and concisely the need to wrest outsourcing of manufacturing back to the US, but that it would mean higher prices or a lower standard of living. But that a free market would find its equilibrium and that he had confidence that Americans would be resilient.

'D' was for Defense. A great country needs to be militarily strong, as well as economically strong, and not afraid to use it when the cause was just, and the cause was right and the aims were clear. He saw many men and women in uniform nodding in agreement. But the next point he knew would be contentious.

'G' was for gun control. To a strong murmur from the crowd, he explained that to him, gun control meant a tight grouping. The uniformed people and many 'good ol' boys' cheered. But he then went on to say how by tightening the laws surrounding guns, then responsible gun owners would be protected, and criminals would find it harder to get guns. This, like health care, was met with a mixed response, but when he said that penalties for illegal use of guns would increase and that truth in sentencing was paramount, that was met with smiles and nodding heads.

"After all," he said, "responsible gun owners who have the right to bear arms," (added for effect) "would be the first to take away the guns from illegals to protect their communities."

He chose his words carefully to hit just the right chord. A quick reference to the bill of rights and the use of the word 'illegals' rather than 'illegal gun owners' gave just enough impact while still providing deniability and obscuration. He knew that those words would be analyzed later, *ad infinitum, ad nauseum.*

'E' was for the environment. A sensible program for carbon emissions that did not impact jobs in the short term, but created opportunities in the long term, while clearing the skies and cleaning the seas. This was, he said, the least we could do for the future of our kids. "But let's not throw the baby out with the bath water," he said. "It must be a sensible timeline to protect jobs. For once it got underway, it would gain its own momentum without government having to step in and close down factories."

"Let's make the Middle East and Arab oil irrelevant!"

Mick kept referring to the first-person plural: "We need to do this," and "It is up to us." His Australian accent bore testament that he was 'not from 'round here', but his words made him one of them. This Australian was talking about how to make, and keep, America the greatest country in the world. He had been on stage for less than five minutes and already he was proving to be the most popular of the day's speakers, but then again, it may have just been his accent.

* * *

In Washington, a group of men stood around a large mahogany boardroom table in the House of Representatives listening to the speaker phone sitting in its center. They could hear the applause and the clapping and Mick's voice on the line as he addressed the Iowa State Fair's *Political Soapbox*. One of them, his white shirt half turned up at the sleeves and his tie hanging down as he leaned in with both hands on the desk, showed his concern on his face. It was the government whip who, shaking his head, let it drop in frustration.

"What the hell is he doing!?" is all he could say. "He's going to undo all the good they've done so far. Get Maye on the phone and tell her to get her ass down here, now!"

* * *

In a small office in The White House, a similar scene was playing out. The images from Iowa were streaming onto a laptop, glowing on the faces of the two men and one woman that crowded around it. The door opened with a thud and President Troup walked in. The three of them stood up, Troup motioned to them to sit back down.

"What have they said? Anything?" asked the president.

"Universal health care, gun control and the environment," replied one of them.

Troup smiled. That would be their undoing.

"What do you have for me," said the president to the woman tapping away. She turned her computer to face him, and he read the paragraph she had written. He took the computer and began tapping out a tweet. He pressed 'Enter' and his tweet went out into cyberspace.

* * *

In the office in the House of Representatives, all the phones of all the men whistled a chirp. One of them grabbed his phone to see what had arrived.

"Troup's watching O'Rourke and he's tweeted," he exclaimed.

The whip closed his eyes in frustration and signed heavily. "What did he say?"

"Young's foreign boyfriend wants socialism here. The US does not need an outsider telling us what Americans need. #Troup2020"

The government whip yelled out again to one of his underlings who was on the phone outside the meeting room, "Hurry up and get Congresswoman Young down here now! NOW!"

* * *

Back in Iowa, Mick wrapped up his speech and the emcee called for questions. Immediately, the media cried out in unison, shouting questions or calling Mick's name. He pointed to one reporter.

"Major O'Rourke..."

"Mick," he responded.

"Mick!" she yelled, "President Troup has just tweeted that you are a foreigner and that you have no business telling Americans what we need. What is your response to that?"

"Well, I'm glad President Troup is watching what we're doing," he said, and with that he started waving around the crowd for theatrics, as if looking for the camera that was providing the feed to The White House.

"Hello Mister President," he cried out, looking down the lenses of all the phones and cameras. "Nice of you to join us here in Iowa."

"I am not telling you what I think we should be doing; I am telling you what Congresswoman Maye Young's platform is. But, if it's of any interest, I agree 100% with her, and I think it is a great platform foundation," he explained.

"These five points, these HEDGE points: health care, economy, defense, gun control, environment—these five points are Maye's platform. They are the 'five points of Maye'. One could even say that they are the Cinco de Maye."

With this the crowd laughed. They understood the play on words of *Cinco de Mayo* and Cinco de Maye. Mick motioned for another reporter to pose a question.

"Miss Young's five points seem to be at odds with Republican Party ideals," yelled the reporter from the media area. "Does this mean that you are going against what the Republican Party stands for?"

Mick knew he had to be careful with what he said. A wrong answer here, and not only would the GOP dis-endorse Maye, but it would create a sound bite that would be played over and over and could cripple the campaign.

He paused for a second as he gathered his thoughts. In the two rooms in Washington, where the Republican power brokers listened intently, and somewhat tensely, they also awaited his response. Was the Australian going to dig himself deeper into this hole?

Mick was just about to respond when there was an audible gasp from the crowd. Someone was climbing the steps to the stage and was heading towards Mick.

He turned to see who had caught the attention of the crowd. Stunned, he was frozen to the spot.

74

Take a Knee

Sally-Anne pushed her up the steps onto the stage where Mick was being hounded by the media. She walked towards Mick, and all eyes in the audience turned to look at her. She could even hear the gasp from the crowd. Mick also turned to look at her, he was frozen for a moment. Only the emu plumes in his slouch hat waved in the breeze

Maye gave a wave to the crowd, which erupted into applause and cheering, as all lenses turned towards her. Mick smiled and stepped forward; arms outstretched. He dropped the microphone which landed with a thud on the stage, squealing feedback for a second.

Maye had definitely surprised everyone, including Mick. She met his embrace and he pulled her into him, their lips meeting in a most passionate kiss. Of course, the crowd went hysterical with delight.

It could not have been scripted better, thought Sally-Anne, but this was not her doing. The text message she had received in the RV, just as Mick had revealed Maye's five-point platform, had been from Maye letting her know that she was arriving at Des Moines airport unannounced (and in disguise) to stand in for Mick on the podium. Unfortunately, she had arrived a little too late to do that, but from all accounts, her Australian boyfriend had acquitted himself well, even if the message had not been received as well as was hoped.

She looked terrific, as if she had just stepped out of a salon, and of course Mick looked dashing in his Army uniform. Mick whispered to her that it was wonderful to have her in his arms... but that maybe they should give the crowd and the cameras some extra loving, and then he kissed her again.

After they had stopped kissing, Maye motioned for the crowd, still applauding and cheering, to quieten down so she could say something. The emcee retrieved the microphone and handed it to Maye, as the crowd began to quieten.

The women in the audience were visibly delighted. The romance between the two was impossible to avoid in the media. Maye was the darling of women all over the US, and was on almost every magazine cover. She was even a sex symbol to the males. Mick was admired by men and had proven extremely popular with women. Now they were both in Iowa, together, and the crowd could not be happier.

Maye put the microphone close to her mouth.

"Hi, Iowa," she said, and the crowd erupted again. She paused to let the noise subside, and then continued.

"I have a question for you," she said to them... and then paused, turning to Mick and looking at him.

"Actually," she said looking into his eyes, "I have a question for you." And with that she got down on one knee.

For a moment there was silence... but only for a moment. When people realized what was about to happen, the sound was deafening. It was like an explosion as women screamed hysterically and began applauding. The camera lenses suddenly began waving, and the push of reporters and cameramen became a scrum as they elbowed each other to get into position to capture the moment. With the instinct of a photojournalist they knew that this might be a defining moment in history, that photo that defines a time. That one image that captures the world's imagination. Right now, right in front of this crowd in a pavilion in Des Moines, Iowa, the female Republican candidate who was campaigning to oust a sitting Republican president—and who may even win—was about to propose to her Army officer boyfriend in front of the world.

Maye put the microphone up to her mouth again. In Washington, the men in the room in the House of Representatives were listening intently to what their man in the crowd was telling them as he described the scene unfolding on stage.

In the White House, President Troup and his three advisers watched the live stream from their agent in the crowd. All were transfixed. Troup realized what was happening and started swearing at the screen as he saw 'that Southern Bitch' kneeling in front of the 'Goddamn Australian', arm outstretched.

With the experience of a seasoned sitcom actor, Maye waited until the crowd's applause and cheering died down before she spoke.

"Michael John O'Rourke," she said, and paused while the crowd again gasped, Mick's eyes as wide as saucers, "will you do me the honor of being my husband?"

The crowd fell silent, except for the clicking of cameras. Outside the pavilion the sounds of the fair still brought the merriment of the fete wafting through the summer Iowan air. Outside the pavilion the fair-goers had no idea what was happening in that marquee. The Democrat speakers were stunned and watched, just like the rest of the crowd. Those amongst them that were not transfixed by the moment muttered, "You've got to be fucking kidding me!" through clenched teeth.

The crowd waited for Mick's answer. It seemed to take forever for him to form the words.

"Yes," he said, and Maye breathed a sigh of relief.

Off to the side, Sally-Anne—her hands clasped together so tightly in anticipation that her ring cut through the skin of one of her fingers—squealed with delight. Not only was she happy for them both, but the mileage she knew she could get out of this was gold dust. Her job had just become very complicated from a technical sense, but also much easier from a selling sense. She could easily sell this good news story, but more importantly, she was so happy for two people that had come to mean so much to her.

Of course, the crowd—again—went crazy, as Mick reached down and, with both hands, helped his now fiancée to her feet, taking her in his arms and kissing her again. They looked into each other's eyes and said something to each other before they turned to face them, each one's arm around the other's waist.

Once the crowd had calmed down, Maye pointed to one of the reporters screaming for attention.

"Mick," she said, "did this come as a surprise or was this planned?"

"Oh, this was definitely a surprise. I was not expecting to see Maye until next week, and I certainly did not think when I woke up this morning that I would be engaged by the end of the day!"

"How do you feel," she added.

Mick paused and thought for a moment. The question was trite, but immensely appropriate.

"I feel so honored that such a beautiful, intelligent, kind and wonderful woman would want to have me as her husband, and that she would ask little ol' me. I mean, she could do *much* better!"

The crowd laughed and cheered.

"And guess what?" said Mick to the crowd, letting them settle down.

"I will become an American citizen... and before anyone asks, No! I didn't say 'Yes' just to get a 'Green Card'!

The crowd erupted again, their faces beaming with smiles, except for the Democrats and their teams, some of whom turned and walked away. Mick then led a chorus of "U.S.A! U.S.A!"

The cameras captured Mick and Maye, arms around each other's waists, punching the air with each letter: "U.S.A! U.S.A!"

* * *

A thousand miles away in Washington DC, the President of the United States grabbed a coffee cup from the desk and threw it against the wall. A few blocks away in the J. Edgar Hoover building, two FBI agents smiled. It would be much easier to deal with an American citizen than an Australian. It could all be handled within the Department of Justice without having to worry about the State Department or the Australian Embassy.

75

⚛

Off We Go, Into the Wild Blue Yonder

As fall arrived and the leaves began to turn, the shadow campaign continued to cause a split in the Republican party.

Many in the GOP wanted to remain with the president saying that it was better to 'not change horses in mid-stream', while others were being convinced to take a risk with the 'new girl', and still more were already fervently behind Maye as 'the way of the future'. It was twelve months until the general election and there was much to do, not the least of which was to come up with cohesion in the Party.

At first, some state party organizations said that they would still support President Troup as the incumbent, and that to show their support they wouldn't bother holding primaries. This was disastrous for the nomination process for Maye. What's more, Maye's five-point plan had worried many of the members, but it had also buoyed many others. It had such an impact that there was internal movement of support within the Party. Conservative die-hards were polarized towards Troup while more centrist and progressives became Maye supporters, urging the Party to mandate primaries to allow the rank and file to make the decision.

And it was the rank and file that ended up doing exactly that. Those county and state committees that had announced they would not bother holding primaries came under significant pressure by their members to hold primaries, or risk widespread resignations and abandonment. After a week of internal and external pressure, the national committee mandated that each subordinate committee was to hold a primary 'in order to provide clarity and direction'. This was welcome news to Maye and her team. At least now they had a shot of getting the nomination. Again, Troup was furious with the Party.

The Democrats, in the meantime, were finding it hard to counter Maye's five-point plan. It was stealing the thunder of their own progressive policies. What's more, they found it almost impossible to attack Maye personally, also. To do so would be disastrous. She had been so gracious towards her Democratic Party opponents during the midterms campaign and had never played negative politics. Now she had earned a reputation for being a fair and generous campaigner. In fact, she made it public that she would not engage in negative politics, and that became the foundation of her five-point plan. "A positive way forward based on positive campaigning". Partisan politics was wearisome to the American public and Maye was saying and doing all the right things. She was like opening the drapes and a window of a dark and musty room. All the creepy crawlies slither and scurry away, and the room is filled with fresh air and light.

But outside the party planning rooms the public was more interested in the wedding than in the campaign!

There was a lot of deliberation about the wedding, and how it should be run. The Party was ecstatic that it was to occur and saw it as a great way to garner publicity. Their PR people tried to hijack it and wanted to make it a spectacle: 'our very own royal wedding... but for the Republican Party!'

The Democrats cried, again, 'Republican Stunt!' But after a day or two of very public debate, and very heated private debate, Mick simply turned to Maye and said, "Wherever you want to get married, I'll be there. We can go to City Hall right now and get it done! It might be simpler. Or how 'bout Vegas? I've always thought about getting married by an Elvis impersonator!"

Maye laughed, but Mick was sitting at the computer and had found a place on the web.

"Hey, how about 'The Wee Kirk 'o the Heather' as a venue?" We can register at Clarke County courthouse, shoot some craps and then hire a limo and get married by Elvis! No blood tests!"

He saw Maye looking through brochures of places in DC and in Atlanta. Behind her on the mantle were pictures of her time in the air force.

"How about the Air Force Academy chapel?" he suggested. "You're still in the air force reserve."

Maye looked at him and a smile shone. "Perfect," she said, and came over and kissed him. "I could wear my mess dress and you could wear your uniform. It'll look very smart."

Mick thought about this for a moment. He had always pictured himself marrying a woman in a traditional dress. "You wouldn't want to wear a white dress?" he asked.

She kissed him again, placed her arms around him and straddled him, saying cheekily, "I think my days of wearing white to my wedding are long gone, as you would know!"

He chuckled. "Yeah... especially after what you did to me last night. White is *definitely* out of the question! But, if you were to wear a traditional dress, we could put it out to the public to help you choose it. Make it something where people could give you their opinion and make them a part of your decision-making."

"Oooh!" said Maye, "The Democrats would hate that. 'Republican stunt! Republican stunt!'" she cawed.

She thought for a second. "I *would* like to wear something traditional. I didn't get to do anything special for my first marriage... but I would have liked to have worn my wings and my ribbons."

"Why not do both?" asked Mick. "Wear an air force-blue sash with your dress, and we can have your wings and decorations on it. That's what they did in the royal wedding in Britain."

She loved it. And so would the public. But the question arose as to when to hold it. It was now August and by the start of February they had to be in full gear for the primaries. It would be an incredibly busy time, with none left over for any sort of wedding shenanigans.

"The last week of January!" said Mick. "Five months away."

"Five months?" said Maye incredulously. "That's not very far away. And January in Colorado is risky."

"Yeah, but if it's a clear day—fingers crossed—we'd have the snow-capped Rockies in the background. It would look spectacular. Better than anything the Brits could do!"

There was, of course, method in Mick's madness. Whilst he wanted Maye to have the wedding she dreamed of, there was no harm in it helping her campaign. The last week of January would put the wedding just a few days from the Iowa caucuses and a week from the New Hampshire primaries. If they could get a good showing in those two primaries, then they would be on track as a viable competitor against Troup. The wedding would put them in the forefront of everyone's minds.

76

Being a Trouper

President Troup continued to be a great ally to the campaign, even if he didn't mean to be. Every time he tweeted, he managed to alienate those who supported him, and cement the opinions of those who opposed him. But there were still enough Republicans in Congress who believed it would be dangerous to dump the incumbent for the sake of an unknown.

He demanded the RNC bring her back into line, but after a few weeks of her shadow campaign, the RNC had what they wanted: a viable alternative candidate to put before the voters and who seemed to be a hit with them. The RNC finally announced that it would allow the decision to be made by the voters, because 'after all, that was what democracy was all about.'

Like a querulous child, Troup continued his cyber rants, each tweet more vitriolic than the last. And with each the support for Maye merely increased. The public lapped up the drama of the president's ire, juxtaposed against Maye's dignity and her preparations for the wedding. Hollywood couldn't write a better script.

As the Christmas season approached, the big question was who would be invited to the wedding. It was no surprise that all of a sudden Mick and Maye became very popular with Republicans in Congress. But not only them: the rich, the famous, and the influential all wanted a seat at the table.

Mick suggested to Maye that any member of Congress that was serving in the reserves or the national guard would be invited, regardless of party. Of course, the RNC was not consulted on this, otherwise they would have stacked the invitation list themselves. But when that was announced to the media it left both the Republicans and the Democrats with nowhere to go. The public-relations value was inestimable.

When the Governor of Colorado heard about this, he immediately offered C-130 Hercules transport aircraft from the Colorado Air National Guard to bring people into his state, and Chinook helicopters from the National Guard to transport them from Petersen Air Force Base to the US Air Force Academy. He had already arranged it with the commandant of the academy who had to seek permission from the Secretary of Air Force, a Troup appointee. She was a fan of Maye's so she agreed to allow the wedding to take place at the air force academy, and hoped the president wouldn't put two and two together. The Governor, a Democrat, knew that Troup would be furious, which made arranging this for Congresswoman Young all the more sweeter. Besides, it was an election year so if Troup decided to take his revenge by withholding federal funding to his state, it would be at his own peril… and if Congresswoman Young was nominated and won, then he'd be in her good graces. For him it seemed a win-win situation.

The congressional wedding guests jumped at the opportunity to ride in the back of an air force aircraft, at least those that had not experienced it before. It was certainly not comfortable or salubrious, but the photo opportunities of them walking down the ramp of military transports, while the unchosen ones arrived in limousines, would be PR gold. But for Mick, the greatest coup would be to have Democrats and Republicans traveling together. That was an even better image for Maye's campaign.

* * *

Back in Australia, the Prime Minister was ecstatic. Not a night would go by where there was not a story about 'Their Mick'. Of course, the women's magazines were going into overdrive. Whilst it was a fact that Maye had not yet won a single vote to even be considered the Republican nominee for the presidential election, this fact was lost on most Australians who did not understand the rather convoluted American election process. As far as they were concerned, 'their Mick' could be the husband of the next President of the United States. But Mick and Maye knew that their real challenges still lay ahead during the primaries.

Even more giddy with excitement were the Prime Minister's advisors and communications people. They saw new ways to exploit the commodity that was Major Michael O'Rourke. But there was a problem of which these civilians were unaware.

The Chief of Army advised the PM that if Mick was to marry an American citizen, and took up dual nationality, that would pose a problem for his position as an officer within the Australian Army. He would have to make a decision about his future. He could remain an Australian citizen and remain a commissioned officer on extended leave without pay, but that might be a problem for the American people. They may not appreciate a foreigner being the spouse of the president with no intention of becoming a US citizen. Or he could take dual nationality and be an Australian citizen and a US citizen, but that would disqualify him from holding a commission in the Australian Army. Whilst it was true that President Troup had a foreign-born wife, she had become a naturalized citizen. If Mick was to do the same, he would have to resign his commission. In fact, he would most likely have to relinquish his Australian citizenship altogether.

The Prime Minister had his concerns about O'Rourke giving up his Australian citizenship. He was hoping that he could be convinced to assume dual nationality as an Australian and US citizen. Now the Chief of Army was telling him it was one or the other.

"Why can't he be a dual citizen and still be in the Army," asked the director of communications, Jenny Deakin.

"Because Commonwealth law forbids it," replied the general without even bothering to look at her. Instead, he maintained his gaze at the PM who could see Major General Braddon's patience being strained. The general wasn't in the mood to explain the law to this media spin doctor. A soldier could not be loyal to two flags simultaneously. It opened up issues of security and commitment to duty. What if one country demanded their citizen returned home to fulfill national service obligations but that citizen was doing the same in another country? What if both countries began hostilities against each other? It was a simple concept if one bothered to think about it for five seconds.

His head of communications could not understand why this problem could not be overcome. She then started to try to convince the Chief of Army of the importance of influencing Mick's decision. She was not so much concerned about him and his relationship as she was about how it would affect the Prime Minister's re-election chances.

"Surely you can tell him what to do, General?" she said. "I mean, can't you appeal to his patriotism? Make him resign his commission."

The career military soldier could hardly contain his contempt for this woman. Her whole career had been about manipulating others, including the PM. It was unconscionable to think that her advice would have an impact on the lives of his soldiers. For the first time, he was about to speak his mind to the PM without a filter.

"Major O'Rourke is a professional soldier who has followed orders his whole career, including some rather dubious ones that began in this office, Prime Minister," he said as calmly as he could. "Every order he has followed he has done so out of his sense of duty and sense of patriotism, so don't ever question any soldier's loyalty in front of me," he said to both of them. He then looked the Prime Minister directly in the eye and gave him an ultimatum.

"And Prime Minister, if your bitch here doesn't back off and get back in her kennel, I will make sure that the media knows about the conversations that have taken place in this office and which, I am ashamed to say, I was a part of. If there is justice in this world you will not be in this office after the next election and you and your professional peroxided liar will be a dim and embarrassing memory."

"You wouldn't dare," gritted Deakin. "You would destroy your own reputation," she rasped coming out from behind the PM to stand toe-to-toe with the general. It was a ridiculous sight. Deakin stood all of five feet five whilst Lieutenant General Braddon towered a full head taller, and yet she thought she could stare him down.

The Chief of Army deliberately bent down theatrically so he could meet her eye-to-eye.

"Perhaps you are just appealing to my sense of patriotism," he said quietly. "I am already ashamed to have been a part of this. My only redemption is honesty. If that means I destroy my reputation, then so be it."

His whole life had been about assessing the enemy and where their vulnerabilities were. He knew right then that these two political puppeteers could twist the truth. After all, Deakin had a communications background, so she was trained to distort the truth, and the PM was a politician, so naturally he was a career liar. He picked up his hat and turned to leave, but not before firing a warning shot at them both.

"Do you honestly think that I don't have recordings of our conversations?" he said, patting a bulge in his pants pocket. "We have a term for it in the military, it's called the 'commander's reserve'. The thing you keep aside, just in case."

And with that he left Deakin and the PM staring at the door he slammed behind him, speechless, trying to process what the Chief of Army had just implied.

The chief walked down the corridor and down the steps and headed to the Parliament House car park where his driver was waiting. When he knew he was out of view he reached into his pants pocket and pulled out his 'commander's reserve', a packet of mints. He poured a couple into his mouth and crunched them. His interactions with the PM and his staff always left a sour taste in his mouth that even mints could not take away.

77

The Silly Season

The end of November arrived, and Congress took its break while the excitement surrounding Mick and Maye's wedding continued. But other events were coordinated to maintain the momentum over the Thanksgiving and Christmas holiday period.

There were surprise visits to kids in hospitals where the media was deliberately not invited. That was by design, though. This was a genuine desire to bring some happiness to the families that were experiencing pain and sadness at Thanksgiving. Besides, there was no need to get the media involved when everyone had a camera in their pocket and were eager to sell their stories to the news. Even if Mick and Maye wanted their visits to be private, parents and staff were eager to let everyone know that 'the first couple of the United States' had paid them a surprise visit.

But perhaps the greatest coup was when Mick and Maye turned up in Iraq on Christmas Day to spend it with the troops that were still there fighting ISIS, the Islamic State in Iraq and Syria, and those that were providing aid to Syrian refugees. This caught everyone in the RNC and DNC by surprise! At first the RNC leadership was angry that they had not been informed, but when Maye was given a flight suit to wear with captain's rank insignia, her previous rank in the air force, she became the most photographed woman in the US, and the optics looked terrific. Of course, it helped that she was given a form-fitting flying suit by a female pilot. They even had a set of wings embroidered with a new nickname for her: Congresswoman Maye 'Mayday' Young. Her fit body filled it perfectly and all the soldiers there wanted a picture of themselves with the hot ex-air force congresswoman, 'Mayday' Young.

Mick wasn't excluded. At a visit to an army unit, he was given an opportunity to shoot with the soldiers on one of the firing ranges there. He had brought along his uniform and even though it wasn't protocol or proper that he should wear it while he was not on duty, he knew that the Chief of Army would be given a boost if he did, as would Maye. And so with his Australian uniform on, he joined the American soldiers on the firing range and did a practice shoot with them. Mick had worked it just right and Sally-Anne wrangled the cameras with aplomb and got them into the best positions.

But perhaps the piece-de-resistance was something that was completely unplanned and that would send President Troup into a social media frenzy, not that much was needed for that to occur.

Mick and Maye were talking to a group of soldiers when one of them, a young sergeant, said that when Maye was elected, he would be proud to serve under her as commander-in-chief. Sally-Anne had managed to get footage of that, and it was on social media not twenty minutes after the soldier uttered it. President Troup, sitting in the West Wing, saw it on his Twitter feed... and went berserk.

And when they made an unscheduled visit to Australia to lend their moral support to the firefighters battling the country's worst bushfires in recorded history, they could seem to do no wrong. It was a welcome diversion from all the bad news that Mick's home country was experiencing.

78

Beach Blanket Bingo

While Maye had involved the women of America in her search for the perfect wedding dress, Mick had asked the 'men of America' to suggest what he should do for his buck's party. He termed the party his 'Call for Fire Support: the last hooah!' tour. A title that would tickle the fancy of military men and women, past and present.

His only proviso was that it be 'kept clean… relatively.' The response was overwhelming. The hashtag #callforfiresupport grew and grew, and in a few days he had over fifty thousand followers and dozens of offers to help. Hundreds of suggestions were made ranging from cookouts at local fairs to huge parties to adventurous pursuits. But one suggestion really stood out from the rest and played perfectly into the campaign. It was a five-day 'moving beach party' down the coast consisting of skydiving, scuba-diving, football matches and beach parties, culminating with a blowout on Fort Lauderdale beach with a Cuban theme. The party would start in South Carolina and move south through Georgia finishing in Florida.

Of course, Ben, his best man, would be a part of it. So would Rob and Jesús. The four of them looked like they had just stepped out of a diversity meeting, but they had all become very close in the pressure cooker of the campaign. The #callforfiresupport bucks party was quickly underway and gathering steam.

And it was a roaring success. Starting in South Carolina, he held a party at Hilton Head on the beach and invited anyone who wanted to come along. It ended up getting somewhat out of hand, but the local economy thrived in what is normally its low season.

A quick stop at Savannah in Georgia and a visit to the 160th Special Operations Aviation Regiment, of which Ben's father was a part when he disappeared, and a special tour of the base and a chance to say hello to the troops. They even took them for a skydive from one of their Chinook helicopters, both of them strapped to an instructor each. Both of them remarked that it was quite a different way to leave a Chinook than they were used to. A unit cameraman jumped with them and captured Mick and Ben surrounded by freefalling special forces soldiers at eight thousand feet. It was a great and unexpected addition to the party and played well for the media.

But perhaps the most successful events were in Florida. A session with the Jaguars football team in Jacksonville. They had won their division, but lost during the playoffs, so their season was over. But they put on a special training session for Mick's buck's party and for their fans.

But further south is where Jesús's seven-months of intensive language coaching had really come to the fore. The days of deep conversations, the multitude of lunches and dinners at Mexican restaurants where he was only allowed to speak Spanish, the constant news feed from *Telemundo* and their re-runs of *Friends* and *Seinfeld* en Espanol, (*¿Rachel está muy bonita, non? Y Kramer! Ay, ay, ay!*) Mick was able to converse in Spanish good enough to give interviews to the Spanish-language papers such that every one of them was crying out for more of '*El rey Australiano*'. The Latino population lapped it up. A big party on the beach near Miami was even bigger than the one in South Carolina. Rebel flags were everywhere along with the flags of Puerto Rico, the Dominican Republic, Mexico and Cuba. Jesús had become a minor celebrity as '*el hombre detrás del hombre*', 'the man behind the man.'

The final day's partying descended into the night and the boys had had way too much sun and way too many Cuba Libre cocktails, rum and cokes. It was unseasonably hot, even for Miami, and it brought out thousands more to the party. By 9 p.m., the diehards were still going strong and, as the quartet was drinking and dancing and shaking hands with everyone—and Mick and Jesús were screaming out cheers in Spanish, much to the delight of everyone, there started a chant of *"Cuba! Libre! Cuba! Libre!"*

Though Mick had meant to chant the name of the drink rum and coke, it didn't occur to him that it was also a political statement.

And with their heads spinning and their ears ringing, the four of them stumbled back to their hotel rooms, sunburned, drunk and much the worse for wear.

* * *

At 9 a.m., the four met in the hotel restaurant for a big breakfast of bacon and eggs and sausage and anything else that had grease in it. All of them were less than at their finest. Rob was looking the best of the lot of them, but the other three, over a decade Rob's senior, admitted that their partying days were definitely in the rear-view mirror.

As they sat at the table, Jesús returned from reception with a copy of the *Miami Herald*. On the front page, above the fold, was a photo of Mick, Ben, Rob and Jesús dancing with a bevy of bikini-clad Latina beauties with the headline, 'The blunder from Down Under'. What followed was a scathing article on how it was unbecoming for the partner of a presidential candidate to be cavorting with 'loose Latinas' just days before his wedding.

Jesús began reading it and Mick's heart sank. He buried his head in his hands. This was not a good look for Maye's campaign.

When his phone buzzed and Sally-Anne's number appeared, his heart sank further. He knew he was in for a tongue-lashing. The *Miami Herald* was syndicated so he assumed that the photo of him and the boys partying had probably made it across the continent. Who knows what was playing on the morning news bulletins as people would be waking up to this image, and any other image that was caught on phones by party-goers and supplied to the media, showing them at their partying best, but at their campaigning worst. A bit of a steamy scandal during the cold, northern winter.

"Hi Sally-Anne," Mick said sheepishly. "Is everything OK?" He waited for the dressing down.

"Not as OK as it is in Miami, by the looks of it," she replied. Mick couldn't tell if she was seething or not. His phone was not working well and had been playing up for a while now. He kept telling himself to get rid of it... and right now he wanted to throw it into the sea.

Just at that moment Mick's phone chirped, along with the phones of the other three.

"Hang on, Sally-Anne, I have a tweet," he said, delaying *the talk* for a few more seconds. The four of them grabbed their phones to see what it was. It was yet another Troup tweet, but this one featured Mick with the picture of him partying with the bikini girls.

@theRealTroup #thatforeigner not displaying the standards of an Army officer. Pretty lame. Disgraceful behavior before his wedding. Not White House material. #Troup2020 #MAGOM

"Did you see Troup's tweet," asked Mick. Now he *knew* he was in trouble.

"I sure did," said Sally-Anne. "I'm looking at it now. In fact, we're all looking at it. I'm on speaker. Maye and Pam are with me. Mick looked at Ben and closed his eyes, slowly shaking his head.

"Hi honey," a contrite Mick squeaked. "It's not as bad as it looks." Mick had put his phone on speaker hoping that it might keep things a little more civil. "You're on speaker, too. All the guys are here, and they say 'hi'."

Ben, Rob and Jesús gave a timid 'hi' to Maye. They all had desperate expressions on their faces as they looked at Mick. They were glad they were not in his shoes.

"Hello, darling," she replied. Her tone sounded like she was smiling, but it was that tone of one that is holding the moral high ground, a tone of exasperation. "Hello boys. It looks like you are all having a lot of fun. Has Jess called you yet, Ben?"

Ben's eyes closed and it was his turn for *his* head to sink. Rob and Jesús were glad that they were both single.

"Hi Maye. No, she hasn't yet." He sounded like someone resigned to his fate of sleeping on the couch for a week or two. And then there was his commanding officer back at the battalion. To be featured on the front page of newspapers across the nation... Oh, this was not good!

"Do you want me to put out a statement apologizing?" Mick asked. His pained expression and drooping shoulders testament to his contrition.

"Oh, it's too late for that," replied Maye, with a voice of condescension, "I've already been interviewed this morning," she revealed. "In fact, I have been on three morning breakfast shows. My day started at 4.30. That's 4.30 a.m." She placed a lot of emphasis on the 'a' and the 'm'.

Rob and Jesús and Ben glanced at each other. Their Australian mate was a 'dead man walking'. And they were aiding and abetting him! There was a silence while she let that sink in. The boys were at a loss for what to say.

"The main question they wanted answered," she continued, "was did I think it was appropriate for the potential First Gentleman of the United States to be cavorting with bikini girls and shouting, 'Free Cuba!'"

This last part jolted them.

"We were shouting 'rum and coke' not 'Free Cuba!' pleaded Mick. This could have serious international implications with the Cuban dictatorship. It was then that Jesús held up his phone excitedly. The online article from the Spanish-speaking weekly, *Diario Las Americas*, had reporting that was somewhat different. Instead of lambasting Mick and his entourage, it raved about the new age White House, *la neuva casa blanca*. Jesús quickly scoured the story, looked at Mick pointing to it, and gave it a thumbs up.

"You certainly are the Golden Child, aren't you honey," said Maye.

"Um..." Mick stumbled, not sure where Maye was going with this. The *Herald* was negative, the *Diario* was positive. Exactly what did this all mean?

"The response to my interview has been overwhelming. About ten percent negative and ninety percent positive. They're online. You can see them now."

Ben and Rob scrambled for their phones and started searching for the ABC, NBC and CBS breakfast shows on their websites and on YouTube. Each interview started out as a negative, asking questions like was it appropriate for campaign funds to be spent on such debauchery, or is it appropriate behavior for a presidential candidate's fiancé. But with the expertise of a veteran politician, Maye was able to sway them to her point of view.

She let each breakfast show know that no campaign funds were expended, and that Mick and the boys had paid for everything out of their own pockets, including the bus hire and the signage on the bus. Any other event was held by local organizations as part of Mick's bachelor party.

She also let them know that if she was elected, then Mick's life would change drastically. It would be unfair of her to not let him have one last big party as a bachelor, and it would be unfair of the American people to judge him negatively for that.

"I love my fiancé," she told the reporters. "I trust him completely. He has been my rock; my confidant; my number one fan. He deserves some down time. It's the least I can do for all that he has done for me."

She had done such a great job that by the end of each interview, the hosts were either neutral or supportive of Mick's sojourn. The male hosts in particular seemed very much onside.

As they said goodbye to Miami and headed across the Everglades to pick up I-75 northbound to Atlanta—with a quick stop at The Villages for a reception by some Republican boosters—they scoured the comments on any video posted that showed them partying. They were not only gauging the response, but were also looking for anything that may be controversial. After all, towards the end of the evening, things were a bit blurry.

There were literally hundreds from the whole buck's party: from partygoers at Hilton Head; from their visit to Savanna, Georgia; at the Jacksonville Jaguars' training session; and the Fort Lauderdale beach party. All of them were complimentary for the most part, in English and in Spanish. Rob and Jesús featured in many of them with pleas from many girls in the comments for the two accidental stars to contact them if they were ever in Florida again.

The various hashtags had begun springing up: #MANDM (#M&M took them to the candy); #MickandMaye; and others. But someone had created the hashtag #FGOTUS, First Gentleman of the United States, and it was certainly trending and becoming the 'go to' hashtag for any-one's post that related to Mick.

This may have been premature. Mick wasn't even married to Maye, yet. And what's more, she hadn't even competed in her first primary. She may not get the popular vote of the Republican party's rank and file, and her campaign could end sooner rather than later.

The Republican caucus in Iowa in just a few weeks would be hard to predict. Troup was extremely popular in the conservative Midwest. And the New Hampshire primary the following week was also just as hard to foretell. If she didn't do well in those two primaries, and failed to get the support from the Republican voters there to even nominate, well the campaign would be dead in the water.

But right now, it was time to get ready for the wedding. A stop to see the retirees at The Villages, and then back to Atlanta.

His phone rang. The caller ID country code said +61. It was a number from Canberra in Australia. This wasn't good. It was the Chief of Army.

79

Here Comes the Candidate

The end of January had come quickly, and the excitement surrounding the wedding was whipped up into a frenzy by the media. There had been a lot of jockeying for invitations by members of Congress from both sides of the House and Senate. Mick's choice of the US Air Force Academy chapel was a stroke of genius. It was huge! And it allowed for scores and scores of people to be invited. In the end, twelve hundred guests, the capacity of the chapel, had accepted. It was a diverse invitation list: 'A' listers right down to 'D' listers. Mick had a soft spot for stars from some long-canceled sitcoms and so a smattering of former 'A' listers who had slid down the alphabet to the 'D' list were there, and very grateful for the opportunity! Of course, there was also a generous sprinkling of members of the armed services.

The virus that had been causing the Center for Disease Control and the World Health Organization such heartache over the last few weeks had been named as Severe Acute Respiratory Syndrome Coronavirus 2, or Novel Coronavirus 2019—Covid19, for short. So far, the US had gone about its business as it always had, but the deaths in China were climbing and the evacuation of US citizens from Wuhan was about to commence. But that seemed a world away. Today was America's own royal wedding.

The congressional invitees all took the opportunity to arrive at Peterson Air Force Base by Hercules where they were met by Chinook helicopters. The units' commanding officers found their excuses to be onboard the aircraft so that they could have some face time with the captured audience of senators and representatives. For many of the career politicians and their partners, it was a great thrill to be aboard military aircraft. A red carpet was laid out on the tarmac of the airbase to allow for the parade and a photoshoot. The backdrop was the line of air force aircraft and the snow-capped Rocky Mountains. Something that could not be replicated in any Grammys or Emmys or Oscars. No big noting rappers with their entourages, nor A-listers with agendas and questionable fashion statements could be seen, just dignified members of Congress, still serving in uniform, and their partners.

Sally-Anne had made sure that all the media had dossiers on each congressional invitee, and it made the whole event run smoothly. Even though the temperature was a chilly forty-five degrees, the sky was a brilliant and cloudless blue. The ladies were able to show off their dresses and, if they were members of Congress, make a quick plug for whatever cause they thought needed it. Others said hello to their constituents while others congratulated the happy couple. The wedding was being televised live and it was, so far, going extremely well.

The politicians currently serving with the national guard or a service reserve numbered only two dozen: fifteen Republicans and nine Democrats, and so they were given special treatment. Of the Republican invitees, it was a way to assess what sort of support Maye had within Congress from her own party. She was somewhat disheartened by the response. It seemed Troup had threatened dire consequences to any member of the party that accepted an invitation to the wedding. He even threatened the Governor of Colorado with withholding funding for his state and its national guard if he dared authorize them to participate in the wedding. The Governor, knowing that it would be political suicide for Troup within his state, doubled down on the threat and became even more resolute in his support for the wedding and his contribution, much to the delight of his state and the businesses in Colorado Springs and Denver, which would stand to gain with over two thousand visitors from the wedding and media. Again, the Mick and Maye show had brought a boost to the local economy during the state's low season. Furthermore, with it being a marginal state which could, if handled correctly, possibly swing to the Republicans, Troup was advised by the Party that it was unwise to make such rash threats. The Governor's prediction had been realized, and President Troup backed down. The Governor was the hero, and the victor.

He was singled out by Sally-Anne to have his photo taken with every member of Congress who was invited and kept the Colorado news agencies close at hand. Sally-Anne was giving the Democrat Governor a spike in his approval ratings, and yet again, this did not go unnoticed by those that understood the nuances of bi-partisan politics.

Soon, Chinook helicopters from the Colorado Army National Guard started up, and the guests disappeared inside each to be whisked away to the academy chapel.

By the time the guests had been deposited at the chapel by the helicopters, and those that were to travel by limousine had arrived—and after their own red-carpet event had concluded—it was almost time for the bride and groom to make their entrances.

The guests had all taken their seats in the magnificent academy chapel, and large television screens had been erected to display the televised event. Mick arrived in a Chinook helicopter, piloted by Ben and the guard unit's commanding officer, which landed in the forecourt of the chapel grounds. Mick looked the part in his dress uniform.

Ben thought it prudent to have Mick invite their unit's commanding officer from Fort Rucker to the wedding. It would go a long way to giving Ben a Teflon coating for his part in the beach party incident, know nicknamed 'beachparty-gate'. The CO leaped at the opportunity and he and his wife made their way from Fort Rucker to Colorado to participate. The national guard unit's commanding officer—who also happened to own three hardware stores in Denver—flew as aircraft captain with Ben as his co-pilot. After landing, a standby crew who traveled with them took over the controls and Ben and the guard unit's CO did a quick change out of their flight suits and into dress uniforms in the cargo compartment. The four officers: the two unit COs, and

Mick and Ben, then emerged from the cargo compartment and down the ramp stepping out into the bright, Colorado sunshine. Their arrival was caught on camera and beamed around the world, as well as to the screens in the chapel.

Mick and Ben both turned and saluted the Colorado Army National Guard CO, who was the more senior of the two commanders, and then, for good measure, Ben saluted his CO, who also returned the salute. Mick and Ben then walked into the magnificent protestant chapel and took their places at the altar near the priest standing beneath a huge, stylized sword, at least forty feet high. (Mick thought briefly that it reminded him of the sword of Damocles!) Now it was time to await the arrival of the bride.

Maye's Chinook had departed the air force base for the nine-minute flight to the US Air Force Academy. Television and computer screens around the world showed Maye, strapped into the seats of the Chinook helicopter in her wedding dress, wearing a flight helmet, her face covered by its dark visor. Never was there such a unique wedding-day image. The British royal family may have the tiara-adorned bride arriving in a glorious coach with uniformed attendants and pulled by six magnificently appointed horses, but Maye Young arrived to her wedding strapped into the bench seat of an army helicopter, wearing a flying helmet rather than a tiara... and she wouldn't have had it any other way.

Soon, the wedding Chinook arrived and, stepping off the ramp, beneath the Stars and Stripes that hung on the cabin's ceiling, was Maye, being escorted by the Governor of Colorado and, to everyone's surprise, the Secretary of the Air Force! Behind her were two female air force cadets holding her train in the rotor wash of the giant helicopter. Maye had suggested that because her father was dead and her grandmother too frail requiring her mother to look after her, and their fear of Covid—however irrational that was—that she didn't have any family to attend. She suggested that asking the Governor of Colorado to give her away, and the Secretary of the Air Force, herself a lady from Wyoming and a qualified pilot herself, then that would be a good way of smoothing things out for the day. Of course, both of them were eager to be part of the spectacle.

The Secretary of the Air Force, Abby Wilcox, had not asked the president's permission to be a part of the day. As a presidential appointee to her position, it put her in a difficult situation. She figured that she would 'continue until apprehended.' Anyway, if she got the sack, she didn't really mind. She'd be happy to go back to her ranch and her horses in Wyoming. Washington politics wasn't fun anymore... except for Maye's potential candidature, which she thought was wonderful drama, and which she supported whole-heartedly.

An honor guard of air force cadets took post—after all, it *was* the Secretary of the Air Force—and they flanked the bridal party, their rifles at present arms. And as the wedding march began to play on the magnificent organ above the chapel's entrance—its four thousand pipes blasting out the Bridal Chorus better than Wagner ever could have imagined—Maye, the Governor and the Secretary, walked down the aisle, with Jess—her matron of honor—walking close behind the two female cadets attending to her train.

Maye's wedding dress was exquisite. White taffeta and lace with pearl and diamond highlights. Dress designers had been falling over themselves to dress her. She wore a light-blue sash which fell from her left shoulder across her chest tied with a red, white and blue rosette on her right hip, her air force wings and her service ribbons displayed proudly. (The Secretary of the Air Force approved this departure from the dress manual). The British royal family would have been jealous.

Mick looked at her, her beautiful face covered by a shear, lace veil. He thought he loved her as much as he could yesterday, but today he was proved wrong.

80

When Duty Calls

The wedding and reception occupied much of the news cycle, a stark contrast from the worsening stories coming out of China, and the dire warnings of the CDC and WHO, the UN's World Health Organization, about this new virus.

President Troup, eager to distract the attention of the nation from the wedding and Maye's tilt at power, proclaimed the virus 'the Chinese Flu Strain' in contravention of WHO's guidelines on naming diseases after people or countries. He coupled that with 'the foreign sickness', and 'the foreign flu'.

When asked about Maye, he made polite comment about their marriage saying that 'he hoped the Congresswoman and her Chinese relatives and her foreign husband' had a great celebration.

His comments were thinly-veiled rancor and their petulance was not lost on the nation. Pundits quickly jumped on his words, and they were analyzed continuously for the three days leading up to the Sunday, the day before the Iowa caucuses.

Since the buck's party, Mick had fielded a number of calls from Australia. The Chief of Army, or the PM's office seemed, at first, to be very critical of the reporting of the partying in Florida, but quickly changed their tune when they saw that what should have been a negative story turned out to be a positive one. It seemed that a huge cross section of the American male population approved of Mick's behavior. If they weren't keen on a female president, they were certainly keen on her fiancé, now her husband, more so than President Troup or any of the Democratic candidates.

Parallels were drawn between Mick's influence and that of Jacqueline Bouvier Kennedy, but in reverse. Where she had been the doting wife of Senator John Kennedy and, as the potential first lady, had posed dutifully in her pillbox hats, and influenced debates on women's looks and their abilities, Mick had done likewise, but in a manner more appealing to the men of America. Jackie's contribution to the campaign, and the influence she had on women, was a major factor in JFK's election. Her influence, though, was confined to a newspaper column she wrote, and interviews conducted at home due to her pregnancy. Mick, on the other hand, was getting out and doing as many masculine things as possible, mixed with refined dinners and speaking engagements befitting an Army officer. The polls had his popularity in the high sixties amongst registered Republican males and low sixties amongst females. But more importantly, registered Democrats found him more appealing than any spouse of a Democrat candidate seeking the party's nomination. Unfortunately, only two of the Democratic hopefuls were female, and their husbands were well into their sixties, so the comparison between them and Mick was unfair. But when did political campaign spin doctors ever let facts get in the way of a good story or twisting statistics?

However, since the wedding, the one question that seemed to be raised more than any other was that of his citizenship. Of course, being married to a US citizen meant automatic permanent residency and a relatively easy path to citizenship, however there was still paperwork to do and a waiting period of months or years. And then there was the problem of his commission in the Australian Army. If he was to take US citizenship, or even dual citizenship, it would be at the expense of his commission.

Maye and Mick had spoken about this on a number of occasions, but because it was so sensitive and painful, neither had pushed it to a logical conclusion. Mick had been given leave to remain with Maye until 'after his honeymoon' which, he told his superiors in the Australian Army, would be towards the end of February after the Iowa and New Hampshire primaries and Super Tuesday. They figured that by then they would have a good idea of Maye's chances to be nominated by the Party. If she won enough support, the race would continue. If she didn't, then the point was moot, and she would cease campaigning. February would be critical for Maye's future, both politically and as a wife. She had even said to Mick that she seriously contemplated making a decision after Iowa and New Hampshire and, if she was not likely to get the Party's endorsement, quit the campaign, see out her term as congresswoman, and then move to Australia to be with her army officer husband.

So on the weekend before the Iowa caucuses, Republican and Democrat candidates had gathered in the freezing Midwestern state to try and convince the voters to side with their camps as they competed with each other for their parties' nominations.

* * *

By lunchtime the day before the caucuses, Mick and Maye had been to four separate events. Mick was in uniform, at the request of the Party, which had coordinated two huge events at two VFW posts. The two of them were welcomed like superstars and everyone wanted a chance to congratulate them on their marriage and to get selfies. Now, at a lunch given in their honor by the Des Moines and Ames Chambers of Commerce, where Maye was to give a speech on her platform and participate in a Q and A, they were once again being mobbed by the media.

The *Des Moines Register* had its representatives there, just like back in August at the Iowa State Fair. This was not lost on the two of them, because it was at the state fair that Maye had surprised Mick and had proposed to him. The local network affiliates were there, although PBS, again, was not, and all the major networks sent extra crews to cover as many events as possible.

During the Chambers of Commerce event, the media had cornered Maye and she was up against the ropes explaining her progressive (for a

Republican) five-point plan, especially the health care and environment components. President Troup was very popular here in Iowa, so the local media smelled blood and they were not going to let Maye's pseudo-progressive policy platform go without a few jabs.

She won support with her discussions of ethanol as being a resource that was under-utilized (Iowa provides much of the corn-based ethanol in the country), but the idea of a type of universal health care for all Americans was an alien concept and smacked of President O'Conee's health care system that had been bastardized in Congress.

It was soon time for her to escape the media scrum and mount the stage. She was tired, and Mick could see it. The last few months campaigning against Troup's bottomless pockets, while they had to keep the momentum on a shoestring, was starting to take its toll.

The sad thing was that Mick could see just how good a president Maye could be. She was smarter than Troup; more worldly than Troup; more likeable than Troup. The country would be much better placed with her in the White House than the current buffoon.

Over the past few weeks he had been playing over in his mind various scenarios involving their future together. He really missed her during his moving buck's party two weeks prior. But it was the phone call from the Chief of Army when they were leaving Miami that had really caused him a lot of concern. His appointment as commanding officer of the army aviation school had been held for as long as possible and the Australian Army wanted him back in two weeks' time. His promotion had already been approved but he did not tell his wife that she was now sleeping with a lieutenant colonel. He chuckled to himself that he didn't want her to be intimidated by his rank, notwithstanding the fact that in less than a year she could conceivably be the most powerful woman in the world.

But all kidding aside, his career was calling him home, and the army had been very generous in letting him stay and have free rein, even if it was in the PM's best interest. And as much as the PM and his communications adviser wanted the Chief of Army to make Mick stay, the chief was making a stand and letting the PM, the Minister for Defence and the Chief of the Defence Force, his boss, know that none of them had any right to influence the career of an army officer who had been following orders faithfully up to this point. At least they had no right to influence his career without the risk of their interference being made public. It certainly would not be a good look for the Australian Government or the Australian Defence Force to be seen trying to influence US politics, especially when Australia wanted to maintain its strong alliance. Nor did it want to jeopardize their submarine deal that was still being negotiated. The Chief of Army had told the PM's communications adviser exactly that when she tried to throw her weight around yet again. To be precise, he told her that when duty calls, a good army officer will answer. Something that she would not be able to comprehend.

As Mick sat there, he caught himself in the reflection of the water pitcher. The reflection of him in his uniform only served to remind him of his duty. From his viewpoint there were two options. The first was to head home in two weeks and take up his command, and let Maye continue the campaign without him. If she didn't win office, then she would see out her term as a congresswoman and then either she moves to Australia, or he moves back to the US.

His second option was to forgo his posting and take leave without pay and remain in the US until the end of the primaries in August and see if Maye got enough votes to get the Republican nomination as its presidential candidate. Then, if she did, she would contest the presidential election in November... but that was as far ahead as he had thought.

In any case, his imminent departure in two weeks was all he could see on the horizon.

But he had to put that out of his mind, because right now his wife (it was still strange to call her that) was mounting the stage, and the media was going to keep giving her a hard time about her five-point plan. Right now, his duty was to support her.

81

I Owe Her

Maye's presentation went down reasonably well with the invitees of the Des Moines and Ames Chamber of Commerce Caucus Lunch, but Mick could tell she was not at her best. Her five-point plan was a good and sound plan, but the media was going to do its best to challenge her, to find a chink in her armor, and then exploit it.

"Does anyone have any questions for me?" she asked taking the microphone from its stand so she could walk the stage. The reporters' hands all shot up and they called out for her attention.

She pointed to the reporter from FOX 28. The FOX network had usually been friendly in the past, but here in Iowa they may be more partial to Troup. The blond reporter called out her question.

"Your platform on gun control seems at odds with party policy. Are you proposing that gun owners must pay more to buy and own a gun?" she asked. The subject of gun control was a touchy one here in Iowa, and it was obvious the reporter didn't have a grasp on her policy. It was not to stop gun ownership, just increase the penalties for illegal gun ownership, and increase the requirements for background checks and the safe storage of firearms.

Maye braced herself to answer. She just had to get through the next thirty hours 'til the start of the caucuses. She looked down at the reporter and all eyes—and camera lenses—looked at her... and then something happened at the edge of the stage that diverted their attention from her to it.

She looked at the steps leading up to the stage and saw her husband ascending. If he was going to come and stand by her while she answered these questions, then that was exactly what she needed right now. She was tired, and she didn't feel her best, but here came her knight in shining armor, looking dashing in his Australian Army uniform.

As Mick approached her, he took the microphone from her hand and kissed her on her cheek. Placing the microphone back on its stand, he leaned into it to address the crowd and media. The cameras bore down on him, and the still photographers clicked away, their flashes punctuating the scene. Others in the crowd held up their phones to capture Mick and Maye together on stage.

"Ladies and Gentlemen," he said into the microphone, his arm around Maye's waist, "this woman is the most remarkable woman I have ever met in my life."

Maye smiled and blushed and looked away. The cameras loved that, and the shutters clicked. It was a brief reprieve from the media grilling.

"Her drive and determination have brought her here today, standing before you, asking you to believe in her and her ideas for this great nation. It has brought her here from her family that escaped communism and its brutality to settle in a land where people can be free and where they can live in peace and can make whatever they want of themselves if they are willing to try. It brought her here from her hard work at school that saw her attend the US Air Force Academy, graduating with honors. It brought her here from her service flying in war zones and on humanitarian missions as a pilot in the United States Air Force. It brought her here from an abusive relationship that she escaped. It brought her here from her service to her community as a member of the US House of Representatives. And her drive and determination has now brought her remarkable journey here, to the great state of Iowa, which is the crucible of one of the great examples of democracy, the election to decide the President of the United States. Iowa is, and will continue to be, the shining light of the American democratic process."

He waited while the audience of business owners and their guests applauded and cheered, and then finally settled down.

"And even though I am from half a planet away, Iowa will always be held closely in my heart, because it is where this remarkable woman defied convention, and proposed to me, in front of the people of this great state, and the people of this great nation. She defied convention and took control and got down on one knee and asked me to come with her on this journey, a journey that has brought us back to Iowa, as husband and wife."

The crowd lapped this up, and Maye reached out and took his hand, and kissed him on his cheek, pausing just a little longer so the cameras could capture the moment.

"Unfortunately, my country has called upon me to fulfill *my* duty," he said, bringing a murmur from the audience.

"Duty is a concept that is not lost on Americans. If there was any nation in the world that understood the meaning of the word, it is the United States! But I, too, understand the meaning of duty. My country has asked me to return home in two weeks, to resume my duties as an officer in the Australian Army, where I am to assume command of a unit as a newly promoted lieutenant colonel."

This last statement caught everyone by surprise. Some began to applaud the news of his command and promotion, but when they realized they were in the minority, they quickly quietened. For it was not good news. This news meant that Maye would be left alone to finish her campaign for the primaries and the presidency.

It was seen on Maye's face as she looked shocked. The cameras switched quickly to Maye, cameramen pulling close ups to capture her eyes, which underscored her anxiety at what Mick was saying.

At one of the tables near to the media, a husband and wife filmed the drama being played out on the stage. The man had an earpiece with microphone and was narrating the event. She was filming and transmitting from her phone. Her images, and his narration, were being beamed straight to Troup's team in a Des Moines hotel. The president and his new CREEP, the Committee to RE-Elect the President, had been closely monitoring Maye and her appearances in Iowa. Since the wedding her popularity was soaring and Troup, not being able to effectively kill her campaign through the Party, was now resorting to close monitoring. He was ready to pounce on any weakness, and it looked as though Young's husband was about to destroy her greatest strength and their trump card—their partnership on the campaign trail.

Troup's campaign team were just as shocked as everyone else at the luncheon. But their shock was one of eager happiness. They were on the verge of giving each other high fives, only containing themselves long enough so that they could hear Maye's response to her husband's shock announcement; that he was returning to Australia. The Mick and Maye dream team was about to have a major setback, and her campaign would, no doubt, suffer. And at just the wrong time for her. The caucuses were to be held tomorrow; and next week were the New Hampshire primaries. Along with Super Tuesday, these were the three most important events in the primaries race.

"That's right!" said Troup transfixed on the screen displaying the images being captured by his spy's phone camera. "You tell her that you're scuttling off back home to Australia. Just go home and let the grown-ups run America." He snapped his fingers at one of his assistants, beckoning for a whiskey. This was going to be a celebration.

* * *

Back in the Chambers of Commerce luncheon, the atmosphere was not as joyous as that in the Trump camp. The mood had become tense in the space of just one minute. All eyes—and camera lenses—were fixed on Maye, and how she was reacting to Mick's announcement. And how would Mick handle her reaction? The cameramen and women could tell instinctively that this scene would lead all the campaign stories that evening, so eager was the public for news of their relationship and their campaign trials and tribulations. Mick continued.

"But in every person's life there will come a cross-roads moment; a moment when a decision must be made that you know will have life-changing consequences. I had that moment here in Iowa just five months ago when the most amazing woman in the world asked me to be her husband. I owe her for the happiness she has given me and for the amazing journey of which she has asked me to be a part. I owe her everything. I owe her, Iowa!" he said, not hiding his play on words.

"The least I can do," he went on, "is to show my love for her... by making *her* my duty. *She* is now my duty."

He looked into her eyes and made sure his words were captured by the microphone. The crowd was at a hush, just the shutter clicks of the cameras breaking the silence.

"So I make this announcement, not with a heavy heart, but with a greater clarity of what my life's calling actually is, that I shall resign my commission in the Australian Army so that I can remain with my wife and," he turned to the crowd and to the media, "will seek citizenship of the United States of America... if you will have me."

In the banquet hall of the Des Moines Marriott Downtown, the invited guests of the Des Moines and Ames Chambers of Commerce cheered and applauded as Mick removed from his epaulets the insignia of his rank as Major—two silver crowns— and placed them in his wife's hand, squeezing it affectionately.

"Are you sure?" she whispered to him, her eyes glistening.

"More than anything else I have done in my life," was his reply. And with that she embraced him to the strobing flashes of cameras; the shouts from the media; and the applause and cheers from the crowd.

* * *

It was 4 a.m. in Canberra when this remarkable scene transpired in Iowa, and so, as the news agencies flashed the story, the Australian correspondents in the US representing the various Australian networks, picked it up and immediately created a piece and sent it to their news directors back home.

As the morning shows went to air, their lead story was Major Mick O'Rourke resigning his commission to take up American citizenship. Jenny Deakin, senior communications adviser to the Prime Minister saw the news as her hands grasped her morning coffee.

"NO!" she screamed at the TV. The way her heart leaped into her mouth, the PM's spin doctor would need an actual doctor!

The Chief of Army, with the sound turned down on his TV, also saw the bulletin. The scene that was played out in the Des Moines Downtown Marriott only a few hours before, of Major O'Rourke with Congresswoman Young embracing, was being replayed. The ticker-tape along the bottom of the screen proclaimed: *"Mick O'Rourke resigns from Australian Army to become US Citizen."*

The Chief turned up the volume to hear the hosts discussing it.

"Goodonya, mate," he said, looking at the smiling image of Major O'Rourke... and, smiling himself, wondered how the PM would take the news.

82

Survival of the Most Cunning

That Sunday evening, and the following Monday morning, all the news of the Iowa caucuses were led by the story of candidate Maye Young's husband resigning his Australian Army commission so he could take up US citizenship.

So, as registered Republicans readied themselves to attend the caucus meetings in school gymnasiums and town halls, and other meeting places around the state, they were inundated with images of Mick and Maye. And so too were Democrats, who were doing the same thing as they decided which, of the half-dozen candidates that had nominated for the Democratic Party ballot, they would support. The more cynical in the Democrat camp called Mick's announcement 'another Republican stunt'. The more sentimental however, preferred to think he did it for love. In either case, the news coverage was very positive... and the Democrats hated that.

Of course, for President Troup, this was another headache. As a businessman used to getting his own way, the fact that he could not bring the GOP into line was frustrating. They could have pulled Young's candidature straightaway and left him—an incumbent President—to go to the polls uncontested by another Republican. He had let anyone that mattered know—including members of the GOP national committee, and anyone in his government—that any assistance to Maye Young's campaign would not be forgotten, and that he would take action. He had already demonstrated that he meant what he said when he sacked the Secretary of the Air Force for participating in Mick and Maye's wedding, and any other member of his government that had attended and who held an appointed position 'at the president's pleasure'. The ensuing re-shuffle on Capitol Hill saw Troup loyalists replacing several rebels who had sided with Congresswoman Young's campaign.

President Troup was touring the state. He rarely attended any events, preferring to show up, make a few comments and shake a few hands, then move on. He was getting more and more irritated that the media was only concerned about a potential split in the GOP in general, and Mick's gesture and his wish to become an American in particular.

"We'll have to see if he is a fit and proper person," came Troup's surprising response. "I mean, can we trust him? He is a foreigner who wants to marry a candidate for the most important position in the world. It sounds to me that he may have an agenda, I'm just saying."

One of the reporters beat her colleagues in pointing out that Troup's wife was also foreign born, a former businesswoman from Slovakia.

He ignored that comment and began to move on. Agent Henry 'Bruce' Lee politely made way for the president to move through the throng. He had also been the subject of some of the photographers' interest. He was not often seen since the attempted assassination, and the interest in him 'taking a bullet' for the president had made him a national hero, and somewhat of a minor celebrity. The secret Service did not appreciate that sort of attention on one of their agents.

But the news cycle moved on and Agent Lee kept as low a profile as possible. Troup, ever the showman, demanded that Lee be his 'point' man, a constant reminder that he had survived an assassination attempt. In fact, he would try and wend that story into any interview as an example of how he was a 'no-nonsense world leader and that other countries wanted him gone because he was "making America great once more".'

'Bruce' Lee had been in the US Secret Service for over five years. He had spent eight years in the US Marine Corps prior to that, serving as a military policeman, before gaining entry into the program. He had to have a visible tattoo surgically removed before he could apply, but once accepted he found the training relatively easy compared to his marine corps training.

During his initial training he applied for the Presidential Protective Detail after graduation, the most highly sought-after role within the service, but which was almost never granted to a new graduate. To his surprise he was successful but had to spend a year in counter-surveillance while a re-shuffle in the PPD was made and a position became vacant. Soon he was inducted for the detail's specialized training.

At first, his appointment was seen as yet another example of political correctness and tokenism, especially by his peers. He was a veteran (and the service was seeking to increase its number of veterans from below nineteen percent to at least twenty-five percent) and he was not a white male, having Asian heritage. But he persevered, and found himself finally detailed to provide protection for Troup.

It was early in 2018 at a Republican fundraiser in Vermont where Troup was delivering a speech that a man rushed the stage next to where Lee was posted. The agent threw his body onto the would-be assassin, cameras capturing the drama. Soon, the sound of a shot, but the agent kept him in a bear hug, hitting him over and over. Agents next to the president rushed him off stage while other agents swarmed to Lee's aid, pulling the gunman from him. Agent Lee fell back, his jacket opening to reveal blood all over his chest and shoulder. Mayhem ensued, the media's cameras thrusting as close as possible into the fray.

The following day, every news outlet carried the footage of the president visiting Lee in his hospital bed interspersed with footage from the drama. The bullet, a .22 caliber, had missed the agent's body armor and had entered his shoulder. The wound was not life-threatening fortunately, and he would make a full recovery, but not before becoming a celebrity. For the next two weeks the news focused on the assassination attempt and the 'failures of the intelligence community to identify the threat.'

The secret service allowed some limited interviews with Agent Lee, but after a day or two any further requests were declined. By then, the main story was 'who was this assassin and who did he work for, or was he a lone wolf?'

It had been discovered that he was from the former Tajikistan, near the border where it meets China and Afghanistan. He had entered Afghanistan and then came to America through Pakistan where tracking his whereabouts became lost. So, between entering Pakistan, and the assassination attempt, he had somehow entered the US, possibly through Canada. The FBI was uncertain how long he had been in the country, but it had been for at least three months. He had been recognized as being a resident of a cheap hotel in Trenton, New Jersey for the past nine weeks, paying cash.

While he was in protective custody at a federal prison, he was found unconscious in his cell, beaten beyond recognition. He had died without regaining consciousness. So, the FBI was not able to totally ascertain exactly where he had come from other than Tajikistan, nor what his motives were in his assassination attempt on the president.

But that did not worry Troup. He immediately blamed Pakistan and capitalized upon his 'miraculous survival' from the assassin's bullet. Of course, the media ignored the fact that a bullet from a .22 caliber pistol was unlikely to be fatal in most cases, but why let facts stand in the way of a good story?

And today, that 'miraculous survival' was rehashed as Troup made sure Agent Lee was always nearby... just as a reminder of what an important world leader he was that people wanted him dead.

83

It's Green in New Hampshire

The Iowa results were somewhat disappointing. Even though they had only narrowly been beaten by Troup, fifty-two percent to forty-eight percent, they had gained nineteen pledged delegates that would vote for her at the Republican National Convention, while Troup would get the other twenty-one.

"What I'm concerned about," said Sally-Anne with the other members of the campaign management team, "was that we had good press after Mick's grand, romantic gesture. Our campaign was lead story that Monday. We should have won more delegates."

"That's only the first primary," re-assured Maye. "And Iowa is very pro-Troup. I think things will be different in New Hampshire," she said.

"I hope so," said one of the campaign managers supplied by the GOP. "If we don't get a good showing in New Hampshire, we'll probably not do too well at Super Tuesday, and that will mean the campaign will be dead in the water."

New Hampshire would be a hard nut to crack. Like Iowa, its population was very conservative and very white. Maye's background and Mick's background, not to mention the great visuals provided by Rob and his rebel flag gesture, and Jesús as Mick's right-hand-man, were not likely to be as impactful as they might be in, say, Texas, or New Mexico, or Florida. Rob had split the black community. Some African Americans saw him as a traitor to blacks all over the country, while the more educated saw him as a role model for those that wanted to have more say in politics; to have a voice in the room within the Republican Party. The Party, it liked to think, cared more about the merit of a person than it did about diversity for the sake of diversity. It adhered to the precepts of Martin Luther King Jr by judging people on the content of their character, rather than the color of their skin, something that the liberal left seemed to have forgotten along the way to the divisiveness that the country was now experiencing. But be that as it may, the reputation of the Republicans, rightly or wrongly, did not make it the poster child for diversity.

"Isn't our first event at City Hall in Manchester? Well, let's find the closest Immigration Services center and I'll submit my application for a marriage green card. That should get some coverage. I mean, I don't want to be sponging off my wife! Now that I'm not a soldier anymore, I've got to get a job," said Mick, half-jokingly.

"That's how we can spin it," said campaign manager number 2. (Mick and Maye and Sally-Anne had kept the GOP's helpers at arm's length and nicknamed them 'Number 1 and Number 2'. But they had been coming in handy when Sally-Anne was overwhelmed and needed some assistance... so they couldn't really complain. But it was obvious that they were communications professionals. Everything was cut-and-dry, and none of their ideas had much imagination. It was Mick, Sally-Anne and Pam that had come up with most of the driven ideas for the campaign.

"Congresswoman Young's husband sets out on his own in the US," she said.

Mick thought it sounded condescending, but smiled, letting her have her moment in the spotlight.

"I think a better way to present it," said Sally-Anne, being careful not to use the word 'spin', "is that it is the first step to Mick's citizenship. After all, he is a grown man who was an army officer. I'm sure he's 'set out on his own' many times before. If we say it like that, it sounds like he's leaving home for the first time."

Mick was glad that Sally-Anne had stepped in with some common sense, and he could certainly work with that idea. Pam found the details of the Immigration Service offices in Manchester, New Hampshire and started the ball rolling. It would be another dog and pony show for the local media in that small New England state... but that was necessary if they were to have a chance against Troup. Iowa was a good result, but it could have been better. New Hampshire needed to be won by Maye. If she didn't get a majority of delegates, it would be hard to recover. With Super Tuesday the first week in March, the single day when primaries are held in fourteen states, including the almost three hundred delegates from California and Texas alone, then a good showing in New Hampshire was vital.

84

Fear and Loathing at 36 000 feet

Troup was furious. While Maye had again failed to win a majority of the vote in the New Hampshire primaries, her forty-five percent was still very respectable, and she picked up ten delegates who would go to the Republican National Convention and vote for her. On the Democrat's side, the outcome of their primaries saw two of the six candidates pull out of the race, having not been able to gather enough effective support during the Iowa caucuses nor the New Hampshire primaries to be considered as viable candidates for the Democratic nomination.

But Troup didn't care about the Democrats. He'd beaten them and their 'bleeding-heart policies' before, and he'd beat them again. It was Maye that he was concerned about, and her candidacy for *his* job! Every time Troup did not defeat her resoundingly in opinion polls—or now in the primaries—*his* stature was chipped away a little more. She had gleaned forty-eight percent in Iowa and forty-five percent in New Hampshire. That was too close for his liking. And the GOP was not intervening, much to his chagrin.

Super Tuesday, just three weeks away, would most probably be the deciding factor.

But in the meantime, he still had to contend with this virus that was starting to be a problem in China. He was getting briefings from his intelligence people and had made sure that the head of the NSA and his health intelligence team had traveled with him to New Hampshire to keep him updated. In response, he had instigated travel bans to and from China, but his main concern, and that of the media, was the campaign.

The president was not shy in dressing down his staff. During one of his many rages while they were on Air Force One, heading to California for a campaign event before returning to DC, he demanded that an investigation be carried out into 'that foreigner'. The head of the NSA let slip that he had heard the FBI was looking into some suspicions about Mick's background. There were a couple of years before he joined the Australian Army that had left a question mark. This was a period where he had gone traveling around the world, including a long stay in China.

Troup immediately demanded to see the reports and to know more. He wanted the Director of the FBI in the Oval Office as soon as they got back to the White House the following day. No excuses!

The secret service agents aboard Air Force One kept their distance. Only a minimal presence was needed in the presidential reserved area, his private office or outside his sleeping quarters.

Agent Lee was standing at his post when he saw one of the other agents down the long hallway signal that the president was on his way towards him. He straightened his suit and got ready to assist Troup should he need anything.

The president made his way down the hallway, his larger than average frame—made a little larger since he took office—filled the narrow passage.

"Good evening, Mister President," said Agent Lee to Troup who was looking rather distracted. Startled from his thoughts he saw the secret service agent, took a second to register who he was, and responded.

"Hello Agent Lee."

Not being one for small talk, he was ready to ignore the agent after this brief exchange of pleasantries, but it was Lee that spoke.

"Is there anything I can do for you, Mister President?"

Backhandedly, Troup replied, "Only if you know how I can get rid of a congresswoman who is proving to be a pain in the butt."

"I serve at your pleasure, Mister President. Anything you need from me, just ask."

Troup paused and looked at the agent. That was an odd thing to say. Was the agent being polite and dutiful? Saying he was here to fetch him a coffee or a sandwich? Or was his meaning being deliberately obscured by his choice of words? Perhaps he was saying that he was prepared to do something a bit more serious for the sake of the election. Troup studied his face carefully for a second, but Agent Lee kept it inscrutable. He would be a whiz at poker.

"Thank you, Agent Lee. I may call upon you at some time later," replied Troup, deliberately vague and watching for a reaction.

"Yes, Sir. Anything you need, at any time, just let me know. I'll be close at hand, Sir." And with that he took his post standing next to the entrance of Troup's private bedroom. They would be landing in Sacramento in about three hours, and he wanted to grab a nap. He closed the door behind him, Agent Lee's offer playing on his mind.

85

The Director of the Feds

Director Herbert Wilcox was a thirty-two-year veteran of the FBI. As an agent, and later as a special agent-in-charge, he had worked in nineteen of the field offices of the bureau all over the country. Later, as he was promoted through the various directorships, he spent more and more time in DC and less in the field offices until, finally, his orbit would remain in the capital. He had been director of the FBI for almost two years under the current administration.

He was not a fan of Troup's. The president had called upon the FBI to conduct investigations into his political enemies before, and that had put Wilcox into a difficult position, because there was no reasonable cause to conduct an investigation if the person had neither done, nor said, anything illegal. Speaking one's mind was not a crime, unless it could incite a crime.

Today was a bit different. He actually did have reports on one of the president's 'enemies', the husband of Congresswoman Young. He flicked through the file while he waited for the president to come into the Oval Office. Assistant Special Agent-in-Charge Gus Gilmer had submitted the report. When Major O'Rourke, a foreigner, became involved with a member of the US Congress, the Department of Homeland Security requested the FBI undertake a background check. Some unanswered questions generated a more thorough investigation which grew to active surveillance as his profile grew, thanks to the media's interest in

Congresswoman Young's very successful campaigning tactics during the mid-terms.

Troup walked into the Oval Office with his chief of staff.

"What have you got for me, Director?" asked Troup, taking his seat behind the desk. He rarely sat on the couches with his office visitors as his predecessors had done, preferring visitors to the Oval Office to stand before him. He found that they were less likely to keep talking if they were getting tired, and that's why he had the chairs in front of his desk removed.

"For the most part, Mister President, he's clean. There are no flags, however there is a part of his life that is a blank. After he graduated high school, he took some time off to travel. This is not uncommon for Australians. What is uncommon though, is the fact that he spent at least half a year in China. He claims he was teaching English to schoolkids; however we can't find any evidence if that was true."

Troup was handed the dossier with a picture of Mick taken from his early days in the Australian Army, alongside a more recent one of him on the campaign trail with Maye.

"We have asked the Chinese through official channels for information on his visa, but initially they denied our requests. After we kept pushing them, they claimed that those records were destroyed in a fire in 2003 before they could be digitized," Director Wilcox told Troup.

The president considered this for a moment. He may have found a chink in the Mick and Maye armor.

"We have also asked the Australian Government for details on his security clearance, and they have provided us with his records. He doesn't deny being in China in his bio, but we cannot be sure that the dates are correct, and the Aussies cannot be sure either."

As he flicked through the file, the president found an image of Mick speaking with an Asian man sometime during the campaign. He held it up for the Director to see.

"What's this?"

"We're not sure," he admitted. "We cannot identify who that is. That was taken while they were campaigning for the mid-terms in Georgia by agents from our Atlanta field office."

There were more photographs of Mick, and in a few of them another Asian man could be seen in the background. His face had been circled in three of the photos.

"And who's this?" asked the president.

"We're not sure of his identity, either. He has been seen at a number of events. We're still trying to put his face through facial recognition programs to see if he's from a foreign intelligence service. So far, nothing."

As he looked over the file, he asked what the status was on the investigation.

"We have elevated the case, Mister President," said the Director. "O'Rourke is under surveillance until we can be sure that he is not a security threat."

Troup seemed to like hearing this.

"We will continue trying to fill in the blanks from his time in China," he continued.

Without asking the director, he placed the file in his drawer and looked at his chief of staff and nodded. Taking up a pen he began writing notes and, without looking up from his desk dismissed the director with a "That will be all..."

Director Wilcox, taken aback that the president would take an official file, was then guided to the door by the president's chief of staff.

"I need that file back," said Wilcox.

"Thank you, Director," he said. "We'll get it back to you."

86

We Serve at the Pleasure of The President

As Troup was finishing up for the day, he stepped out onto the long colonnade past the White House's rose garden heading for the Executive Residence, his two secret service agents shadowed him. He had been thinking about Agent Lee's comments.

"Where's Agent Lee?" he asked one of the pair.

"He's just handed over duty, Mister President. I think he's about to sign out."

"Tell him I want to see him," Troup demanded.

The agent spoke into his microphone to the comms center, inquiring as to Lee's location. A short time later came the response into the agent's earpiece.

"He's downstairs in the Secret Service Office, Mister President."

Troup stopped, pondering the garden. Though the roses were not blooming at the tail end of this cold Washington winter, during the spring and summer they were magnificent.

"Tell him to come and see me." And with that he turned on his heels and went back into the Oval Office.

A short time later, the president's secretary showed him into the Oval Office, and he stood before the president's desk. Troup looked him up and down. They had spent an inordinate amount of time together

372

after the assassination attempt, much of it at the behest of the communications people who wanted to milk it for its positive PR. No other agent had had so much exposure to the president, and him being called into the Oval Office certainly raised some questions with his supervisor.

"You take your duty seriously, don't you Agent Lee?" asked the president. "I mean, you took a bullet that was meant for me."

"Yes, Sir," he responded, looking straight ahead and not meeting the president's gaze. Instead, he focused on the glass panes of the window behind the president's chair.

"You offered to do anything for the president when you took your oath, didn't you?" Troup chose his words carefully, and Agent Lee could instantly tell that he was being led.

"I took an oath to faithfully serve the president, yes, Sir," came his response, gently correcting the words used but remaining equally vague. He then looked directly into the eyes of Troup. "To serve the president as the need required."

Troup, a businessman, had been in many negotiations before—billion-dollar negotiations—and had prided himself on being able to read other men. For an agent to meet his gaze like that spoke volumes. And for him to choose those words, those specific words, told the president what he needed to know before he ventured further.

"If I was to ask you what the biggest threat to this office is at the moment... the biggest threat to the President of the United States, what would you say it was?"

Agent Lee paused to consider and was circumspect in his response.

"Notwithstanding internal threats to your physical security, Sir, I would say foreign influence on the election process."

This response shocked Troup. It was not what he expected from the agent. The president had been accused of fostering interference from foreign intelligence agencies during the 2016 elections but had managed to fend of the accusations even though there were moves to have him impeached. Was this what Lee was referring to? Or was he being a bit more direct? Lee could see the slight change in the president's face, a micro-expression they called it.

"So, if I was to ask you to help ensure the..." Troup paused as he considered his words, "...continued safety of this administration, would you be... comfortable... with doing so?"

The question was deliberately abstruse.

"Sir, if you require me to perform my duty to protect this administration, I am duty bound to do so," came the response.

Agent Lee then put his finger to his lips. Troup looked at Agent Lee, stunned. Who was this man to tell the president not to speak?

Lee then took a pen and notepad from his jacket pocket and wrote '*Talk in private, Sir*' and held it up for Troup to read.

Troup was initially dumbfounded. For Agent Lee to write a note meant that he suspected that the Oval Office had listening devices. Troup had never considered that. He would need to be careful in future. Regardless, he looked at Lee and nodded his head.

"Sir, if there is nothing else," said Lee as he wrote another quick note. He held it up for the President to read. It said: "*I am on detail tomorrow from noon.*"

"Um, no, thank you. That will be all Agent Lee. Thank you... and thank you for your service."

"I serve at your pleasure, Sir." And with that, Agent Lee left the Oval Office.

As he headed downstairs to sign out, his supervisor pulled him aside.

"What did the president want with you," he said suspiciously.

Lee took out his pass and scanned it, signing off duty.

"The president wants me to be involved in another PR thing for the election," he lied. "I told him that I serve at his pleasure but that it might be an idea to run it by you, from a security point of view. I told him I would prefer not to, but if my supervisor was happy to authorize it, then I'd do it," he lied again. "He said he would call you up to the Oval Office to discuss it," he lied for the third time.

His supervisor was both annoyed and excited at the thought that the most powerful man in the world would be seeking his counsel, and permission.

"If you can get me out of it, that'd be great," said Lee. "I'm tired of being 'the guy that took the bullet for the president'. I just want to do my job and stay out of the spotlight." These were the words one would expect from a loyal member of the US Secret Service. Of course, they were all lies.

"Well, if the president wants you, then we serve at his pleasure," said the supervisor, with an air of authority fostered by his newly found power. "I'll let the president know that I'll approve his request. Expect to be assigned that task after I speak with him," he said with more than just a hint of pride and self-importance.

Lee feigned a slight look of annoyance but resignation that he would be forced to carry out an unwelcomed duty. "OK boss," he said. "If you say so."

87

⚜

Making Things Happen

The next day, in a fake file delivered with the president's dossiers, was a note from Lee suggesting a meeting in the kitchen off the president's secretary's office. It was a small room with just a fridge, a microwave, a benchtop and sink.

The president asked his two secretaries to run a special errand for him to buy a private gift for the First Lady, something he did not want his official staff to do 'for personal reasons.' He was then able to use the vacant office and its kitchenette for a private discussion with Agent Lee.

Immediately after the clandestine meeting, he summoned Lee's supervisor to the Oval Office and told him of the 'task' he would like his agent to undertake: a PR task that may have an impact on the secret service roster.

"I am seeking your advice and permission," Troup said to the senior agent, stroking his ego as suggested by Agent Lee, "unless you think it is not becoming of a secret service agent to be photographed with the president."

Lee's supervisor 'gave' the president permission to use his subordinate for the task telling the president that he could organize the roster such that he would be available for the president's use. "I can make that happen for you, Mister President," he told him.

Troup was ready to rip shreds from him for his arrogance but held his tongue. *"Of course you will make that happen, you twerp. You work for me. I don't work for you, you piece of shit,"* he thought to himself.

As Agent Lee walked his supervisor out of the Oval Office, he was given his instructions.

"Until further notice Agent Lee, you will be at the disposal of the president. We'll re-staff your position until this project is over, and he releases you. We'll then put you back onto the duty rotation. Clear?"

"Yes, Sir," responded Lee. "I think he wants me to spend time with the communications people starting right away."

"OK," thought the supervisor. "We'll send someone up to replace you asap. Let me know when you're finished, and we can get you back to your normal tasks." And with that he went downstairs back to the secret service offices to re-arrange the duty roster, happy he was able to help the president.

Agent Lee paused for a moment. All around him staff hurried to and from the various offices. A press conference was being held in about half-an-hour and last-minute changes to notes were being checked and staffed. The campaign, and the virus, were all anyone wanted to report on. His jacket pocket bulged, and he moved his notepad and pen from one pocket to the other. He had to get home to his computer.

88

Wednesday's Child is Full of Woe

Super Tuesday was not as super as they had hoped.

The Republican National Committee demanded that every committee in every district and state aligned their voting system to a proportional system, which Maye and her campaign team welcomed. By keeping it proportional, they would be guaranteed of a pro-rata number of delegates based on the vote. A winner-take-all result gave a disproportionate advantage to the winner of the primary, giving him (or her) all the delegates.

Of course, Troup denounced the decision and made his feelings known via social media. The little blue bird was crapping all over the Party once again, as one observer wrote, resurrecting a theme used all too often. Troup was hoping to sweep the floor with a winner-take-all majority in the larger states, but none of the subordinate Republican committees gave any real objection to the proportional system for this special situation. After all, it wasn't often that a sitting president was to be challenged from within his own party by a candidate that had such a high profile in such a short amount of time. The female members in particular, were very vociferous in making this change. In effect, the national committee was ensuring the purist popular vote possible, and with only two candidates on the ballot leaving the waters unmuddied, this was easily achieved.

Unless delegates who pledged to a candidate reneged at the national convention *en masse*, by the end of the primaries—or even sooner—the 2020 Republican presidential candidate would be known. The convention would merely be a formality to crown the candidate officially... and a celebration for the party faithful.

Colorado's popular vote was won easily by Maye with a resounding thirty of the thirty-seven delegates pledged to her. The wedding being held in that state certainly helped, as well as the elevation of the Governor in the eyes of Coloradans. Troup did not trouble himself with the smaller states and didn't even bother to visit the Centennial State. This was also reflected in the primaries in Oklahoma, Alabama, Arkansas, Tennessee and Maine where Maye won the majority of support and delegates. But it was in California and Texas where they were let down, and this brought an air of foreboding to her campaign.

Texas remained a dyed-in-the-wool Troup state where he won seventy percent of the delegates. And although California's results were better than expected, Maye did not get enough support to gain a lead over Troup. Combined, those two states accounted for more than a third of the other states voting on Super Tuesday. Florida, New York, Ohio and Pennsylvania... those were the big-ticket primaries now. If a majority could not be gained in those states, along with many of the smaller states, then Troup would have the numbers, and nothing would be able to prevent him from getting the Party's nomination. Maye's tilt at the election would be over, and she would become roadkill on the highway to the election.

Now, they were on the campaign trail once more, heading east from Colorado to Michigan and visiting as many mid-sized towns as they could. But anyone could tell that the wind had been taken from their sails.

The GOP's campaign team that had been appointed by the national committee to help could tell that they were being used as they should. They had been sidelined by Mick and Maye who, buoyed by their successes in the mid-terms in Georgia, had decided to 'go with their gut' on almost all campaign decisions. But the losses in the Iowa caucuses, the New Hampshire primary and the Super Tuesday primaries had delivered body blows. They demanded to be heard.

"We know how Troup thinks," said Perry Houston, previously referred to merely as Number 1', he was a seasoned campaigner and former deputy lead on Troup's campaign. He had deliberately not been brought into the inner circle because Mick, Maye and Sally-Anne had doubted his allegiance. Was he a plant by the GOP as a conduit to Troup? They weren't sure. But the last few weeks he had seemed genuine, and now that they hadn't performed as well as they would have liked in the opening shots of the campaign proper, they were keen to explore *all* possibilities. Now it was Perry's turn to shine.

"Troup won't bother with the smaller states," he said, "and especially those ones that are safe."

Perry pulled out a diagram of the US with all the states marked in dark blue, light blue, white, light red and dark red. The dark blue meant safe Democrat, whereas the light blue meant a Democrat state with a majority of less than five percent. The red colors meant the same except they represented Republican-held states. The white were swinging states or undecided. He pointed to the map.

"Forget the dark blue. They are Democrat states. And don't worry about the dark red. They're safe Republican. You need to focus on the states that are in the middle."

Sally-Anne piped up. "But this would be for a general election. We're trying to get purely Republican support. The Democrats are immaterial," she said to him.

"That's right, this does reflect voter outcomes in the last election. But what Sly and I found was that the tendency of the state reflected in the tendency of the voter's views, even down to within the party."

Sylvania 'Sly' Screven, Houston's off-sider, formerly known as Number 2', threw her opinions into the mix.

"The party is like the state in microcosm," she said. "If it's a safe Republican state, then the average of the party members will tend more to the right. If it's a safe Democrat state, then the average views of the members of the Democrats will tend more to the left. If it's a state that's somewhere in the center, then the views will be more moderate. And if they're moderate, then they can be influenced to change."

Applying that logic to the map, that meant that Ohio and Arizona could be easily turned away from Troup; North Carolina and Nevada remained as swinging seats; and Florida, Pennsylvania, Rhode Island and Vermont as Democrat states but with a winnable margin. So, the focus became clear: those were the key battlegrounds.

Mick was eager to ask the team their opinion on how best to maximize their coverage. Should they stay together as a couple, or would it be more advantageous to split up?

"Our advice," said Houston, "is for Maye to head for the big-ticket states that can be turned, and Mick, you go for the safer states and try your luck with them. Your campaign to Iowa went down well with the smaller states, and now that we didn't get a majority in California and Texas, we'll need them. Plus, the president probably won't go there. He'll assume he'll do well in those seats regardless of whether he visits or not."

Sly took the map and turned it to face Mick and Maye. Sally-Anne stood next to the table as the bus lurched, examining the map intently.

"Maye, we'd recommend you hit Michigan hard, but from there the problem is going to be Florida and Illinois. We're already in the north, so Illinois is close and convenient, but Florida cannot be left without coverage, especially because Mick was such an influence there with his buck's party events. So, you'll need to make a choice: remain in the north and do Illinois and maybe make a start on Wisconsin, or try and cover as much of Florida as you can. It has one hundred and twenty-two delegates alone. Illinois and Wisconsin have one hundred and nineteen between them," said Screven.

"What about if I go to Florida?" Mick offered. At first blush this appeared to be a good solution to spreading Maye's message to Republicans. After all, Mick was incredibly popular there, and had proven to be a valuable asset to the campaign. With the Latino population enamored by him in the Sunshine State, it was an obvious choice.

The only problem was transportation. The campaign did not have Troup's war chest. The president had gathered a significant amount for his nomination in party campaign funds as well as donations from his billionaire friends and supporters, whereas Maye's campaign budget was less... significantly less. The problem was that the campaign vehicles and campaign staff could not be split. There were simply not enough assets to be divided up.

"How about if I hire an aircraft and do a fly-in, fly-out tour of the smaller states *en route*?" he offered.

The team thought about this and how it would play for the media. It would have its problems, like making it hard for media agencies to follow him and conduct interviews on the road. They would have to leapfrog from airport to airport or town to town, but the optics would be good. It was Maye who then dressed up the idea.

"How about if we *both* do that?" she said, coming up with a novel plan.

89

The Great States Air Race

It was all the media could talk about. The Republican campaign for the party's nomination for president, something incredibly rare, was now becoming the most unique in living memory.

The young, intelligent, attractive female veteran candidate and her exotic foreign husband, who could possibly become the first ever 'First Gentleman of the United States' were to split up and, using hired aircraft, compete with each other to see how many states and towns they could visit to spread the word of Maye's platform.

Abby Wilcox, the former Secretary of the Air Force, sacked by Troup for her role in Maye's wedding, had returned to Wyoming and her ranch leaving the snake pit of Washington politics behind her for the big sky of her home state. When she heard of Maye's idea—which made the lead story of every news bulletin, and which infuriated Troup—she offered the candidate her personal aircraft, a twin-engine Cessna 404, for the campaign. Anything to get back at the president.

Sally-Anne and Pam organized a media event where Maye would take the keys from Abby and be wished good luck by the woman who 'gave her away' at her wedding. The governor of Wyoming was invited to participate, much to the delight of his PR staff. The Wyoming primaries would only provide twenty-nine delegates, but every state needed to 'feel some of the campaign love', plus if Maye could get to use an aircraft for just the cost of fuel, then it was worth it.

Abby didn't disappoint. She made a moving speech about how she was proud to have given Maye away at her wedding and send her forth on her journey into married life, and now she had the opportunity to do likewise and to send her forth into Wyoming's big sky and her journey as the first female President of the United States. (That clip lead every bulletin yet again, and, yet again, Troup was incensed! The public lapped it up).

Pam pointed out that because they had extra seats in the aircraft, they could invite a reporter and a cameraman for a ride-along. The two would be a captured audience, and Maye could not only show off her piloting skills but could also sell her '*Uniting these Great States*' message and her five-point plan.

Of course, Mick could do the same thing in his aircraft. And, as Sly pointed out, if Sally-Anne and Pam stayed with Maye, and Mick took Rob and Jesús, then it could also be the 'husband vs wife', or 'boys vs girls' competition. The PR girls were going into overdrive, and Mick and Maye were happy to accommodate them and ham it up for the campaign. (Another Republican stunt!)

Once Mick sourced a suitable aircraft, the two would both get checked out on them, and then blast off on their unique race. Maye would head from Wyoming and stay in the north, while Mick would head south-east. They then invited all the Republican committees in all the states in that area of the country that had yet to hold their primaries, to invite them to their districts, and the two of them would compete to see how many they could get to before the Georgia primary in three weeks' time. That would be the finish line. The big risk to this venture was that they would not be able to attend the primaries in some states, whereas Troup might. But Mick and Maye were counting on the good publicity from this event and showing up Troup and his lackluster campaign. It was a gamble, but so far their gambles had paid off.

And so it was, on a sunny March morning in the great state of Wyoming, at Jerry Olsen Field, a small regional airport near Cheyenne, that Mick and Maye kissed each other in front of the cameras.

"Good luck, sweetheart," said Mick, embracing Maye and looking into her eyes as two dozen cameras trained their lenses on them.

"I don't need luck, Aussie. I'll be waiting for you on the tarmac back home in Georgia! GIRL POWER RULES!" Then she grabbed his face and mashed her lips against his and pushed him away with a wink.

The two of them, with their two off-siders—Maye with Sally-Anne and Pam, and Mick with Rob and Jesús—and each with a reporter and a cameraman for the first leg of the race, then boarded their respective aircraft, started up and taxied out to the runway.

The cameras caught the two aircraft rolling down the runway and lifting off in formation to the east, Maye turning left and Mick turning right. While the media left to file their stories, the campaign support team packed up their gear and drove out of the airport. They would follow Maye to her next destination while Mick and the boys were on their own and would get local support at each of their stops.

90

Shark Attack in Michigan

The 'Great States Air Race' idea was closely followed by the public, and their respective routes were plotted on their campaign website and repeated on news bulletins.

The demand to be included in the 'ride-alongs' by the media was intense, and Pam and Sally-Anne were very selective in which networks and agencies were given the opportunity to sit in the 'co-pilot' seat in either Mick's or Maye's aircraft.

Each day, footage from the campaign was uploaded to YouTube, and Pam and Rob ensured that all their social media accounts were kept up-to-date, and even up-to-the-hour, for every one of their legs. At each airport, be they regional, local or capital city, the local Republicans had organized events close by. Of course, the veteran community was actively encouraged to be a part of whatever was being coordinated, and most offered to help the Republican committees, even if the veterans themselves normally voted Democrat. 'Supporting other veterans is greater than supporting a party' was the catch cry that the VFW and American Legion suggested be their policy with regard to this unique campaign. The results were turn outs better than either of them could have imagined.

By the third day Maye was in the lead. She had visited fourteen individual airports and had spoken at sixteen individual events. Mick was not far behind at thirteen and fourteen respectively. At the end of each day, Maye and the girls were met by the campaign convoy that was leap-frogging each day's destination in as much of a straight line as possible while Maye's track zig-zagged hither and yon. Mick and the boys did not have a support convoy, but the local Republicans or veterans made sure that they were never left stranded, and there was always someone ready to transport them wherever they needed to go.

On the fourth day, as Maye was heading to Michigan, and the interest continued to grow and grow. She had flown into Oshkosh in Wisconsin and the huge aviation fraternity greeted her like she was the re-incarnation of Amelia Earhart. After she left there, she and her team were cruising at three thousand feet and had just passed Sheboygan. They were almost half-way across Lake Michigan tracking for their destination of Grand Rapids when her flight was intercepted by two Michigan Air National Guard A-10 Thunderbolts. These attack aircraft—ungainly but threatening—formed up close on either side of Maye's Cessna 404. Shark's teeth and angry eyes painted onto their noses made them frightening to behold, which was exactly the point. What was more frightening was the huge Gatling-gun that they sported, capable of easily destroying their aircraft. About three hundred yards away, a smaller twin-engine propeller aircraft, also in military livery, flew alongside. The reporter and Sally-Anne and Pam were concerned, perhaps a little frightened. The two gray aircraft seemed uncomfortably close, close enough to touch. They saw the pilots in their cockpits, visors down, oxygen masks over their mouths giving them a ghoulish appearance. They could be easily seen looking at the occupants of Maye's Cessna, their helmets painted like skulls with their black visors making them appear as though they were the black eyes of the undead. For the reporter, Sally-Anne and Pam, it was quite unnerving.

Maye, on the other hand, was not scared, although she *was* very concerned. She thought she may have inadvertently flown into the restricted airspace of an Air Defense Identification Zone and was being assessed by these attack pilots as to whether she was a threat or not. After 9/11, aircraft that were in airspace where they were not supposed to be, were considered a threat. In this case, however, she would more likely be escorted to land at a military base or shooed out of the air-space. If she had strayed into military airspace it would be an incredible embarrassment for her. She could imagine it on the news. It would be a terrible blunder on her part and her heart raced as she tried to fig-ure out how she could have made such a mistake. Normal practice was for the intercepting aircraft to contact the 'bogey', the name given to an unidentified and potentially hostile aircraft, on an emergency fre-quency and give the bogey instructions, and force it to comply. If it did not, it risked being shot down. Checking her navigation charts, trying to figure out how she could have made a blunder, she waited for the ex-pected radio call from the interceptors. Soon enough, it came.

"Seven Three Tango, this is the Michigan Air National Guard," came the call. "The Governor, the honorable Jackson Calhoun, sends his re-gards, and has asked us to escort you to your destination. Welcome to the great state of Michigan, Ma'am."

The reporter squealed with delight as did Pam and Sally-Anne. The cameraman was turning himself into a pretzel trying to get just the right shot of these two shark-mouthed killing machines flying escort to Maye and her team in the Cessna 404.

That evening, the footage of the two warplanes escorting Maye's air-craft was all over the news. The third air national guard aircraft was ob-viously a camera aircraft and the images, both still and moving, were spectacular. The might of the US military escorting a presidential hope-ful as she piloted her own aircraft on her own campaign. The images were replayed around the world.

Troup's campaign team was beside themselves. These events were be-yond anything they could have dreamed up nor anything that would be possible to orchestrate within their program. Troup was about to turn seventy and was an overweight businessman. What exciting images could they possibly create with that lump of clay? And what's more, his response to the Covid pandemic was not garnering much support for him. Thousands were dying and he seemed to be more pre-occupied with the campaign than with running the country. He was a hard sell to the public.

91

An Executive Order

Agent Lee received a simple cryptic message from the president on his phone.

"Y"

It meant 'Yes', and was his go-ahead to take action to ensure the president's campaign was not hindered by the upstart congresswoman from Georgia.

Agent Henry Lee, former marine and now loyal member of the secret service, sworn to protect the presidency, was planning his next move. He had been watching Congresswoman Young's journey from Wyoming to Michigan, and he had traveled from DC to Ann Arbor in Michigan where she would be landing at the municipal airport so she could address a Republican fundraiser for her campaign at the nearby Holiday Inn.

The meeting with the president in the kitchenette of the secretary's office was where the chief executive of the United States had given him his instructions on how he wanted the problem of Congresswoman Maye Young handled. And so now he was in Michigan, and had checked into a small motel under a false name and with fake ID.

Even though he had spent less than a year in counter-surveillance with the secret service, he had managed to acquire more than enough of the skills necessary for this task. He kept his face obscured always, now made easier by the need for face masks due to Covid, and he never, ever, looked anywhere near a camera. He adjusted his gait and changed his clothes often, and avoided outdoor parking lots, sidewalks or anywhere where he could be watched, and where he could not readily detect an observer.

At the Holiday Inn he registered to attend the fundraiser and was handed a pamphlet on social distancing and what hygiene and disinfectant products were available for his use. It was open to supporters and there were plenty of veterans wearing their garrison caps with the name and number of whichever VFW or American Legion post they belonged to, as well as three or four hundred members of the state's various Republican committees and well-wishers.

It was soon after that Maye arrived at the hotel. Lee was watching from an upstairs reception area that overlooked the courtyard. Maye's campaign RV had just pulled in after collecting her from the airport. It gave her time to freshen up and get changed before the lunch event. Media vehicles followed the Winnebago into the parking area.

He found out from an overly helpful middle-aged woman assisting with the registrations that Maye had requested some time for herself alone, so a room had been reserved for her and she was going to take some time in solitude and review her speech, and then enter the function room after the other speakers had finished. Lee would make his move when she was alone.

Looking around, he saw some attendees loitering outside the doors. They seemed to be quite wary of being in such an enclosed area with so many others. Covid had made people paranoid. One gentleman, he looked Japanese, was busily washing his hands with disinfectant. His partner did likewise. They didn't seem to want to step inside until one of the organizers ushered them in. Nervously looking around, as if they were seeking a way not to enter, they reluctantly walked through the doors. Covid, it seemed, had made everyone jumpy.

9 2

Garbage Time

Two months later

It looked like Maye's campaign was over. Mick had worked wonders in Florida and Maye had received over seventy percent of the one hundred and twenty-two delegates on offer, but Illinois did not receive her or her message as well as was expected. She did well in Alaska, North Dakota and Wyoming, but Ohio and Virginia let her down, and those were where some of the big numbers were to be had.

By the end of May, Troup had already secured nine hundred and fifty pledged delegates from Republican primaries and caucuses. The only way Maye could guarantee the party's nomination is if she could win over sixty percent of every remaining primary election, and that was almost an impossibility.

The 'Great States Air Race' had been a roaring success, and had generated lots of interest, lots of incoming funds, and had translated into great results, but Troup's initial lead proved very hard to beat. They had been clawing their way towards his numbers, but the primaries season was almost over with just a few weeks to go and the commentators and analysts, many of whom had been supporting Maye's bid with positive commentary, now had changed their tune. In news stories, phrases like 'virtually impossible to win' and 'an unassailable lead by Troup' were being used more so than phrases like 'potential first woman president'.

Troup's incumbency and campaign backing proved too strong, and the competition for the White House from now on would be more-or-less 'garbage time', when the campaign play was expected to no longer see one hundred percent effort.

Maye remained upbeat and kept her team enthusiastic. "We still have a chance," she would tell them, and Mick was giving his all, but the others were not as confident. They would still give her their best effort, but more so out of loyalty, affection and admiration rather than the possibility that she could get the party's nomination.

"How can you remain so upbeat?" asked Mick when they were in bed together. "You've done spectacularly, but it will be hard to convince the committees that most of their pledges should go to you. Troup and his guys in the national committee have a strangle-hold on them."

"I reckon we still have a chance," she said to him, running her fingers through the hair on his chest, her head nestled in the crook of his neck. "Our campaign has been the most thrilling that's ever been," she proclaimed proudly. "Some of the images will go down in history."

"That's true," her husband replied. "Those selfies I took with the bikini-babes in Miami are as good as any picture Roosevelt was in," he joked.

Maye bit his ear lobe as punishment, and Mick let out a whimper.

"I really believe we have a chance," she repeated, looking into Mick's eyes. "Are you still with me?"

"Right 'til the end, and then beyond," he said, kissing her.

* * *

In DC, during a late-night campaign meeting, the head of the GOP and his senior staff discussed the new campaign to re-elect President Troup. It was time to bring the party back together under one banner and one nominee.

They began making phone calls to the leaders of the state GOPs in each of the remaining states that had yet to hold their primaries telling them to cancel any event that they or their sub-committees had planned. They would be a waste of money and the GOP national committee would not provide any support. It was time to fall in line behind President Troup and concentrate on him being re-elected in November.

As good a candidate as Maye was, she was not going to be able to defeat the millionaire business tycoon that held the Oval Office. As unstable as *he* was, he was still 'their boy', and as far as they were concerned, he would be for the next four and a half years.

Congresswoman Maye Young would need to be cut away.

93

Canceled, Due to Popular Demand

As the pair sat down to breakfast in their Baltimore hotel room reading the mixed stories in the paper and online, Mick was trying to get his phone to download the Washington Post without much success. He was still having trouble with it. Maye's phone buzzed. It was Sally-Anne.

"Good morning, Sally-Anne," said Maye. "You're up early." She then heard what sounded like sobbing. "Are you crying? What's wrong?"

Mick looked up from the article he was reading on his phone, Maye's expression underscoring the concern in her voice.

"What do you mean it's been canceled. Who told you that?"

Maye was due to address a Republican muster at Gettysburg, and then another in Philadelphia that evening in preparation for that state's primaries, while Mick had been invited to address the graduating class at the US Naval Academy at Annapolis. Sally-Anne informed Maye that when she contacted the organizer at Gettysburg she was told that the muster had been canceled by order of the state committee, which was following orders from the national committee.

"Why would Pennsylvania cancel its primaries?" she asked, half not expecting an answer.

"You don't understand," cried Sally-Anne. "It's not just Pennsylvania.

It's all of the presidential primaries that are still to be held... Delaware, Indiana, New Jersey. They're all canceled."

In the mirror on the wall, the TV—its sound on mute—was reflected. Mick saw Maye's campaign image flash up during the morning news program. The bottom third caption read, 'Troup election'.

Mick got up and turned up the sound. Sitting at the end of the bed he watched the bulletin.

"Hang on," said Maye to Sally-Anne. "It's on the news."

"In a surprise announcement this morning, the Republican Party has confirmed that it will cancel the forthcoming presidential primary elections and caucuses of those states still to hold them for this year's general election. In a statement released early this morning, the Republican National Committee said:

> *'Though Congresswoman Maye Young ran a fantastic campaign, and the Party allowed its members the democratic right to listen and to decide for themselves who the Party's nominee for the presidential election should be, the current support base will not be able to effectively combine to provide the pre-requisite number of delegates for Miss Young to be the successful nominee at the Republican National Convention. Therefore, in light of this fact, and the administrative burden of ensuring the primaries are Covid-safe, we shall suspend any further voting for a presidential nominee by means of a primary election. President Troup has the required support and so will be the sole Republican candidate for the upcoming presidential election.'*

Mick looked at her in disbelief. His phone rang, and Maye's 'call waiting' beeped also. The phones were about to go into overdrive as a dumbfounded public came to terms with the end of an exciting campaign. Supporters and friends would demand answers: What did this mean for the campaign? What did this mean for the election? And what about those that had sided with Maye? What would be the fallout for them? How would the Democrats respond to this?

As Mick and Maye started to make calls, and field calls, so did the GOP. The president also found himself on the phone and on Twitter, praising the GOP for a sound decision that will help *Make America Great Once More*. Troup made some more calls and sent some text messages.

* * *

In an apartment in the suburb of Chevy Chase, just outside DC, secret service Agent Henry 'Bruce' Lee received a text message. He read it and put his phone away. It was the president canceling his services.

94

Damage Control

Mick and Maye arrived at Annapolis. Now that her events at Gettysburg and Philadelphia had been canceled she needed to put on a brave face, and it would be good to have Mick next to her.

The superintendent of the academy welcomed the offer for Maye to address the graduating class along with Mick. If there was one thing he learned in his forty years in naval service, it was to be flexible and to take advantage of opportunities that come your way. Congresswoman Young's fight had been an inspiration to the cadets, especially the female ones, and now that she had been dumped by her party, her offer to address the class could be not only historic, but it could also be a great lesson in life about handling disappointment.

The superintendent was well aware of that hard-learned lesson. He should have been an admiral by now but had been passed over twice for fleet deputy command by others that he considered 'less capable' than he. So what if he got into trouble for allowing the congresswoman to address the ceremony? She was a veteran and a woman, and her husband was a veteran, also. It was a much better effect than getting a career politician to speak who had never donned a uniform!

He could, however, foretell that there may be a lot of media interest, so it would be prudent to find a way to accommodate their requests lest they make a nuisance of themselves.

Mick was more than happy for Maye to give the address in lieu of him. He would be happy just to be her 'arm candy' while she answered what would undoubtedly be pointed questions about how she felt about being dumped by the party, and what were her thoughts on the election even though she had gained almost fifty percent support from the rank and file of her party. What about her future? Would she return to Congress or, if not, what was she going to do?

She and Sally-Anne and Mick had started writing some talking points.

* * *

The graduating class of young naval officers looked resplendent in their white uniforms with the cadets of the US Marines in their black tunics standing out. They were eager and fresh young faces, not yet creased by the lines that bore testament to worries and disappointments and stress. There was plenty of time for the military to 'issue those worry lines' later.

Their families were unable to attend and so now, more than ever, in a country racked by the effects of the pandemic, words of inspiration were needed as these young officers prepared to take their posts in a world that was becoming more and more uncertain.

When Maye took the stage, she was met with resounding applause. The female cadets, now newly promoted to ensigns and second lieutenants in the US Navy and US Marine Corps, took to their feet. The male cadets, taking the lead from their female classmates, did similar, all keeping six feet apart. They were eager to hear what this former commissioned officer cum politician had to say, on the day that she had been dumped by her party.

"Officers of the United States Navy and the United States Marine Corps, ladies and gentlemen. Today is a day that will long be remembered by all of us, some with warmer feelings than others." The young officers chuckled at this. They knew exactly what she was referring to.

"There will often come a time when you and your life will be sent off its expected trajectory by events not of your doing, and how you respond will be a testament to your character.

"Today, as you may well have heard, is one such day that held one such event for myself, and if you permit me to indulge, I will let you know what happened and how it made me feel so that if something similar happens to you, you will know that your situation will not be unique, nor will be your feelings of pain and disappointment.

"Last night, in a room of faceless men, a decision was made that mocked the very core of the democracy that this country stands for, and that you have sworn to defend. Faceless men made a decision about a woman and her career without the courage and honor to tell her to her face, but instead to issue a press release. I did not have a chance to speak up for myself nor to defend my position. Instead, I was beaten into submission by men who sought their own agendas, regardless of what I wanted, or what the country wanted... and now what it so desperately needs.

"But this is not the first time that this has occurred to me, and at the moment I am addressing all the women in the audience, so that you know that indecencies committed in secret must be brought into the open... because sunlight cleanses all.

"As a junior officer, I was the victim of abuse—physical abuse—by my partner. I was ashamed and I was alone. I did not feel that I could turn to anyone in my chain-of-command. My injuries I had to hide, and I did not feel that I could approach anyone in uniform."

The officers and cadets, and the media looking on, hung on her every word. This was a revelation about Maye's background. Mick was surprised that she had brought it up at this event, but if the party was going to dump her so unceremoniously, then they brought it upon themselves.

As she continued, she spoke of her deep shame. How she would put make-up on her bruises and then go to class and try and pay attention even though she was in pain. Or how she had to be careful that the make-up didn't run when she was doing PT and was perspiring. The audience was mesmerized by the story, and some of the female junior officers and cadets were weeping. So were some of the reporters. She finished with her counsel for these new graduates.

"Whatever life throws at you, whether it is physical abuse by a trusted partner, or the demolition of your career and aspirations by a room of faceless men, how you pick yourself up and move forward will be determined by your strength of character. So I implore you to protect those that cannot protect themselves: the citizens of this great nation and the subordinates who look to you for advice, protection and leadership. Because it is leadership that they need, and leadership that this country needs, now more than ever. God bless you, and God bless the United States of America."

As she sat down, Mick took her hand. He was taken aback that she had been so honest and open, and while he liked the swipes at the party and at Troup, he was of two minds as to whether Maye's dramatic speech was prudent. She still had to serve out her term as a congresswoman, and it would be made harder if she returned to Capitol Hill as the embittered, man-hating bitch that had split the party.

But for now, the officers of the US Naval Academy had received her speech well and applause resounded in the academy's grounds. The evening news would be interesting, made even more so by the interviews she was about to give to the media.

* * *

That night, all that could be talked about was the dumping of Maye by the Republican party and the room of 'faceless men' and her revelations of the domestic abuse by her first husband. Female hosts of news programs were having a field day of outrage. Even overtly left-leaning 'female gabfests', as they were often derogatorily known, featuring has-beens from the last decade, were one hundred percent behind Maye and her predicament.

News programs had pundits discussing everything from politics to domestic abuse, and every conversation or opinion was centered on Maye, her campaign and her story of being abused by men, particularly today. The GOP was being described using exactly the same words that Maye had carefully chosen: 'a roomful of faceless men'. It was a message that was being played over and over and over. Even the hundreds of deaths of Americans due to Covid seemed to take a back seat to this latest drama in the 'Maye Young for President' campaign. If she had hoped to 'unite these great states', then it was not a good look as she divided the Republican party.

And so it was that in Washington DC, on the corner of 1st and D, not far from the Capitol Building, the GOP's leadership quorum held a 'damage-control' planning session. How were they to respond to this outburst?

The National Chairman, Adel Cook, spoke first. "I don't care what Young has said about her past. That was before she joined the GOP. What she said about the Party is inexcusable. We took her in. We built her up. We gave her a home. For her to treat us like that cannot be left unanswered."

He ran his hands over is forehead and what was left of his gray hair. He looked fit for a man in his sixties, but at the moment his face looked haggard. The campaign had taken a lot out of him, especially Troup's anger at letting Maye run. He took off his glasses and rubbed his eyes. It had been a long day.

"The media is baying for our blood!" said his deputy. "We should have released a statement earlier."

"What's there to say?" suggested Preston Webber as legal counsel. "We made a decision based on simple calculations that any further effort to find the most appropriate nominee for president was rendered moot by virtue of the fact that she could not gather the required number of delegates. It is a simple product of our party's constitution, and it is simple math: 'win more delegates than your opponent and you get the nomination.' She didn't have the numbers, so she wasn't going to get the nomination. It's simple logic."

"The problem is that many people, especially in the media, are immune to logic! If they see a story with an emotional tagline, then that's the story. It's all about feelings, not logic. The truth is immaterial," Cook said angrily.

"She will pay for that outburst. Preston, is there any legal action we can take? Is defamation an option?" asked Cook.

Preston shook his head. "No. She mentioned no names, and she wasn't specific about any event in particular. We don't have any legal recourse. All we have is whatever punishment we can dole out within the Party's constitution."

"Where's our Goddamned media people," rasped Cook looking around the room.

From the back, standing in the shadows, stepped forward a silver-haired man in a charcoal suit wearing a Republican-red tie.

"That's me," he said quietly.

Cook pointed to him. "What do you think we should do, um... I don't know your name."

"Fulton, Robert Fulton," he said. "I know this woman... and it is my opinion that she should be destroyed."

95

Outflanked

Robert Fulton had left Georgia angrily. That stupid soccer mom and her idiot husband that ran the GOP committee in Atlanta had no idea what it meant to play in the big league. It was here in DC where the real decisions were made, not down in the sticks.

Cook, Webber and the rest of the GOP leadership listened intently.

"Congresswoman Young is a second-term member. She was selected based purely on her looks and her sex when there were more suitable candidates—men and women—with more experience and more runs on the board who could have been a more viable and amenable selection. If there is to be any blame for the mess the party is currently in, then it falls squarely on the choices made in this room," he said accusingly. The senior leadership looked pained and insulted, but the essence of Fulton's accusation was correct.

"When you go for looks over substance; emotion over logic; then you are destined to fail. What is needed now is to put a muzzle on her. She will dominate the news cycle for the next two or three days, and then one of two things will happen: events will overtake this story, such as what is happening with the pandemic; or the story will be dredged up for a week, especially if the media detects disunity within the Party or she panders to the female indignation that the media will stir up," he opined.

"Every day longer of her slinging mud on the party means more soundbites, more clips, and more oxygen for the Democrats. That is the real battle; winning against the Democrats in November. Congresswoman Young is a side-show, and it is time for that clown to pack up her circus and fuck off and take that Australian prick of hers with her!"

Cook listened intently. Fulton was somewhat right, notwithstanding his obvious enmity towards Young and her husband. She had been chosen primarily because she looked good compared to Troup. The fact that she was smart and was able to hold her own was a bonus. And that Australian, well he was an outlier who served the campaign and the status of the GOP well... then.

But facts are facts. In his opinion, the two of them ran a great campaign, and did very well, but she simply did not have the numbers to get the nomination. Troup may be an idiot, but he was in power and that is where he needed to stay. The fact that Maye fired some shots at the party as she left, which hit a nerve with the current mood of the public, is where the damage lay. Cook agreed. Maye needed to be removed from the equation and Troup's re-election made the priority.

"How do we do it?" asked Cook. "Disendorse her? We don't want to lose her district in Georgia."

"She might jump ship and go to the Democrats," replied Fulton. "She's shown that she has liberal leanings and has a good reputation with the left, so it's not a big ask. They'd want her because of her profile. The best way to take her out is to discredit her so that neither party wants her."

"How do we do that," asked the deputy.

"Easy," said Fulton. "We release a statement saying that we informed her that the Republican voters did not vote for her in enough numbers such that she could not win, and we recommended that she withdraw her nomination but that we were very happy with her performance and were looking at her for the position of running mate for Troup's re-election. She'd be VP under Troup."

"Well, that's more-or-less true. She *was* slated to be on the ticket for VP, and then she didn't win the numbers for nomination," said Cook.

"Exactly. And we have enough of a paper trail to prove that."

"But how does that discredit her?" asked the national chairman.

"Well," continued Fulton, "we add that when we informed her that she didn't get the votes, she became irrational and incensed and insisted that we nominate her. We'll say that she threatened us with accusations of misogyny, sexual misconduct and abuse, and that she would reveal that in the most public and shocking way to destroy the reputation of the GOP."

Fulton paused to allow that to sink in. Looking at the other men in the room, he continued.

"Her speech at Annapolis was the realization of those threats, even after we had generously offered her the position as VP, the first woman to be given that role in the history of this country, in appreciation for her hard work for the people of Georgia and for the Republican Party and because she had done so well."

The group thought for a minute. She would be poison in politics, and no-one would want anything to do with her, and the GOP would be made to look like the jilted lover, trying to do the right thing by her and by the country, only to be sullied by the vitriol of a woman scorned. Preston was the only one to offer a counterpoint. "While it is almost true, if we accuse her of threatening us, then we all need to be on the same page."

"That's easy," replied Fulton. "We say she delivered the ultimatum in writing and it was read out during a meeting of the senior leadership. That way we all have the same recollection of what was said."

"OK," said Cook. "Let's do this. We'll need to create the words she used to threaten us."

Fulton pulled out a piece of paper from a folder and placed it on the table. "I have her threat right here. We 'printed out her email' and this is a 'copy' of it," he said, further concocting the story. "If everyone reads it, we can then discuss its contents and then we'll all be on the same page."

Cook looked at the fake email which had her address block, yesterday's date, and other details that pointed to it being from her. "How did you know to do this? We hadn't even decided on our course of action."

"That's what you pay me for, Mister Chairman. I am here to predict problems and provide solutions. The current problem we have is Congresswoman Young going off the reservation when she didn't get her way and deciding to poison all the wells as she left. I'm the sheriff bringing her in. Now's the time to lynch her."

Just as the fake email was being circulated around the table so that everyone would have the same 'recollection of events', it appeared that the solution to destroy Miss Maye Young's reputation was being brought to fruition by a canny ploy by Rob Fulton. As each man read it, he passed it on. They were, in fact, 'creating the truth'. The news shows the following morning would tell the story of how Congresswoman Young sabotaged the Republican Party and threw a tantrum when she didn't win the votes at the primaries, threatening them unless she got her way. This would neutralize her as a threat and discredit her in the process. Troup and the Party would be the winners.

The knock on the door of the committee room at well past 10 p.m. was highly irregular. Webber opened the door. It was the security guard from the lobby escorting a man in sweats.

"I'm sorry to trouble you," said the guard. He didn't know who Preston Webber was, just that he must be important if he was in a closed-door meeting with the Chairman of the GOP. "But this gentleman insisted he needed to speak with you. He says he's from the secret service."

96

The Queen and King of America

The three days since President Troup announced that he would not be seeking re-election had been a whirlwind. Congratulations had been flowing in from friends and associates, even those that had not been wholeheartedly in support of Maye's campaign in competition with the president.

The reason for President Troup's decision was never made clear. The official line was that the president wanted to pursue business interests which he had let languish while he was in office, but insiders gossiped about some sort of memo or other evidence that the president had engaged in something underhanded, and when the Republican Party leadership had found out they were eager for him to move on and move out. In any case, Miss Maye Young, representative of the Georgia 11th, was now the sole Republican Party nominee for President of the United States and would go to the general election unopposed by anyone from within her party.

The Democrats had settled on John Berrien as their nominee who would be announced at the Democratic National Convention in August, Covid permitting. He was a seventy-eight-year-old former senator from New England: another 'stale, pale, male', as the female hosts on TV news programs discourteously referred to him, even if they were Democrat supporters, which most were. There had been mass protests across the nation after a white police officer killed a black suspect during an arrest and the mood of the nation had shifted significantly. Protest marchers were pulling down statues of any person even remotely connected with the Confederacy and even though the campaign no longer included him, President Troup condemned their actions stating that 'they'll probably pull down statues of George Washington next.'

And while there was more and more division in the country during the protests, the good news of the political campaign for the Republicans was the excitement about the fact that Maye was running unopposed, and that she was extremely popular with both conservatives and liberals, a lot of the interviews in those first few days were interested primarily in the allegations of marital abuse that she had suffered in her first marriage, rather than her prospective policies for the nation, now gripped in the throes of the pandemic and the anti-racism marches.

She would go on TV or on the radio and make skirting references to her relationship, just enough to keep them happy, but not enough to give them too much. Instead, she would turn the conversation around encouraging women who were in abusive relationships to seek help and to find options to get out. She promised that if she was elected, that one of her first orders would be to establish spousal abuse as a hate crime under federal jurisdiction.

And while that was not part of her remit as president, nor would she have the power to do so, that fact was lost on the average person. But it had the desired effect: it put virtually every woman on her side.

Opinion polls had her leading significantly over the Democratic nominee. Most had her in the high fifties, while some even had her in the low sixties. At these numbers, the election was a foregone conclusion, and November could not come quickly enough.

The GOP had decided to keep the VP, Jasper Greene, in his current role 'for stability'. So the man that Maye was originally going to replace after the GOP dumped him, was now going to be the one who was showing Maye the ropes. The Young/Greene presidential ticket had not been lost on the PR people. 'Young and Greene' sounded like they were inexperienced and immature, but by putting their Christian names into the mix, Leigh Young and Jasper Greene, well that mitigated the effect. *"Leigh Young and Jasper Greene, Uniting these Great States"*.

But the spousal abuse theme continued to be appended to her and her background. She was 'a survivor of domestic abuse' and was a 'courageous and outspoken opponent of misogyny'. The frenzy was being whipped up and the women's chat shows were competing amongst themselves trying to get her to appear as a guest.

In Alabama, Ben and Jess followed the journey of their dear friends and sent Maye messages of support and gave her any help she needed. They had direct access to her and Mick through private phone messaging, and if the two needed a place to stay, or someone to run interference for them, away from the media circus, then they were happy to facilitate it.

Jess was proud to say that she created the next POTUS and FGO-TUS—President of the United States and the First Gentleman of the United States—to anyone who would listen. And when the media referred to them as "The Queen and King of America", she called herself 'the Queen Maker'. The fact that the queen can't have a king but has a royal consort was lost on the media, although it did cause some chuckling over in Britain.

After Maye had sold her huge house on Lake Allatoona, that she had bought all those years ago from the divorce settlement, she and Mick had moved to a more secure condo near her congressional offices. If and when she was sworn in, she would be moving to the White House, but if she didn't win the election, then she'd return to Atlanta and figure out her next steps then. That's what she told Mick and he was happy to help in any way he could.

He had become almost as much as a celebrity as Maye and, by virtue of his support of her campaign and his popularity, and by virtue that he wasn't the abusive husband that Maye previously had, Mick had been elevated to status of demi-God. Well maybe not demi-God, but he certainly was a hit with women and with men.

Ben was laughing at Mick's latest embarrassing appearance on TV where women were throwing themselves at him trying to get selfies and autographs.

"You'd like that to be you, wouldn't you, honey," snarked Jess as a blond nymphet rushed the stage to kiss Mick while he was on a talk show. "I'm sure you'd love to have bimbos kissing you."

"You know you're the only bimbo I want kissing me, babe," he volleyed, right back at her.

His phone then buzzed. He looked at the message. It simply read, *"Must talk. Utmost privacy. Steve B."*

97

Vicodin and Lies

Ben had left Dothan after dropping of Jess at the airport and had driven to Birmingham in northern Alabama. Jess was headed to Atlanta to spend a secret night with Jess. She needed a break and some time with her bff, so Ben had two days to find out what Steve Buchanan, Maye's first husband, wanted.

Ben disliked Steve intensely since they were both posted to Texas, when he and Maye had become friends. Or, as she was known back then, Leigh Buchanan.

He had had a brief talk with Steve on the phone after his cryptic message, and Steve begged him to come and see him, and to tell no-one. At first, Ben was suspicious, but the desperation in Steve's voice when he was begging him gave rise to a genuine concern that he was in some sort of trouble. Anyway, if he tried anything again, then Ben would 'kick his ass'. He'd already done it once before.

His GPS guided him from the interstate into Steve's sub-division, a rundown neighborhood not too far from downtown Birmingham. It had certainly seen better days. He looked at the houses and the streets. It wasn't what he expected, and certainly not the neighborhood that an air force officer would be expected to live in. Low wire fences enclosed overgrown front yards where kids' toys, some obviously left out in the weather for weeks, if not months, were strewn.

An EMT ambulance and a police car were down one end of the

street where a crowd of onlookers watched a gurney being wheeled out of a house, the sheet pulled up over the head. Another victim of Covid, most likely. The virus was spreading through struggling neighborhoods where low incomes meant low expectations of life.

He arrived at the address and looked at the house. A small, single-level on a bare block. It was neat, neater than the others, but it was certainly not what Ben was expecting. He wasn't sure if he was at the right place. The name on the letterbox didn't say 'Buchanan', it said 'Clinch'.

Nor was Ben expecting to be greeted by the man who answered the door. It was Steve, but he had aged terribly, and had put on a lot of weight.

"Hey man," said Steve, reaching out his hand and smiling a genuine smile beneath his mask. "Thanks for coming. I really appreciate it."

Ben, somewhat shocked, did not take Steve's hand but offered his elbow, the new manner of greeting people in the age of Covid. Steve bumped elbows with him and invited him in. He assured him that he did not have the virus and had seen no-one for the last several days. Inside it was neat and it was clean, but it was not for a fighter pilot. The furniture was cheap, and the pictures on the walls did not point to any evidence that Steve was once one of the air force's finest.

Steve motioned for Ben to sit and, at the fridge, held up a can of beer. Ben nodded and Steve returned to the table with two cans. He came back to the table, but not easily. It was obvious that he struggled somewhat. Seeing Ben looking around at his home he started.

"Not what you were expecting, huh?"

Ben was embarrassed to say yes. He took a gulp and shrugged. "Not really. I don't see any pictures of aircraft."

Steve merely said, "My air force life never happened, as far as I'm concerned."

Ben sat for a second, studying the overweight man sitting in front of him. His hair had way too many grays in it for a thirty-five-year-old, and was thinning unceremoniously, giving him a tall forehead. How did he end up like this?

"What happened to you," he finally said, looking around once more.

It was then that Steve told Ben the whole story. How, after a couple of years of marriage, he had followed Maye to Texas when she was given an opportunity to attend language school. He told Ben that he was very much in love with her but by the time they were in Texas, she had fallen out of love with him. She had changed dramatically after she started her language lessons. She'd often go out without him, and he suspected she was having an affair. When she wanted a divorce, he said no; that it was not in keeping with his beliefs, and that he'd prefer to try and work things out and get marriage counseling. He had already given up his position as a fighter pilot to be an instructor so that he could be with her, but she wanted out of the marriage entirely.

He then said that he offered to resign from the air force and follow her on her career; that he was hopelessly in love with her, but she did not feel the same, and she just wanted out.

Then she disappeared for a few days during the teaching semester and messaged him that she needed some time to think. Soon after, Steve was visited by the US Air Force Police and asked to accompany them to see his CO. He was then informed that Maye had accused him of assault but was not pressing charges. He told his CO that that wasn't true, but the CO showed him photos of bruising and cuts on her body.

Then one day he came home, and she was gone. He then heard that she had shacked up with Ben and went over to confront him. He thought that he was the reason she did not want to be married any more, because she was having an affair with Ben, even though Ben was already married.

"I couldn't believe it," said Steve. "When I was told that she had moved in with you, and that you had left your wife in DC, I was distraught. Her disappearances and her change in personality now made sense because she had fallen in love with you. I mean, I was beside myself. How could a man do that to his own wife and steal another man's?"

"But I didn't steal her," said Ben.

"I know... now... but at the time that was what I was told. I didn't know that you were just letting her sleep on the couch. I mean, you guys got pretty chummy, and everyone saw you two hanging out all the time, at the Officers' Mess, on the weekends."

"You know we were just friends, don't you?"

Steve looked down at his beer and nodded. "Yes. I do. But at the time I had no idea. The other guys in the squadron said that I should dump her because she'd shacked up with you. And then when you beat me up, I thought that was proof that you two were involved."

Ben shook his head. "I beat you up because you keyed my pickup."

"What? No I didn't"

"Yes you did. It cost me nine hundred bucks to get it re-sprayed."

"I don't know what you're talking about, Ben. I never touched your truck. All I know is that one day you appeared at my place, and I was beaten up. Then I was grounded by the CO and the rest is history."

He then told Ben about how he ended up leaving the air force and got a job flying freight out of Kansas until they somehow found out he had been accused of wife beating. His boss decided that it was time for him to go and they made things hard for him. Uneven rostering, early starts and late finishes. He had to break Federal Aviation Regulations just to keep doing the shifts. When he told his boss that he wasn't prepared to continue to break regulations he was fired for some trumped up nonsense. His reputation was shot, and the online aviation bulletin boards warned people about him. Job offers would suddenly be withdrawn. He moved to Birmingham on the promise of another flying job, but that fell through also.

So, he took six months off away from flying. The divorce came through and he was left with very little afterwards. The six months turned into a year, and a year into two years. He started drinking a bit too much and never went back to flying.

After changing his name, and a couple of years of driving trucks for UPS, he had an accident when he was T-boned by an eighteen-wheeler driven by a trucker high on amphetamines, and he ended up on social security and insurance payouts. He now lived here. He looked around at his very modest existence.

"I am in pain most days so I'm on Vicodin. I don't sleep because of the drugs, so I sit in that chair over there and watch TV for eighteen hours a day."

Ben wasn't sure if he could believe him. It seemed so far-fetched. But what Steve had not told him was why he had called. What was the reason for Ben to be here?

"I've been watching Leigh and her campaign," he said. "She's been doing a good job, and her Australian husband seems to be popular," he said.

"Yeah," said Ben. "Not too many people can say that the president used to sleep under their roof," he said, trying to lighten the mood.

It didn't help. Steve looked crestfallen.

"I've been watching her interviews. She's been really pushing this domestic abuse story. It's only a matter of time before someone joins the dots and knocks on my door. And what happens to me then? I become the loser that used to beat up the president."

Ben still wasn't totally convinced. Steve must have had an angle. Maybe he had some way of blackmailing Maye and just wanted Ben to 'see' how he was living... or maybe he wanted his fifteen minutes of fame some other way. In any case, Ben was suspicious.

He got up to leave and head back to Dothan. Steve walked him to the door. Sitting down at the dining table for too long made his back ache and it was causing him grief. Ben wished him luck, not willing to commit to anything, but stopped at the door. He had to ask.

"Steve, why am I here? What is it that you want from me... or Maye? Do you need money?"

Steve looked at Ben in amazement.

"No. I don't want your money, or her money. I just needed you to know my side of the story. And maybe you can get her to ease up on the 'wife bashing' stuff. I never touched her."

Ben still wasn't convinced. He wasn't buying that 'I don't get divorced because I don't believe in it' stuff.

"I'm sorry... but I don't believe you. I mean it's too bad that your life didn't turn out the way you wanted it to," he said looking at his house and yard, "but I know Maye, and I know how scared she was when she was with you. We talked a lot... I mean a helluva lot... and you can tell if someone's telling the truth or not when you speak to them for hours on end."

Steve sighed heavily and looked down, crestfallen again. He realized that it was no use trying to speak with Ben any more about this. He offered his hand.

"Thanks for driving all this way. Have a safe drive home." He then turned to go back inside as Ben started for his truck. Backing out of the driveway he headed for the interstate. The whole day was a waste of time.

98

Victims to the Virus

The next few months passed quickly.

Covid was ravaging the country, and Troup was having a field day blaming the World Health Organization for kowtowing to China who, he claimed, manufactured the disease and had weaponized it.

With Troup's administration in its final months, he had nothing to lose. His tweets became even more erratic, and he did not hold back in criticizing the GOP, or anyone else who did not share his world view.

As Covid case numbers rose, and new variants were detected, the hospitals were filling to capacity and health care workers were strained to the limit of their capabilities. Nurses were being brought out of retirement, and trainee nurses were being fast-tracked through their training. Anything to increase the patient to nurse ratio.

Inconsistencies reigned across the country as state governors ignored federal advice or orders. As much as Troup bombastically demanded the states fall into line, there were plenty of political pundits and constitutional clairvoyants who asserted that what was being experienced was the purity—and the shortcomings—of the federal system, with the states exerting their rights. The left would cry that if the right wanted small government, this is what they got. The right, on the other hand, claimed that it was left-leaning state governments who were enforcing the more restrictive rules to the detriment of their citizens. In a country already divided, it was increasing the schism.

And while the Covid cases rose to more than five million, and deaths approached two hundred thousand, mass events continued to be canceled, or would be converted to 'virtual' events. This included the national conventions of the Democratic and Republican parties.

In the Democrat's camp, John Berrien, who had won the primaries, was to be nominated. He had chosen a black woman, Carla Haralson, to be his running mate which, while welcomed by a large cross-section of Democrats, was a blatant gesture bowing to political correctness rather than selecting the best person for the job. With the number of female potential candidates significantly smaller than the number of males, and then the number of black candidates even smaller still, it did not take a mathematician with an advanced degree to do the calculations that a black female candidate was unlikely to be the best choice for rational decision-making, intelligence and experience. The selection pool was way too small for that to be likely. A few interviews with the media and it was obvious that she did not have the intelligence, the experience nor the political acumen that some of her colleagues had, male and female. If she was confronted with a question that was difficult for her—and that happened more often than not—she would brush it off or laugh inanely. It was obvious she was not up to the task, and that performance was being sacrificed on the altar of perception. But if there was anyone in the Democratic party that objected to her selection, then they were quickly silenced, or branded a racist or a sexist. In that way, it appeared as though the choice was unanimous from the Party. The fact that she had accused Berrien of racism during the primaries debates, but was now his running mate, seemed to be lost on the media.

Then, of course, there was 'smilin' John Berrien' himself. He had also seen better days. Easily confused, and a mumbler, he did not inspire confidence in those around him or who were watching him on TV. And it wasn't long before questions were being raised if that duo was the best that the Democrats could muster? Furthermore, was Haralson, once a critic of Berrien, just biding her time until he 'shuffled off' and she could take the reins? Consumer politics had become a virus, and it was just as deadly to the quality of America's leaders as Covid had become to its citizens.

In September, the virtual national convention was held and, as expected, the Berrien/Haralson ticket was chosen to lead the party to the elections in November. With Troup withdrawing his candidacy and not seeking re-election, and the primaries well and truly over, the GOP had only one choice and so the Republican National Convention was canceled, much to the chagrin of many of the delegates who were looking forward to the event. But the pandemic was not only taking lives, it was also taking livelihoods. Massed events, whether sporting, celebratory, commemorative, political... they were all victims of the virus, and the Republican National Convention was the latest.

99

G.U.

The presidential debates were a walk in the park for Maye. Berrien, dazed and confused, did not do himself nor the reputation of the Democratic party much good. At least when O'Conee was president he was intelligent and convincing. Maye was articulate, knowledgeable and attractive. And while she did not have the same number of years in politics that Berrien had—he had been a senator for more than sixteen—she did have some key attributes on her side.

Firstly, she was young. In a world where technology had seen much disruption in the way things were, those that were able to grasp technology were at an advantage... and that was the young.

Secondly, she was a woman. Humans have biases; some overt; others inherent. There was an inherent bias towards a woman candidate by women voters. This was not news, and the Republicans were more than aware of this human condition and played upon it well. They were also well aware that it was a double-edged sword.

The Republican queen makers knew what was needed. The power coaches, most of them women, would school the senior leadership, mostly men, on how best to re-create Maye into the candidate they needed. They would tell these men that women see other women—especially young, attractive, successful women— as threats, either consciously or subconsciously; an internal manifestation of an external locus of control. To make things even more complicated, women want to see important women as reflections of themselves. Of course, this only served to confuse the men who just wanted to know how best to make Maye into what women wanted.

"It is important that Maye be seen as 'Jane Allwomen'", said the senior coach, "and not as a threat or a competitor. If we make sure that Mick is always with her, then that will definitely help. Because she has become somewhat of a sex symbol in the media, it makes her a threat. We can mitigate that threat by putting her husband in the picture, beside—but behind—her. A married woman was no longer a threat, no matter how attractive and intelligent she is." And so her second attribute was enhanced by this simple ploy that made her, subconsciously, less of a threat.

Her third greatest asset was that she knew her stuff. The Republicans had put a lot of effort into coaching her, and she had risen to the task. Besides a few early butterflies in the debates, she found her stride, and was able to run rings around her opponent.

And VP Jasper Greene was no slouch, either! He easily outshone Carla Haralson, making the Maye Young / Jasper Greene ticket all but unbeatable. If that wasn't enough, he enjoyed working with Maye on the campaign also, and their partnership was seen as more natural and more comfortable than that which he had with President Troup.

But there was one event that sent the GOP into a frenzy, and the media also.

As the Covid numbers became more and more critical, and the morgues were overflowing, the race was on to find an effective vaccine. Pharmacological companies in Europe, America, Asia and Australia were putting their trials into overdrive. Soon the European and American vaccines were showing more promise and, with greater financial backing, were streaking ahead of the rest of the world. The Australian trials ceased, having not shown signs of efficacy, as did those in Japan and South Korea, but not in China.

The Chinese Communist Party announced that their scientists were making headway into a polyvalent vaccine that appeared to be active against the Covid pathogen and its mutant strains, not just the 'alpha' strain. The genomic sequencing had been altered in the proteins to make the vaccine recognize the underlying virus chain and target that. If the underlying virus is killed, then the mutations that had made viruses immune to earlier versions of a vaccine, would naturally become orphaned and would die.

Knowing that the reputation of their country as being the origin of the worldwide pandemic, along with SARS and bird flu prior, the Chinese were eager to share their technology. To help underscore their research, they named it G.U. which, when said as Zhee Yoo, means 'cure' in Chinese.

They offered a thousand doses to the Center for Disease Control for their assessment, provided that American pharmacological companies were not given any samples until the Chinese were happy to share the technology.

President Troup immediately rejected the notion, but the public outcry was too great. There were so many patients in hospital that almost overnight, two hundred thousand people suffering Covid's effects volunteered to trial the drug for the CDC's assessment.

Once the lawyers weighed in, and big business demanded of the government that the trails be conducted—after all, they were losing billions because of this pandemic—Troup authorized the CDC to conduct the assessment on volunteers provided they indemnified the federal government and its agencies.

And this was done.

Within two days, almost seventy percent of patients began to show signs of improvement, with their breathing becoming easier and their pain easing. Those with pre-existing and underlying conditions had mixed results, but some showed improvement. Overall, the assessment was positive, and the CDC reported that while there were improvements to be had, the Chinese G.U. vaccine seemed to be the most effective against the multiple strains of the virus. But it also warned that more testing was needed, and more caution advised until it could be definitively ascertained that there were no side-effects.

The public and business, fueled by the media, demanded more access to the G.U vaccine, as the economy continued to sputter and falter.

Troup, whose popularity had only been enhanced by his tough stance on China during the trade disputes of his presidency, was loath to credit China with creating a potential cure. As far as he was concerned, that nation needed to be brought under control and put in its place, even if they had a vaccine. But Maye didn't share this view.

In an announcement that pleasantly shocked the country—and the world—she said that one of her first acts as president, if elected, would be to help China find a cure for this virus and with China and the United States working together, help the world return to some sort of normalcy where people can feel safe in being with each other and the international economies re-opened..

And even though she was just a presidential nominee, and the American public still had weeks before going to the polls, that announcement was welcomed across all sectors. The Dow Jones Industrial Average and the S&P 500, both of which had languished for six months, both had their highest spikes since March as business and industry were heartened by her comments. And if that was not enough, the General Secretary of the Chinese Communist Party, Jaw-Long, made a public announcement that he and the People's Republic of China looked forward to a resumption of normal relations between the two countries if Congresswoman Young was elected, and that China wished for further cooperation with the US under her leadership to help solve the world's challenges.

For a country, and a world, that was expecting US-China relations to continue to sour, and maybe even turn to conflict, these words were most welcome. If Maye had not been seen as 'The Free World's Greatest Hope', she certainly was now. And yet again, Troup was furious. So was Berrien. Many saw the Chinese comments as blatant interference in US politics by China. Others saw them as hope for the world.

After the debates, Maye's approval rating was fifty-eight percent. After her comments about cooperation with China to cure the virus, and China's complimentary comments in return, it was sixty-four percent. World leaders began calling her directly... and she hadn't even been elected yet. But as far as the world was concerned, her election was a *fait accompli.*

100

Civis Romanus Sum

The following January, after the inauguration...

The first week of President Young's administration was a honeymoon.

As soon as she took office, she spoke to the leaders of America's allies to reinforce the bonds between each country, and that she looked forward to meeting him or her in person, Covid permitting. This was reciprocated with gracious compliments of how the new administration was a breath of fresh air.

She then overturned many of her predecessor's less popular decisions, but when it came to national security, she was ruthless. Political pundits marveled at how she could impress both sides of politics simultaneously.

In another orchestrated media event, President Young requested the Director of the US Citizenship and Immigration Services to fast track the three-year citizenship process for the First Gentleman. A special civics test was to be held for Mick that was going to be televised. He was now a major in the US Army since his induction and swearing in on Inauguration Day. The president had the Secretary of the Army push the induction and administration for him. It was a good look to have the First Gentleman in uniform and helped cement that link with the military, a relationship that had helped her throughout her career and which had been critical for her campaign. Now she was intent on the Executive being a friend to the military, not a hindrance.

But today it was Major O'Rourke's citizenship test on the subject of civics to be held in the Oval Office. It was another media event, obviously staged for the public's consumption. And though she did not need to campaign anymore, it could not help but boost her standing with the people of America, and that of the First Gentleman.

The civics test is a mandatory test that must be passed by anyone seeking citizenship. Twenty questions from over one hundred and twenty-eight possible options are asked at random, with a pass mark of a minimum of twelve correct.

The president stood nearby in her Seal of the President of the United States mask, along with a bevy of White House staff, all of whom had warmed to the First Gentleman and his laid-back ways, and who were silently cheering him on from behind their Stars and Stripes face masks.

The USCIS Director commenced the questions as the cameras recorded.

"How are changes made to the US Constitution," he asked.

Without pausing, Mick responded "Through the amendment process."

The director nodded and fired another question. "How many amendments does the US Constitution have?"

"Twenty-seven."

"Name the three branches of government."

"The legislative, the judicial, and..." he nodded towards his wife, the president, "... the executive."

The director smiled and the staff chuckled. It certainly was the most unusual civics test the USCIS had ever held.

Mick continued to answer question after question, each one correctly.

"Who is your US representative?" The director looked up from his paper at Mick, peering over his bifocals. This was an unusual question with an unusual response.

"Well," said Mick, and paused. The director immediately regretted asking that question. The First Gentleman was unlikely to know this answer as he had been a resident in DC for only a few weeks and had been educated outside the US. He would look foolish, and it was the director's fault.

"When I was in Georgia in the Georgia 11th, my representative was Congresswoman Maye Young," he said with a grin and a wink at the president, "but the District of Columbia has no voting representative in the house but has a non-voting delegate... and she is Amelia Horace Newton."

The director sighed with relief. This guy was good! He continued with the questions and each one the First Gentleman answered correctly. Questions on the Civil War. Questions on the war in Afghanistan. Questions on Colonial America. He even answered a few questions as a question, referring to the director as 'Alex', a nod to Alex Trebek, the late host of *Jeopardy*, to the delight of the staff, and later to the people watching on TV.

He was up to the final question. Even though he had passed with flying colors, the president and the staff were silently cheering him on to get the final one correct. The director flicked through the one hundred and twenty-eight questions and settled on one.

"What is the rule of law?" he asked.

Mick again paused. He knew the answer, but decided to couch it in a particular way that he thought would play well in Peoria.

"Everyone must follow the law: the government, our leaders, everyone. No-one is above the law."

There was a pause. The director looked at him solemnly. For a second, Mick thought he had gotten it wrong. But when the director smiled, he knew he had it in the bag with a clean sweep of answers.

"Major O'Rourke, may I congratulate you on becoming a citizen of the United States." The director held out his hand and Mick offered his elbow in return. Embarrassed, the director returned the new Covid-compliant compliment.

The president, on the other hand, embraced him and held him for a minute while the White House photographer captured the event. They had both become adept at holding a pose so that they could be captured by camera. She looked at him, her hands holding his arms. They had taken their masks down so that their mouths could be seen.

"I am so proud of you Major," she said. "Welcome to the citizenry of the United States."

The staff applauded and he went over to thank them for their support, all of whom were eager to bump elbows.

The Defense Liaison Officer to the White House, a US Navy commodore, offered his elbow and with a smile said to him, "Now you can get your security clearance!"

It was ironic that the man married to the President of the United States, and an officer of the US Army, was not allowed a security clearance because he had not been a citizen.

"Sorry for the inconvenience," said the commodore.

"Don't be sorry, Sir," Mick replied to the naval officer who, by rank, was more senior than he. "I am a citizen of the United States... and no-one is above the law of the United States."

That innocent interaction between the commodore and the major, between a senior rank and a junior rank, a most ordinary and understandable interaction to men and women in uniform, was captured on camera unbeknownst to either of them. It was played over and over and over on every network, to resounding approval from pundits and punters alike. And with a nod of approval by those serving in uniform.

This administration, this White House, really *was* the new Camelot.

101

Something Stinks in the Rose Garden

Mick had been appointed 'special adviser for Indo-Pacific relations which, at first, was met with disdain at the State Department. But after Major O'Rourke met with the various desk officers that looked after intelligence on, and relations with, Australia, New Zealand, Indonesia, India and the other nations of the area, they were duly impressed with the First Gentleman's grasp of the delicate balance in which the area exists. His suggestions on how communication flow can be improved between the nations and the US, and between the State Department's Indo-Pacific desks and the White House were, in their eyes, positive and a marked improvement from the last administration. He assured them that he would not be someone who would be interfering, but an involved and interested go-between for the president and their baili-wick. This, in particular, made them extremely happy.

President Young spoke of the need for a re-vamp of the nation's se-curity: smarter spending on new technologies and smarter ways of mil-itary operations. "We shan't be using a military option unless it is a last resort and unless we have specific and attainable goals, suitable support from our allies, and a clear and unambiguous exit strategy," she told the nation. "I do not want to sacrifice American lives for a wasted effort, but let me be perfectly clear... if we, as a nation, do decide to use the military option, then we shall do it with full gusto and determination, and not with a half-hearted attempt to please commentators. Our military leaders are best placed to conduct military operations. Politicians should not get involved unless it is to facilitate military decisions or to rein in largess." The armed forces loved that.

When a president's progress is measured in the first one hundred days, President Young had made significant progress in only ten, and she was just getting started.

She was definitely the media's darling. Soon, her nickname became 'The Great American Hope' and moderate Democrats whispered amongst themselves, "Thank God she won, and Berrien didn't." And the Republicans? Well, they couldn't be happier. After a string of sub-par Republican presidents, they had scored a winner with this one. The brief unpleasantness after the primaries were cancelled and her talk of 'faceless men' had long since been forgotten by the national committee who saw eight years of power in their future.

Mick had encouraged her to reach out to China as soon as possible. It would be a good way to show off her language skills. Plus, it was a good idea to start the normalization process with the Chinese Communist Party. "The whole world is on edge," he said to her. "You can help calm things down if you reach out to them."

She considered this, and while she was not a fan of the communist Chinese, her grandmother being a staunch nationalist Chinese woman still fostering a bitter resentment towards them, she had said that she would look at areas of cooperation with them as the world searched for a vaccine if G.U. proved not to be the magic bullet all had hoped. But right now, there was an immediate matter that needed her attention.

When she agreed to grant an interview to the media, it was in the rose garden. Her secret service detail escorted her from the Executive Residence to where the camera crew and reporter had set up. Upon her request, Agent Lee had become her primary agent when he was on the roster. He had definitely become the poster boy of the US Secret Service and everywhere that the president went, Agent Lee was usually close at hand. Some even joked on Capitol Hill that they were having an affair, but that was usually the ill-mannered and small-minded who hated having Maye as president, and who didn't care for the First Gentleman, either. Some had even intimated that his relationship with President Troup may have been anachronistic, perhaps too close. But Agent Lee seemed to be nothing but loyal and dutiful to the administration. Wherever the president was, he was there, and today was no exception. He walked ahead of her and stood nearby as she was prepared for the interview with make-up and microphone.

The reporter, appropriately distanced, took off her mask and commenced with the stock standard questions about how she was settling in, and had she spoken to other world leaders. She was then asked some personal questions about the First Gentleman, and married life in the White House. President Young was happy to discuss them and give a human touch to what are normally staid questions about politics, and the day-to-day intrigues of Washington.

But then the reporter took the questioning down a different path.

"So, Madam President," she began, "you have attained the position of the most powerful woman in the world, but there was a time in your life when you were, let's say, powerless. Of course, I am referring to your first marriage and the domestic abuse you suffered at the hands of your then husband."

President Young did not appreciate the questions taking this turn. She had wanted to remain on the subject of domestic issues and foreign policy. But the reporter cornered her with a follow-on statement.

"What would you say to the thousands upon thousands of women who are in destructive and abusive relationships? What words of advice or encouragement can you offer to these women?"

She was trapped. She could not deflect such a sensitive question. She had to give a response.

102

Let Sleeping Dogs Lie

Ben and Jess watched a recording of the interview of their friend, the president, that had been filmed the week prior and had already been televised the day before. She looked terrific sitting in the White House's rose garden.

Soon, the subject of Maye's marriage to Steve Buchanan was raised, and she was asked to give words of encouragement to women in abusive relationships.

"I can't believe they're digging that up again," said Jess, a glass of wine in her hand. "Can't they concentrate on more pressing issues?"

Ben watched the screen. He thought about his meeting with Steve back in September, five months ago. He never told Jess about the meeting. He thought it better to let sleeping dogs lie. Now the subject was being aired once more.

But then a surprise that made him sit up anxiously. The interviewer began filling in some details of Maye's time in the air force, about her posting to San Antonio to the military language course, and her marriage to a fighter pilot.

Suddenly, a photo of Steve when he was Lieutenant Steven Buchanan, fighter pilot, appeared on the screen. They had 'outed him'.

They then showed a reporter outside the modest brick house in Birmingham that Ben recognized as Steve's home. In the fashion of sensationalist journalism, the cameraman was running down the street to try and intercept Steve who was trying to escape the TV crew and reporter.

"Oh my God," exclaimed Jess seeing Steve trying to get into his truck. "Is that Steve? He looks terrible."

The program continued in that manner; in the way those sorts of shows do. A mobile car wreck that seems to go on forever, and from which you cannot avert your gaze.

At the end of the program Jess spoke about how she was so glad that that part of everyone's life was over, and how the time in Texas was hard on everyone, especially Maye.

"But I'm glad I came down from DC to check out this chick that was sleeping on your couch," she said. "'Cos, I got a best friend... who is now the most powerful woman in the world! And it's all because I thought she was trying to steal you from me."

She got up to get ready for bed but stopped and bent down to give her husband a kiss.

"You're a good man for looking after her," she said, and headed off to put the wineglass in the dishwasher.

"Remember that townhouse you were living in when you took Maye in," she asked from the kitchen. "That was quite a nice place. Except for the garage door. That thing was so noisy. I'm sure it woke everyone in the complex up when you were on night duty." She headed up the stairs. "See you in bed."

Ben thought about what Jess had just said. He had forgotten how loud that garage door was. It would always squeal when it opened, especially when it was forced open, which he had to do a couple of times when he locked his keys in the condo and he had to get into the garage to get to his spare.

How *did* Steve open the garage door to scratch his car without waking everyone up? He couldn't have come through the front door, that was dead-bolted. The only answer was Maye. Maye must have let him in!

Just then his phone rang. It was 10 p.m. Late night phone calls were never good.

"Hello?" he said warily. It was the Birmingham PD. They had found Steve Clinch's body in a vacant lot near the rail yards. He was in his truck with a hose from the exhaust into the window. There was a note with a letter addressed to Ben.

103

Pillow Talk Diplomacy

Six weeks into President Young's administration, and with the Covid death toll rising continuously, the calls for the G.U. vaccine became louder and louder. And while those on the right side of politics were wary of 'getting into bed with the Chinese', as they put it, those on the left were eager to get a solution to the pandemic that was killing so many Americans, especially minorities, whose health was already compromised. As far as they were concerned, the benefits of saving hundreds and thousands of lives far outweighed any potential security risks, which they felt could be managed anyway.

Big business was eager for a solution, also. A virus that prevented workers from being able to get to the factories and retail outlets and any other place of business was killing the economy. The only sector that was not keen on getting G.U. out on the street was big pharmaceutical. It was still trying to perfect its own vaccines.

For the general public, the CDC's assessment that the Chinese vaccine was, in its early development, effective—particularly for those that were in critical condition in hospital—was enough for opinion to sway in favor of getting the G.U. vaccine rolled out before any American vaccine was developed and tested.

But there was still significant doubt about any deal with the Chinese. They had been very public about their intentions to expand their influence world-wide through its foreign policies such as the Belt and

Road Initiative, so if America was going to partner with them to save its population, then would it be beholden to China?

The president wrestled with the conundrum. She was vehemently opposed to doing deals with the Chinese Communist Party, but each day saw new records broken in infections and deaths. At this rate, the US would be crippled within five years, and its economy in tatters within two.

"I'm really at a loss for what to do," she confided in her husband that night in bed. "The State Department is ready for the White House to make an announcement either way," she said, "but the strategic policy guys are extremely wary, and Defense doesn't want a bar of it." She looked at Mick, troubled.

"You're damned if you do and you're damned if you don't," he said.

"What do you think?" she asked him. "Should I reach out to Jaw-Long? If I did, my grandmother would disown me," she said trying to lighten the seriousness of the conversation.

"Well sweetheart, this is something that I cannot weigh in on," said the First Gentleman, "this is something that you need to decide."

The president leaned on one elbow. "You're kidding, aren't you?" she asked incredulously. "During the campaign you had an opinion on everything, and your gut feeling was usually right," she said. "You always gave me good advice, and if there was ever a time when I need good advice, it's now," she implored him.

Mick looked at her. She was looking very tired. Late nights and early mornings were not being kind to her. Hopefully, as her knowledge and capabilities got better, and her staff became more in tune with the tempo and her needs, things might become smoother... but for now, it was riding a roller coaster.

"Well," he started hesitantly, "if the G.U. vaccine is effective, and the CDC and Department of Health and Human Services have found nothing of concern, then it might be a good idea to start introducing it," he said. "The Chinese might even license the production of the vaccine here," he said. "Then it will be a matter of handling the ongoing relationship with them. But if we don't stop this virus from killing Americans, then you'll have no America left. Better the devil you know..."

She looked at him with some curiousness. "You've never been totally opposed to the Chinese, have you?"

"Not really," he said. "I mean, it's obvious that they want to take their place at the big boys' table, so it's a matter of how you handle that."

The president thought about what her husband had said. How the Chinese want to be taken seriously as a world player.

"OK. Let's do it," she said. "Time to harness the dragon and save American lives. I'll get State to contact Jaw-Long's people and we'll set up a visit to Beijing."

104

Politically Incorrect

The entourage had boarded Air Force One at Joint Base Andrews. As is typical, the media and staff boarded via the rear entrance leaving the president and the First Gentleman to board via the front door. The two of them ascended the airstair and paused to wave at the crowd of well-wishers and media, just as so many of their predecessors had done. The cameras snapped the couple next to the Seal of the President of the United States as they embarked on their first international engagement: the historic visit of a serving president to the People's Republic of China, only the fourteenth time a presidential visit had been undertaken. Before President Nixon, the US had visited the moon six times. Traveling to the moon was easier than traveling to China. But still, in the more than forty years since Nixon, there had been only twelve visits to China by an American leader.

The VC-25, a military version of the Boeing 747, took the members of the president's party, some media and members of the State Department, including translators, desk officers and strategists, across the Pacific with a quick stopover in Hawaii to 'show that state some love'. Air Force Two, a C-32—the military version of the Boeing 757—was to accompany the delegation, along with two US Air Force C-17 transports carrying the president's vehicles and security. On the way back from China, President Young was going to see the Japanese Prime Minister to discuss defense arrangements, a Clean Pacific program to combat plastics pollution, and to sue for the cessation of the Japanese whaling program. These last agenda items were warmly welcomed by the environmental lobby. It seemed that President Young was hitting home runs at every turn, and her popularity remained high. She was proving to be the best, and most effective president, the country could remember. Even President Kennedy, whom people remember through rose-colored glasses, was not as successful as folklore would have one think. A cursory look at history would show that he had more failures than he had victories. But so far, Maye Young had exceeded the expectations of her detractors and had continued to win friends and supporters, at home and abroad.

As the president did the rounds on board greeting the members of the entourage and the media, she agreed to do interviews a little later while she prepared for her visit. She had had a Chinese tutor accompany her for the last few days to help her brush up on her Mandarin and she wanted some time alone with him and the China specialists from the State Department 'to get up to speed.'

Mick continued his wife's soft PR campaign, as she called it, by engaging informally with the staff and media. Never before had they enjoyed so much access to the president and her spouse, and it was paying dividends. All the federal government departments were eager to come within the orbits of the president and the First Gentleman, who had proven amiable and easy to deal with, and the media continued its glowing reports, both left- and right-biased news agencies.

The First Gentleman came to a gaggle of State Department officials and asked them what their roles were. There were the usual desk officers and specialists and officials who were going to undertake 'counterpart visits', where they meet with their equivalents in the Chinese government. Mick saw one gentleman, an Asian fellow who, he thought, looked familiar.

"Hi, I'm Mick O'Rourke," he said extending his hand.

"Good morning, Sir," replied the stranger, "Yes, I am quite aware of who you are," he said with a smile. Mick had a knack of putting people at ease with his informality. "I'm Dawson Chiroki. I'm with the Japan desk and I'll be helping coordinate the president's visit to Japan," he said.

"That's terrific," he replied studying his face more closely. "Have we met before? You look very familiar to me."

"I don't think so, Sir," Chiroki responded. "I've been in DC for quite a while working for State. Have you had any dealings with the Japan desk?"

"No, I can't say that I have," he said. "But you do look familiar."

"You know how it is," replied Chiroki, "we Asians all look alike!" he said with a smile.

The other members of his team grimaced and one whispered hoarsely that 'you can't say that!'

Mick saw the discomfort in them. "Hey, lighten up!" he said. "It's just a joke." He then turned to Chiroki whose expression had changed to one of contrition. He had just embarrassed his colleagues and the Department of State in front of the president's husband.

"Well, Dawson," said the First Gentleman. "I like a man with a sense of humor who can make fun of himself. Political correctness is killing humor and it's strangling America." This last comment was a slight dig at his colleagues who were now breathing a sigh of relief that offense had not been given.

Mick saw their faces and decided to throw Chiroki another bone. "You sound like a fun guy. Come back to the quarters and have a drink with me and tell me about the Japan visit."

Dawson Chiroki picked up his gear. He looked at his supervisor who looked shocked and concerned.

"Do you want me to come also, Sir?" asked Chiroki's supervisor. "Agent Chiroki has only been with State for a short time. If you have any questions, I might be better placed to assist with your enq..."

"No, that won't be necessary," said the First Gentleman, cutting off the supervisor in mid-sentence. "I've got some good jokes that Dawson might appreciate. They may be a bit too un-PC for others," replied the First Gentleman.

Chiroki's supervisor and colleagues looked wounded. They knew that they, and their political correctness, had just been put in their place, albeit subtly, by the husband of the president. The supervisor, in particular, seemed quite anxious, but the First Gentleman paid him no heed.

Mick led Dawson down the corridor to the executive suites. Outside the meeting room where the president was speaking with her tutor and the China specialists stood the ubiquitous Agent Lee and another secret service agent.

"G'day Bruce!" said Mick to Agent Lee, who he had jokingly dubbed 'day-time husband' to his wife in response to the accusations that they were having an affair.

"Good morning, Sir," he responded with a forced smile.

Dawson, nervously, did not make eye contact with Agent Lee who watched him carefully. Mick could see Lee's concern.

"This is Dawson from the State Department. We're going to talk about the Japan visit."

"Yes, Sir," Lee replied, and resumed his post.

Arriving at the executive suite, Mick poured Dawson a drink.

"Not too early, I hope?" he said, offering him a glass with bourbon and ice.

"It's afternoon somewhere in the world, Sir," came the reply. Mick had taken an instant liking to this guy.

"Here you go," said Mick handing over the glass. "Boy, you sure do look familiar."

105

⌾❦❧⌾

Tearing Down the Great Wall

In Beijing, President Young surprised and impressed not only Jaw-Long, the Chinese president, but also all of the official delegation with her poise and elegance, but mostly with her command of Mandarin. Back in the US, and around the world, televisions and computer screens showed shots of her with her Chinese counterpart, wearing masks with their country's flags, meeting and discussing the way forward.

Besides the G.U. vaccine, the president was discussing a plan to resume and normalize trade relations that had soured under President Troup. He had built a wall between the two countries and President Young was tearing it down. And against State Department advice, she also took time to gently bring up the subject of intellectual property rights, an area in which China often showed scant regard.

By the end of the visit, agreements had been reached on supplying the US with the G.U. vaccine at the rate of one hundred thousand per week for the first two weeks and increasing to one million doses per week thereafter. The Chinese felt that their production capacity could be increased to accommodate their own domestic demand as well as the needs of the US. Once the US had stabilized its infections and its death rate—"as China had done", claimed Jaw-Long—then China could start supplying the rest of the world. He even intimated that they may share their technology in polyvalent vaccine manufacture which had proven to be more promising than they had expected, especially in the field of cancer research. President Jaw-Long said that they had found that two of the trial patients had cancer, but since the Covid G.U. trial, their cancers had gone into rapid remission. This unexpected event surprised the scientists, and so a supplementary program had been initiated to look into this possible side effect. So far, the results had been surprising and positive.

At one stage, President Young and President Jaw-Long dismissed their translators and minders and took a long walk alone in the gardens of the former Imperial Palace, conversing in Mandarin. The media jockeyed to capture images of the two, together, alone. She really was America's greatest hope for the future.

Mick, in the meantime, had been taken to Shaanxi province to visit the Terracotta Army of China's first emperor Qin Shi Huang. To everyone's surprise, he was able to converse with the delegation guides in reasonable Chinese, something that was completely unexpected, and which greatly impressed the media scrum that was escorting him.

He informed them, as they clamored for an explanation, that he had taught English in China before he joined the Australian Army. Then, as a joke, he informed them that it was "Australian English... you know, the correct English."

For the Chinese people, this visit by the declining superpower helped cement their faith in President Jaw-Long and the status of China as being a world leader and, possibly, the savior of the human race.

106

The Last Supper

After further rapid trials by the Department of Health and Human Services, President Young signed an executive order initiating the distribution of the G.U. vaccine. Noting how the less advantaged socioeconomic areas were suffering the effects more so than the more affluent, she decided that the southern states of Mississippi, Alabama, Georgia and Louisiana would be the first to be given the vaccine.

She enlisted the help of the governors of those states who had their national guard activated to help distribute the vaccine to their more remote areas. And even though there were critics who thought the distribution was unfair and favored minorities, for the most part people understood why she was doing it in that manner.

The communications advisers suggested that perhaps a tour of those states to see the distribution would be a good look, to which she agreed, and so she and Mick boarded Air Force One for a tour of the south and to see the distribution and to touch base with the governors. They decided to take some time to visit Ben and Jess and to have a private dinner with their good friends.

* * *

As they toured the outer counties of Georgia and Alabama they were met like heroes. Crowds of masked Georgians lined the roads waving American flags and rebel flags and holding up hand-made signs of support, welcoming her 'home to GA'.

They were spending three days in Georgia and had some time to visit Rob Early and Sally-Anne Atkinson and Pam Spalding, all of whom had moved on to different jobs since their campaign days, but who were still considered dear and close friends. A private dinner at a restaurant that was closed for the occasion allowed Mick and Maye time to relax away from the media with the people who helped get them to the White House. Jesús Emmanuel flew in from Texas, and Ben and Jess drove up from Dothan. Carol Coffee was still looking after the office of the 11th District, but her new boss was "...not as nice as you, Maye... I mean Madam President." These were the closest friends Mick and Maye had, and it was a welcome relief from official dinners and photo opportunities. The only photographer permitted was the official White House photographer who was tasked with taking candid shots of the event for the First Couple and their friends.

Mick asked the kitchen staff if they would make up some finger food for their secret service agents and the media waiting outside, and to deliver it with some sodas.

The following night they would have a function for the GAGOP, but tonight it was just the First Couple and their friends.

As the evening wore on, and they reminisced about the mid-term campaign and the lead up to the primaries, Ben took Mick aside for a private chat. These two army buddies had been through a lot together since their first meeting over ten years prior as trainee Chinook pilots at Fort Rucker. But Ben was a bit more serious this evening.

"Did you hear Steve Buchanan killed himself?" asked Ben.

Mick had to think for a second, then realized who Ben was speaking of. He couldn't help but feel a bit guilty that he wasn't sorry to hear the news. After all, he had been beating his wife, who was now Mick's wife.

"He says that he never laid a finger on Maye," said Ben. "He called me and asked me to visit him in Birmingham, so I did. He wasn't in a good way."

Mick listened with curiosity. Ben had no love for Steve. He had 'kicked his ass' in his own words. So why was he so concerned now?

"He was living in this dump and was hooked on pain killers. His career ended when he was kicked out of the air force, and he couldn't get a job without his past catching up with him." Ben took a gulp of his scotch. "Anyway, they found a letter in his house after his body was discovered. It was addressed to me, and it was him pleading with me to believe him, that he never hit Maye, ever."

"Do you believe him?"

"I didn't at first," replied Ben, "but then I thought about some things he said, and I think there's some truth in it. Like I now think that he couldn't have keyed my pickup unless he came into the house first."

He paused for a second, wondering if he should tell Mick his suspicion. "I think Maye let him into the house," he said, with trepidation.

Mick looked at his friend, shocked. Why would Maye let her abusive husband into the house? It made no sense.

"I guess she may have wanted to talk to him. Maybe talk some sense into him, I don't know," said Ben. "But I don't think he could have entered the garage in any other way."

"I don't get it," said Mick. "If she did, and he then went into the garage and keyed your car, then why didn't she just admit to you that she had let him in."

"Maybe she was embarrassed, or ashamed. But that's the only explanation I can think of for how Steve got into the garage without Jess or I hearing. But, if you believe what he said to me and what he said in the letter, he had nothing to do with it. In fact, in his letter, he claims he didn't even know where my condo was!"

Neither of them wanted to say it out loud... but was it Maye who scratched the pickup? Did she do it and blame it on her husband? Maybe she wanted reasons for the restraining order. Or perhaps she concocted the story to get Ben on side.

"I don't know what to say," said Mick as he processed this bizarre turn of events while trying to figure out possible alternatives.

"You know what else is also strange?" asked Ben. "When I went to

Birmingham to speak to the police and the coroner, his lawyer had to speak to me by phone to ask what my relationship with Steve was. Apparently, he died intestate and so they needed to track down his family and friends to inform them that there was no will, and that his personal effects would go to his next of kin.

"He told me that he had handled Steve and Leigh's divorce from back in 2013. I asked him how did Leigh do so well in the settlement, but it appeared that Steve had not. You should have seen his house and the neighborhood. Not nice. Anyway, you know what he said?"

Mick shook his head. All he knew was that Maye, who was previously known as Leigh, had done very well from the divorce, so much so that she was able to buy a two-storey lake-front house in Cherokee county.

"Well, he said that Leigh did not get anything because she didn't want anything. She just wanted the divorce finalized. And anyway, there was nothing to split up. Because they had lived on base or in service housing since they were married straight out of the academy, they had virtually no personal possessions except their cars and whatever savings two young lieutenants could scrape together that they hadn't spent on partying."

Mick looked over at the table. The president was happy letting her hair down. She had had a few too many drinks and was relaxing with her friends, laughing. She saw Mick looking at her and beckoned him over, excitedly.

"Honey," she said, "listen to this. We were talking about the campaign and how we didn't get the numbers and how disappointed we were when the GOP canceled the rest of the state primaries. Well, I said, 'Why the hell did Troup pull his nomination?' and listen to what Sally-Anne said. Go on, Sally-Anne. Tell him what you just told us."

Sally-Anne, glass of wine in her hand, and three or four more already under her belt, smiled and related the story. "So you know how I'm married to that asshole, The Chairman?"

Mick smiled and nodded.

"Well, one evening, he was hosting some GOP heavies at our place, and I overheard them saying that the national committee had been blackmailed by someone who had a recording of Troup making arrangements to interfere in the campaign... *our* campaign. Apparently, it was pretty damning. It was something that he could be impeached for, and it forced Troup to pull his nomination."

She held up her glass. "And that, ladies and gentlemen, cleared the way for the best president the country has ever seen."

"Here! Here!" they cried in unison, clinking their glasses together.

107

Off the Books

The G.U. vaccine roll out was going well. The initial criticisms began to wane as images of less fortunate families in the rural areas of Mississippi and Georgia, mainly black communities, were being immunized first. The six million doses would go a long way to alleviate the strain on the health facilities in those states and in Alabama and Louisiana. With about forty percent of the population estimated to be infected, and with deaths exceeding eight hundred thousand, it was good news that the nation needed, and desperately.

The president was confident to tour the country to show that she was in charge and in control. Her executive order to get the roll out going was quickly responded to by the state governors, and their national guardsmen were setting up clinics, or getting to those that were unable to attend.

Mick visited his old battalion at Fort Rucker where he was an instructor less than four years prior. Now he was the First Gentleman of the United States. Every soldier wanted a picture with him in his US Army uniform. The president was invited to address the airmen and airwomen of the 94th Airlift Wing at Dobbins Air Reserve Base in Georgia, just north of Atlanta, where she was once stationed and, likewise, she was welcomed with open arms, figuratively speaking. Of course, all welcomes were done at a distance and masks were now ubiquitous.

As an odd twist, Agent Lee was also the subject of some celebrity, and he was asked to address some gatherings, but politely declined, even though the director of the secret service had encouraged him to accept. After all, the service was always looking for new recruits.

Knowing that the president was going to be in Atlanta, one of the deputy directors of the CDC requested to speak with her about the roll out of the vaccine. He went through the director and his chain of superiors in the Department of Health and Human Services, seeking a chance to address her. He held some concerns about the rapidity of the program that was being executed without, what he considered, due diligence, but his concerns were not shared by his superiors. They were satisfied with the report from the Chinese tests and the tests that the CDC had conducted earlier.

"We would know by now if the vaccine had any major negative effects," they told him, "otherwise China would not be administering it to their own people."

But these bureaucrats, for the most part, were public servants, or appointees without a medical or research background, and their eagerness to help bring the economy out of its stagnation by defeating the virus biased them towards haste, rather than caution.

The deputy director, without permission or a clearance from the White House, made it to near the president's party, where the CDC's people were assisting with her presentation at the Georgia Institute of Technology. Based on his credentials as a deputy director of the CDC, he was able to get past the police cordon and close to the auditorium where the president's party was.

"I need to speak with the president," he said, flashing his ID to one of the secret service agents. But his eagerness was not couched in common sense. The process for speaking with the president was strict and thorough, and during a busy schedule if it had not already been approved, then it certainly would not now. Had he given it more thought, he would have been more prudent in his approach.

The secret service agents instructed him to leave the area, and to contact the White House through normal channels, but his insistence only brought greater concern by the secret service, and more agents gathered to help calm the situation before it got out of hand.

The disturbance was seen by members of the staff who were off stage. The First Gentleman's EA looked towards the agents concerned and at the disturbance they were trying to control. Mick, watching his wife on the stage, saw his EA was distracted, and looked towards the edge of the official party where the secret service was quietly, but forcefully, removing the man.

Mick could see that he was flashing an ID. He was not struggling, and he was not raising his voice. He did not appear to be a threat. Instead, he looked like a businessman with a genuine concern.

"I'm just going to see what's going on over there," he told his EA. Shocked, she told him that that was not advisable, but Mick was gone before she could finish her plea. His secret service detail shadowed him, and the lead agent strenuously told him the same thing. The First Gentleman ignored him.

"What's going on here," he asked as he approached the group. Agent Lee spoke first.

"Sir, sorry for the disturbance. This gentleman was insisting on seeing the president, but he is not authorized and has not gone through appropriate processes. We are escorting him away. Sir, may I advise that you return to your staff. We cannot spread our security too thinly, I'm sure you can understand." And with that, Agent Lee nodded to Mick's security detail as if to say, "Get him out of here."

"Wait!" said Mick, holding his hand up as the agents gently, but with purpose, marshaled him away. His voice had the authoritative timbre that he had not used in the White House. It made the agents pause.

"What do you need, Sir?" he asked the man being physically held by the agents.

"Sir," the man replied, "My name is Doctor Trenton Dade. I'm a deputy director at the CDC, and I need to speak with the president." He held up his ID which Mick took and examined.

The First Gentleman whispered to his senior agent to get online and to check if he was who he said he was.

"Let's go over here and have a quick chat," Mick said to him. The agents looked towards Agent Lee who, processing this sudden wrinkle in his tight security plan, had no choice but to nod. The man was let go, but the two agents stood close to him, ready to intervene, while another patted him down.

"Sir, I have a preliminary report on the G.U. vaccine, and some of our people have doubts about it. The problem is that the program has been rushed through so quickly that we cannot get any traction on our concerns through our normal chain."

Mick, surprised, tried not to let it show. His senior agent came over and returned the ID telling the First Gentleman that he was who he said he was: Deputy Director for Public Health Science and Surveillance at the Centers for Disease Control and Prevention. Mick handed the Deputy Director back his ID.

Deputy Director Dade then went on to explain how normal protocols for testing were bypassed for the G.U. vaccine, in opposition to all processes the CDC uses. Even the most basic scientific research and trials had either been fast-tracked or dispensed with in order to get the vaccine out as per the president's executive order. He just wanted to convince the president that the best option would be to stop the roll out until trials could successfully determine that the vaccine was perfectly safe for humans. Or even if they were imperfect, then at least the side effects would be known, and appropriate caveats and mitigations put in place. And if the roll out was not going to cease, then allow the trials to be funded so that they could be carried out simultaneously, but with enough rigor and resources to make them a true and legitimate test. As it stood, there were no in-depth trials by order of the Director of the CDC and the Secretary of the Department of Health and Human Services.

"Me and two other scientists did some research off the books. We've explored the protein sequencing of the vaccine, but we haven't been able to quantify or qualify its efficacy. We've seen it work, but we're not sure what it's long-lasting effects might be, but our initial trials indicate that it may have an effect on reproduction, based on some of the compounds we've found.

"The side effects of cancer remission had us concerned. It sounded like the G.U. vaccine had an angiogenesis inhibiting effect." He saw the slight look of confusion on the First Gentleman's face. "Angiogenesis is when blood vessels spontaneously split. Cancers need that to grow. If G.U. inhibited angiogenesis such that it aided in normal cancer therapies, then the cancers could be inhibited, or even get reduced.

"But about two decades ago, we found that thalidomide had the same effect. Do you know what thalidamide is," asked the deputy director.

"Yes," responded Mick. "It was sold in Australia during the sixties to pregnant women but was banned in the late sixties or early seventies."

"Yes. Well it was never sold in the States, but we watched carefully as it was sold in Britain, Germany, Canada and a bunch of other countries, and we saw the resulting birth defects from its use. Anyway, two decades ago we did some trials on the compound, not on pregnant women, of course. It was found to have some positive side effects, and that's what led some of the scientists at the CDC to do their own tests on G.U. What we found were some racemic compounds. They are compounds that will self-replicate into a mirror image version of itself but in reverse so that it has the same genomic make up, but different qualities, sort of like a Jekyll and Hyde situation. This is why we're concerned. We don't know what these racemic compounds will do in the long term, but we suspect that birth defects or sterility may result. That's why we need to stop the roll out and do proper trials."

The First Gentleman listened intently. The secret service agents stood nearby. Agent Lee, supervising them listened to the deputy director also, and seemed agitated. He waited for the First Gentleman to finish indulging this man so he could get his agents back to their posts and continue the security.

"Do you have any evidence of this," asked Mick.

Dade pulled out a folded document with what appeared to be his hand-written notes. "Just these," he said, "our 'off-the-books' results."

"Can I have a look?" asked Mick. "Would I be able to understand it?"

"Yes, Sir," he replied. "I wrote it so that the president could digest it, so it's written in layman's terms, but it's imperative that she gets it without it going to the director or through the secretary of the department."

"If I take this to give it to her, would that help?"

Dade's shoulders relaxed and he closed his eyes. "That would be great, Sir, yes..." he said, "please take it."

Mick took the documents and offered his hand to the deputy director. "Thank you for your service, Sir. I'll make sure the president reads this, and I'm sure she will be in touch. If G.U. is harmful, we'll need to action it immediately."

Dade shook the First Gentleman's hand with relief and thanked him effusively. Agent Lee then politely, but firmly, instructed the two agents to escort Doctor Dade away from the event and make sure he got to his car and then they were to double-time it back and resume their posts. He then extended his hand to direct the First Gentleman showing him the way back to his position where his agents could better protect him. The last thing this man needed was Major O'Rourke pulling crazy stunts like that again. This guy was going to make him prematurely gray!

Mick resumed his position off stage to listen to the end of the president's speech and the beginning of the Q and A, but not before he gave the notes a quick once over and discretely hid them away before he made a phone call.

108

Shirk Not That Which is Difficult

There were positive signs beginning to emerge. Business confidence was growing now that there was a light at the end of the tunnel. The Dow opened higher, for three straight days, looking to claw back some of the losses with jumps of three percent or more each day. It was almost unheard of.

President Young decided to address the American people and give the public her view of the state of the nation and the continued fight against Covid, and to assign 'an Executive Task Order'. She praised the efforts of the southern states in a smooth roll out and, with millions more vaccines arriving, the other states would be getting their allocation as soon as possible. She informed the nation that negotiations were underway for the licensed production of the G.U. vaccine in the United States to help finalize the full immunization of the nation, and then to help the rest of the world.

But the most surprising part of her speech was her 'Executive Task Order'. She spoke of the tumultuous times of the sixties, when the threat of nuclear war with the Soviet Union was only averted by mutually assured destruction and careful brinkmanship diplomacy, sometimes with a stick in one's hand, and how even though we had sent our fighting troops to a war in South-East Asia, we had still managed to pull together to create a space program and put an American flag on the moon.

"And so I ask of all Americans to gird their loins for the war we are currently fighting against the microscopic enemy of Covid, and at the same time look to the heavens, for that is where hope for mankind lies. And so, to fulfil our manifest destiny to know what is beyond that river, to know what is beyond that mountain range, to know what is beyond that sea, we shall go further and explore what is beyond our skies.

"It is my wish, and my order to our scientific and military communities, that we shall work towards establishing a permanent unmanned scientific station on Mars within the next four years, that will be self-powered and self-contained and, using unmanned vehicles and unmanned aircraft, able to explore the regions of the Hellas Planitia Basin, and the possible existence, either now or in the past, of water.

"The United States will lead a multi-national effort of like-minded countries including the United Kingdom, Israel, India, Japan, Australia, Canada and China, and partnering with private enterprises that have an interest in space exploration, to make this into a reality... for all mankind. We shall share our technology for the benefit... of *all* mankind.

"And so, my fellow Americans, may I echo the words of President Kennedy when I say that this will not be easy, but we shall decide to do this and the other things, because we, as Americans shirk not that which is difficult."

The following day, all the newspaper headlines read 'Shirk not that which is difficult', and millions googled the Hellas Planitia Basin. Once again, President Young had demonstrated her inspirational leadership.

Someone pointed out that in H.G. Wells's *The War of the Worlds* it was the Martians that came to earth and were defeated by microscopic bacteria. Now the Earthlings will go to Mars while defeating a microscopic virus on Earth.

It almost went unnoticed that while researching the delta variant of Covid, a protocol breach at the CDC labs sent a number of workers to hospital for observation and isolation. This formed part of the daily

Covid brief to the president by the Department of Health and Human Services but didn't even rate a mention on the evening news.

109

Kung Pao Chicken

The FBI had tapes and photographs of the First Gentleman speaking Chinese into his phone as he walked the Kennedy Garden outside the East Wing of the White House. A translator had provided a transcript:

"We don't know how long it will take... I will let you know once it is finished. But secrecy is of utmost importance."

"Who was he talking to?" asked the director of the FBI.

"We're not sure, Sir," replied the executive assistant director overseeing the investigation, "but have a look at this." He placed a photo on to the desk in front of the director. In it was a screen grab from some surveillance footage taken during the tour that the president and the First Gentleman had finished in the southern states. In the crowd at Georgia Tech was the same Asian man that had appeared previously.

"Did he try and make contact with O'Rourke?" inquired the Director.

"No, Sir. We didn't even know he was there until we started reviewing some of our surveillance imagery."

"We're still investigating. We've tried our facial recognition programs again but still no luck. It doesn't match any Chinese agents that are known to us. We're looking into North Korean agents and Vietnamese."

The director looked at the image of the First Gentleman on his cell phone, walking the grounds of the White House. He then looked at the image of the Asian man. "What about the Aussies. Any luck with them?"

"No, Sir," came the reply. "The Australian Security and Intelligence Organisation has no details on any affiliation back in Australia but they're looking into it. He did work in a Chinese restaurant after he left high school, though."

"A Chinese restaurant? Hell, my son worked in a Chinese restaurant to put himself through college. You've gotta have something more concrete than that because it doesn't sound to me like he's discussing the ingredients to Kung Pao Chicken! Did we get anything from the Chinese since our last queries?"

"No, Sir. They've shut us down. Nothing coming in or out."

The director got up from his desk and walked over to his window. He looked down onto Pennsylvania Avenue below. Less than a thousand yards away up that very road, in the White House, the First Gentleman was gaining in popularity with the American people, but not with the Federal Bureau of Investigation.

"Keep on it," said the director.

I I O

Dade is Dead

The morning military brief informed the president that another C-17 had arrived at Travis Air Force Base in California from China with another four million vials of G.U.

Ordinarily, the First Gentleman would not be privy to this information, and not being part of the president's security meetings, he was not. But when he was at the State Department doing his liaison with the Indo-Pacific desk, it was mentioned to him, as if he was already aware, that the aircraft had to make an unscheduled stop in Japan because of an electrical fault. The Indo-Pacific desk had been asked to assist with arrangements to keep the vaccines suitably refrigerated. They had been liaising with the Defense Attaché in the US Embassy in Tokyo to source his contacts within the Japan Self-Defense Force who might be able to assist so that the State Department could put in place the necessary requests and thank yous.

The First Gentleman had given the briefing notes that Deputy Director Dade had given him to pass on to the president, who had assured him that distribution would be stopped for at least four weeks while they conducted more tests on the angiogenesis factor. That was only five days ago.

"Can you look up an agency director for me," he asked the Japan desk officer who immediately agreed. "Director of the CDC in Atlanta."

After getting the number he took his cell phone and, finding a quiet corner where he could talk, but where his security detail could still monitor him, he gave it a call.

"Hello Director? This is Major Michael O'Rourke, the First Gentleman, how are you?" On the other end of the phone his Australian accent was recognized, and pleasantries exchanged.

"I was just wondering how the trials were going for the angiogenesis. Deputy Director Dade was overseeing the..." He was cut off by the Director.

"I'm sorry, Sir," she said, "Trenton Dade was killed in a home invasion three days ago. His projects have been put on hold until we can find a replacement. I'm embarrassed to say that his key scientists are in hospital after a protocol breach and they were infected with a Delta variant of the virus," she told him.

Mick did not react. His demeanor was calm. This information seemed to not be novel to him. "How are they doing?" he asked.

"Not too well. One will make a full recovery, but the other is not in a good way. Both are on ventilators, and we are just waiting," replied the director.

The First Gentleman discussed the loss of Dr Dade and thanked her and hung up. He thanked the team from the State Department and assured them that he would keep the president informed of the good work they were doing.

I I I

The Vegemite Was Too Thick

Arriving at the Executive Residence, he dismissed his security detail. They dutifully took their positions at either end of Center Hall while the First Gentleman went into the kitchen at the end of the West Sitting Hall to make a sandwich. He loosened his tie and undid his tunic.

He did not like having people wait on him for simple tasks that he was quite capable of doing himself. Besides, they never got a Vegemite sandwich right, anyway. They always laid it on too thick. Plus, he liked tomatoes on his Vegemite sandwiches, and he had been craving one for a couple of hours now.

He was dropping crumbs everywhere, so he grabbed a tray and placed the plate on it and started slicing the tomato, gingerly placing each slice on the bread. He could smell the saltiness of the Vegemite and his mouth started watering. The president was, no doubt, down in the Oval Office, so he thought that he'd take a break from everything and watch some TV in the Private Sitting Room, just off the president's bedroom, their bedroom. The North Queensland Cowboys were playing the South Sydney Rabbitohs in the National Rugby League back in Australia, and the game had already started two minutes ago. It was being live-streamed and he could watch it in peace. This was his chance to spend some time by himself, a rarity these days.

The First Gentleman dropped a tomato which burst on the floor

462

of the kitchen. Quickly cleaning up the mess, he grabbed the Vegemite and some more bread, another tomato, a slicing knife and a dish towel, and threw them all onto a tray, put an apple in his mouth and a soda in his pocket, and darted across the hall into the dressing room entrance that would take him into the bedroom, and then into the sitting room. He didn't want the staff to see that he had made his own sandwich, (nor his uniform undone) otherwise they would come and tell him, yet again, that they were more than happy to make refreshments for him... and he wasn't in the mood to make small talk or be polite to the staff when all he wanted to do was watch the football.

Pushing the door open with his back, he entered the dressing room foyer. The door was on a hydraulic arm, and he deftly maneuvered his tray so it wasn't hit by the returning door. He heard Maye speaking to someone in the bedroom.

"We know the First Gentleman can speak Chinese, Madam President. The FBI has been monitoring him and has asked the secret service to conduct surveillance on him," said the voice of a man. It sounded like Agent Lee.

Standing there in silence, he heard them talking about him. Immediately his thoughts turned to some concerns he had but which he pushed deep down away from his consciousness. He did not want to believe that Maye and Agent Lee were having an affair. But now he could hear them in the bedroom, talking. Was he about to find them in bed together? He kept as quiet as he could, barely breathing with the apple still in his mouth. He would stay in the dressing room so he could hear their conversation. He just didn't want to hear them having sex. That would crush him.

Just as he was about to put down the tray, the door closed behind him with a loud 'click'. Mick heard his wife say, "What was that?"

Within a second, a Glock-19 pistol was pointed at him as he stood there, apple in his mouth and tray in his hands.

Agent Lee cocked his head indicating that he wanted Mick to come into the President's Bedroom, the pistol pointed menacingly at his chest.

Entering the bedroom, he saw the president with the written papers by Deputy Director Dade in her hand.

112

Hope has Died

"Breaking News. The President, Maye Young, has been shot in an incident at the White House. No further details are as yet available. Initial reports are that she has been admitted to the Walter Reed National Medical Center in Bethesda, Maryland, just outside DC, and is undergoing emergency surgery. The First Gentleman is currently assisting police with their inquiries. We'll keep you updated as more comes to hand."

113

"She's Still Alive!"

"When we heard the shots, I entered the president's bedroom and saw Major O'Rourke standing there with a pistol. It appeared to be a Glock-19. Standard issue for a secret service agent. Agent Lee was on the floor and the president was on the floor also, next to her bed. They were both stationary and bleeding. I drew my service pistol and identified myself as secret service, and aimed it at Major O'Rourke, and ordered him to drop the weapon."

"Did he say anything?" asked one of the committee members.

"No Ma'am. He dropped the weapon and raised his arms."

"What happened then?"

"The second agent entered, and I told him to check the president. He did so and said that she was dead. I told him not to touch anything and to take some photos for the investigation and to get them into evidence."

The crowd murmured.

"Did Major O'Rourke cooperate?"

"For the most part, Ma'am. We were required to restrain him when he tried to resist."

Mick turned to his lawyer and whispered, "That's not true. I cooperated fully."

"When did you discover that the president was still alive?" the agent was asked.

"After we had taken Major O'Rourke into custody, I did another check on Agent Lee. He had a knife wound through the chest which appeared to have entered his heart. I assumed that Major O'Rourke had stabbed Agent Lee, and then took his service weapon and then shot the president.

I then did another check on the president and saw that the blood from her chest wound was exiting in short, rhythmic pulses. It could only mean her heart was still beating."

"What did you do then?"

"I yelled out 'She's still alive!' and grabbed a dish towel that was on the floor and pressed it against her chest wound."

This was the most graphic account of the events in the president's bedroom on the day of the shootings heard so far, and it mesmerized all who listened. Photographers snapped images of Major O'Rourke as he listened calmly to the testimony, his face showing no emotion.

114

Major O'Rourke, Chinese

"I entered the bedroom. Agent Lee had his pistol pointed at my chest. He told me to put down the tray on the bedside table and put my hands up. I put the tray on the bedside table and, because I had an apple in my mouth, I raised one hand and with the other, took the apple from my mouth and placed it beside the tray, then raised my other hand. He then said that he knew I spoke Chinese."

"Do you, Major O'Rourke?"

"A reasonable amount, Senator," he replied. "Enough to get by."

"So, what happened then?"

Mick continued. "Well, Agent Lee said that I had been suspected of espionage for the Chinese Communist Party, and that he was placing me under arrest. I looked at the president and asked her 'is this some sort of joke?' She shook her head and said 'no'."

"I denied it, but she said that it didn't matter, because she had authorized the G.U. vaccine and no matter what I did, she was going to make sure that she used the Chinese for everything she could. That didn't make sense to me. She said that she was going to make sure that as much of the vaccine as they could get from the CCP would be given to Americans and there was nothing I could say or do that would stop America from getting more from the Chinese."

The senator representing Utah then chimed in, "Why would you want to prevent Americans from being vaccinated, Major O'Rourke."

"I didn't, Ma'am," he replied. "My only concern was that the CDC had not done effective trials and it was brought to my attention that they had not. I had given the president the initial trial results that had been conducted off the record and subsequent to the start of the roll out. I told the president that it might be an idea to cease the roll out of the G.U. vaccine until proper trials could be conducted. She said she wanted as many Americans as possible to be vaccinated as soon as possible. She had promised that, and she meant to keep that promise. She also said that the Chinese vaccine was the world's best hope for the future."

"After this alleged conversation with the late president, what happened then?" asked the representative from South Carolina.

"It was then that Agent Lee took a handkerchief from his pocket and reached into his jacket. He took something and offered it to me. It was obscured by his hand and the handkerchief. He said 'Here, look at this', and I put out my hand and he placed a revolver in it. At first it did not register what had been handed to me. I looked at it and it confused me as to why he was handing me a weapon. When I realized what he intended to do, I immediately threw it onto the bed away from me and put my hands back into the air."

The senators and representatives leaned towards each other, absent-mindedly breaking the social distancing rules. They were conferring, discussing the plausibility of this absurd story. The crowd, too, murmured amongst themselves. It was incredibly far-fetched and obviously concocted. Why would a suspect be handed a loaded weapon, and in the presence of the president? It made no sense to even try and make people believe that story. If this was the idea of his legal team, then he was not being well served by them.

"Major O'Rourke," said the Senator from Utah, "I, for one, find that story to most likely be fiction, but we shall come back to your version of the events surrounding the shooting later. I would, however, like to discuss your connections with the Chinese Communist Party."

Mick was calm. He showed no emotion. "I have no connection to the Chinese Communist Party," he said.

The senator looked at him for a moment. "You don't?"

"No Ma'am, I do not."

The senator turned a page and, glancing at it momentarily, took off her glasses, pointing one of its arms at Major O'Rourke.

"Would it surprise you to know that President Young regained consciousness briefly while at Walter Reed Hospital and was heard to say," she looked down through her glasses at the words, "'Major O'Rourke, Chinese'."

The room seemed to heave a collective groan and cameras flashed, looking for a reaction.

"What do you think the president meant by that," asked the Senator.

"I couldn't say," Mick said simply.

"Perhaps she meant to say, 'Major O'Rourke is Chinese,' or 'Major O'Rourke is working for the Chinese', or 'Major O'Rourke's a Chinese spy.'"

"Like I said, I couldn't say," Mick replied.

* * *

"In another day of surprising testimony, a link was alleged between the former First Gentleman and the Chinese Communist Party," said the female anchor on the evening news. "According to evidence presented for the committee investigating the assassination of President Young, it was claimed that as the president was dying in the Walter Reed Medical Center in Bethesda, Maryland, she uttered the words, 'O'Rourke' and 'Chinese'.

"In other news, the vaccination rate of American adults has increased to sixty percent with the target of ninety percent on track to be reached in three months. US-manufactured vaccines have replaced the G.U. vaccine from China after importations from that country ceased on order from President Greene after his assumption of office in the wake of President Young's assassination. The negative side-effects of the G.U vaccine have given rise to several class-action suits against the Government by people affected by its rapid roll out."

As the television was turned off by the Representative from North Dakota, the other members of the Joint Select Committee sat in the chamber adjacent to the hearing room discussing the events of the day and how the following day's testimony would transpire. Each day the evidence was more damning on Major O'Rourke, and his affiliation with the Chinese Communist Party was the subject of ongoing investigations by the FBI.

A committee coordinator entered the room and spoke to the chairman who listened intently.

"Ladies and Gentlemen," said the committee chairman, "we have a request for a special testimony for tomorrow which will require some extra coordination."

115

⊙⊗⊙

Australian Interference

When the crowd entered the hearing room the following day, a large curtain-covered cubicle had been erected with a covered walkway leading from a side door. Obviously, a witness was going to be testifying and they wanted his or her identity to remain secret.

The media immediately filmed and photographed it from all angles. It was highly unusual, but had been used before, especially after the 9/11 terrorist attacks, and the special investigation 'navel gazing' that had occurred thereafter. One could only speculate that the witness was a member of the intelligence community and was still active.

As yet, Major O'Rourke—Mick—had barely defended himself. Besides his preliminary testimony where he claimed that he had been handed a revolver by the secret service's Agent Lee, a story that was so far-fetched as to be dismissed as a falsehood, he had not elaborated on the events of that day. So far, the testimony had been from Walter Reed Medical Center, the medical examiner's office, the other secret service agents, the FBI, Department of State, CDC and others. The former First Gentleman was to be taking the stand for further questioning today, but with this new witness, his opportunity to answer further questions by the committee would have to wait.

By the time the committee had convened, and various announcements made about proceedings and processes, it was time to hear testimony.

Mick and his counsel were in position at their table. The curtained witness stand was novel, and both could not help but wonder what new hell this would be.

"Ladies and Gentlemen," began the chairman, "we will be hearing evidence out of sequence from the program. This is on request from the Central Intelligence Agency, so we ask your indulgence. The Agency has indicated that it had evidence that has a significant weighting on this hearing, and which may skew further evidence and testimony, and so we have amended the interview program to accommodate this request."

Behind the curtained walkway, the top of a door was seen to open and then close. From the loudspeakers the sound of a microphone being adjusted could be heard which, it could only be assumed, was for the anonymous witness' benefit. The committee chairman spoke into his microphone.

"Witness X, are you ready to proceed?"

"I am, Mister Chairman," came the response.

Mick thought to himself that he'd heard that voice before.

A committee coordinator could be heard giving instructions on placing a hand on the bible and taking the oath and whether the witness was prepared to give truthful evidence, so help him, God, to which Witness X responded, "I Do."

"Witness X, can you please give the hearing an indication on what your role is?" asked the chairman.

"I am an operative for the Central Intelligence Agency," the invisible witness said, "and I was a member of a team assigned the task of investigating and establishing if any links existed between the US Government and the People's Republic of China."

The senator from Utah, a Democrat, and the one committee member that had been the most vociferous, immediately interjected. "The CIA's remit is for overseas intelligence gathering, not investigating US citizens or other domestic operations," she said. "That is the purview of the FBI. Why were you assigned this task, and by whom?"

"I cannot tell you by whom, Senator," Witness X responded, "but it was authorized by the Foreign Intelligence Surveillance Court by warrant. It fell to the CIA to investigate due to our international presence. Domestic operations to be carried out by the CIA were authorized by that warrant."

The senator from Utah was obviously angered. She had been a vehement opponent of the Patriot Act and the subsequent hobbling of the Freedom Act which would have curtailed many of the aspects of the former. To hear that the CIA was conducting surveillance on an American citizen on American soil flew in the face of everything she stood for.

The chairman stepped in before more objections were made by the senator from Utah.

"Did you find evidence of foreign interference or links with the US Government?"

"Yes, Sir, we did," he responded. The crowd, its own beast, groaned and shuffled. The chairman of the committee waited for the audience to quieten down.

"And which country or countries were involved in this interference?" he asked.

"The People's Republic of China," was the response. The crowd murmured again. While it was not surprising to hear that there was interference from China, hearing it as testimony from a member of the intelligence community undertaking an active investigation, brought it to reality.

"Were any other countries involved?" asked the chairman.

"Yes, Sir," Witness X replied, "Australia."

Mick's head swung to face his lawyer. His cool expression had been replaced by horror.

116

This is Not a John Grisham Novel

When the crowd in the room ceased its clamor after hearing this revelation, Witness X was allowed to continue answering questions by the committee.

"Were any individuals identified as being linked to these foreign countries, China and Australia?"

"Yes, Sir," said Witness X, "There were three individual agents that were working on behalf of their governments to influence events within the US Government. Major Michael O'Rourke was one such agent."

The audience rumbled. The testimony thus far had painted the First Gentleman as most likely a foreign agent. The FBI reports had been damning and had left too many questions unanswered. Now the CIA was confirming that Major O'Rourke had been influencing US politics. It seems that the blanks were now being filled in.

"That's not true," demanded Mick in an urgent whisper to his legal counsel.

"And who were the other two?" asked the chairman.

Witness X paused. He knew he was oath-bound to tell the truth, but he hesitated none-the-less. Their investigation was ongoing, and to say their names would effectively kill it off. Slowly, and reluctantly, he revealed their identities.

"Secret service Agent Henry Lee was an agent for the Chinese government," he said cautiously.

The cameramen and women were forced to capture the shocked expressions on the faces of the committee members. They so much wanted to pull back the curtain and photograph Witness X. The crowd voiced their horror that the hero of the US Secret Service, feted in the media, was an agent for the Chinese. It was unimaginable that a foreign intelligence agent could be within the White House, and so close to the president. It was already impossible to believe that the president's husband had been a foreign agent. What was happening in their government?

The chairman banged his gavel a few times to encourage the audience to quieten down again. After several seconds and more raps from the gavel, the audience finally acquiesced to hear further evidence from Witness X.

"Witness X, that seems highly unlikely, and we would ask you for further evidence to verify that claim," the chairman said.

"Yes, Sir," came the response. "I have evidence to confirm what I have just told you."

"Very well," said the chairman, "we look forward to hearing that evidence, but you said there were three agents. Who was the third agent involved in political interference?"

The pause seemed interminable. Witness X moved his microphone and there was a momentary squeal of feedback from the speakers. He answered.

"The late President of the United States, Miss Maye Young," he said.

The committee room erupted. Cameramen and women leaped to their feet to get close to Major O'Rourke, to capture his expression. Any semblance of social distancing was long forgotten. The room strobed to the lightning of scores of camera flashes, and committee coordinators and Capital Police struggled to keep the melee from becoming totally uncontrollable as the media completely disregarded their limitations and tried to get close to the former First Gentleman.

The chairman banged his gavel as though he were in some John Grisham court room, but it was drowned out in the cacophony of yelling.

117

Acting as an Enemy of the United States

For the second time in as many minutes, Witness X's testimony had shocked the audience. His claim that the president, the hope of America, and her secret service agent—and national hero—Agent Henry Lee, were operatives for the Chinese government, was too much to bear.

Witness X was allowed to explain the history of the investigation into Maye Young, Henry 'Bruce' Lee and Michael 'Mick' O'Rourke.

He related how the CIA had been tracking Chinese operatives recruiting members of the US military at installations overseas, but then it was discovered that contractors to the US military, including one operative at the US Air Force language school in San Antonio, were part of the intelligence network. "It became clear during our later investigations that this operative in Texas had successfully recruited at least half a dozen junior officers and NCOs, mainly through financial incentives or blackmail," he revealed.

Captain Leigh Buchanan, or Maye Young as she was now more commonly known, was one officer who had been recruited, but, at that time, had not come to the notice of the intelligence community.

"She was still unknown to us when she joined the Republican Party in Georgia," continued Witness X, "and it was only after she had been elected to the House of Representatives as a congresswoman that she was seen to be in contact with a known operative, Agent Henry Lee."

The crowd in the committee room grumbled at that admission; that a foreign operative was allowed to keep her position as a member of Congress. Witness X went on.

"Agent Lee was already being tracked when he joined the secret service. The CIA kept his status secret in order to flush out any other operatives, or to discover which members of the Chinese intelligence service could be compromised and, perhaps, turned. A phone call to then Congresswoman Young in Chinese had the agency commence tracking her to see what her involvement was. It was only then that we started looking into her past, and it was that vetting that revealed that she had had contact with a Chinese tutor at the US Air Force language school in San Antonio, who, we discovered, was an operative for the Chinese intelligence services. That discovery led us to uncover the other members of the military that he had recruited."

"Wait a minute," said the senator from Utah. "You knew that a member of the US Secret Service was working for the Chinese, but you allowed him to continue in his role of guarding the President of the United States?"

The audience grumbled again.

"Yes, Senator," said Witness X. "We assessed the risk, and we knew that it was highly unlikely that a foreign operative, so close to the Oval Office, would wager revealing his status—and any connections he might have—when he was so close to the seat of power. The likelihood that he would do harm to the president was extremely remote. He would be of more use to his masters in Beijing if he was able to gather information."

What Witness X did not tell the committee was that the potential to lose President Troup was considered less important than the threat to the entirety of the US Government. Troup could be replaced immediately if he was assassinated, but if the US Government and Armed Forces were riddled with informants and agents, then that was a more serious concern, because it was at legislative-level, not executive-level, where policy and decisions were made.

The senator guffawed again. "So you let him gather information? From the White House?"

"No, Senator," he replied. "We fed him false information, or information that was no longer of use to us, just to keep him 'sniffing around the trough', as it were. As began looking more closely at Congresswoman Young," he continued, "we saw the reports of domestic abuse and her resignation from the air force to take up a consultancy job in DC. But of immediate concern was her purchase of a house in Georgia that seemed beyond her means. She had claimed to friends that it was from a divorce settlement, but our investigations found that to be false. We were uncertain as to how she was able to raise the money to make that purchase."

"She had then taken on an international sales rep job with a Taiwanese company that took her to Asia often. We assess that it was during this period that she had semi-regular contact with her handlers, but we cannot be sure. We can only assume that it was during this period that she decided to, or was encouraged to, enter state politics, and she joined the Republican Party in Georgia," revealed Witness X.

"If she was a person of concern," asked a committee member, the representative from Wisconsin's 3rd District, "and you admit that you learned this when she was a congresswoman, why did you not intercept her when she commenced her presidential campaign?"

"We had no evidence that any intelligence or other information of note had been fed to the Chinese Government by her," replied Witness X. "All we had were indications that messages had been passed between Lee and the Chinese, Young and the Chinese and, on at least one occasion, between Lee and Young. If we were to arrest her, it would have been difficult to prove that she was conducting espionage, and we would have shown our hand to the Chinese. They would have shut down their operations, or gone further underground, making it harder for us to track them. So we had to play them. And the reason why we did not intervene during her presidential campaign was that we, at the

Agency, were of the opinion that she would not win the nomination of her party. And we were right. She did not get the support to beat President Troup. Had he continued with the nomination process during the primaries, he would have been the sole Republican candidate, but he removed himself from the presidential nomination race. That was unexpected and took us by surprise. We then thought that the Democratic Party may have had a chance at winning the White House, which would have been the best scenario for us and our investigation."

"Why do you say that?" asked the senator from Utah.

"Because Congresswoman Young would have returned to her duties as a representative from Georgia. That would have made the investigation much simpler. We were surprised, again, at how popular she became, and the influence that Major O'Rourke had on the election campaign."

The committee members looked at each other and conferred. A few got up from their seats and gathered with the chairman in a huddle away from their microphones. The representative from South Carolina, the committee's chairman, then questioned Major O'Rourke's involvement.

"What interference did the Australians conduct?" he asked. The thought that a staunch ally of the United States would interfere in US politics was anathema to Americans. They might expect it from the Chinese or the Russians or the North Koreans, but to be told by the CIA that Australia had been interfering in America's government system was shocking. "Was Major O'Rourke a spy working for the Australian Government?"

Witness X paused. A little too long for Mick's liking.

"Not exactly," said Witness X. "Major O'Rourke was a legitimate officer of the Australian Army posted here as an approved exchange officer with no hidden agenda by him or his government. His role over here was purely as a flying instructor attached to the US Army.

"According to Agency representatives in Australia, when it became evident that he was romantically involved with a US Congresswoman, he was encouraged to pursue the relationship by his government in order to be in a position to further ingratiate the US towards Australia to further their foreign policy. He was, for all intents and purposes, made into a political lobbyist for Australia. It was then that we started tracking him and later we were able to place a script on his cell phone so we could listen to his calls or his conversations."

It then dawned on Mick why his phone kept acting strangely.

"So there was no espionage?" asked the representative.

"No, Sir. He conducted no crimes against the United States. He was, however, encouraged by his Prime Minister to become a part of a US political campaign. In that sense, and in that sense alone, he had been an agent interfering in US politics. But I must emphasize that the interference was in the same way as any American representing any organization on a political campaign team would be an agent interfering. No crime was committed by Major O'Rourke against the United States or any of its laws," said Witness X.

"Mick closed his eyes and took a deep sigh, relieved."

"Right up until he shot the president," said the representative, cynically. This comment underscored the whole committee and was the reason it had been convened. These revelations of spying and accusations that the president was actually a Chinese spy were inconceivable.

"Actually, no," said Witness X. "Major O'Rourke was justified in killing the president."

These words bore home like a diamond drill into pumice. How can anyone be justified in killing the president?

"How do you mean?" asked the representative, to the eager expectations of everyone in the room.

Witness X paused, his explanation shining new light onto the whole sordid affair.

"Major O'Rourke came to our attention when he met Congresswoman Young in Alabama, and then when they started dating. It was then that we opened an investigation into him and found that besides some poor record-keeping by the Australian immigration service surrounding some of his travels, he was not involved in any activities that would raise any concerns. Except for six months in China teaching English, Major O'Rourke's background has revealed nothing of note from an intelligence point of view.

"We tracked him when he accompanied Miss Young on a clandestine romantic visit to Vancouver, Canada. And then during the midterm election campaign, and the presidential primaries campaign, we were close at hand to monitor him and Miss Young. When Miss Young proposed, and they were married, he became eligible for US Citizenship," said Witness X. "He did not have to take US Citizenship, but he announced that he would."

"But this was at the expense of his eligibility to hold a commission in the Australian Army, which he gave up, as required by Australian law. After he resigned his commission in the Australian Army, he was a civilian who was an Australian citizen, legally married to a US citizen, and an authorized permanent resident of the United States. In that status he was legally allowed to remain in the US and he was legally allowed to join the US Armed Forces, even if he wasn't yet a US citizen.

"When Miss Young was inaugurated, her first act was to induct the then Mr. O'Rourke into the US Army. When he was asked during his swearing in ceremony if he would faithfully serve the United States and, on oath, agreed, he was binding himself to the Uniformed Code of Military Justice, and was thus legally bound to defend the US Constitution against all enemies, foreign or domestic. When it became obvious that President Young was a Chinese operative, she was, in fact, acting as an enemy of the United States, even though she was the elected president. And," he added for effect, "as we know from our civics lessons, 'No-one is above the law'." Mick could not help but smile at this. It would play well in Peoria.

The crowd could not help but process this information out loud. It cut deeply that the American public could be duped into electing a person to the nation's highest office who was working for a foreign government, and to be beguiled by her as a modern-day Kennedy. This information would, no doubt, lead to some serious deliberation by the Supreme Court.

"Major O'Rourke was legally bound to defend the US against, well, the president. His shooting of her was legally justified. It was also morally justified. You could say that when the president inducted him into the army and made him take the oath of service, she had inadvertently signed her own death warrant. She made it her husband's duty to," he had to choose his words carefully, "terminate her role as a hostile foreign agent."

Yet another shocking revelation produced restrained hysteria in that room as everyone digested this. Every person had a comment and the rumbling fomented.

The senator from Utah weighed in. She was a noted liberal and had ardently opposed the Young/Greene administration saying that it had too close a relationship with the military community in America.

"How can you claim that the killing of another human being is both legally and morally justified, Witness X? You were not there, so you cannot make that judgment. We are here to ascertain the events surrounding the assassination of President Young. Notwithstanding your claims that the first female president was a Chinese spy—which I personally find very hard to accept—we cannot be sure that Major O'Rourke did not act in the role of assassin."

"We have audio recordings," said Witness X.

"Audio recordings of what?" demanded the senator.

"Of the shooting."

This revelation brought the room to a standstill.

"Are you saying that you have audio recordings of the shootings?" The chairman was incensed, as were the other committee members. "How did you get recordings from inside the White House? And why were these not provided to this investigation?" demanded the chairman.

"The presidential bedroom was authorized by warrant to be bugged prior to President Young moving into the Executive Residence," said Witness X. "It was hoped that the actualities of the afternoon of the deaths would be brought to light by this committee without the CIA's involvement, and that the truth would become known that Major

O'Rourke's actions against of Agent Lee and the president were legal," he said.

"But what the Central Intelligence Agency has been seeing is that this joint committee has not been on track to reveal the truth, and that the last two days of testimony have made it appear that there would be a significant miscarriage of justice. The director of the CIA ordered that we provide this information to the committee to ensure the truth was, indeed, made clear, even though it will now significantly hamper our investigation of foreign intelligence activities involving the US Government."

118

I'll Throw it in the Potomac

The recording was played. On it could be heard Agent Lee speaking with the president.

"We know the First Gentleman can speak Chinese, Madam President. The FBI has been monitoring him and has asked the secret service to conduct surveillance on him," they heard.

There was a click. *"What was that?"* the president could be heard asking.

Pause. Indistinguishable sounds.

"Come in, Sir. Keep your hands where I can see them. Put down the tray... over there."

The recording was riveting and those listening, who had heard the last two days' testimonies, could see in their mind's eye what was happening. A number of blown-up pictures of the president's bedroom had been used as evidence, so in their imaginings they could clearly picture the scene.

Agent Lee, pistol drawn, pointing it at the chest of Major O'Rourke who, in the space of less than twenty minutes, had gone from the most hated man in the United States, to its new hero.

They heard the discussion and accusation about the G.U. vaccine, and the reason for the rapid roll out.

President Young admitting that it was her order to get it rolled out

485

as soon as possible "to hasten the process of China's ascendancy" and the descent of the United States to the role of subordinate superpower.

They heard the interchange between Major O'Rourke and Agent Lee and the revolver being handed to him and him throwing it away. But Agent Lee's admission that it didn't matter if he had it or not, evidence of him handling it was all he needed, just as Major O'Rourke had described it.

They listened, and pictured Major O'Rourke, realizing that there was no escape, deliberately turning his back on Agent Lee.

Lee demanding that O'Rourke turn around but O'Rourke refusing, saying *"If you're going to shoot me, be the coward you are, and shoot me in the back. Splatter my blood against the wall and get ready to answer some awkward questions to the investigators."*

The sound of Lee's voice demanding he face him... and then the sound of him physically trying to force O'Rourke to turn around so the bullet would enter his chest. But then, the sound of a struggle, and a sharp groan as the carving knife from Mick's sandwich tray is thrust into Lee's chest.

The sound of the president yelling *"No!"*

Some more sounds and grunts, then the sound of a shot, then another, and what sounded like something heavy being dropped, or falling to the ground. Most likely the body of the president.

The crash of a door opening and the shout of, *"Secret service! Drop your weapon!"*

Various other sounds of orders being given: to check on the president and Lee; to take photos; and cautions to not touch anything.

The sounds of accusations and cursing, then *"you son-of-a-bitch"* and then what sounded like a punch and a loud groan, and more punches followed by gasping and coughing.

Mick turned to his lawyer. "They gave me a bit of a tune up," he said, referring to the beating by the secret service. The representatives of the US Secret Service looked embarrassed and could not make eye contact with the committee members who could tell, by the sounds of grunting and coughing and swearing, what was happening... some summary justice at the fists and feet of the secret service.

One of the agents turned to Mick, obviously embarrassed. Mick just smiled and winked at him; the whole event caught on audio file. His beatings in Fort Leavenworth had been much worse.

Everything that Mick had said was proven true by the recording from the listening device placed in the president's bedroom by the spooks who were following him. Witness X, of the Central Intelligence Agency, had just saved Mick's skin. He would have loved to have met this guy, whomever he was, but he thought he was destined never to see his face. It was too bad really, because he would have looked very familiar to him.

* * *

As the United States turned to navel-gazing, and pondering how, exactly, they could have been so easily led to follow the wrong person, the most hated man in America became its most celebrated. But where he had previously been happy to be in the spotlight to help his girlfriend's—then his wife's—campaign, now he was not so eager to place himself in its harsh glow.

When there was talk of bestowing him with the medal of honor, he was quick to point out that the medal of honor was for valor in combat, and because the US was not at war, then it would not be appropriate... "and besides, you don't do things to earn a medal, you do it because you believe in something." He underscored his view by saying that if anyone tried to give him a medal, then he would "throw it into the Potomac."

The pandemic continued to wreak havoc across the country. The hope that the G.U. vaccine had briefly given the public, turned to rage when it was revealed that it had been causing infertility in young females. This was not detected at first because most of the initial recipients were older and more vulnerable citizens, mainly black, in rural communities. All anyone saw were significant improvements in health by those that had been vaccinated, and it had lulled them into an eagerness to get more vaccines to beat the disease, but at the cost of due diligence.

Any remaining stocks of G.U. were immediately incinerated, and the CDC and Department of Health and Human Services began a long period of explaining why they had not heeded what the late Deputy Director Trenton Dade had warned about. In the meantime, class action lawsuits were being prepared to be filed against the CDC and the Department, and civil actions were being drawn up against its directors for gross misconduct eventuating bodily harm.

Not long after his public exoneration, Mick disappeared from public view, avoiding interviews and allowing the news cycle to regenerate without him. After all, there was still a pandemic to battle, and people needed to support President Greene who, at least in Mick's estimation, was doing a good job.

* * *

The CIA sent Witness X to meet with Mick in private. They thought it prudent to provide the former First Gentleman with details of the tumultuous last two years so that he may find some sort of closure and, perhaps, peace of mind.

Mick sat on a shaded bench near the reflecting pool, not far from the Lincoln Memorial. The walk from the Metro station had aggravated his ankle and it was throbbing. It probably would never be one hundred percent again.

The breeze was cool, bringing relief from the Washington heat and humidity. When Witness X appeared Mick immediately recognized him from Air Force One as Dawson Chiroki, the man from the Department of State who had been working on the Japan desk. He did not divulge his surname, but told Mick his first name actually was Dawson, and that he had been impressed with how he had conducted himself during the whole campaign, his arrest, his incarceration at Fort Leavenworth and then through the hearings.

He told Mick in confidence that the CIA had obtained samples from the autopsies of President Young and of Agent Lee, and had found genetic markers indicating that they had common great grandparents. In other words, they were second cousins, and that they had come from the Lee family in Nanking via Shanghai. The agency wasn't exactly sure of the connection, but Mick thought that it probably had to do with Maye's great uncle, who had disappeared fighting for the nationalists back in 1947. Was Agent Lee his grandson? He would never know. But perhaps Maye's grandmother may have, had she not died the year prior.

Dawson lit up a cigarette and gave him the full story. He told him that the CIA had been tracking Mick throughout the campaign in Georgia for the mid-terms and then for the primaries. Dawson had been at a number of the rallies and events. Even as far back as before the campaign. Back in the parking lot where Mick had defended Rob from the two rednecks, and even before that; when he had first met Maye at that dinner party in Dothan, when Jess had set them up.

"I've kind of been a part of your relationship from the start of the story," he said, "like I was following Ross and Rachel," he joked.

He found his mind drifting off to that happy time at the dinner party, when he and Maye first met, that muggy Alabama night, where he was mesmerized by her personality and those beautiful almond-shaped eyes, and how she smiled when she met him for the first time. He would think fondly of all the adventures along the way that took him from Alabama, through the real America, to Washington. It was funny how the last two years of agony and beatings and the accusations seemed to dissolve, and he was left with the happy thoughts of his time with Maye, but they always ended up in the President's Bedroom...

Dawson was still talking about why the CIA had to intervene during the hearings because it looked as though the FBI had provided incomplete evidence; evidence that had made it appear that the First Gentleman had some inconsistencies in his past, and which seemed to be leading the committee to a wrong conclusion and a possible miscarriage of justice. But Mick had zoned out. He tried not to think about how his wife, scrambling for the revolver that was on their bed, had picked it up and pointed at him, her husband. And how he hated remembering fumbling for Agent Lee's pistol and how his wife, whom he loved so deeply, fired at him trying to kill him, and how he had no choice but to shoot back. He tried to put out of his mind the look of shock—and sorrow—in his wife's eyes, as she fell to the floor.

When she fell, she fell facing away from him. That was the moment the secret service agents burst through the door, and so he never got to see her face that one last time. As he was on the floor, being kicked and beaten, he looked over towards his wife's body and reached out to her. He was then dragged away.

His last vision of Maye had been her look of shock—and sorrow—in her beautiful, almond-shaped eyes.

119

Nice Place. Good People

Horn Island, Torres Strait

The couple looked like typical American tourists. Checkered shirts and shorts, white socks and sneakers. Loud and friendly.

"Your pilot will be with you shortly," said the booking clerk, "and he'll take you out to the chopper."

A short while later, a very tanned man with a graying beard, wearing a short-sleeved shirt with epaulets, shorts and boots appeared. He had a slight limp.

"Mr. and Mrs. Rockdale? I'm Michael. I'll be flying you out to the resort today. Are these your bags?"

The Americans confirmed that they were, and Michael gathered them up and carried them out to the Bell Jet Ranger. It was a garish yellow and purple with the words 'Torres Adventures' emblazoned on the side. After giving them their safety brief and loading their bags, he did a final check of the aircraft and strapped them in.

Taking his seat at the controls he made sure they could hear him through their headsets and started up the chopper. Lifting off from the airfield he headed north-east over the azure-blue seas of the tropical north of Australia. Thursday Island passed by their left side with its houses and old government buildings from when the island was a northern outpost of Australia during the time of sail and steam, and which saw traders and pearlers and poachers of bêche-de-mer plying their trade. On their right, the ocean stretched almost uninterrupted all the way to Peru. In front of them, just over the horizon, about eighty miles away, was Papua New Guinea with its virtually impregnable mountains and stone-age tribesmen still maintaining their traditional ways. But these two were headed for a remote resort on Mabuiag Island, about thirty minutes' flying time away.

"It's so bright and clear," said Mrs. Rockdale. "And so remote."

"Yes, you're almost as far north as you can go in Australia," said Michael. "There are a lot of people here who just want to get away from it all and live a hermit's life." For a brief second, he thought about the old Chinese woman in Vancouver and the tarot card with the hermit on it.

"Are you from here?" she asked.

"No, I'm from down south, but I wanted to come north where the weather is warmer," he replied.

"It's funny," said Mr. Rockdale, "when you say you're going north back in the States, it sounds like you're going to colder weather. But here, you're going to hotter weather."

"Yeah, that is funny," said Michael, even though it wasn't.

"Say," Mr. Rockdale said, "have you ever been to the States, Michael?"

"A couple of times a few years back," he replied. "Nice place. Good people."

"We think so," said Mr. Rockdale, "but don't get me started on our politics. It will drive you to distraction! Have you read the latest dumb thing our president has done? He's pulling down statues of some of our nation's founders. President Troup said years ago that would happen..."

As the helicopter flew through the sky that was clear and blue, and the same color as the ocean below it, it seemed to have no horizon and that it went on forever. He liked being here, it was peaceful, and he was able to see clearly where his life would go. He found himself calm and listened quietly as Mr. and Mrs. Rockdale recounted to their pilot, Michael O'Rourke, all about the craziness that was American politics and their president's latest blunder. His thoughts meandered to how one chance meeting can cause so much upheaval and drama in a person's all-too-brief stay on this planet.

But such is life.